OUR
BEAUTIFUL
BOYS

OUR BEAUTIFUL BOYS

A Novel

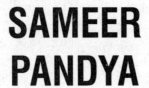

SAMEER PANDYA

Ballantine Books

New York

Published in the United States by Ballantine Books,
an imprint of Random House, a division of
Penguin Random House LLC, New York.

BALLANTINE is a registered trademark and the colophon
is a trademark of Penguin Random House LLC.

LIBRARY OF CONGRESS CATALOGING-IN-PUBLICATION DATA
Names: Pandya, Sameer, author.
Title: Our beautiful boys : a novel / Sameer Pandya.
Description: First edition. | New York : Ballantine Books, 2025.
Identifiers: LCCN 2024059130 (print) | LCCN 2024059131 (ebook) |
ISBN 9780593726167 (hardcover ; acid-free paper) |
ISBN 9780593726174 (ebook)
Subjects: LCGFT: Novels.
Classification: LCC PS3616.A368 O97 2025 (print) |
LCC PS3616.A368 (ebook) | DDC 813/.6—dc23/eng/20241210
LC record available at https://lccn.loc.gov/2024059130
LC ebook record available at https://lccn.loc.gov/2024059131

Printed in the United States of America on acid-free paper

randomhousebooks.com

1st Printing

First Edition

Book design by Elizabeth A. D. Eno

For Ravi and Ishan

The echo in a Marabar cave is not like these, it is entirely devoid of distinction. Whatever is said, the same monotonous noise replies, and quivers up and down the walls until it is absorbed into the roof. "Boum" is the sound as far as the human alphabet can express it . . .

—E. M. FORSTER, *A Passage to India*

Part I

END ZONE

ONE

Except for the Native Caves—tucked high in the hills above town—the city of Chilesworth presents nothing extraordinary. During the day, the three large craggily black holes set against a lion-yellow hillside were something: a historical artifact, a geological occurrence, a living thing, an astonishing view. By dusk, they were mostly abandoned, the dirt path leading to them framed by cactus, sage, and the occasional beer can left by generations of teens looking for a secret place. And at night, the caves had a register and intensity of darkness that made it hard to tell up from down, side from side, boy from boy. Late one night, that darkness would pull all four boys into the largest cave, their arms and legs soon flailing and tangled, the click-click of their bones against bone, their grunts and cries echoing off the smooth walls.

TWO

Now, looking down, the scene below the caves could be West Texas (1972) or eastern Michigan (1988). But it was a bright Southern California (2019) fall afternoon, one of those where when you looked up, the blue stretched in every direction, and a bird, no matter how low or well winged, looked like nothing more than a jittery black dot. Roughly fifty teenage boys, in full pads, were draped around one another, waiting for practice to start. And right before it did, a new kid walked onto the field, mostly on his heels.

"Bin Laden is *playing* now?" one of them asked the thick boy next to him.

"I thought we dumped his dead ass in the ocean," the other responded.

They both burst into mocking laughter.

–––»»»»»–––

"Did you read it?" Gita Shastri asked her husband, Gautam, later that evening. She'd watched him walk into the kitchen, glance briefly at the yellow Post-it note with his name on it and an arrow pointing to a permission slip she'd left on the counter, and head straight to the refrigerator. This first stop for a beer had been a recent thing.

"Isn't he a little old for field trips?" Gautam asked, cooling his hand on a bottle.

"You didn't read it?"

"You saw me not read it."

The two looked at each other, neither wanting to proceed down this particular path. Gita had trouble recalling her once young husband's handsome face, now covered in week-old gray stubble because he'd run out of razors; Gautam just looked away.

"Apparently, Vikram was walking down the main hallway yesterday when the football coach noticed him. He asked if he had any interest in the game and whether he wanted to come to practice after school to take a look."

Gita was conveying the story and staring at the discoloration on their oak cupboards, now lightened and worn by sun and overuse. They'd bought the house new nearly two decades before, a small development in a neighborhood of old, seventies-era stucco tract homes. As the older houses were bought, sold, and remodeled with each turn of boom and bust, their house, once the shiny new thing, now looked frayed and outdated. The old, drafty windows let in too much dust, a patch of shingles on the roof needed to be replaced, and the lawn out front, while still green, had large holes from the gophers living below. In most everything she did, Gita operated with order, cleanliness, and just the right amount of sheen, and while the rest of the house was warm and inviting, the kitchen in particular had become the object of her sustained frustration. No matter how much she scrubbed, it never got the right kind of clean. And with every hole she plugged, another would appear with a fleet of ants coming in, mocking her about the one grain of sugar she had failed to clear from the counter. The remodel she wanted—an added island with a stainless steel six-burner stovetop, walnut cupboards, thick wood floors—would cost them roughly seventy-five thousand dollars, maybe more if she got the exact green Rajasthani marble counters she'd discovered on their last trip to India. Gautam had insisted that they couldn't afford it, that the cupboards were perfectly functional, and that maybe he could slap a coat of paint on them. She'd been annoyed by his use of *slap* as a verb. She wished he was actually handy around the house.

"He checked it out yesterday," Gita continued, turning away from the cupboards and now looking at the stained grout on the counter. "He went to practice today and loved it and now wants to play." She paused and then added, laying out her argument, "He also thinks having a second sport would be good for his apps."

Vikram was upstairs in his room; their daughter, Priya, was in her first year of college and barely called.

"He thinks or you think?"

As the words were coming out of his mouth, Gautam leaned slightly forward, as if doing so might let him suck them back in.

"Let's leave aside for a moment how little you've done to help him think through any of it."

"Isn't the loss of one kid over all this college admission madness enough?" Gautam asked.

Gita looked straight at her husband. When her mother had died, her father, in a rare show of raw emotion, had said that after fifty years, he could no longer distinguish between his own thinking on things and his wife's. She took all our memories with her, he'd said, his eyes filling with thick tears. For the past few years, Gita had in-stead felt herself inch further and further away from her husband, greedily hoarding her own thoughts and memories.

"Sorry," Gautam said immediately.

"I think we both did that. But we can certainly argue over who was *more* responsible. And I would win that argument."

Gautam looked away, took a deep breath, and had a sip of his beer. After the first couple of sips from a bottle, the rest was just disap-pointing.

That morning, Gautam had arrived at work at his open-floor-plan office—the kind of space with a kitchen stocked with cereal and protein bars and quinoa bowls to be delivered at lunch, a Ping-Pong table that all the programmers called *table tennis,* and clear sight lines between the CEO's desk and the intern's. He wished they still had cubicles so that he could disappear into one for the day. For years, he'd made a very good, consistent income as a programmer. But at some point, he'd realized that programming was the dentistry of the tech world: solid and steady, but without the glamour or the paycheck of being a doctor. He'd watched the sales guys, who knew nothing about the architecture of the software they were selling, making absurd year-end bonuses based on the zeros and ones Gautam had carefully constructed. And so, a few years back, he'd decided to switch to sales.

Gautam had been the twenty-fourth employee hired by a startup called VirtualUN. "Never Be Misunderstood Again" was the tagline on their marketing material. There were other video-conferencing companies on the market, but theirs was the only one that had real-time translations in more than a hundred languages. If a German speaker and a Mandarin speaker got on a call, the German speaker heard only German from the Mandarin speaker, and vice versa. When Ryan the CEO and Bryan the head of sales—RyanBryan in Gautam's mind—had originally interviewed Gautam for the job, he had told them that he would come on as a programmer to help them refine the accents attached to each of the languages. It would give him the time to learn the guts of the technology. But then soon after, he wanted to move into sales. I'm the perfect translator for this product, he'd said in his pitch to them. I can move between tech and sales, between Hindi and English, between Asia and America.

The mood at work that morning had been liminal. They were past the collective exuberance from having received an infusion of big boy, Series A funding. Now, if they wanted to get to Series B, they needed to make something of it; they needed to sell their product far and wide. Gautam found himself in a similar in-between space. He was older than most other people in the company. He knew and understood the programmers—young Asian American kids fresh out of college and older H-1Bs from India and China—but now he was spending his time with the salesmen, mostly fit white guys who seemed to have an endless supply of crisp button-downs that never wrinkled. No matter how intimately he knew the product he was selling, no matter his deep love and precise knowledge of the history of Pac-12 basketball, the buyers simply didn't buy from him. He knew why, but to admit it openly meant that he would need to return to the sanctity of coding and algorithms. He was not ready for safety yet. But he was getting there.

He had originally taken the job because he liked the CEO. Ryan was in his late twenties, had a programming background, rode his bike to work, and had the air of an ascetic even before he'd made his millions. Most tech CEOs only put on the Buddhist bit with eight figures in the bank. Gautam did not, however, like his immediate boss, Bryan. A week before, Gautam had had a meeting with the two of them and Bryan had pressed Gautam hard about how little he'd sold. "You convinced us to hire you based on your translation skills, but that hasn't quite translated into actual accounts." I hope you're saying this to *all* your sales guys, Gautam had wanted to respond. Coming to work was becoming a chore and by the end of the day, he was exhausted and anxious and short-tempered. It didn't help that Gita liked to casually remind him how well their Bay Area Indian friends were doing, with their IPOs, their trips to Kerala in the winters, and their children getting into Princeton.

"Have you ever watched a football game?" Gautam asked Gita now, taking one more sip of the beer before placing it aside. "I mean really watched it. And listened to the bodies crashing against one another. It's brutal. He can try out for water polo. I hear that they grab each other's balls, but at least he wouldn't be banging his head in. It's the new white flight sport. Lacrosse is over. Colleges assume you're a rapist in training."

"*Now* you have all these opinions?"

"I've always had these opinions. No one has asked."

"It's not our job to ask."

This time Gita paused, realizing that dipping into old arguments in new forms was not going to help Vikram play football. She wasn't excited about the idea of football either. But she did like the ironic juxtaposition with golf, a sport that Vikram did play exceptionally well.

"He really wants to do it. He's never asked much of us."

Their daughter, Priya, had always been the hard one, spending a better part of her senior year in high school not speaking to either of her parents. She didn't trust her father and found her mother too overbearing. She was now a freshman at Humboldt State studying sociology and horticulture, details that Gita didn't like to advertise.

"This isn't my fault," Gita continued, now trying to lighten the mood. "He gets his size from the Punjabi side of your family."

There was no Punjabi side of the family. Both Gita and Gautam were Gujaratis, or more accurately, Gita was born in America to Gujarati immigrants and Gautam had arrived in the country in his very early teens. Gautam was a big, strong guy, and Vikram had inherited the weight of his feet, the thickness of his thighs, and the width of his shoulders. From his mother, Vikram had inherited the handsome angles on his face, his deep, striking eyes, and a head full of lustrous black hair, attributes Gita could have leaned on through the years at school and work, but purposefully had not. Gujaratis, for the most part, were known for being slight; Punjabis, their neighbors to the north, were known for being big and strong. It was a bit of low-key interstate parochialism that crumbled under any actual consideration.

Gita's family had been heavily fortified with fancy degrees going back several generations. Her grandfather had earned a PhD in chemistry from MIT in the 1920s and had returned home to India, first becoming a professor and later making a small fortune developing and manufacturing industrial cleaning supplies for newly independent India; her father had two graduate degrees in electrical engineering from Carnegie Mellon and had spent his entire academic career at UCLA; she'd studied economics at Cornell. Gautam's family, on the other hand, had arrived at degrees more recently. His parents had both attended small state schools in India and then migrated to the Bay Area, where they had opened and still operated the Gandhi Restaurant, a strictly vegetarian place on San Pablo Avenue in Berkeley, which started doing really well once the customers had discovered that the menu was largely vegan. Gautam had graduated with a degree in computer science from Berkeley and worked at the restaurant as a waiter throughout high school and college.

Gautam liked to intone that the men in Gita's family were effete, ineffectual intellectuals who had squandered the fortune the soap maker had amassed; Gita replied by saying that Gautam's family were a bunch of farmers made good. It was a bit of banter that had spanned the twenty years of their marriage.

"The joke is getting old," Gautam said, looking straight at his wife who, somehow, miraculously never seemed to age. And then added, "It was old the second time you used it."

"Fine," Gita snapped.

"He can't play," Gautam said. "The game is pure madness. Only the poor kids play. And the white kids get to be quarterback, well protected and untouchable. They just want his body."

"Are you making all the decisions now?"

"You asked me what I thought. This is what I think."

"There are only three games left," Vikram said as he stepped into the kitchen. "And they're not even going to put me in."

"How long have you been listening?" Gita asked.

"All I heard was Dad saying that they only want my body." He paused. "Well, at least somebody wants my body."

The comment released some of the hot air that had gathered in the kitchen.

Vikram was showered and clean, wearing shorts and a T-shirt. He was big and strong and self-contained, like a semitruck idling at a stop sign. He walked over and gave his father a kiss on the cheek, now having to slightly lean down to do so.

"We have to win at least two of the remaining games to make the playoffs. I won't get any playing time. There have been a bunch of injuries and so they need to have people on the sidelines just in case there are more."

"The injuries should be the red flag," Gautam said.

"I know. But there are plenty of guys ahead of me who want playing time. Honestly, I only want to do it because the college essay practically writes itself. 'How I Went from the Gandhian Nonviolence of My Ancestors to the Violence of the Gridiron.'" He had a slight smile on his face as he said this, as if he knew how absurd it was and how he'd hit essayistic gold before he'd written a single word or played a single down. "I'm just a cliché if my only sport is golf. Golf and football together? And an Indian kid? Admissions counselors will gobble it up."

"How did you become such a cynic?" Gautam asked, winking at his son.

"It's not cynicism," Gita said. "It's practicality."

Gautam looked over at his wife, annoyed that she'd interjected.

"And this is all coming from him," Gita said. "I'm not thrilled about him being on that field either."

Yes, Vikram getting into a good college was important to her. Perhaps more important than she cared to fully admit. Where he'd get in, and where he would end up going, would be a reflection of the success of her parenting, a preview of his and their collective futures. He'd scored high on his SATs without really studying; his GPA was well north of a 4.0; he'd tutored disadvantaged kids in math. He just needed a few more key, properly curated pieces for his applications. Gita had taken her daughter's indifference to college personally.

"You had to pick the one sport that would make your great-grandfather turn in his ashen, watery grave?" Gautam asked. "You can't just be the big body in basketball instead?"

"Dad, I didn't pick it. It picked me."

Gautam enjoyed his son's ironic bravado.

"Easy there. They're watching."

Gautam motioned to an 8x10 framed black-and-white photo hanging on their living room wall of Mahatma Gandhi striding at the Salt March in 1930, surrounded by a few other marchers, including Vikram's teenage great-grandfather. Gautam could not remember a time when the photo wasn't a part of his life. Like his parents before him, Gautam had hung the photo on his family's wall, in the same way other families might have a cross to remind them of their faith. The great man and his beatific smile, watching and reminding them to remain austere and humble, to keep things simple, and yes, most of all, to chill on the violence. Gandhi's omniscient presence in the family had never been preachy or insistent, and yet for three generations a certain Gandhian ethos had seeped into the family marrow. Gautam's father had never raised prices in his restaurant for the sake of increasing profits; Gautam felt the need to keep his work ambitions in check; and Vikram, when picked on in junior high, seemed to instinctively know that the way to deal with a bully was not to punch him in the nose.

But was there any sport more un-Gandhian than American football?

"I'll be careful," Vikram said to his parents. "I promise. They teach you ways to protect yourself when you tackle and when you get tackled. And I liked how exhausted I felt after practice today." He paused and then slightly lowered his voice, as if to make sure Gandhi didn't hear. "I don't know, I've never used my body in this way. You know? Plowing into other players. It was kind of fun hitting them. And getting hit was not nearly as bad as I thought it would be. You bounce right back up."

Gautam looked at his son, then his wife, and then back to his son. Vikram had apparently already had his first practice. And they had clearly strategized about how to make this pitch. Standing there, still feeling the residual effects of a rough workday, he felt a little lonely. He walked over to the other side of the kitchen and signed the release form, which Gita had signed already.

"Don't say I didn't warn you," Gautam said, taking a final sip of his warming beer before pouring it out in the sink. "Necks aren't elastic."

Neither Vikram nor Gita heard him.

Before she knew exactly what they were, Veronica Cruz had wanted to live in a Craftsman. She'd seen them around when she was an undergraduate at Berkeley and loved the dark of the wood, the comfort of the low ceilings, the luxury of the ample front porch. When she was a bright, ambitious senior, one of her professors had held an end-of-term dinner at her house in Rockridge and as the class sat around a book-filled living room, eating quiche, drinking Malbec, and discussing Judith Butler on performativity, it had all made a deep, lasting impression. Now that Veronica had the designation of *full* professor at UCLA and finally owned a Craftsman of her own, she had decided that she would never leave it. She had paid careful attention to every detail when she was refurbishing it, spending a ridiculous sum to fix the stained-glass window on the front door, getting marble countertops in the kitchen, and carefully curating the built-in bookshelves in the living room with the three hundred or so books that were particularly important to her. Most of them had her name on the first page—"V. Cruz"—along with the month and year when she first bought the book and little penciled checkmarks throughout the pages: an analog archive of the things she'd found meaningful as she read. Tucked among Moraga and Anzaldúa, Eduardo Galeano, Morrison, Roth, Lispector, Paz, Natalie Davis, Ranajit Guha, Eric Williams and Raymond Williams, and many others, were the three books she'd written herself. Her remaining library of well over a thousand volumes was in her office at work.

She even liked the look and feel of the redwood mailbox, which she was now standing in front of, about to get her mail when her son, Diego, walked up to the house. If he'd continued his short-lived freshman-year wrestling career, he'd probably now be a junior heavy-weight, with his broad shoulders and his thighs and legs thick and strong. And yet despite all this growing manliness, he still had his beautiful long lashes and the remnants of the soft curves on his face that had made people wonder if he was a boy or girl when he was a child.

"What's up, stinky?"

"I'm starving."

Diego was always hungry; Veronica's hunger had mostly subsided.

"Practice good?"

"Hard. But good. We need to win these final games. I think Coach is riding us just a tiny bit more because he thinks he might get fired if we don't make the playoffs."

"Did he say that?"

Diego shook his head. "There's just a different intensity to him right now."

From as far back as she could remember, Diego had always been attuned to the emotional tremors of others. This was only one of the reasons she luxuriated in her son's presence. They could talk without speaking. They were a unit, the two of them. A tight, unbreakable pair.

And yet Diego's emotional radar also meant that he absorbed the feelings of others, infusing him with a melancholy that Veronica had first noticed in his moist brown eyes when he was a baby. Football was the one thing that freed him from all that; he liked running through people.

"But that guy is still coming down?" Veronica asked. "There's not much time left."

That guy was the coach's friend from college, who was now the running backs coach at Cal. Around midway through the season, the coach had taken Diego aside after a particularly strong game and told him that he'd sent a few videos of Diego slashing through de-fenses to the Cal coach, who would make a quick pit stop to check out Diego in person when he was in Southern California.

"He's not said he isn't. One of these remaining Fridays, I guess."

"Shower up. Dinner will be ready soon."

Diego went in the house; Veronica retrieved the mail.

Among the magazines and flyers and bills, there was a thin envelope addressed to her, with her name—her birth name—written in large block letters. A name she purposely hadn't seen or used in years. A few weeks earlier, when she'd received a similar envelope without anything inside, she'd had a small panic attack, right there on the street. At first, she'd suspected it was her ex-husband, Diego's father, sending her tiny threats. He had recently lost yet another bid to get even more alimony than the generous amount he already received. But she knew his handwriting and there was no way he could muster such clear block letters. She recognized the writing, but like a fading memory, couldn't quite place where and to whom it belonged. She assumed it was one of her envious colleagues. This new envelope was empty too. She had ripped the first one into tiny pieces, but she folded this one and placed it in her pocket.

She took a deep breath and turned to the piece of mail she'd been looking forward to receiving: a hard copy of the latest *New York Review of Books*, which included a glowing write-up of her recently published book. She had read it online already, but she went and sat on the steps leading to the porch to read the review again, luxuriating in the paper it was printed on. It made her heart flutter anew.

Veronica had trained as a historian of Latin America, and her first book, which had earned her tenure, had been a social and economic history of a single slave ship that had traveled between West Africa and Brazil. It had won a prestigious prize in her field; the selection committee had pointed to the brilliance of one particular chapter on the music that had traveled on that ship. In her second book, she had taken a well-known moment of *marauding* in Brazilian colonial history and recast it as *rebellion* by carefully rethinking and rereading the state archive. And this, her third, was an overarching intellectual history of Afro-Latino identity across music, literature, and film. It was big and ambitious, and as the reviewer had written, "the book we need now to move historiography, Afro-Latino studies, and human-istic studies more generally into our new century." The review was written by the preeminent scholar in Veronica's field, a white woman who was part of the first generation of women to insist on their rightful place in the academy. She'd spent her entire career at Co-lumbia and now seemed to be arguing, in this very public forum, that Veronica was the logical choice to take up her soon-to-be-vacated Simón Bolívar Chair in Latin American History. Sure, Veronica loved her house and the neighborhood, but she could be persuaded to move into a sprawling apartment on the Upper West Side over-looking Riverside Park.

The reviewer spent considerable time in the review praising the narrative built around Slave Z.105.

In graduate school, Veronica had been studying in the colonial archives in São Paolo when she'd discovered mention of one slave who had brought a small instrument with him: a wooden flute. She didn't find anything further on him. But she had referred to him as Slave Z.105—named after the archival number on the file in which she had found him. She'd used him as a device to dramatize her ar-guments about the movements of people and music across the At-lantic. And with each successive book, she'd built a larger and more complex world around Slave Z.105, and so now, by the end of the third book, she had imagined his entire life, based on meticulous ar-chival, ethnographic, and genealogical research.

At this point in her career, she'd negotiated things so that she only taught two classes per quarter, one quarter a year, and lived well over an hour away from campus. The rest of the time, she was flying business class to universities to give keynotes. While no one could accuse her of not being prolific, many could accuse her of making a very good living from correctly assessing the life of the downtrod-den. Though she traveled a lot, she had never missed a single one of Diego's football games.

She had grown up in a family where the men—her father, her brother, her uncles—liked watching the Raiders on Sunday afternoons. It seemed silly to her that she'd spent all this time making up for being left out of those gatherings. But left out she had been. And somehow, her only son being the star running back on his high school team made her feel better. Even as she knew that the game was violent and horrible, she felt a genuine elation, an elation unmatched by any other moment in her life, when her son broke through one tackle, one more, and then with the slightest bit of daylight, would kick his legs high and break out for thirty, forty yards and, in a move that she had told him dozens of times not to do, would slow down inside the five-yard line and saunter in like he was sauntering into the front door of their home at the end of the day.

Veronica finished reading the review and looked up as the evening sun filtered through the enormous oak that anchored her front yard. She went back inside and stood in front of her wall of books, scanning her choices. She pulled down her first book—this hardback thing with 350 pages of text and 50 more full of endnotes that had laid the groundwork for the comfort and safety she now enjoyed. Inside was an old clipping from the school newspaper at her first academic job about the publication of the book. In the accompanying photo, she is leaning against her desk in a book-filled office, her thick brown hair down her shoulders, wearing a stylish peasant blouse she'd treated herself to from an expensive boutique in Rio. She looked thin, even though she'd only recently given birth to Diego. Now she had to work hard to stay in shape, her hair was cut to a more practical length, and she usually wore tailored pantsuits with a crisp white shirt for work. When she looked at the photo, a sudden longing for the earlier Veronica washed over her. She carefully placed the clipping back, along with the envelope from her pocket, and then returned the book to the shelf.

When Diego came into the kitchen after his shower, Veronica was ladling a hearty beef stew into two large bowls. Veronica liked to cook, but lately she'd joined a service that dropped off a different ethnic meal each weeknight. Monday was Italian. She appreciated that the company didn't take the unimaginative way out by having tacos on Tuesdays, which were reserved for regional American. Wednesday was Mexican. Thursday was open Asian night—Thai one week, Indian another, Vietnamese when the chef was in the mood for noodles.

"A new kid showed up to practice today," Diego said as they sat down to eat.

"This late?" Veronica asked.

"Some of the other kids were pissed."

Playing on the team in the fall meant enduring an entire summer of practice. Two-a-days in the blazing heat.

"The O-line is getting too thin," Diego continued. "He's a big, strong guy who can open up some holes."

"If he can block for you, then that's a good thing."

"That's what I figured. But one of the coaches was clocking his forties today."

"And?"

"Pretty fast for an Indian guy."

Veronica cocked her head slightly. From an early age, she had trained her son to be aware of and sensitive to all forms of race talk. She'd taken Diego with her on research trips to Brazil so that he knew his familial roots and the enormous privileges he now enjoyed.

"He's in Calc with me," Diego continued. "Nice. Smart. Dependable if your eyes need somewhere to land during a test."

Veronica didn't pay this any mind. Diego was very good at math and had no reason to cheat.

"And I didn't realize he's also in AP English with me until he told me today."

"If he can catch, he could be a pretty decent tight end for a few plays," Veronica offered. "You've been pretty empty there all year."

Given the opportunity, Veronica and Diego could talk football and football strategy for hours. Every Sunday in fall, they watched the Niners together. And no matter how the high school team did for the rest of the year, Diego was in the midst of a pretty good season. He had gotten some college recruitment nibbles, but he'd have to finish the season strong to convert those into something more substantive and genuine. Veronica didn't care about who was coming onto the team as long as it didn't mess with Diego's touches. If it did, that was a different story.

—〉〉〉〉〉〉—

"Is it too much to request that you wash your feet and put on some shoes for dinner tonight?" Shirley Berringer asked her son, who went by MJ: Michael Jr.

"More advanced societies don't wear shoes in the house," MJ said, standing in the kitchen, sweaty from practice, his feet filthy from the day.

"But they do wear them outside and wash their feet when they come in."

"I'm happy to wash them."

For a better part of the past month, MJ had stopped wearing shoes, inside or outside the house. He went to school barefoot and he went to parties barefoot. The only shoes he put on were the cleats he wore for practice and games. He could pull all this off because he was bright and handsome and had a rifle for an arm that had earned him a verbal commitment from Yale. He was in his senior year, which he had finished even before it really began.

His parents had noticed the change and thought of it in the same way that they'd thought of his mullet in junior high, his freshman-year mustache, his walking everywhere this past summer to avoid the use of fossil fuels: phases that passed more quickly if they didn't question him directly about them. But for MJ, the bare feet were less a phase and more a piece of a broader philosophy: unburdening himself from the thingness of things.

"Your grandparents are coming over for dinner and I'd love it if you could take a shower and put on some shoes and a shirt with buttons."

MJ had a particular affection for his grandparents and that was the only reason he considered doing what his mother was asking.

"How about a shower and some socks?"

"This isn't a negotiation," Shirley said, winking at her son. "Go. And not those horrible woolen ones."

"Fine. I'll borrow some argyles from Dad."

"Don't mock the argyles," Michael Sr. said from his leather chair in the adjoining family room. Even though he didn't actually wear argyles much, his casual uniform often included a Lacoste polo, which he'd realized was a worthy object of his family's mockery. He'd been listening to the exchange. He appreciated Shirley's ability to talk to their son without getting agitated, something he'd been unable to do lately. "They're making a comeback. You'll see."

Shirley had grown up in the old, very spacious colonial they lived in. All white with black shutters, it had a row of bluish-purple hydrangeas up front that seemed like they were in perpetual, perfect bloom. It was the type of house with rooms that led to other rooms that led to other rooms. The type of house where, when the children's friends were over, Michael and Shirley could have a quiet dinner and not hear any ruckus. She'd inherited it when her parents died, along with the nineteenth-century English furniture, Persian rugs, American landscapes and European pastorals on the walls, with an abstract here and there, and a certain formality in the air. In the living room, where Michael and Shirley had drinks when guests came over, there was a couch that a master furniture maker had built for her great-grandmother. Every decade or so, for the past forty years, it had been re-covered in the same blue chinoiserie imported from a London fabric designer. The ornate liquor cabinet that served as the centerpiece of the room may or may not have been built by the slaves of Shirley's English ancestors. Attached to the living room was a formal dining room that housed a table that sat twelve comfortably.

MJ and his younger sister, Kelly, spent most of their time in the family room, watching TV and doing their homework. It was the only place downstairs where they could breathe easily.

Michael loved the house and the comforts it afforded and at this point, he'd stopped noticing that he was living his life among another family's artifacts, thinking they were his own. When guests came over for the first time, he loved walking them over to the painting hanging above the fireplace, a self-portrait by Erich Van Royen, roughly a contemporary of Rembrandt's who had, as Michael liked to say, been unjustly written out of history, as if the one art history class he had taken in college gave him authority on the subject.

Michael's parents used to come over every week, but now that they were getting older and slower, their visits were less frequent. The less they came, the more insistent Shirley became on making the dinners with them more special. She'd grown up with her parents throwing frequent, extravagant dinner parties at the table she was now setting. For all their wealth and access to good health, her parents had died unexpectedly and relatively young in their late fifties, when Shirley had barely finished college and was working abroad. Their only child, she didn't need a therapist to tell her that their deaths—her father first from a heart attack and her mother six months later from grief—had left a hole inside her that she'd been trying to plug ever since by maintaining a household with clean, shiny surfaces and full of dinner guests.

"Who're you playing on Friday?" Michael asked when MJ came down after showering.

"I don't know."

"Shouldn't you know?"

"It's the same old thing. We play. We win. We lose."

The deeper MJ got into his senior season, the less and less he seemed to care about football or school. Mostly because he didn't need to care. He'd been recruited by Michigan, UCLA, and Notre Dame but had chosen Yale as his father and grandfather had. He was now indifferent about how the rest of the season went. But his parents, and Michael in particular, wanted him to go out on a high note.

"Sometimes it feels like the season is more important to you than it is to me," MJ said.

"That's not fair," Michael said, feeling stung. "I'm just doing what I've always done. Don't blame me for being interested."

"I appreciate it, I really do," MJ said. "But I'm not sure I even like the game anymore. I liked it when there were flags involved and I even liked it when I started high school. But I'm not sure I like it now."

"What's going on?" Michael asked.

"Nothing," MJ said. "That's the problem. I don't know if I can do four more years of this."

At this, Michael's back began to sweat, far more than it should have from his son simply saying that he was tired of being hit, Friday night after Friday night. For some time now, he had sensed that MJ was moving further away from him. This was to be expected from a teenage son. But the turn he was making—the days without showering, the shoelessness, and now this about not wanting to play—felt too sharp and sudden. Someone had to be whispering in his ear.

Before they could continue the conversation, the doorbell rang.

"We'll talk about this later."

"There's nothing to talk about," MJ responded.

When Michael opened the door, his mother looked overly cheerful and his father, as usual, was dour.

"Sorry we're late, honey," she said.

"We're not late," his father responded.

If she said one thing, he said another.

Michael led his parents into the living room and sat them down. His mother was still steady on her feet; his father less so. He poured a glass of Chardonnay for her and vigorously shook Manhattans for him and his father.

"Easy," his father said. "Don't bruise the bourbon."

Bourbon didn't bruise; gin did. Michael's father knew this and said it only to needle his son for marrying into a family where the bruising of gin mattered.

"Don't worry," Michael responded. "I don't use the good stuff when I'm mixing drinks."

Michael's father cracked a tiny smile. He'd been the first in his family to go to college and he'd maintained an outsider's spirit as he made his way through Yale, law school, and a long career, first working for others and later building his own lucrative practice.

Shirley came and greeted her in-laws. Michael appreciated how genuinely warm she was with his parents. If she didn't set up these dinners, Michael would see a lot less of them.

When MJ walked in, his eyes lit up for his grandfather in a way that they never did for Michael. Equally, the grandfather's mood suddenly lifted. Michael watched all this and tried not to feel too hurt.

"Hey, sweet boy."

MJ went and sat next to his grandfather.

"Hey, Gramps. You reading anything good?"

"Do you know about this Harry Potter business?" the grandfather asked.

MJ smiled. "Of course. They're great books. Which book are you on?"

"I just finished the last one."

Now retired, Michael's father had read an average of two books a week for the past fifty years. Mostly biographies and histories, occasionally a collection of essays or a book of letters, and plenty of novels. Every winter, he reread *The Brothers Karamazov* and *For Whom the Bell Tolls.* And when the Pulitzers were announced, he'd buy all the books, except the poetry. He and MJ shared a love of books. Michael had never been much of a reader, but he always awaited the annual birthday book he received from his father, reading it immediately to decipher what his father was trying to say to him. What did he mean in giving him Chekhov? That he wished Michael had become a doctor? He couldn't get through *The Sound and the Fury,* but he told his father he did. He'd loved Naipaul's *A Bend in the River,* even though he wasn't quite sure he understood it. The second he'd read it, the powerful first line of the novel had tattooed itself on his frontal lobe.

"You have a home game this Friday?" the grandfather asked.

"I do," MJ said. "The remaining three games are at home. We're playing Bonaventure this week. Can you come to one?"

MJ looked excited about this prospect. They were his last set of high school games.

"I can pick you up," Michael offered. He knew his father couldn't manage to park and walk to the stadium on his own anymore. He used to come to a lot of MJ's games. "We can make a night of it."

"Yes, let's do that."

Michael felt a bit of relief. He wasn't sure what MJ had been threatening earlier when he said he was tired of playing football.

"Dinner's ready," MJ's sister, Kelly, said, sticking her head out from the dining room.

As the family headed to the dinner table, Michael's father remained seated. Michael went to give him a hand up off the couch.

"I can get up on my own," he said, struggling.

He finally stood and looked at the painting above the fireplace. "I've looked at this hundreds of times, but I didn't realize until now just how ugly this guy is. Are the Dutch usually that ugly?"

Michael sipped his drink. He didn't quite know how to respond. "I don't know. I've always found them to be a hearty, handsome people."

"Tom Regan called me today," the grandfather said, moving on to the next thing.

Michael knew the name well. The sweat on his back from MJ's doubts about football came from the same general source that was making him sweat now with the mention of Tom Regan.

"He said he's been trying to get in touch with you and you won't return his calls."

"Really?" Michael had ignored two messages from him. "I haven't gotten the messages for some reason. I'll give him a call first thing tomorrow morning."

"Make sure you do. I consider him a very good friend."

"I know," Michael said. "And I appreciate you sending him my way. I've really taken good care of him. He's done quite well."

Michael ran a boutique investment firm and many of his clients over the years had come from the actual Rolodex his father still kept on his desk.

"Let's go eat," Michael said. "Shirley's cooking seems to get better and better."

"Funny. Your mother's gets worse and worse."

Later that night, after his parents had gone home and Shirley was pretending to be asleep, Michael stood shirtless in the bathroom, brushing his teeth. He had a weekly squash game and took long bike rides in the hills, but he'd liked the sensation of food and wine in his mouth too much, and now the truffle fries here and the second bottle there had all migrated down to his belly. This has to be a thickening mirror, he thought as he sucked his stomach in. While he still looked perfectly fine in his pressed button-downs, he didn't feel confident in them anymore. And though she'd never said anything, he knew Shirley judged him for the weight gain. She was tall and naturally thin, still the same weight she'd been when she was a stellar setter on her high school volleyball team.

On the uppermost part of his right arm, he had a tattoo that he'd gotten for his fiftieth birthday two years ago. When he'd floated the idea to Shirley, she had reacted with disgust, as if he'd suggested they bring a third person into their bed. But he had gotten it nevertheless, as some form of deep rebellion that he felt compelled to keep mostly hidden. Shirley was the only person who knew about it. And since then, on the occasion of their semiannual tiptoeing into sex, she insisted he wear a T-shirt so that she wouldn't have to come in contact with the ink.

"It's dry," Michael had said that first time.

"So am I," she'd said, turning away from him.

With every passing year, the Naipaul quote he had chosen, written in a faux Old English script, seemed to mock him more and more:

> *The world is what it is;*
> *men who are nothing,*
> *who allow themselves*
> *to become nothing,*
> *have no place in it.*

THREE

A large thicket of boys was standing on the field, talking all at once.

"Dude. 7-Eleven is back."

"Maybe he can do our math homework."

"Hey, Bruce Lee. Is Bin Laden Asian?"

"I don't know. But I know that your dad was over at my house mowing our lawn last night."

"He mentioned that. He also said that your mom kept a close eye on him."

"You going to marry your cousin?"

"How many kids you have? Six? You know, K-Y isn't birth control."

"Are you yellow? Gray?"

"Pink. Like your mom."

"Fuck you."

"No. Fuck you."

"Why is that ass so bitchy?"

"Do you Venmo the guy before he sneaks you over the border or after?"

"Shut up, bitch tits."

"You Samoan, or just fat?"

"Is that a boner? Why do you have a boner?"

"Because your sister just texted me."

"Fuck you, cunt."

"That's some gay-ass shit."

"Everyone, shut up," Diego yelled. He and MJ were team co-captains and that gave them some authority. "Coach is here," MJ added.

When the head coach walked onto the field, trailed by his staff, the boys went instantly silent.

"Start running, gentlemen. Ten laps."

Coach Gary Smith was a new breed: fit, his beard trim and properly groomed, his khakis lean and pressed, his entire right arm a tattooed sleeve. On game day, he wore clean Stan Smiths. His temper was always under control; he outsourced the yelling to his assistants. During the schoolday, he was a physics teacher, and Newton came up often when he was trying to explain the transfer of energy required in tackling. Increasingly, his job was to manage a team sport that half of the school thought represented everything that was wrong with America and the other half supported with a certain lust on Friday nights.

The boys continued to linger for about a second longer than they should have.

"What's the matter with you?" one of the assistant coaches yelled. "Are you all deaf? I think Coach was about as clear as the day is bright."

A few of the kids started running.

"Am I done talking?"

The kids stopped.

"Never walk away when I'm talking," the assistant continued. "Now run. All of you. And if you slow down, you might as well run your asses home."

The boys waited for the slightest beat, making sure there was nothing else.

"GO."

And they were gone.

There was a front guard: the wide receivers and running backs who moved ahead quickly. And there was a rear guard: the stout linemen and the players who never entered a game. After the first minute, Vikram found himself closer to the front, getting farther and farther ahead of those behind him.

"What's up, new guy," MJ said, catching up to Vikram.

"Hey," Vikram replied tentatively.

Though Vikram and MJ had been in a couple of classes together, MJ spoke to him as if it was the first time they'd met.

"Can I give you a bit of advice?" MJ asked.

"Sure."

"First, don't stop running until you've run your ten laps. It's on the honor system and the coach knows when you've been dishonorable. Second, don't pay much attention to what the coaches say when they're yelling. And third, don't listen to the other kids. They lose their minds when they get on the field. Once you start helping the team, they'll love you."

"That's a lot of pressure. Helping the team."

"Just keep your head down and you'll be fine. We're good guys. Most of us. We just take some getting used to."

Vikram had remained silent during the earlier chorus, wondering if he was making a terrible mistake being on this field. He'd never experienced any type of hazing on the golf team. When he tried out his freshman year, despite not having quite grown into his body, he'd outdriven the seniors by fifty yards off the tee. He knew all the name-calling he'd heard here was just how the boys talked, and the lines directed straight at him were still pretty tame. And yet, he'd heard plenty from grade school on—the 9/11s, the 7-Elevens, the curry munchers, the ragheads—and the pit in his stomach never ceased to know that the move from words to fists was just a matter of time and circumstance. Over the years, Vikram had learned to listen, but never respond.

Vikram and MJ ran together, getting farther in front of the group. Once they finished their ten laps, they stopped.

"We've been in class together, right?" MJ asked. "Drawing last year?"

"Yep," Vikram said. "The hardest A ever. Harder than AP Chem."

"I got a B-plus," MJ said. "The teacher kept saying my lines were off. Too straight or not straight enough."

Vikram shrugged. "I guess I'm good with my lines."

After they were all done running, the kids broke into their positional groups. It was as if one enormous school of big thick-thighed fish had separated into five smaller schools.

MJ remained with Vikram, giving him a quick tour of the team breakdown. He started with a group of enormous young men, each hovering around 250 pounds. "Easily the best defensive line in the league. The Great Wall of Oaxaca."

MJ paused. Vikram looked over at him.

"That's what *they* call themselves. I don't even know if they're from Oaxaca. They don't let anyone through and they feast on quarterbacks. Most of them are graduating and so they've been going extra hard these last games. Did Coach say he was going to put you there or the O line?"

"I don't think the D line needs my help. He said O."

"Oh. Excellent. We've been having a tough time there. I'd like to say the sacks are their fault, but I'm just not getting the ball away quick enough." He pointed to the side. "The wide receivers and corners are right there. I usually practice with them. And then the running backs and tight ends over there. You know Diego?"

"Just from classes."

"He and I've been in these trenches for a while. He's cool. You can ask him whatever."

Vikram stood there, unsure of where to go. The feeling was foreign to him.

Coach Smith walked up to the two of them and tapped MJ. "Be where you need to be, bulldog."

"Yes, Coach." MJ jogged away obediently.

"So you've never played?" Coach Smith asked, his voice quiet and deliberate. "Not even when you were a kid?"

"On the playground," Vikram replied, feeling nervous standing there next to the head coach, in pads and a uniform he didn't quite know how to wear yet.

"Did you know you run such fast forties?"

"I won some ribbons in elementary school for the fifty- and hundred-yard dash."

"Any other sports?"

Vikram shook his head. "Just golf."

"There are only a couple of other kids on the team who run the forty faster than you. Diego is *fast*. But there's no one who runs the first twenty faster. You're out of the blocks like a beast. You've wasted your time playing golf."

"That's not what my coach says," Vikram replied, not recognizing the bluster until the words were out of his mouth.

Coach Smith smiled. Vikram slightly cocked his head to the left and grinned.

"How far can you drive?"

"Three twenty-five when I get after it."

"And your short game?"

"I do most of my scoring around the greens. Soft hands." Vikram held up his palms, as if the sharp lines that predicted wealth and multiple children, and the long delicacy of his fingers, were a clear explanation for why he was a wizard with a wedge.

"Let's play a round when the season is over." Coach Smith pointed to the running backs coach. "You're going to run today."

"I thought I already did," Vikram said.

"You're just getting started."

Vikram walked over to the running backs, now even more nervous. The day before, when he was put with the offensive line, he could hide his lack of knowledge of how the game was played by blocking really hard. But there was a particular skill involved in running with the ball. Mistakes here got you punished with a vicious hit.

Diego was the only one he knew from his classes and he walked toward him as if he were a life raft.

"Yo, man," Diego said. "You hanging with the grown men today?"

"That's what Coach said."

"Welcome to the terror dome."

Vikram didn't know exactly what that meant. But given the friendliness in his voice, compared to the light menace he'd heard earlier from the team, he stuck close to Diego.

Vikram spent the next hour with the backs, watching Diego first before stepping in and sharing the ball with him, playing fullback to his running back. Mostly, he ran with the ball, but also blocked and caught some short, hard passes. He always brought the ball in, even when it was off target. He just didn't know the plays, which left him feeling confused.

Despite sensing that Vikram was indeed going to get some of his touches, Diego tried explaining the different plays to Vikram by mapping them out on his palm. For stretches of the season, they'd been a very good team, while in other inexplicable stretches, they'd been shamefully bad, the bad usually emanating from an anemic offense. It was hard to know which team was going to show up in a given week. Diego knew that he needed some real help if they were going to win these last games.

At one point, during a water break, the two stood side by side and watched MJ throwing one perfect spiral after another to the wide receivers. The ball looked like it had been shot out of his arm as it traveled in a perfect, high arc through the afternoon sky.

"Damn," Vikram said, louder than he intended.

Out of the five throws MJ delivered forty yards down the field, four were dropped. From a distance, it seemed like they were dropped on purpose; the receivers were bringing the balls in before they slipped through their hands. With the final drop, MJ removed his helmet and screamed out into the ether: "Catch the fucking balls."

"Hippie boy is my boy," Diego said. "And he's hippie most of the time. But he really loses his shit if you keep dropping his perfect balls."

"He's got perfect balls?" Vikram asked.

"Apparently so," Diego said, trying to keep a straight face. "And a bit of a temper. *And* a trust fund. And yet somehow he's not a douche. Unless you drop his balls."

"I'll remember that," Vikram said.

"Let's ask Coach to run us some options," Diego said.

They worked on some set plays.

"How was it?" Coach Smith asked Vikram at the end of practice.

"Tough," Vikram said, exhausted and drenched in sweat. "But really fun. I've got a lot to learn."

Vikram felt a strange tingle of desire in his fingertips. He wanted to keep practicing. He wanted to stay on the field. He wanted to lay down some more hard blocks.

"You do. But you looked good out there, all things considering." Coach Smith handed him a small binder filled with pages. "You're going to have to learn the playbook as fast as you can. What math class are you in?"

"Calculus. With Diego."

"I may have the smartest backfield in the league. Some of these kids need months to learn the plays and still don't get it. I've a feeling you'll only need a solid day."

Vikram nodded. He got this kind of thing from his teachers a lot.

"Really, it's not that complicated of a playbook. We run, we throw, we tackle. I saw you chatting with MJ earlier."

"We ran together."

"You ask him or Diego whatever questions you have. Those two have a little ESP thing going on the field. Now go get your stuff. I'll see you tomorrow. And learn those plays. I'm going to quiz you."

Just as he stepped off the field en route to the locker room, Vikram's friend Tyler Chen walked by.

"You checking up on me?" Vikram asked.

"I am," Tyler said. "You still in one piece?"

"Barely."

Vikram and Tyler had met in the seventh grade and had been almost inseparable since. They'd coordinated taking nearly every class together once they entered high school and now held two of the higher GPAs in the junior class. As Vikram had continued to physically grow, Tyler had remained a slight 160 in socks. And yet on the golf course, where the two of them spent a lot of time together as teammates, Tyler had far and away the more beautiful, rhythmic swing. He was simply the better player. Both had gotten some college recruitment interest, but Vikram's had come from schools in the South he knew he wouldn't attend. Tyler, on the other hand, was getting California love. Vikram was both excited for him and a little envious.

When Vikram had initially floated the idea of playing football to his friend after the coach had approached him, Tyler had been clear. "That's a dumb dick move. It's going to ruin your golf game and you're going to dip on me."

"It's not and I'm not," Vikram had assured him.

But now as Vikram stood there talking to Tyler, he wanted to finish up the conversation and join his teammates in the locker room. He'd liked chatting with MJ and Diego. They were clearly in a higher social class than Tyler and his other friends from the golf team and Vikram liked his newfound proximity to them.

Tyler pointed to one particular place in the hills above the school. "That your next stop?"

Tyler was looking up at the caves, at that moment lit up by a late afternoon orange glow. They both had heard about the parties that raged up there. Invitations were hard to come by.

"Yeah, I don't think being the last-resort running back is getting me any invites."

Tyler smiled. "Wanna get a drink? I'm heading over to the store."

"I can't. My mom is picking me up. Call you later?"

The two gave each other the handshake they'd devised in junior high—they brought each of their index fingers and thumbs together, took a hit from an invisible joint, joined the burning tips together, and then flicked them away. Then they parted ways. Neither had ever smoked a real joint.

FOUR

Gita sat in her car and watched as practice ended. She couldn't locate Vikram in all the pads and helmets. She had always liked this part of the job: waiting during Vikram's practices and tournaments. They'd driven all over California together as he played junior golf. She was too nervous to watch him play and so she spent hours in the car, paying bills, occasionally needlepointing, sometimes reading, and having arguments in her head with Gautam about why the management of the family and the house was, indeed, a *job*. Where Gautam had one succinct to-do list, she had several in the notepad that was always with her: "Household," "Finances," "Remodel," "College: Vikram," "Emergency Preparedness," "Back to Work(?)." Her college friends were busy working and raising their own kids and so they saw one another maybe once a year. Though she'd made friends with other moms in town over the years, she mostly just stuck to herself and her family. In recent months, she'd been making weekly trips to see her aging father, who refused to move in with them.

When she had been pregnant with Priya, there was no part of her that thought she'd never return to her office, or any office, after she went on maternity leave at the end of her thirty-seventh week.

Gita had always worked: at McDonald's when she'd turned fifteen and then in a series of jobs at the local mall—toy store, sporting goods, sunglasses, and then finally, for the last year of high school, Emporium-Capwell, where she made serious commissions at the cosmetics counter. As she was headed to Cornell after high school, with a substantial wad of book and spending money lining her pockets, the store manager had offered her the position of head of the cosmetics department. She was barely eighteen. She thought her boss was kidding at first and she kindly declined without thinking about it or consulting her parents.

She concentrated on coursework in her first year in college, but during her sophomore year, she started working as a research assistant for an economics professor and at the campus coffeehouse, both at once along with a full load of classes. After college, she spent a year as a journalist in Albany. She absolutely hated New York politics and asking awkward questions to state senators, though she loved writing clean, sharp stories on deadline. And so she found herself, like so many of her friends from college who'd studied econ, heading into management consulting. Sixty, seventy hours a week, traveling around the country, telling fat companies how to become lean. She'd loved work because of the basic transaction: she gave her labor and in exchange she got money, now lots of it. It wasn't lost on her that the essence of her new job was to put other people out of work.

The management consulting firm she'd worked for had a grueling hiring process, but once she was in, she could choose to work out of their New York or San Francisco offices. It didn't matter much, since she'd be on the road nearly every week anyway. After college, most of her friends had moved to New York City, but now, in the early aughts, they were all heading west to San Francisco, right as the first dot-com boom was busting and booming. The first decision Gita needed to make was where she wanted to live. Most of her friends were moving to Noe Valley or the Mission so that their commute to the South Bay would be easier. As much as she liked these neighborhoods, and the gimlets that were pouring out of the bars, she was honest with herself: she didn't care for their rough edges. And so she'd found herself a large sunny studio in the Marina, a place whose urbane fanciness she appreciated more and more after spending her workweeks in the American interior: Boise, Kansas City, Colorado Springs.

After she'd been with the company for roughly a year, she was sent off to her first solo job. For that first year, she'd been the junior accompanying a senior consultant. This time, she'd flown into Little Rock, rented a car, and checked in to the best Best Western in a town of ten thousand people. Her firm had been hired by a fifty-year-old family-owned chicken farm that had seen its profits decline steadily. The family was ready to sell their business but wanted to take one last shot at making it profitable. Over a two-week period, Gita had pored over all their financial spreadsheets, met with the management team, and interviewed workers, many of whom had joined the so-called chicken ranch, as it was known in town, soon after they graduated high school. She had toured where the chickens were raised and then she had quickly walked through where they were slaughtered and plucked and carefully portioned off into breasts, thighs, wings, and drumsticks. At the end, when she wrote her final report with an executive summary and charts and graphs in color, she felt a bit embarrassed at what her firm had charged for her to come up with a simple solution: the chicken ranch needed to either process a lot more chickens more quickly to keep up with the demand, or hire cheaper contract workers, replacing some of the longtime employees. Ideally, they could do both. Arkansas was beginning to have an influx of migrant workers and Gita had pointed to "alternate workforces" in her report. Depending on how one looked at it, her report was either Econ 101 or Marx 101.

When she was done with the assignment, the thing that stayed with her was not the looks of exhaustion on the workers she wanted fired, but rather the constant shrieking of the chickens. She couldn't understand how the workers were able to stand the maddening sound of existential angst coming from the birds. If she were in their place—and she would never be in their place—she thought she could manage the floors made slippery from blood and stray guts. But she couldn't bear the noise. After she flew out of Little Rock, she never touched a piece of chicken again, no matter how humanely it had been raised. She never cooked it at home for her kids.

She'd kept up the long hours and travel through her early days of marriage and until her belly was enormous. Her plan was to take four weeks off, get a nanny in place, and be back on the road. It wasn't that she'd always dreamed of being an excellent management consultant, in the way that perhaps her grandfather had dreamed of discovering a new element when he'd started his PhD in chemistry or in the way her father loved the poetry of mechanics. But she was really good at her job—instinctively knowing where the fat resided in a company—and she couldn't imagine a life without work. But three months of postpartum depression clicked a switch in her, brought all her internal gears to a halt. She had been working and working and working since she was a teen and she was now absolutely exhausted. Gautam was making good programming money, and her parents had approached her with a modest proposal. As the only child, she would inherit a decent sum of money when they both passed. But why wait until then? They wouldn't give her everything she would get, and they certainly couldn't match the salary she would give up if she quit her job, but it was a solid supplement to Gautam's income. And she wouldn't have to work. Ever. She thought about their offer, thinking it was deeply unfeminist to just stop working. During the fog of her depression, she hadn't been able to get the sound of shrieking chickens out of her head. But once she took her parents up on their offer, the sound disappeared.

When she made her decision to stay at home, she promised herself that she wouldn't become an overbearing mother and that she'd sketch out some ideas for a book—perhaps about her grandfather the chemist, or something more personal. Maybe take on a freelance consulting gig here and there until she was ready to go back full-time. Now, all these years later, she'd seen her share of overbearing mothers and she wasn't sure she wasn't one of them. And there hadn't been much writing.

As she watched Vikram walk toward her, she knew that he'd be off to college soon. And she had no idea what she wanted to do with herself when the house went empty. This worried her deeply. What workforce was she going to reenter? Could she reenter? Who would she be?

"My god, you smell," Gita said when her son got into the car. "How was it?"

"Interesting."

"Good interesting?"

"There isn't a bad interesting," Vikram said. "Interesting implies good."

"Not really. Interesting is neither good nor bad."

"It was fun. I only got the wind knocked out of me once."

Gita quickly turned to him.

"I'm kidding. They're careful about hits in practice."

He had, in fact, gotten the wind knocked out of him during practice. One of his teammates tackled him really hard when he was running without the ball, as if to tell him that he needed to learn the plays immediately.

Vikram went into his bag and brought out an old book. It wasn't that he wasn't a reader. It was just hard to tell these days because his phone was the only thing in front of his face.

"What's that?"

"A book."

Gita flicked his ear. He smiled and showed her the tattered paperback. *A Separate Peace.*

"Kind of weird, but the quarterback gave it to me after practice and told me to read it." He reached into his bag and took out the binder. "And the coach gave me the playbook I need to learn. Essentially by tomorrow's practice for the game on Friday if they play me."

"Are they actually going to put you in?" Gita asked.

"Relax. Not if some of the other players have any say about it. They don't like that I just showed up."

"Don't worry about them," Gita said. "It's their problem if they can't keep up. I can help you with the playbook."

"It's not chemistry homework."

"It can't be harder than chemistry homework."

"True."

Gita started the car and then pointed to a tall, lanky kid.

"What's that boy's name? The one who used to come around the house."

"Stanley Kincaid," Vikram said, too exhausted at that moment to bother with anger.

Stanley was animated, looking like a pale, red-haired, caffeinated giraffe. He was talking to a subdued MJ, who looked like he wanted the conversation to end.

"He plays?"

"No. I don't know what that asshole is doing here."

Usually Gita was a stickler about bad language, but she didn't say anything. Stanley had brought a strange energy the few times Vikram had him over to their house. That first time, Stanley had stepped into the kitchen and opened the fridge, looking for something to eat. Gita had made him a grilled cheese sandwich and he'd been very polite in thanking her and asked for a second, this time with more cheese.

Vikram had met Stanley in Spanish 1 his freshman year. He happened to take the seat next to Vikram on the first day. In those early days when the kids were still trying to feel one another out and get a sense of how the cockfights operated in high school, the two had spent some time together, at Stanley's urging, walking around a dying outdoor mall in town on the weekends and playing basketball after school. Vikram was mostly indifferent to Stanley; he was fine spending time with him, fine not spending time with him. Stanley had taken that indifference personally.

At some point during aimless walks through stores where neither had the money to buy anything, the two had begun talking about their parents. Stanley had shared that his fought constantly and that he was just waiting for them to get a divorce. Vikram's parents bickered, but nothing like what Stanley was describing. Feeling bad that he couldn't agree with Stanley and tell him that his parents were equally at odds, Vikram had shared something else. That he never heard his parents seriously argue, but he always knew when they had because the house went completely quiet after and his parents were clearly in a standoff. Neither wanted to break the silence. The one who did was admitting defeat. Once they'd gone over to Stanley's house and left before they opened the front door because the yelling inside was so intense. Vikram had heard nothing of the sort in his life. Loud and aggressive and threatening. After that, Vikram had begun pulling away from Stanley.

Vikram had forgotten about this shared moment of intimacy as the year continued and the two stopped hanging out. One day before the start of class, Stanley had asked loud enough for the whole class to hear: "Hey, Vikram. How are your parents? They still not talking to each other in the same house?"

The questions came out of nowhere, and, in Vikram's mind, were unprovoked. All he needed to do was take a breath and respond: I'll take silence over all the screaming that's happening in your house. But, perhaps feeling bad for him, Vikram had said nothing.

Vikram could sense the other kids looking at him funny after that day in class, as if Stanley had confirmed something they already sensed about Vikram being from a different tribe. Had things ended there, Vikram might have moved on and thought of Stanley as nothing more than a fleeting irritant.

But toward the end of that first year, Vikram was walking from the school field back to the locker room at the end of PE. The greatest challenge in the class was not the pull-ups, the sit-ups, or the awkward coedness of it all, but to make it back to the locker room without having your gym shorts pulled down by someone bigger and stronger and faster. Somehow Vikram had avoided this bit of humiliation. Until he didn't. When it was his turn, not only were his shorts pulled down to his knees, his boxers came down with them. It was an unwritten code among the kids: shorts were fine; leave everything else alone. The second it happened, and he could feel the cool breeze everywhere, his face turned bright red. And by the time he'd pulled everything back up, most of the boys and girls in the class had *seen* him, including Stanley. Vikram knew from that stupid grin on Stanley's face that he had been the one that did it and then slipped away. Stanley didn't have the soft hands or the agility to pull down just the shorts. And even he knew that he couldn't get this one thing right.

The moment had been seared into Vikram's body. Thinking about it now, nearly two years later, his cheeks still burned from anger and embarrassment.

"I haven't seen him around for a while," Vikram said to his mother. "I wish he played football. I could knock him around without getting into trouble."

"You stay away from him. I don't like that kid."

Vikram hadn't told his parents about what had happened in PE.

As they began driving away, they passed by Diego, who turned to look at Vikram. He waved. Vikram waved back.

"New friend?"

"A guy on the team. Seems nice."

"Is he Indian?" Gita asked, smiling.

"Yes, he is. Diego Cruz. South Indian, I think. Maybe even a Brahmin."

FIVE

Diego's favorite part of the day was not second-period calculus when he sat directly behind the luminous Erin Greene, who smelled so good that he was convinced that she might be the fix for everything that ailed him. Nor was it practice, which he loved just slightly less than the actual games. What he loved most was the calm and quiet of the walk home after school. He had friends in all his classes and he usually ate lunch with the Oaxacans. By the end of the school day, he liked the meditative time on his own.

Chilesworth High School was located at the northern end of Vanderbilt Avenue, which separated the east and west sides of town. The west side was full of small houses built after World War II, large apartment complexes, Mexican grocery stores, and the best mole in town. Here, the people did their best to keep the outside from spilling into the inside of their homes. The east side, where Diego, Vikram, and MJ all lived, was leafier and shadier, with plenty of breathing room between houses. In the mile stretch of neighborhood that separated Diego's and MJ's houses, the homes became older and more stately, and homeowners paid architects large sums of money to re-design houses so that there was an organic movement between inside and outside living. Vikram's house was several neighborhoods over, on the newer edge of the east side where the developments had been built.

Diego liked to stop at a corner convenience store halfway between the high school and his house. And whenever he walked in, the Jordanian owner always posed the same question: "Diego, how's the football?"

"Very good," Diego would reply. "How's the business?"

"Very, very good. Please give my regards to the Scholar."

"I will."

And then Diego would proceed to figure out what he wanted to buy.

"Big game this Friday. I know a guy who can get you tickets." Even as he said it, Diego sensed that maybe he shouldn't have. Every time he'd walked in the store, Karim was always working. He'd never once seen anyone else behind the counter. He had no idea where Karim lived or whether he had a family to go home to at the end of the day.

Karim's place was known in town for the incredible lamb and chicken shawarmas he made behind the counter, along with the fresh mint lemonade that he prepared each morning. As he poured out a customary glass, Diego walked up and down the short aisles looking for something savory. He grabbed a bag of sea salt chips that he knew would pair well with the lemonade. He then briefly stopped in front of the candy section. From where he stood, Karim couldn't see what Diego was picking from the shelf. He'd been in the store before when there were other high school kids there and while Karim knew not to follow them around too closely, he did keep a watchful eye. He didn't need to do the same with Diego and perhaps because he didn't need to, Diego eyed a small box of Mike and Ikes. He certainly had more spending money than he needed. And yet, he quietly slipped the box into his backpack. He'd never done anything like that before and he didn't know exactly why he'd done it now.

Diego went to the counter and took a sip of the lemonade that Karim had poured and marveled at the taste—a perfect combination of lemons, honey, and mint. Just then, another customer walked in and Diego turned to see her. He noticed a circular mirror he'd never seen before attached to the wall, which allowed Karim to stand behind the counter and still see what was happening in the aisles. Diego suddenly felt hot all over.

Diego looked back at Karim and his thick mustache and was certain that his eyes were now full of sadness.

"Good luck with the game," Karim said, ringing up two dollars for the chips. He never charged him for the lemonade. "I'm sorry I can't be there."

"I'm sorry, too," Diego said.

He looked at the register, placed a five-dollar bill on the counter, grabbed the chips and the drink, and quickly made his way out.

By the time Karim noticed the money and said, "This is too much," Diego had already stepped out of the store, hearing the Mike and Ikes banging against the cardboard box they were in. Certainly Karim could hear them too.

When he was about a block away from home, and he'd finished his chips and the lemonade, he stopped, opened his backpack, and retrieved the candy. He knew he wasn't going to be able to eat them now. He also tried to avoid all sugar during the season. At 5'10", Diego was the perfect size for slipping under defenders on the football field. And because he wished he was taller, he obsessed over the body he had, regulating his calories, being the first in and last out of the team weight room. And now that his braces had been off for six months, he was slowly creeping toward vanity.

He opened the box and dumped the multicolored candies in a bush. But the shame he felt all the way home melted away once he got to his driveway and saw that there were two cars where there was usually one. His mother's white Tesla and a beat-up old yellow Jeep.

"When did you get here?" Diego asked, walking into the house, barely able to contain himself.

Diego went to his mother's younger brother, Alex, and gave him a long hug.

"I've been waiting here for hours. Where have you been?"

"Some of us have responsibilities."

"I actually just got here," Alex said, pawing his nephew's shoulders. "Man, those are big."

"Just grinding, little man."

Diego saw his father once, maybe twice a year, a fact that Diego didn't like to admit left him feeling adrift, no matter how hard his mother tried to play the role of both parents. And he saw his uncle even less than that. But he felt closer to him, even though Alex looked nothing like Diego or his mother. Alex had blond hair and green eyes; his mother had olive skin. Diego came in at a shade darker than his mother. Years ago, when Diego had asked his mother about the discrepancy, she'd said something about a recessive gene and Diego had left it at that.

"How long will you be here?"

"As long as your mom lets me stay."

Alex had all the top-shelf ingredients of a ne'er-do-well brother. The shitty Jeep, the mop of dirty blond hair, the sudden showing up, the lack of plans. But in fact, this was the affect of a man who had spent a better part of his twenties and thirties working eighty-hour weeks in various investment banks, never taking vacations. And at thirty-nine, two months shy of his fortieth birthday, he had handed in his resignation, having done the math and figured out that he could live well for the rest of his life without having to work again. He'd sold off or given away the suits and watches and cars he'd bought through the years and had spent the next year traveling around the world by himself, trying to find a reasonable response to the very tired maxim: *Know thyself.* A lot of guys he knew, all of whom had struck gold in finance or tech, were trying to figure that out for themselves. He thought he now knew himself a little better, but he had also discovered that he really missed working. And so now he was back at it, but this time only working the hours and days he wished. Some weeks that meant way too many hours, other weeks none.

It was not lost on Veronica that her son seemed more excited than he had in months. Alex brought a certain subdued bantering masculine energy that Diego loved.

"You playing this week?"

"Friday night at home."

"Perfect," Alex said. "Maybe I can take you and your friends out for dinner after."

"That would be great," Diego said, even though he knew that when his teammates—particularly the Latino ones—met Alex, it would only further confirm Diego's deep bougie status, a catch-all term they used for the neighborhood he lived in, the butchered Spanish he spoke, the skin that was more olive than brown. He tried not to be bothered by their ribbing, but he was.

"Why don't you shower up," Veronica said to Diego. "Then we can all eat."

Veronica waited until she heard the shower running before turning to Alex, who had arrived barely five minutes before Diego.

"Why are you here?" Veronica asked, her tone softer than the question.

Veronica and Alex had grown up in the Bay Area—Richmond to be precise, mostly known then for its high murder rate—in a stucco house built for returning GIs after World War II. It had two bedrooms and was barely a thousand square feet. Unlike her son's, Veronica's walk to high school and back was filled with social land mines. She and her brother had always shared a bedroom, though sometime during her junior year, Alex had started sleeping on the couch to give his sister some room. It was a small house, but their parents had filled it with warmth. Besides normal arguments over curfews and the cost of things, Veronica and her parents had mostly agreed, though they'd never been close and she always felt a little trapped in the house.

It was not until she left for college at Berkeley that she finally felt something new: freedom. The more time she spent away from her parents, the more she realized that she was nothing like them. She saw herself in a world much bigger than the one they'd created for themselves, reading books that they had no interest in reading, meeting people they would never meet. And all this made her feel really guilty. They were perfectly good, loving people. During her college summers, she stayed in Berkeley, telling herself that she wanted to let Alex have the room to himself. After graduation, she went to the East Coast for graduate school. And when she got married, she had a quick courthouse ceremony so that she didn't have to invite any of her family. She reasoned to herself that it was perfectly normal for a child to grow distant from her parents.

But over the years, she and Alex had maintained a closeness, even if they were not always regularly in touch. He'd gone to USC on scholarship and then left for New York to work in finance. They'd have a meal together when she happened to be in New York for work; he'd visit them whenever he could. More recently, they saw each other a few times a year and she trusted him more than anyone else. They knew how to fall into old conversations quickly and effortlessly. Over the past year, he'd sent Diego a series of postcards from everywhere he'd traveled. Dharamshala, Cairo, Tokyo, Lima, and on and on.

"If I'm honest, that question hurts my feelings," Alex said.

"Since when do you have feelings?"

"I'm serious."

"I'm sorry."

"I can go."

"No, no," Veronica said immediately. "Clearly, he likes you being here. And I do as well." It wasn't that she kept Diego's father, Andre, at a distance. He'd had his depressive struggles and said he had trouble being around his son. The house suddenly felt warmer with Alex's arrival. "How's unretirement? Is it investment banking, hedge funding, private equitying? Or is it used cars?"

"Venture capitaling," Alex said. "But why the hostility?"

"It's actually envy for the cash."

Alex looked around. "I think you're doing fine here. This house, as usual, looks beautiful. How's everything?"

"I can't complain, which means something is about to go wrong." Veronica hesitated, wondering if she should say what she wanted to add. She needed to talk about it but she was not accustomed to having another adult around. "Someone is sending me little threats. Maybe Andre. But he has no reason to do it."

"Threats?"

"I've gotten two empty envelopes in the mail with my name written in large block letters."

Alex didn't immediately respond but seemed about to say something.

"What?" Veronica asked, suddenly feeling accused and agitated. "Say it."

"The threats are shitty. No question. I can call Andre if you think it may be him."

"I don't need you on this. I can handle it. But why the pause?"

"You've gotten yourself into this. I would have gotten out of it long ago."

"That's the difference between your job and mine," Veronica said. "You can be whoever you like, as long as you're making money." She shook her head. She didn't want to keep talking about it. Diego would be back any second; he took quick showers. "Can you make us some kind of drink while I finish preparing dinner?"

"I learned how to make pisco sours in Peru."

"What were you doing in Peru?"

"Learning to make pisco sours."

"Honestly," Veronica said. "Why are you suddenly here? Is she sick? Is he?"

"She," Alex said, sounding subdued.

Veronica felt hot all over.

"How bad?"

"She had a heart attack. But not a huge one."

"Why are you just telling me now?"

"Because I just found out yesterday. Dad called after they got home from the hospital. She seems fine now. I talked to her. I'm going to drive up tomorrow and figure out if she needs follow-up appointments. Come with me. Bring Diego. It will make her happy."

In some ways, she'd known a version of this news was coming. Her parents were getting older. She wished that at some point she and her parents had actually had a major argument so her prolonged absences would make some sense. But they hadn't. The time between visits had simply become longer and longer. And the only real explanation she had was that she didn't like going back to that house and the person she'd been. Hearing this news of her mother, she felt the same guilt that she'd felt years ago when she left for college and could feel herself able to breathe for the first time. But this time she had trouble catching her breath.

"Mom likes you," Veronica said, her voice cracking without warning. "She's always liked you. I can't say the same for me. She's not going to want to see me."

"That's not true," Alex said. "It's just the story you like to tell yourself."

"I felt it, even when I was a kid. The way she looked at me and then looked at you." Veronica took a sip of her wine. "I really don't want to feel all these weird emotions right now."

"I'd be worried for you if you didn't feel them. Can you at least think about it?"

Veronica had not seen her parents since Diego started junior high.

"Can you just make us that drink? The bar is right over there."

Alex walked over. "Why are most of these bottles still sealed?"

Veronica pretended not to hear the question.

Right before they sat down to dinner, Veronica checked her phone. One email caught her eye: "Final Offer." It was from Mary Stone, her department chair. She left it unopened so that she had something to look forward to after dinner, the moment in the day that she felt the most listless.

As they ate, Alex dazzled Diego with stories of his travel. Afterward, Veronica offered to clean up while Diego and Alex settled in front of the PlayStation. Veronica had furnished the family room as if *Dwell* magazine had envisioned a man cave. A large TV (but not so large as to overtake the room), a comfortable leather couch and chairs so that spills could be easily wiped off. The shelves were filled with books that Diego had read through the years, along with the Lego sets that he particularly loved, including a fully built Death Star. When Diego's friends came over, they could be in this separate room, and yet Veronica could listen to them if she wanted while she cooked in the kitchen.

"*Madden?*" Alex offered.

"I don't need to pretend," Diego said, searching for the right game on the TV. "I do it on the field already."

"Alright then," Alex said, smiling.

"*NBA 2K?*" Diego asked.

"Of course."

"Who do you want to be?" Diego asked, scrolling through all the available professional players. "Larry Bird should be here somewhere."

"If you remember the last time we played, you might have been close to tears after I doubled your score."

"I had allergies," Diego said. "And I barely knew how to play."

"I'll take Steph," Alex said.

"Everyone takes Steph. He's the new Bird."

"That's a little complicated," Alex said. "I'm not sure how to feel about that."

Diego played this game with his friends more than any other

and had spent an inordinate amount of time constructing an avatar of his own—a shooting guard with point guard handle and the upper body strength of a power forward who could take a charge from a player six inches taller and fifty pounds heavier. But what Alex noticed was not the skill set but the skin. The player was roughly Diego's shade of brown, but he had blond hair and earrings in both ears. More like the Latino bassist in a thrash band than an NBA player.

"Is your hair natural?" Alex asked.

"It's a game," Diego replied. "You ready to lose?"

And then they were off.

Veronica had not heard the substance of their exchange, but from their tone, Diego sounded at ease. He had plenty of friends over to play video games but usually the competition was punctuated by jokey denigration. He and Alex sounded relaxed, as if they were fishing by the side of a lake and occasionally sharing an observation about the nature of trout.

After she finished with the kitchen, she finally opened the email. Since her last book had come out and continued to receive so much attention, other universities had begun getting in touch with her, gauging her interest in possibly moving. She had no immediate desire to move to a new job but had used the interest to extract more from her own university.

Dear Veronica,

I've genuinely pushed this as far as I can. In addition to the terms agreed upon already, we can offer a year without teaching and a 20 percent raise over your current salary. The dean has made clear that this is the last and final offer. He won't budge on the *Distinguished* designation. I know that is what you have wanted, and I'm in full support of it. But he's not. If you can let me know your decision and how you would like me to move forward as soon as you can, I'd appreciate it.

Yours,
Mary

PS. I read the piece in *The New York Review of Books*. I think it's essentially a job offer. When you have an official offer, I'll certainly take it back to the dean. I'm sure he'll give you everything you want then. He has Ivy envy.

Veronica knew that several of her male colleagues across the institution had gotten the *Distinguished* designation for a lot less. There was one part of her that wanted to accept the offer, which was already far more than what her colleagues in her own department had, many of whom were openly resentful of Veronica and all the perks she enjoyed. But there was another part, the part that enjoyed the art of the counterpunch, that wanted to fight for what she actually deserved.

She wrote Mary back:

Thank you for all your help and hard work with this, Mary. I really appreciate it. I'm going to take a moment to think through it. But in the meanwhile, I think I'll set up a lunch conversation with our dear dean. And thanks re: review. I've always thought the *Review* was racist and never paid proper attention to nonwhite scholars. But now that they've given me a rave, and so much space, I love them :).

It was only after she finished the email and closed her laptop that Veronica allowed herself to think about her mother. Yes, she'd been the one to keep her distance. But still. Didn't she deserve a call from her father?

SIX

"Hi, Mr. Berringer," Sara Humphries said as she walked in the front door. "MJ here yet?"

"He should be soon," Michael said. "We were expecting him for dinner, but practice must have gone late. Can I get you something to drink?"

Sara and MJ had been dating for well over a year, and together made quite the handsome, smart pair. Because she was athletic and attractive, Michael avoided prolonged eye contact with her lest he seem like a creep. The person who did happily make eye contact with her was MJ's younger sister, Kelly, who looked up to Sara's ability to dig up a spiked volleyball, no matter how hard an opponent had hit it. Shirley liked her for the clarity and certainty of her opinions.

They went into the kitchen. Michael opened a bottle of bubbly water and poured two glasses.

"I don't think we've talked about your college trip this summer. How was it?"

"My mom absolutely loves these trips. I think we took our first one when I was in the eighth grade when my main criteria was the size of the school's football stadium. Things have changed a bit. This trip was to really narrow things down."

"And what did you narrow down to?"

"We started up north. The Maine schools were quite beautiful but out of the question. Too cold and isolated in winter. Cornell was depressing; not just the place but the idea of it. No thank you to Dartmouth. New Hampshire scared me with all the *Live Free or Die* business. Brown was a little better. I absolutely hated Boston. Loved, loved Columbia and NYU. And the colleges were super nice. Williams, Amherst. Penn was a little too gritty."

Michael noticed that she didn't say anything about New Haven. "New York City is really nice. You can't go wrong. The Upper West Side is so perfectly contained. And the Village? Well, you can live your whole life there and not crack the surface."

"My mom wants me to apply to Smith early decision," Sara said, nearly eating the words as they came out of her mouth.

"She went there, right?"

"She did. And loved it. And has never really stopped talking about it."

"And you don't want to be tied to it?"

"No. The idea of a woman's college is super important to her. And I get it. But it sounds like a nightmare to me. If I *had* to do women's, Barnard would be much better for me."

"Have you told her that? That seems like a nice compromise between what she wants and what you want."

Sara shook her head. "No. It'll make her so sad, even though she'll be super cheery and positive about it."

"But I bet she'll understand."

Is this what MJ and Sara talked about when they were up in his room? Not disappointing their parents?

"I would just apply far and wide to give yourself the most options," Michael said. "I'm sure any of those places would be thrilled to have you. And when you're looking, check to see the kind of study abroad programs they have. It's one of my main regrets. Not spending a year in Berlin or Caracas or Barcelona. And also: Avoid the South. And by South, I mean starting in Virginia. You're safe in D.C., but barely. Georgetown would be fun. A great neighborhood."

Right then, MJ walked into the kitchen. He was filthy from practice.

"What're you doing here?" MJ asked, looking at Sara and then away. His tone was far more annoyed than inquisitive.

Michael was about to say something about his rudeness.

"You told me to meet you here," Sara said, trying to remain cheery. "We have history homework."

"Yeah, I'm not doing the homework. I don't need to."

"Yes, you do. The test is on Friday."

"I'll take the test. And I'll be fine. Lincoln was big on compromise. There."

"What's the matter?" Sara asked. "Everything OK?"

"Why wouldn't it be OK?" MJ asked, pretending to be incredulous. "Look around. I live in a perfect house, my parents are perfect, I have a perfect girlfriend."

"Now you're just being an asshole," Sara said. "Sorry for the language, Mr. Berringer. It was nice talking to you. I am actually going to head home."

MJ immediately regretted what he'd said to Sara. He was using his words, but they were all the wrong words. He couldn't quite articulate the feeling that had been creeping up on him. He'd outgrown everything and everyone around him. Sara certainly didn't deserve this.

"Tell your parents we say hello," Michael said.

Sara left the house. Before Michael could say anything to MJ, he ran up the stairs.

"Hey, hey," Michael said.

MJ stopped and turned around.

"Why are you talking to her like that?"

"I don't know," MJ said, sounding apologetic. "I'll call her and apologize."

And with that he continued up the stairs. He sat on his bed and typed out a text: "Free?" It was not to Sara, but to another classmate. He didn't know how to tell Sara that maybe things had run their course between them. That while she wanted to hit pause and enjoy their senior year together, he felt like his life was on fast-forward.

Michael went and found Shirley in the backyard, tending to her roses. By any measure, the roses were beautiful—pinks and yellows and coral punctuated by a few reds. As recently as a few years ago, Michael used to spend a lot of time with her in the garden. Even though he liked the feel of dirt between his fingers well enough, he didn't enjoy getting it underneath his fingernails. And so he'd had the gardener build him a couple of raised beds where he grew and tended to vegetables, always wearing proper gloves. Working side by side, she handling the bulbous roses and he picking the cucumbers and cauliflower, had been its own kind of intimacy. But more and more lately, Shirley went out to the roses by herself and the gardener managed the beds.

"Do you have any idea what's happening with your son?"

"Is he a little cranky? Maybe he needs a snack. I can go make him a peanut butter and jelly."

"I don't think blood sugar is the problem here," Michael said, annoyed that his wife was still treating their son like an eight-year-old.

"He's worked hard," Shirley said. "I think he's just a little burned-out. Let's give him a bit of time. He'll come around."

He's not coming back around, Michael thought but did not say.

Just as he was about to go back in the house, Kelly walked out. She'd come from volleyball practice, and she had the flushed, healthy look of a fifteen-year-old who'd played hard for hours and still had plenty of energy left. She gave her father a kiss and went to her mother. The two of them had always been close, somehow skipping over normal mother–teenage daughter conflicts. Standing next to her daughter made Shirley look young and vibrant. It should have made Michael happy, but it just made him feel old and out of shape.

For years, he'd liked joking that his kids got their athleticism from their mother. He didn't like saying that anymore because it was no longer a joke.

———

That Friday evening, Diego ran for thirty-eight yards on twelve carries, scoring no touchdowns. His worst game of the season. MJ went four for twenty, threw three interceptions, and converted only one third down. The team lost 21–14, both scores coming from the defense, one from a pick six and the other from a fumble return. Vikram stood on the sidelines for the entire game, studying the playbook between downs, desperate to go in.

Coach Smith gave the team the silent treatment after the game, a sign that he was seething with rage. As the rest of the team changed out of their pads and uniforms, the coach led MJ and Diego to a quiet corner of the locker room.

"What exactly happened out there?" the coach snapped. "Diego, you looked two steps slow. And MJ, you kept looking at the clock, as if that might make it count down faster. Either of you interested in playing next week?"

"Of course," MJ said immediately.

"I'm sorry," Diego said. "I'll run harder next game. I don't know what happened."

"You two wanted to be captains. So captain. *Do something.*"

And with that the coach walked away.

Vikram watched this exchange from a distance as he got dressed. And later, as he stood outside in the night air with Tyler and a few other friends, he noticed MJ come out of the locker room. Once again, Stanley was there to meet him. This time their exchange seemed more intimate, more subdued. Vikram noticed Stanley handing MJ a small plastic sandwich bag. He couldn't make out what was in it, but it certainly wasn't a sandwich. MJ placed it in his pocket and then walked away from the lights of the field.

SEVEN

For a crash course on the culture of high school football, Gita had Googled "the culture of high school football" and landed on *Friday Night Lights*.

"Will you watch this with me?" Gita asked Gautam, offering less an olive branch and more a piece of driftwood they might clutch together to stay afloat. "Just one episode. So we have some sense of what I've gotten us into."

There was a time when the two of them watched a lot of TV shows together. But now she liked watching Scandinavian murder mysteries and baking shows and Pakistani soap operas, and he'd entered his unnecessary biography reading phase, buying books that he never finished.

"Sure," he said, a bit resentful that he was having to do anything involving football. "I've heard good things about it."

She made popcorn; he split a beer for them into two glasses so that each would remain cold; they settled down on the couch.

They abruptly stopped watching halfway through the first episode when the star quarterback lay unmoving in the middle of the field after a particularly hard hit.

"OK," Gita said, quickly turning off the TV. "Maybe you were right."

"I don't want to be right," Gautam said.

"Yes, you do," Gita said.

"The show is about Texas football," Gautam said, trying to convince himself. "These games aren't nearly as crazy. Let's hope they don't put him in. We just need to get him through one more loss and then this whole thing will be over."

"If they keep losing like last night, they may get desperate enough to put him in."

That first Friday night, they had sat on the edge of their seats so that they could be the first to see if Vikram went in. They'd looked around the packed stadium, filled with rowdy and excited students barely paying attention to the game, parents and grandparents and aunts and uncles cheering on their players, and grown, hefty men who'd played on the field twenty or thirty years before, sitting alongside the women who'd cheered them on. And they'd seen a player from the opposing team get carted off in a wheelchair because his knee looked to be shattered, taken to a waiting ambulance that was always present at games.

"My dad called yesterday," Gautam said, wanting to change the subject. "He said some Gujarati guy came into the restaurant for lunch. My mom prepared him some *pani-puri* and they started talking . . . about the Gandhi photograph behind the counter, about the company the man owns. Dad, of course, told him about me and VirtualUN." His father did this a lot, in a similar way that his mother used to always want to set him up with potential wives when he was single, assuring him that the latest candidate was the best. "But then the guy emailed me today. He's coming through town and wants to meet. I was about to trash the note, but then I looked him up. He owns some *huge* paint and chemical multinational."

"So meet with him."

"Of course I'm going to meet with him. Why wouldn't I?"

"I wasn't telling you what to do," Gita said, resigned to the fact that every conversation they had these days seemed to end with them talking past each other. They'd had a pleasant twenty minutes between Gautam agreeing to watch the show and her switching it off. "I was just agreeing with you." Gita had trouble remembering the last time they remained together in a conversation.

"I set something up for later in the week. Friday."

Vikram came downstairs and headed to the kitchen. He returned with a ginger ale, his drink of choice since he was a kid, and stood at the edge of the family room, where Gita and Gautam were sitting.

"What are you guys watching?"

"Nothing interesting," Gita said.

"What's your plan tonight?" Gautam asked. "You're welcome to use the car if you want to go get food with friends."

It wasn't that Vikram didn't have friends. Tyler would always be there for him. But he didn't have nearly the deep roster that Priya had had in high school.

"I'm good. I'm just gonna play some video games."

Gautam looked at his son, whose shoulders were slumped. "What's up?"

"I don't know. They should have put me in last night. At least at the end. I need to play at least one decent down. I just want to touch a live ball. If the coach didn't put me in last night, he's not going to put me in next week."

"You want Mom to go talk to him?" Gautam asked. "You'll start next week."

"You're kidding, right?" Vikram asked, looking worried.

"He may be, but I'm not," Gita said. "You gotta ask for what you want."

"Please don't say a word to anyone," Vikram said, sitting down on the couch between them. He turned on the TV. The Netflix home page came on, displaying the show that Gita had turned off.

"Seriously?" Vikram asked.

"We're huge Texas football fans," Gita said with a smile.

Since Priya had left for college, the three of them had not quite figured out how to be together in this new familial configuration.

"Wanna watch something?" Vikram asked.

"Absolutely," Gautam said, perhaps too enthusiastically.

"Easy there. I get to pick the movie *and* the dinner."

"I get veto power," Gita said. "On both."

"Pizza and *Creed*."

"Homemade and *Die Hard*," Gita countered.

"Domino's and *Die Hard*. That's a solid middle ground."

She got up to call for pizza; Gautam got himself another beer; Vikram got the movie ready.

Halfway through the movie, with the pizza nearly gone and Nakatomi Plaza in peril, Gita noticed Gautam's and Vikram's large feet up on the coffee table, next to each other, nearly identical, with Vikram's inching slightly ahead of his father's. She had noticed the similarity before and felt only wonder. Now she felt a twinge of longing for how father and son would always be inextricably linked.

After the movie, Vikram went back up to his room, wanting to finish an English assignment that was due on Monday. He had the choice to write an essay or try his hand at a short story.

———— ≫≫≫≫ ————

When his English teacher, Mr. Walters, asked Vikram to stay after class a few days after he turned the story in, he assumed he'd done a terrible job and hoped that he'd get the option to write the essay instead. He had, in fact, plenty to say about Roth's Ozzie Freedman, who reminded Vikram of everything he wasn't.

Mr. Walters remained seated at his desk, still sporting a full head of silver hair well into his sixties, and slid the story toward Vikram. On the first page he had scribbled a sentence. Vikram had always assumed that one's penmanship got better the older one got, but

Mr. Walters disproved this theory. Vikram did, however, make out the sentence: "A knockout piece of bourgeois realism. Bravo."

Vikram first felt instant relief. He'd done fine. He'd taken a chance and come through. But then he reread the line and paused at *bourgeois*. Was it a backhanded compliment? A critique pretending not to be? Was this old man calling him bougie?

"I didn't know you had all this in you," Mr. Walters began. "I know you're strong at math and physics, but you really need to spend more time thinking about the gray area with us. This is remarkable writing. I think the middle sags a bit and we can work on that. But that's quite the ending."

The story was called the "The Walnut Tree." Sixteen-year-old Gautama Das, named after the prince who would become the Buddha, the only child of stern, hard-driving immigrant parents who think that intense studying is the only guarantee in life, finds himself adrift during one long summer. He wants to find a summer job but his parents insist that he spend his time studying for the SATs. And so one hot July morning he decides that he is going to go out to the walnut tree in their backyard with his bedsheet, tie it around his neck, and finish things off. He sees no joy in his future. He waits until his parents go to work, writes them a goodbye note, and then heads back to the tree. What he doesn't account for is that the branch where he ties the sheet is not very strong; he hangs barely a few seconds and then the branch snaps loudly and he falls the ten feet to the ground, landing hard on his right arm. Seconds later, the heavy branch falls on top of him. He lies on the ground, in agony from the pain of what is surely a broken arm. He has to call his parents to ask them to come home to take him to the hospital. Gautama doesn't bother to hide the sheet or to throw away the note.

Both his parents see the sheet and then the note, but neither says anything about them, then or in the days and weeks that follow as Gautama's arm slowly heals. But they are now excessively nice to him, letting him sleep in as long as he wants, encouraging him to look for a job and to spend time with his friends. After years of his parents insisting that he spend all his time studying, which had paved the path to the walnut tree, now, letting him do everything he wants to do makes him unhappy as well. He misses his stern parents. *Maybe I am just supposed to be miserable.* That is Gautama's epiphany, which he realizes as he is sitting under the walnut tree one day drinking a ginger ale, several weeks after he first climbed it.

"I'm wondering if we need to talk to a counselor or your parents about this story?" Mr. Walters asked.

"Because Gautama and the metaphor of the tree is too on the nose?" Vikram asked.

Mr. Walters smiled a big smile. He loved teaching juniors, who had suffered through being freshmen and slogged through sophomore year and were not quite the cynics they'd become their senior year. And he knew, of course, to separate fact from fiction. But he also knew that no matter how much a sixteen-year-old insisted that something was fiction, it seldom was. There was truth lurking everywhere in those pages.

"We don't," Vikram said. "I promise. I was just playing around with ideas. Now, if I'd written this for our memoir unit, that would be a different story."

"You do realize that if something bad happens to you, I am going to get blamed. Do you have a walnut tree in your backyard?"

"I don't even know what a walnut tree looks like," Vikram said. "And nothing bad is going to happen, I assure you."

"All the same, do you mind if I hang on to this story just a little longer? I want to give it another read and give you some proper comments."

Vikram picked up the story and turned to the final page and found a large A in black ink.

"It's all yours," Vikram said, handing it back.

Mr. Walters took the story and placed it in a file on his desk.

"One is not supposed to be miserable, Vikram," Mr. Walters said. "Just as a general rule."

"I know," Vikram said, even though he wasn't quite sure his

teacher was right. He had liked high school well enough. He did well in his classes, he loved playing golf, he enjoyed his time with his friends. And yet it all felt like listening to music on a pair of earbuds when one of them didn't work. Being on the football field was different. Like he could hear sounds and melodies he hadn't before.

"Have you started on the next assignment? I'll be curious what you come up with."

Vikram shook his head. It was an assignment Mr. Walters called "An Archive of the Self." Each of the students in class had to find an archive of some sort—a photograph, a book, a letter, a newspaper clipping, a will, anything really—that illuminated themselves and the history of their families in a fresh new way.

"In the meanwhile, am I right that I hear that you've joined the football team? You know I played football in high school."

Vikram imagined Mr. Walters in a leather helmet, cutting through defenders, sometime after the Great War.

"I didn't know that," Vikram said.

"My back still hurts from it. I regret playing."

"I'm a sideline warmer," Vikram said. "I think my back is safe."

"You're teammates with MJ now?"

Vikram nodded.

"He took this class with me last year. He wrote a brilliant essay on 'The Hunger Artist.' I'm a little worried that he read the story a bit too closely. Is he doing OK?"

"I think he's fine," Vikram said.

"The game is at home tomorrow night?"

"It is. Are you coming?"

"It's not for me. But you have fun. And be careful."

———⟫⟫⟫———

That Friday night, sitting in the stands, Gautam spent the first half of the game explaining to Gita in great detail the meeting he'd had that afternoon with the Indian CEO. "I think we're even the same age. We Google-mapped it and we grew up several miles from one another in Ahmedabad. It was weird. I always play this mind game of imagining who I would have become if we'd never left India. And I think it's this guy, Rohan Doshi. I'd be rich, but then also shorter. But I'd have all sorts of servants. And a driver for my black Mercedes. And I'd be a paint mogul, hawking the perfect white across Africa."

"You'd also have not met me," Gita said, surprised at the hurt she felt that Gautam had not considered this reality. Over the past few years, it had been her who'd rebuffed Gautam's desire to be intimate at night, making vague reference to perimenopause, when in reality she didn't like the sound of Gautam's voice so close to her ear or the weight of him. But she still felt a pang.

"And that's why, of course, I'm glad we moved," Gautam said with a smile. "Anyway, he assured me that he'd let me know sooner rather than later if they want to buy. I have to think it's going to happen. It would be such a huge sale for me."

Gautam was still providing play-by-play about the meeting when Vikram—number 24—finally entered the game at the start of the second half with the team down by three touchdowns and the season hanging in the balance.

"Shh," Gita said, half of her heart settling in her throat, the second half in her belly. "He's going in."

Gita and Gautam found their palms reaching for each other, a very old comfort. Or more precisely, they clutched at each other, hoping that the harder they grasped, the safer their son would remain.

Gita had worked diligently with Vikram to learn the playbook. She'd treated it like he was studying for an exam, running him through a series of rapid-fire drills. As long as she did that, the game itself had remained abstract. But all that abstraction was melting away as he made his way from the sidelines to a spot behind the quarterback.

"What's he doing there?" Gita asked. She'd helped him learn a series of plays with Xs and Os moving around, assuming he was a blocking X because that's what he'd initially said. "I thought he was only going to be blocking."

"Yeah," Gautam said, letting her hand go. "That's not blocking. That's him directly in the line of fire."

The first time Vikram touched the ball, he took a hand-off from MJ and barely took one step before he was knocked to the ground by two large young men, one of whom stood over Vikram as he lay there. The entire stadium seemed to groan in pain, as if that might make him hurt less. Gita found Gautam's hand again. But as quickly as Vikram went down, he sprang back up. On the very next play, the ball went right back into Vikram's hands, but this time, he evaded the defense for several long yards before he was knocked down. And the play after that, he caught a short pass, ran ten yards, and stepped out of bounds. Gita could see him on the sidelines, leaning on his knees.

"Is he alright? Should we go down there?"

"I think he's just exhausted," Gautam said.

When the team couldn't advance the ball any farther for the next two downs, Vikram went back in. This time, he caught a very short pass and began running. An opposing player was coming straight at him, and Vikram lowered his shoulder and kept running directly into his body. The defender fell to the ground on impact, Vikram jumped over him and ended up in an empty part of the field, running toward the end zone. Suddenly the noise in the stadium was thunderous. And by the time he reached the end zone, one side of the stadium was on its feet, stomping down on the metal bleachers.

Gautam could not have predicted how absolutely elated he would feel at that moment.

"Who's the new fullback?" someone sitting close to Gita and Gautam asked her neighbor.

"Some new kid."

"He's a *full*back," Gita said to Gautam, smiling nervously. "Are there emptybacks?"

For the moment, Gautam and Gita forgot to be worried and concentrated on the field, yelling and screaming along with most of the stadium. When Vikram entered the game next, he pretended to get the ball from the quarterback and ran forward. As an opposing player ran toward him, Vikram lowered his shoulder once again and brutally hit him so that his teammate could continue running. When the play was over, Vikram stood over his opponent, yelling something.

Gautam looked at his son on the field and couldn't recognize this version of him. The sound of bodies bouncing off one another made him feel sick to his stomach. And yet despite his continued worry, Gautam was enthralled at his son's fluid movement and effortless strength.

As the clock wound down, Diego took a handoff from MJ, nearly tumbled to the ground as he broke two tackles, and then, around the forty-yard line, broke free. Around the thirty, when it was clear to everyone in the stands that Diego just needed to outrun one last defender to score, the home section of the stadium started chanting: *"Go, Diego, Go!"*

When the game ended, the home team had scored four unanswered touchdowns. Vikram had scored two; Diego was responsible for the other two, including the one that had won the game. MJ had mostly kept the ball on the ground but had completed twelve of fifteen throws and been very sharp in his decision-making.

"You should look happy," Alex said to Veronica in the stands as the time ran out. "They won."

In the final several yards of his winning touchdown, Diego had slowed down just a hint before crossing into the end zone. Probably no one in the stadium except Veronica had noticed it.

"I'm plenty happy," Veronica said.

"You don't look it."

She exaggerated a smile. "Better?"

"No."

It wasn't the sauntering that upset her. It was the fact that someone else was getting the same kind of touches on the ball that were typically reserved for Diego. This was what she'd feared when Diego had first mentioned the newcomer.

"He and that other kid were actually a good pair in the backfield," Alex said.

"Yes, yes, they were. But I think that kid stands around when he doesn't have the ball. A little selfish. Did you see how many blocks Diego laid down to create those holes for him?"

"Except that one huge block that led to a Diego touchdown."

"Fine," Veronica said, this time smiling more genuinely. "I'm not trying to kill our mood, but that chanting at the end was a bit much."

"What were they saying?" Alex asked.

"You need to have some kids," Veronica said. "And soon. It's from a shitty kids' show."

———— ⟫⟫⟫⟫ ————

In contrast to the tense silence of the previous Friday night, the old, musty locker room was now loud and joyful and raucous as the team walked back in.

"Now, that was fun," Coach Smith said, standing on top of a bench, speaking to his team. "I'm proud of you all. Take a moment to enjoy what you did tonight. On Monday afternoon, we'll get to work on what we need to do for the next game. I know quite a few of you are seniors. We're going to do everything we can to assure that next week isn't your last game. We win and we enter the playoffs strong. Now go clean up and get home safe."

The players screamed and hollered.

In batches of ten, the team quickly showered in lukewarm water, wearing their underwear or bathing suits and flip-flops, making sure not to catch any fungus from the dirty tiles beneath them. Twenty minutes later, the players emerged from the locker room, clean, dressed, and euphoric.

"That was amazing," Alex said when Diego walked up.

Veronica ran her fingers through his wet hair.

"It felt really good to get the win," Diego said, trying to play it cool. He tried to overlay the deep sadness of his father's absence with the happiness that his uncle had witnessed the moment. The game winner, with the crowd going crazy. Later, when he was an adult, the thrill he felt might embarrass him, but now he was sixteen and everyone loved him and he was the star. He'd dreamed of this moment since the first time he'd watched the Raiders with Alex and his grandfather. "We need one more next week. I know we had plans for tonight, but some of the boys are going out. Is that cool? I won't be home too late."

"Of course," Veronica said. "Call if you need a ride home."

Diego held out his hand for some money and smiled sheepishly.

Several feet away, Vikram was talking to Tyler and a few of his friends. They were congratulating him on the game and he was trying to figure out a way to tell them that he couldn't go out with them.

"I have to grab a bite to eat with my parents, but I'll text you after," Vikram said, and walked toward his parents.

"Are you hurt?" Gita asked.

"Of course I'm hurt. Did you see the size of that other team? But don't worry, I'm fine."

Gita placed her hand on Vikram's right shoulder, as if her touch might make it hurt less.

"That was crazy," he said, unable to contain the grin on his face. He'd loved driving a golf ball three hundred yards. He'd loved curling in a putt that he had no business making. But this: lowering his shoulder as the opposing players came at him and bursting through them as if he was pushing open doors; breaking free of tackles and running in an open field with the defenders at his heels; lunging at an opponent's body to clear space for others to run. This felt different. Primal and naughty and dangerous and terrible. "And so much fun."

"Which part did you like the most?" Gautam asked.

Vikram paused for the slightest moment. "I liked the weaving through defenders. But I really liked the blocking."

It would take a deeper, more considered dive into his memories, but Gautam had no recollection of a time when Vikram had displayed or enjoyed this kind of physicality. He had never been a toucher or a roughhouser. Even as a young baby, he liked to be left alone. Golf had been a perfect sport for him.

"Let's go celebrate," Gita said. "Chow mein?"

"Some of the guys are going out to eat. It's a bit of a tradition after wins. And they invited me. Do you mind if I go with them?"

Gita was slightly disappointed, and in order to hide it, she reached into her purse and took out two twenty-dollar bills. "Treat your friends to some ice cream."

"Mom. I'm not in the fifth grade."

She reached back into her purse and this time handed him a condom. A lot of his teammates were nearby, talking to their parents.

"What the hell are you doing?" Vikram asked. "I don't want this. And I don't want it from you."

"We saw *Friday Night Lights*," she said, winking. "We know how these things go. I heard all that screaming in the stadium when you had the ball. We can't stop you. At least we can help you be careful."

"Please don't say anything more. I just want the cash and that's it."

Gita handed him the twenties, and like a magician, placed the condom within the bills so that Vikram wouldn't see it. He put it in his front pocket.

"Be home by midnight," Gautam said. "Nice work tonight."

"Thanks, Dad. I know you were worried. But I was careful out there."

And with that, Vikram was gone.

Gautam watched Vikram as he walked away with a swagger. It wasn't that he envied his own son. Then again, maybe he did. All this was certainly not his high school experience.

EIGHT

The plan was for a large group of players to head out together, but when the dust settled, MJ, Vikram, and Diego ended up walking away from the rest of the group.

"Should we wait for the others?" Vikram asked, not knowing the protocol, feeling like he'd said yes too quickly when MJ and Diego had invited him. Maybe they were expecting him to say no.

"In fact," MJ said, picking up his stride, "we should walk away as quickly as we can. Splitting a bill with ten guys is a nightmare. And those linemen always eat too fucking much. And too fast. I can drive."

MJ led them to the parking lot.

"What the hell is this?" Diego asked. "It looks like a turtle."

"It's a Saab, asshole. The best car made in the last thirty years."

"Is it thirty years old too?"

"Not quite," MJ said. "But it still purrs like a cat."

MJ had liked Saabs forever and had been saving for years to get one. He had been trying to unburden himself of things, but nothing was going to come between him and his new old car.

Vikram got into the back seat. MJ turned the key and the engine struggled to start.

"Sounds more like a dying cat," Diego said.

MJ tried again and this time the engine roared. They drove out of the high school parking lot like three kings.

"You've really never played before tonight?" MJ asked, looking at Vikram in his rearview mirror.

"I've watched on TV."

"You're like a football idiot savant, except you're not an idiot," MJ said.

"You pleased with that one?" Diego asked.

"Quite a bit," MJ said.

"Where're we going?" Diego asked. "Even my balls are hungry."

"Well," MJ said, smiling, "you're going to have to get used to that. Whatever is good. That Indian place is usually open late."

At this, both MJ and Diego turned back to Vikram. "You mind?" MJ asked. "I'm not suggesting it because of you. It's just good."

Vikram smiled. "Indian is fine."

As they made their way to the restaurant, they methodically went through each and every decent play that had led to major yards. Their memory failed them when they had to get ready for school or do chores, but here, when the game was involved and they were discussing their victory, they all had photographic memory.

When they arrived at the Masala Palace, the older proprietor looked at Vikram and gave him an approving nod, but then glanced down at MJ's bare feet.

"*Goras,*" Vikram said under his breath, shrugging. He didn't speak any Hindi or Gujarati but knew some surgically important words and phrases. In this case, *Whities.*

The owner smiled and led them to a nice booth for four right in the front of the restaurant, next to the window looking out onto the street. In that moment, having made two touchdowns and now scoring a good table, Vikram could feel his confidence growing next to these two boys who dripped with it.

"What did you say?" MJ asked when they sat down. "Was there a problem with the no shoes?"

"No, no. I just asked for a nice table."

Because Gita was such a good cook, and because she harbored a certain snobbery when it came to the over-oiled excesses of most Indian restaurant food, Vikram and his family seldom ate at Indian restaurants. And because his grandparents owned a very particular kind of vegetarian restaurant, he couldn't recognize most things on the menu. When the waiter came around to take their orders, Vikram asked for the chicken tikka masala. Given his mother's complicated history with fowl and his family's Gandhian and Hindu background, he felt like he was ordering a steak, a whiskey, and the company of the owner's granddaughter for the evening.

"Are you kidding?" MJ asked. "That's a colonial dish. Something to soothe the palates of British fucks who couldn't manage actual spices. I don't want to step on your toes, but can I recommend the butter chicken here? It may be colonial as well, but it's the best thing these nice people cook. I'm also going to order the okra for the table."

"Do you mind if Apu here orders for all of us?" Diego asked Vikram.

"Please do," Vikram said, using Apu's accent and regretting it the second it was out of his mouth.

The waiter turned to MJ, who rattled off several dishes without looking at the menu.

"Are you a regular here?" Vikram asked MJ after the waiter left with the order.

"We usually get it to go. I'm surprised the waiter doesn't recognize me. I'm mostly a vegetarian now, but I make an exception for the chicken in this place."

In the few seconds of silence that followed, all three of them looked through the restaurant window and noticed Stanley Kincaid walking down the street with another group of kids. He stood above the rest.

"Please don't stop," MJ said under his breath.

"I saw the two of you talking last week," Vikram said. "You know that asshole?"

"I know that asshole," Diego replied, feeling a visceral anger suddenly coursing through him. "If he sees us and asks to join, say no. Say that we're waiting for Sara or someone. Just don't let him sit down. It'll ruin the night, I promise."

After the debacle in Spanish, Stanley had moved on from Vikram and arrived in Diego's orbit. Diego was small his freshman year. The two were in an advanced math class together, the only two freshmen. They became class mascots of sorts, occasionally beloved but mostly ridiculed. At some point, Diego began doing well on tests. At first, it was a competition between him and Stanley to see who could get the highest score among those with the lowliest standing. But Diego started inching ahead, and then was bounding by feet and yards. Halfway through the semester, on a major exam that covered most everything they'd learned, Diego had the second-highest grade in the entire class.

Because all the kids were good at math, the teacher assumed they were also good kids. But whenever the teacher stepped out before class started, the students had developed a little warm-up game. Some of the older, bigger boys would take it upon themselves to punch the younger, smaller ones on the arm. The ones who didn't flinch earned their momentary favor. Not respect, but a temporary break from derision. Soon enough, Diego was at the receiving end of the punches, coming from Stanley who was, at that point, much bigger and stronger and the one the older kids had picked to give Diego his beatings. The better Diego did on the tests, the harder Stanley would hit. And the harder Stanley hit, the harder Diego struggled to not break down in tears. The year eventually ended. Summer came. Diego had a massive growth spurt and Stanley never touched him again. Now, whenever Diego and Stanley interacted, Stanley pretended that the math beatings didn't happen. Diego liked to remind him that they had.

Stanley had walked past them, but, as if he had eyes in the back of his head, he turned around and noticed the trio through the restaurant window. He said something to his group, who didn't break stride as they kept moving down the street. Stanley walked into the restaurant and came to their table.

"It's the gridiron all-stars," Stanley said, clapping his hands. "What up, boys? Hell of a fucking game. Is this the victory dinner? Are the cheerleaders on their way?"

Stanley sounded like he was speaking through his nose. It was his everyday voice.

The other diners turned to look at Stanley, who could be heard throughout the restaurant. He was a tall, skinny kid, wearing baggy Carhartts and a Powell Peralta hoodie. It was the look of disheveled indifference that most kids their age wore.

"Was I right or was I right about that Vitamin A?" Stanley asked.

MJ looked uncomfortable; Diego was confused.

"Hey, man," MJ said quietly, avoiding eye contact.

MJ had never been on the receiving end of even a negative look from Stanley because MJ had arrived his freshman year fully formed. He was in charge of himself, never needing anyone. And the more he needed no one, the more everyone needed him—to play on their teams, to be in their groups, to be their friend. Stanley had gotten to know MJ when he was a junior and Stanley was a sophomore. At that point, Stanley was living with his mother and his father was gone. And MJ became a kind of salvation. In his own way, Stanley could be charming and engaging. For his part, MJ never had the heart to shake off the puppy who was nipping at his heels. And so Stanley was suddenly everywhere that MJ was. He tried making the football team but that didn't work. But he was always the one greeting MJ at the end of games. The one trying to set up the hangouts before anyone else had the chance. What Stanley understood about MJ was his one weakness: his inability to set boundaries, to say no. At some level, MJ knew that he had been given everything, and because of that, he hated the idea of rejecting anyone.

"You guys about to eat this dope-ass Pakistani food?" Stanley asked.

The three of them just nodded, each waiting for one of the others to say something to Stanley so that he'd go away. It was a testament to all three that despite the fraught history they each had with Stanley, despite the fact that they had spent the better part of the evening violently knocking people on the ground, none had the heart to lie when he asked: "Is this seat empty?"

Vikram felt like he'd connected with Diego and MJ on the field and off it during the car ride. Now hating Stanley together would seal the deal.

And just like that, Stanley sat down in the fourth seat. When the waiter returned, Stanley ordered the chicken tikka masala.

"And can we all get a round of that great Indian beer you have on tap?"

Stanley said it with such confidence that the waiter didn't seem to suspect anything. Or perhaps he did but was letting it pass because Vikram was part of the group. For the first few seconds after the cold beer came and the boys took sips of it, knowing that they had gotten away with something, they didn't mind Stanley being there. But that lasted for barely a minute. When it had been just the three of them, they could talk about the random details of the game they'd played, move on to colonial culinary history, and come back to a particular defensive scheme that MJ had correctly read to get the ball to one of his backs. But now the rhythm that they'd just created was broken.

"So I hear some rumblings from the guys on the team that they aren't thrilled to have a new player come on this late in the season," Stanley said.

For a fleeting moment, Vikram had thought that maybe in the time that had passed since they used to hang out, Stanley had matured, mellowed. That his growth spurt had not just been in inches. But he was still the same guy, always ready to needle, now with acne on his forehead and uneven facial hair.

"No one said that," MJ said. "We love having Vikram on the team, and we love it that he just helped us win."

"You can't be too thrilled with it," Stanley said, turning to Diego. "Those are your hand-offs he's getting. He's cutting your chances of getting recruited by Michigan in half. Or is it Alabama? I bet you'd like those pretty blond Southern girls."

"What are you doing?" Diego asked. "Drink your beer. We're here to celebrate. We just won a huge game. I'm sure you can still catch up with your friends who you abandoned."

"Yes, yes, of course," Stanley said. "We're all best friends as long as we're winning. Go team."

Stanley had the ability to get to the truth of things. But he also had the inability to stop talking when he was ahead.

He turned to MJ. "I have to say, after seeing you landing your passes on a dime, I don't quite understand why you're wasting your talents by going to a shitty football school. You could be the next Peyton Manning. Smart, cerebral, intense."

"Is that meant to be a compliment?" MJ asked.

"No," Stanley. "It's my motivational speech. Aim higher. Be better."

"How are your college plans going?" Vikram asked. Once, long ago, they'd talked about where they wanted to go. Vikram had said he wanted to follow his dad to Cal. "You still jacked up for Long Beach State?"

Stanley turned to Vikram and for a few seconds just stared him down. "Snobbery is beneath you."

"I'm not being a snob. You told me you wanted to go there."

"You're being a snob, Shastri."

Conflict was Stanley's rhetorical style, his only gear. And Vikram's attempt at replying in kind—going at Stanley—had not worked out. He felt rebuffed.

"I'm going to go to the bathroom and then to check on the food," Vikram said.

"Yeah, why don't you do that," Stanley said.

He hated Stanley for already having messed up the start of a pretty good evening. MJ and Diego nodded to him as he left.

Vikram had once overheard his parents talking about why bathrooms in Indian restaurants were always filthy. They'd said something about caste that he'd not understood. The bathroom in his grandparents' restaurant was always clean, as was this one. And he felt relatively safe in it, protected by Indians he didn't know.

Starting sometime in the seventh grade, Vikram had discovered that the public bathrooms he had occasion to enter—the ones at school—were dangerous and radioactive. The places where some kids smoked and others got smoked. Vikram was always in danger of being the latter. And so part of the reason he got good grades and maintained great relationships with his teachers over the years was that when he had to use the bathroom at school, when it was impossible to hold it, he could wait until he was in class and ask the teacher if he could go when the bathrooms were more empty. Some teachers refused the request from students they thought used it as an excuse to wander the halls, but they never refused Vikram. He got himself in and out of there as quickly as he could. He'd seen classmates return from the bathroom with their shorts gone or their noses bleeding. With every passing year, with every additional inch he grew in height and across his shoulders, the fear of the bathroom never fully dissipated.

Vikram finished using the restroom, washed his hands, and stepped out. At the front counter, on his way back to his table, the elderly owner stopped him.

"You live here?"

Vikram nodded.

"You should come in with your family sometime."

"I will."

Vikram looked over at the table and noticed Stanley, MJ, and Diego leaning in close to one another.

"Before Gandhi comes back, I want to discuss the vitamins," Stanley said.

"You got it from *him?*" Diego asked MJ, looking incredulous.

MJ just nodded.

"Fuck," Diego said. "At least shut up about it, especially with Vikram here."

"I'm just saying that I thought they were good for taking tests, but you two on the field was a whole revelation. They really kicked in during the second half."

From his younger brother, Stanley had access to Adderall. He'd mentioned its availability casually to MJ, handing him a little baggie with two pills just in case he wanted to use them. Feeling really low about the state of the team and his sudden lack of interest in the game, MJ had brought it up to Diego after their humiliating loss the previous week. At first, the two of them had laughed off the idea. Then they started going back and forth, reasoning with each other that it was a do-or-die game, and that certainly their opponents were doing all sorts of other, worse things to gain an advantage, and finally, that it would not make a difference if they took it. So why not? Diego hadn't asked MJ where he got the pills. Do something, the coach had told them.

"I was seeing holes in the defense that I'd never seen before," MJ admitted. "Pure focus. No noise."

"It was fine," Diego said. "I didn't really feel anything."

"Don't worry," Stanley said. "Your secret is safe with me."

It was not lost on either MJ or Diego that the promise of safety was, of course, a kind of threat.

"So what's up now? Vikram is suddenly your new best friend? I get no gratitude for saving your season?" Stanley paused. "Joking and pills aside, you know he's going to take your spot, Diego."

"He's not," Diego said.

"Just because you don't want him to doesn't mean he won't. He's good. He's got size on you."

"You Bill Belichick now?"

"No. I'm simply a guy who can see what's in front of you."

"What's in front of me?"

"Him. You're good and fast. But there's just something about this guy that's different. Even from the bleachers, I can see him hitting a new gear."

"Fuck him," Diego said. "And fuck you. We were having a nice time until you showed up."

"He got lucky in one game," MJ said to Diego, trying to assure him. "And you were the one that opened that huge hole for him. You're good. And yes. Fuck you, Stanley."

Vikram was about to return to the table.

"Do you want one piece of advice from me?" the owner asked.

"Sure."

"Stay away from the American boys. They're trouble."

Vikram almost reminded him that he was an American boy too, but he understood what the owner meant.

"And just this one time for the beer. Because of you. Not again."

"I understand."

"Go. The food is coming right now. I added some biryani and samosas. You're growing boys."

Right after Vikram sat down, the food began arriving and despite the volume of the order, the boys ate quickly and ravenously in a way that only teenagers who had just run around for two hours straight could.

"Was I right about the butter chicken?" MJ asked Vikram.

"That and the okra," Vikram said. "And even the eggplant, which I usually hate."

"You know what I've never quite understood," Stanley said, struggling to scoop his food with his naan. "Why isn't Indian food as popular as Mexican food? I've thought about this question a lot. I think it's the smell. People don't like the smell of curry."

Vikram's body stiffened and blood rushed to his face. He knew Stanley was not just talking about the smell of the food. He was talking about the smell of the people who cooked and ate it. His grand-parents, his parents, the nice man behind the counter.

"Mexican food is popular because this used to be Mexico," Diego said. "Indian food isn't as popular because Columbus fucked up."

"Clever, Diego. You've always been clever. It's your best trait."

Diego took a deep breath. Dinner was almost over. He was still annoyed at himself for not saying anything when Stanley asked to sit down.

"Hey," Stanley continued, sticking with Diego. "I saw your mom after the game. Is that your dad? I've never seen him."

"Why are you concerned?" Diego asked.

"I'm not. It's just that I've never seen your dad at these games, given that you're the big star."

"It's my uncle. He's visiting."

Stanley didn't need Diego to confirm his father's absence. Given that Stanley's father was gone, even when he was around, Stanley could recognize that slight twitch on Diego's face.

"Huh," Stanley said. "I guess you and I are more alike than different."

Of all the things Stanley had said all night, this struck Diego the hardest. "We are *nothing* alike."

"Alright," Stanley said, raising his hands in defense. "Can we just end the night right by doing our top five?"

"What are we talking about here?" MJ asked. "NBA, rappers, freshman girls, serial killers?"

"I was thinking NBA," Stanley said. "But now I'm not sure. So many choices."

As they scraped the last of the food off every plate on the table, there was a lot of back-and-forth about the two-way skills of the actual MJ, the other LBJ, Curry, Shaq, Kobe, Magic. Stanley was particularly adamant about Russell—Westbrook, not Bill. Diego was partial to Kevin Durant.

"KD is a bitch," Stanley said. "He cracks like a stick. And he's never won anything on his own."

Vikram had stayed out of the fray, finishing the butter chicken. He had decided that he was going to come here by himself from now on and order a full plate of butter chicken just for himself. He'd been denied it too long.

"I've got mine," Vikram finally said, and took a breath before starting. "Bird, John Stockton, the Steves—Nash and Kerr—and Vlade."

"Ah," Stanley said immediately. "You got all the jokes. But for the record, Vlade is not white. He's Serbian."

"Dude, Serbs are white," Vikram said. "Bosnians, on the other hand . . ."

"Who exactly are the Serbs?" MJ asked. "Is Dirk a Serb? And why do you know all this shit?"

Vikram shrugged. "I did a report on Yugoslavia in geography. My dad has worked with a bunch of them."

When the bill arrived, Stanley turned to MJ. "You got this, right? I've seen that house you live in."

MJ took the bill. "I'm paying for my teammates because they made me look good tonight. But you owe me thirty dollars."

"I'm good for it," Stanley said, drinking the last of his beer. "I am also good for a party I just heard about. You guys want to come with? Cave House is open for business again."

Stanley held up his phone.

Among their fellow students, parties at the Cave House had a mythic quality. Similar perhaps to the parties teenagers must have secretly thrown at the Colosseum after the fall of Rome, or in Agra when the Taj Mahal was in the early stages of construction and there was white marble strewn about.

"I should probably head home," Vikram said, even though he'd heard about the Cave House and had always wanted to go to one of the parties. He'd never been in a social situation where he could be invited. Suddenly he felt like an extra wheel. And he felt guilty for thinking of going without Tyler.

"This isn't peer pressure," MJ said. "But you should come. We'll leave if it sucks."

"It's not going to suck," Diego said. "C'mon, Vikram. You'll have a great time. We all deserve it."

"Yes," Stanley added. "Give in to the peer pressure. There will be plenty o' bitches and brews there."

This elicited a chuckle from the other three. He could be funny when he got out of his own way.

A few minutes later, all four piled into MJ's car, taking the winding road that led out of the town and up and up into the hills. Stanley insisted on sitting in the front seat because he was tall. Vikram sat right behind him, and every few minutes, he would lean his knee into the seat, making eye contact with Diego as he did so.

As they drove up the hill, Stanley removed a flask from his pocket and took a big swig.

"You guys want to get in on this?" he asked. "My Día de los Muertos drink. Red Bull and tequila."

"Put that away," MJ said. "I don't want a cop seeing it."

"Relax," Stanley said. He took one more drink and then slowly put it away. "No one is going to pull over the star quarterback in his Saab. Now, if Bin Laden was driving, that would be a different story."

Vikram pushed his knee into the back of Stanley's seat as hard as he could. "Fuck off, white boy."

There was something about being on that field and knocking players down that had given Vikram a new confidence.

"If you want, you can come back here and suck my 9/11 dick."

MJ made approving eye contact with Vikram in his rearview mirror.

At the Cave House, MJ was barely done parking the car when Stanley opened his door to get out.

"I want my money," MJ said.

"I got it. I'll give it to you in a minute."

He stepped out and disappeared.

"That dude is really fucking *weird*," Vikram said.

Weird was a catchall for the inexplicable, a type of person they had not yet figured out. They understood the athletes, the nerds, the pretty ones. There was no explanation for Stanley.

"Why didn't one of you tell him he couldn't sit down?" Diego asked.

"Why didn't you?" MJ asked.

As they stepped out of the car, the air was filled with the smells of weed and tobacco, and there was an uncomfortable fall chill.

NINE

Once, the Cave House had been the sprawling faux-Italian estate of a movie producer who had made his fortune on B films in the 1970s and liked to say that the Eagles had written "King of Hollywood" after attending one of his parties. With its grand living room, ten bedrooms, swimming pool, and ornate, vaguely Romanesque statues scattered throughout the garden, the parties would start on Thursday afternoon and end on Sunday evening. But now all that was left was the solid cement foundation, walls stripped down to the studs, and a few unusable toilets. During the day and from a distance, it looked like a house that had been bombed and left to ruin. It was this mood of ruin, and the history of parties past, that gave the place its particular charm, attracting teenagers bearing beer and a certain Dionysian randiness.

Up there, high in the hills, there were no neighboring houses and so no adults to call the police when a party got too loud or out of control. But the real allure and mystery of the place came from the nearby caves. At the back of the property, a path flanked on both sides by an assortment of sharp cactus and native brush ascended up to a small clearing. Here were three caves, each lined up to the next, each a little bigger than the previous one. The openings were roughly five feet high, leading to larger spaces that went back some thirty feet, getting progressively darker, hotter, and narrower. The caves had once been occupied by Native Americans who had lived on the land. There was a rumor that the biggest of the three was now home to a lone mountain lion.

MJ had parked in an open field next to groups of other cars. With Stanley already gone, the three of them walked toward the main crowd of partiers, maybe a hundred kids congregated in and around what used to be the large living room. There were lights strung up on the scaffolding and several kegs scattered around. There were separate clusters of boys and girls and a few groups with a mix of both, many drinking from red Solo cups. And because most of the partiers wanted to signal that being there wasn't that big of a deal, they were all dressed casually in baggy 501s and T-shirts, despite the chill. A group of skateboarders carved the empty pool. A mumbled music filled the air—mostly white kids listening to Kanye and Kendrick.

"I didn't know this place actually existed," Diego said, looking around with a smile on his face as if he'd just arrived at a fair.

"I used to come up here when I was a freshman, but then the cops shut it down for a while," MJ said.

"Does anyone own it?" Diego asked.

"One of those assholes," MJ said, gesturing toward a group of guys in a corner. Most of them played lacrosse; a few played both lacrosse and water polo. "Family property that they don't actually need."

"Your cousins?" Diego asked with a grin.

"Fuck off," MJ said. "Actually, they probably are if you go back far enough."

Vikram went to parties here and there, the kind where a lone warm six-pack was the feted guest of honor. But he'd never been to something like this, where the beer was an afterthought. The dimness of the strung-up lights made everyone look beautiful and dreamy. Across the room, he noticed a young woman from his math class that he'd had his eye on since the very first day of high school. They'd shared maybe five or ten words since then. With the beer from dinner swirling in his head, his heart and belly bumped up against each other.

"Oh shit, Erin is here," Diego said, his own heart bumping up against his belly, spying the same young woman. "The game-winning touchdown has to be worth at least a five-minute conversation with the hottest, least-white white girl in the school." He tried to muster confidence as he said this, taking half a step toward her. But his teeth began to chatter.

As Diego disappeared into the crowd, Vikram reasoned to himself that he wouldn't have known what to say to her anyway. And given the choice, Erin would certainly choose Diego.

MJ and Vikram headed for the beer.

"You know all these people?" Vikram asked, now nervous that he had to make conversation with MJ. He recognized most of the kids from school but didn't really know any of them.

"Most of them," MJ said. "I hope Diego isn't chasing too long. I'm actually ready to go. I don't know why I thought there would be something different this time. It's the same old bullshit. Rich kids and beer."

"Let's give it a moment," Vikram said. "It's new bullshit to me."

MJ went and got them two beers.

"Did you read the book I gave you?" MJ asked, handing a red cup full of beer to Vikram.

"I did," Vikram said, taking a long, greedy sip.

Vikram had, in fact, read *A Separate Peace* in one sitting, the first time he'd ever done that. His father had passed him at one point as he was sitting there reading, paused to look at the cover of the book as if he recognized it, and then continued on without saying anything.

"And?"

"First of all, Devon is a white-ass school. Places like that still exist?"

"They pretend not to, but they still do. My parents wanted me to go to someplace similar. I refused."

"Wanted to slum it with us public school kids instead?"

"Way easier to get into college from a public school," MJ said, smiling. "I'm a dime a dozen at a boarding school."

"I can say this because you seem about as straight as straight can be, but that read like a really gay book to me. Like those two dudes were just roommates? I don't think so. They were totally hooking up."

The last portion of that literary analysis was out of Vikram's comfort zone.

"Of course they were," MJ said. "Finny and his pink shirt. Which, by the way, is a great name for a band. But, no, I'm not hitting on you. I would if that was my thing. But it's not. Though the way you plowed through those tacklers tonight—that was hot."

"I wouldn't shake a branch if we were on a tree together," Vikram said.

"Why wouldn't I be the one shaking the branch?" MJ asked.

"Because Finny is the outgoing, athletic one."

"Is that what I seem like to you?"

"You're outgoing and athletic," Vikram said. "I'm clearly Gene, the smart, envious one who makes Finny fall. But then Finny dies from the fall? That was dark. I wasn't expecting that at all."

"But you're the one that essentially won the game tonight."

"Don't say that to Diego," Vikram said, in a faux whisper. "I think he thinks he won the game. Which officially he did."

MJ grinned.

"We can win next week," MJ said. "And then make a deep playoff run. I was getting bored of the game, but I'm feeling a bit more excited about it. At least for the moment. I'm glad you're playing. The team needed some new blood."

He paused to have a sip.

"However you read it," MJ continued, "it's a good book. Deeply Buddhist without trying to be. One long meditation on removing envy from your body. About clearing your mind."

"Is that why you don't wear shoes?"

"It helps me feel more grounded to the earth. And I'm also sick of wearing them. Nothing against Diego, but those shoes he's wearing tonight are like three hundred dollars. That can feed a whole family in Haiti for a year." Diego usually tended toward nicer athletic wear—lots of Nike, the occasional Adidas, mostly shorts and hoodies. Vikram dressed similarly, though with a lower price tag. They'd both settled into apathetic jock chic. In contrast, MJ had recently discovered thrift stores and secondhand jeans and old T-shirts.

"But they're really nice shoes," Vikram said.

"True. You should give it a shot."

"What?"

"Going barefoot. You'll love it."

Vikram just smiled. "I can't pull that shit off. I'd get sent home immediately. It's about the whitest thing you can do."

"Trust me," MJ said. "I can go whiter."

As they were standing there sipping their beers, a young woman walked up to them. Stephanie Cho. She had been the recipient of the text from MJ the previous week when he should have been apologizing to Sara for being rude.

"Hey," she said, tapping MJ lightly on his stomach. "I didn't think you were going to come up."

MJ was about to take a step toward her but then remained where he was.

"It was a bit of a last-minute decision."

Stephanie, a senior with fashion sense that leaned toward neo-hippie, was wearing a paisley sundress down to her ankles that neither Vikram nor MJ would have guessed cost seven hundred dollars. She was the founder and president of the anticapitalist club at school, which she'd first started as a performance piece for her drama class but began treating seriously when people started showing up and staying for the meetings. They read Marx, planned boycotts, wrote manifestos. Vikram knew her from his classes. She had some kind of Arabic writing tattooed on her wrist. Vikram could not understand how her parents had allowed all this.

There were two rumors that followed Stephanie around. First, that she was from a fabulously wealthy South Korean family, whose money had either been made from Samsung TVs or an endless string of liquor stores and laundromats from Ventura to San Diego and all points east to the Arizona border. The second rumor was that as a sophomore, she had taken the SATs and had gotten one answer wrong on purpose to ensure that she didn't get a perfect score. A small blemish, she had supposedly said, was the key to great success, which might also explain why one of her otherwise perfect front teeth was slightly crooked.

"Do you know Vikram?" MJ said, turning to bring Vikram into the conversation.

"Of course," Stephanie said. "Hey, man. Way to break the code."

"Code?"

"*We* don't play football."

"We?"

"You know."

"What do we play then?"

"Not football."

"*We* also don't get tattoos," Vikram said.

"We?" Stephanie asked, and smiled.

The three of them stood there. Stephanie took MJ's beer out of his hand, took a casual, quick sip, and gave it back.

"I'll see you later," she said, walking away. "Don't leave without saying bye."

Vikram had seen MJ with Sara around the halls.

"What?" MJ asked.

"Nothing," Vikram said, smiling.

"It's complicated."

"I'm sure it is," Vikram said.

Vikram's family hadn't talked openly about boyfriends and girl-friends until his sister Priya had gotten a boyfriend her junior year. Since then his parents had occasionally inquired if Vikram was interested in anyone. He'd had crushes, but didn't feel confident enough to ever be open about it, especially to his parents. But now, taller than most of his classmates and with two career touchdowns under his belt, Vikram looked around the party for Erin.

"Wanna check out the caves?" MJ asked. "I need a little peace and quiet."

Vikram looked down at MJ's feet.

"You sure? Not if there are mountain lions up there."

"That's just country myth. The caves are amazing and completely empty, unless someone is using one as a hotbox."

They didn't make it up to the caves for another twenty minutes. Despite MJ's desire to leave the party, there were plenty of people wanting to chat him up. And he was gracious in his conversation, generous in the exchanges. Vikram stood in the wings and sipped his beer. It was like spending an evening with a politician as he went around kissing babies and shaking hands. Vikram liked being close to MJ's easy charisma.

As they finally moved away from the house and farther along the path to the caves, it got darker and darker. They both used their phones for light, passing several people coming down as they made their way up. They couldn't see each other in the night. When they reached the caves, there were more people gathered near the one farther back and so they entered the first, which seemed unoccupied.

MJ went in first. After he ducked through the entrance, the cave was high enough for him to stand upright. Vikram followed. They took several steps in and MJ turned off his phone light. The darkness mostly ate up the remaining light coming from Vikram's phone, and when he switched it off, Vikram couldn't tell what was up or down, left or right. He'd never been so in the dark.

"Hello," MJ said. He didn't say it very loud, but his voice traveled to the back of the cave and returned to them. *"Hello."*

"Boom," Vikram said, a little louder. The echo returned even louder. *"Boum."*

One second, Vikram was standing there; the next he was completely disoriented. He took one step to the right but hit the side of the cave. He turned ninety degrees and took several long steps, bringing him back out into the night. He had trouble catching his breath; his chest felt tight. He didn't like the constricted feeling of being in there.

"You alright?" MJ asked when he emerged a few seconds later.

"People really hook up in there?"

"If you really don't want to see who you're hooking up with."

They sat in front of the cave and finished their beers and talked football and college and classes. The city below them was bright; the stars above brighter. A little drunk from both the game and the beer, and with the dinner with Stanley now receding from his mind, Vikram felt good.

"Wanna head out?" MJ asked.

"I don't want to go inside, but can we quickly peek into the other caves? Are they different?"

"They're a bit bigger. That's it."

There was a group of kids hanging out in front of the farthest cave, drinking and vaping. It was hard to tell who was who in the darkness. But it was easy to recognize Stanley's high-pitched voice. Just as Vikram and MJ walked up, the gathered group of kids started making their way back toward the house. As they walked by, one of them mumbled, "Stanley is fucking crazy." It was only after she'd passed him that Vikram realized that Erin had been in the middle of the group. He'd seen her in his light and she'd seen him in hers.

MJ and Vikram walked up to the mouth of the final cave.

"I watched you take your shot with Erin," they heard Stanley say. "You need to now step aside."

Stanley and Diego, standing just inside the cave, appeared in their light. Stanley was talking to Diego, who turned and noticed his teammates. Since they'd seen him last, Stanley had grown drunker and more belligerent, slurring his words and looking unstable on his feet. He didn't register MJ and Vikram's arrival.

"I think maybe you want to go back down to the party with the others," Diego said. "And drink some water. We all need some water."

"Just because you can run with a football doesn't mean you can tell me what to do." Stanley finally noticed MJ and Vikram. "I see now. A little three-against-one. This is your version of playing fair? Did you text your pals when you got all nervous and tongue-tied in front of Erin and noticed that I was doing just fine?"

"All good?" MJ asked Diego, stepping into the cave.

The only source of light came from their phones. Outside the cave, the darkness was mitigated by the stars above and the city lights below. But once inside and facing inward, the boys found that the darkness had a register and intensity they had never known. It was hard to tell up from down, side from side, boy from boy. They couldn't tell if their eyes were open or closed.

"We should head down," Diego said.

As Diego stepped away, Stanley stumbled. MJ placed his hand on Stanley's arm to steady him. "Why don't you walk down with us?"

"Don't touch me!" Stanley's voice reached a new octave. "None of you fucking touch me." The command had traveled into the back of the cave and returned as a thundering commandment: "*. . . Fucking touch me!*"

"Let's go, then," Diego said, standing in the entrance. He'd had enough of Stanley. "He can stay up here by himself." Then he added under his breath, with an additional bit of cruelty, "He's used to it."

"Fuck off," Stanley said, his voice louder but not yet very threatening. "Why don't you pussies head back down. I'm good up here."

If they weren't so full of alcohol and adrenaline, the three boys might have heard the sadness and longing in Stanley's voice.

In that moment, one force was leading MJ, Vikram, and Diego down the path and back to the party and more cold beer, and another, entirely different force was propelling them toward Stanley and into the cave.

"Fuck you, dude," Vikram said. "You're such an asshole. You've always been an asshole. You really think Erin gives a shit about you?"

At this question, Stanley lunged toward the stronger Vikram, who just remained standing there. Stanley bounced off him and fell to the ground. In the dark, Vikram wasn't sure exactly what had happened. "What are you doing?" he asked.

The three boys each held up their phone lights and looked at one another for a signal on how to proceed. MJ took a step in the dark, toward the entrance, and inadvertently pushed Stanley with his feet, as if he were sweeping away garbage.

"Get off me, bitch," Stanley said. He started wildly swinging his feet and arms.

"We're just trying to get past you," MJ said.

MJ's words disappeared into the walls of the cave, just as Stanley swept his feet under MJ, destabilizing him so that he wobbled and fell. As if by instinct, MJ sprang back up, swung his fist, and connected directly with Stanley's bony glass jaw. Instead of crumbling, Stanley stood up and swung right back, connecting with MJ's ear, who yelled out in pain.

At first, Vikram and Diego froze at the sudden arrival of the moment. But then each saw the exchange as permission to enter the fray—to help their friend, but perhaps more, to get in a lick of their own and get back at Stanley. Diego began with a kick to Stanley's stomach. Vikram's swing landed unevenly on Stanley's mouth, prompting him to let out a small whimper as it connected.

Over the next minute, with the dark pierced here and there by the phone lights shining up from the ground where they'd fallen in the commotion, there were four sets of arms and legs and grunts and thuds everywhere. Whispers echoed, screams died along the walls.

Vikram's hand began to hurt from connecting with so much bone; he could taste salt in his mouth. Increasingly, Stanley sounded and acted like a cornered cat, pawing and punching and scratching.

"Just calm down," MJ said, breathing heavily. "And stay down."

"No," Stanley hissed. He had been holding his own, landing one solid punch on one of the three boys for each punch he took.

Trying to catch his breath, Vikram picked up his phone and shined it on the other two to orient himself. Vikram stood several feet away and watched as MJ and Diego, like shadow puppets, took turns going in on Stanley, trying to subdue him. Diego wildly took his swings, his fists landing lightly. However, it was MJ who put all his weight into it, driving down one vicious punch after another and using his whole body to keep Stanley on the ground each time he tried to get up. "Stop following me around," he said as he landed one more punch.

"Fuck off," Stanley said, now lying still on the floor of the cave, exhausted.

Vikram took a step forward and was about to give him one last kick but didn't. He shined his light down on Stanley, who had pulled himself up and was leaning against a rock. His hair was disheveled, and yet somehow he didn't look that bad, despite the hits he had taken. He had a bit of a split lip and a slight, defiant smile on his face, as if he had won.

Diego again moved toward Stanley.

"Enough," Vikram said, pulling at Diego's arm. "Let's go."

Seconds later the three of them quickly made their way down the path.

"What did we just do?" Vikram asked himself and then the other two boys. He was breathing heavily and thought he might start crying. He'd never hit another person in his life. "Do we just leave him there?"

"We barely touched him," Diego said, trying and failing to convince himself. He dug at his scalp as if that might give him some clarity about what had come over the three of them. "Let him sober up and then he'll come down."

"Yeah, he'll get a breather and make his way down here," MJ said. "But you know he's going to say some shit about how we attacked him. As long as we stick to the story of how it started, we'll be good. We've nothing to worry about. Everyone at this party will attest to him having drunk too much and being crazy. We did nothing wrong. Let's hang for a little longer and then we can head out. If we leave now and he comes down, it'll be weird that we're suddenly gone."

They stepped back into the party, each their own brand of frayed. MJ's feet ached from banging against Stanley's shins and his arms were scratched; Diego thought a bottom tooth had come loose; Vikram's chest felt like it might explode. And yet despite the fear and confusion the three boys felt, they were exhilarated, the adrenaline coursing through them like it had on the field hours before.

"I'll see you guys in a few," MJ said. "And if I don't, let's meet back at my car in about half an hour. That should be plenty of time."

MJ looked around to find Stephanie. He'd tried sounding in control in front of Vikram and Diego, but he wasn't. His heart was beating wildly. Sure, Stanley had knocked him down, but he was the one who'd gone in with the punches. He just couldn't stop himself.

While he wasn't going to tell her what had happened, Stephanie's simple presence would calm him down. But it was Sara he saw first. Before he could walk the other way, she headed straight toward him.

"Is there something you want to tell me?" she asked.

"What are you talking about?" MJ responded, wondering what exactly she knew. "Are you mad I didn't tell you I was coming up here? We decided last minute."

"We?"

"A couple of the football guys."

"Why was Stephanie Cho drinking out of your beer earlier? Is that where you've been? And before you ask, I have more friends here than you do. And they all have eyes."

"She asked for a sip and I gave it to her. The beer line was long. I know in some cultures that's essentially a marriage proposal, but here, it's just a sip of beer."

"Such the wit. So where have you been all this time? I've been looking for you."

"As I said, I was with football guys. Diego and Vikram. The new kid. I was showing him around. He wanted to see the caves. What's going on? Why are you being like this?"

"Because you're making me this way," Sara said. "You're lying about something, but I don't know what it is yet. You just seem weird. Not just right now but for a while. What's going on with you?"

"I just finished being knocked around on a field for more than two hours. I'm exhausted and probably a bit concussed and ready to go home."

"Then go home and get some sleep. And please, I beg of you, put on some fucking shoes. It's getting really old."

Sara walked away. MJ just stood there, dazed by the sudden turn in the evening.

Vikram had gotten himself a second beer because he realized that with every sip, he could think less about what had just happened in the cave. He went to the empty pool and sat on the ground near it, watching the skaters gracefully drop in at the deep end, riding the length of it and grinding the shallow edges before dropping back down. He'd spent all his junior high years on a skateboard and had become pretty skilled. He'd felt his most free then, skating through the neighborhoods near his house, ollieing over a curb and dropping down from one. But when high school started, he thought he was too old to keep at it. And his mother had worried that he might injure his ankle, messing with his golf game. He wasn't good enough to do what these kids were doing, but he'd be fine dipping into the shallow end and riding around for a bit.

"You going to give it a shot?"

Vikram turned toward the soft voice. Erin was standing over him, her brown hair down to her shoulders, the back of her haloed from the house lights. He stood up. They'd never talked outside of class.

He'd always been too nervous, plus Erin had been in that PE class when Stanley had pulled down his pants. She was pretty in a way that looking her in the eyes made him nervous.

"Not tonight," Vikram said. "I'm a little tired. But these guys are way better than me."

"That was a good game. I hear you've never played before. You're quickly becoming a suburban legend."

"Yeah. I got a little lucky with the catches. You were there?"

"I don't usually go, but I did tonight. It was fun. I didn't exactly peg you as the football type."

"I didn't either."

Vikram looked back out into the crowd of kids. While he had been sitting there, he'd seen Diego a couple of times, circling around, probably looking for Erin. He was not in the house anymore. Vikram felt a little guilty for talking to her. He would explain to Diego that she was the one who'd walked up to him.

The two of them stood without saying anything. Both were a little shy around each other.

"Everything OK?" Erin asked. She then pointed to her lip. "You're bleeding a little."

Vikram used his hand to quickly wipe away the blood. "It must have happened in the game," he said. "It's also been kind of a weird night. I don't usually come to things like this."

"I don't either," Erin said.

Vikram didn't immediately respond.

"Did you peg me as the party-on-Friday-nights type?" Erin asked.

"Not really," Vikram said. "What are you supposed to do here? Hang out and drink beer?"

"Pretty much. And pretend to not care."

She took a sip of her beer. He took a sip of his.

"What are you getting in math?" Erin asked.

"I don't know."

"Sure you do."

"I think an A minus."

"I'm getting an A," Erin said, smiling. "It's still early in the year. You're going to need to work harder."

"Are we competing over math grades?"

"I'm not," Erin said. "You're just catching up."

Vikram was already nervous, but now he suddenly felt more so. He'd been waiting to have a conversation like this for two full years. And here they were. He held a beer in one hand and was not sure what to do with his other. And so he put it in his pocket. He felt the twenties that his mother had given him, but he also felt something else. As he pulled it out of his pocket, it fell from his hand and onto the ground. It was a single condom packet. Erin looked at it and then back at Vikram.

"Big plans for tonight?" she asked, smiling. "Now that you're a football star."

"I didn't even know it was in my pocket."

"It's a solid Boy Scout move. 'Be prepared.'"

Vikram couldn't tell if she was still flirting. He felt discombobulated.

"I should probably go find my friends," Erin said. "I'll see you in class on Monday."

"For sure."

As Erin walked away, Vikram stood there and silently screamed. He couldn't believe his mother had messed this up for him. He was still shaken by what they'd done in the cave, but for now he wanted to luxuriate in the brief conversation with Erin.

But when he looked up, he saw Diego about twenty yards away, glaring at him. How long had he been watching?

The harder Diego had tried finding Erin, the farther away she seemed to be from him. They'd been having such a nice chat up at the caves, talking about the game, when Stanley had come up and started talking to her. He'd tried endearing himself to her by making fun of Diego and how short he'd been when they first met. Since they'd come down, Diego had wanted to find her. What he really wanted was to be with someone so that he wouldn't have to be alone. Diego knew a lot of the kids at the party, but none that he felt particularly close to besides MJ. This was what he and the Oaxacans referred to as a "white party," where the rich white kids from the school gathered. Parties where the alcohol never ran out and the cops never showed up. He desperately wished at that moment that he'd gone and hung out with the Oaxacans after the game. Win or lose, they always went to the same west side taco truck.

MJ had finally found Stephanie in a quiet corner. Vikram just walked around at the edges of the party.

And like this, nearly forty-five minutes passed.

The three of them were all in different corners of the Cave House property when they heard the loud, frantic screaming. "It hurts. It hurts so much." They all went toward the sound. The entire party slowly and then suddenly stopped. Stanley had emerged from the path leading to the caves and was now standing in the middle of the house, looking like a martyr from a Renaissance painting, his arms and legs and face bloodied and covered entirely in sharp cactus spines. He was holding his right hand, which was already beginning to swell like a balloon, and screaming in agony. "I'm on fire. Someone help me."

The entire party's attention turned toward Stanley. Most were figuring out who there was sober enough to drive him down the hill to the hospital; it would take too long for the ambulance to make its way up there. But a small, insistent minority turned on their phone cameras, as if the main act of a concert had finally made his way onto the stage. In the minutes of chaos that followed, Diego, MJ, and Vikram finally found one another. They watched as a couple of their classmates helped Stanley into the back of a car. All three of them looked at his bloodied body, but what they all focused on was his face: his lip was split open, a cut had opened above his right eye with blood streaming down, and his cheeks and the area around his eyes had the color and consistency of crushed purple grapes.

After the car left, the three quickly and silently walked toward MJ's car.

"You OK to drive?" Diego asked. They'd all had two or three beers through the course of the evening.

"Not really," MJ said.

When he opened his car door, the light from inside illuminated his feet. They'd been feeling a little funny. He looked down at them and they were both bleeding.

"You good?" Vikram asked, his eyes following MJ's.

"It's just from the rocks or something. I'll clean it off when I get home."

They began their descent. While it was cool outside, the air inside the car was heavy and warm. And all the way down the hill, each of the three waited for one of the others to say something, to speculate on how Stanley had gone from the way they'd left him to the blood-ied, screaming mess he was now.

"Someone fucking say something," Diego finally said, unable to manage the silence.

"We didn't do that to him," MJ said. "We didn't leave him like that. What the hell happened to his face?"

"But he's going to say that we did," Vikram said. "We're going to be on the hook for it."

"He can say whatever the fuck he wants," Diego said, his voice raised.

"Don't scream at me about it," Vikram said.

"I'm not," Diego said. "I'm just screaming. This is bad. It's going to be bad."

"We have to figure out what we're going to do," Vikram said. "How did he get all those cactus things in him? Is he going to be OK?"

"Let's just think and wait this out," MJ said in the tone of author-ity he used in huddles—Diego, you go this way, Vikram, you block this guy. They had just come off the mountain road leading to the Cave House and were now driving through a residential neighborhood. "Don't say a word to anyone. Let's see what he says about what happened. And then we can respond. And nothing about this on text."

They drove the rest of the way in silence, each of the boys playing out their version of the evening in their minds, knowing that there was terrible trouble ahead.

———➤➤➤➤➤———

On Sunday morning, Gautam, Gita, Veronica, Michael, and Shirley all received the same email:

Dear Parents,

I regret to inform you that your son has been involved in an altercation that has resulted in the hospitalization of a fellow student for very serious injuries. Until we have a better understanding of what exactly happened, I am suspending your child from school and from participation in any extracurricular activities, including athletics. I have set aside time tomorrow at 10 A.M. for us to meet in my office. Unless I hear from you, I will assume you will all be there.

Yours sincerely,
Principal Helen Mitchell

Part II

ECHOES

Monday

TEN

Because Veronica had been busy all weekend, doing errands and getting ready for her trip, she'd not carefully checked her personal email. And so, she didn't see the note from the principal until Monday morning, when she was waiting in the car to take Diego to school. Her plan had been to drop him off and then go straight to the airport. She was flying to a small liberal arts college outside Portland, having lunch with students, giving a public talk in the late afternoon, eating dinner with faculty and the president of the college, and then flying home after breakfast the next morning. (All for a five-thousand-dollar honorarium, plus expenses.) Invitations she received from universities and colleges tended to fall into two categories. In the first, she would give a thickly argued academic presentation to scholars, graduate students, and a few advanced undergraduates. In the second, she was invited to historically white colleges and universities to speak with undergrads and to provide some ideas to faculty and administrators, over oysters and a hundred-dollar bottle of wine, about how the college might enter the twenty-first century in its curriculum and hiring practices. This trip fell squarely in the second category and, lately, she preferred those because she didn't have to gird herself against the inevitable attacks from argumentative male historians still clinging to the faint afterglow from that one book they'd published in the mid-nineties.

She took these trips at least once a month. When Diego was younger, a neighbor she trusted came and slept in the guest room when she was going to be gone for the night. Lately, Diego had insisted on being able to manage alone. As she scrolled through her emails, she realized how much more at ease she felt knowing that this time Alex was around and she wouldn't have to check in between appointments to make sure Diego had made his way home, even though he was far more responsible than she'd ever been at his age. It was nice having another adult in the house. Alex liked cooking; he played video games with Diego. And, after years of not doing so, Veronica and her brother had been talking: about their parents, their childhoods. Alex had gone up by himself to see them and had insisted his mother visit a fancy UCSF cardiologist to make sure she was alright. Veronica had promised that she would see them soon.

Tucked between an email that offered 20 percent off skin treatments at a spa in town and a note about her health care benefits was one with the subject line "URGENT." She read it once and then twice. Her immediate reaction was not to wonder what had happened and how it might affect Diego. Instead: she'd have to cancel her trip, or at the very least postpone leaving this morning. Her talk was scheduled for 5 P.M. She could take a later flight. Trips like this were important to her. She liked the fringe benefits—the business-class tickets she insisted the hosts purchase, the nice hotels, the fancy meals. But what she liked the most was that she was an authority on a subject, and for this particular genre of invitation, her hosts seldom questioned this fact. Over the years she had read and read and written and written, the completion of each book creating in her an unshakable exhaustion. In exchange, the universe had been professionally kind. And yet she had never compromised in the attention she paid in raising Diego on her own. She never said no to a reasonable request from him. She never said she was too busy with work. But when work was finally scheduled, she saw it as her sacred, untouchable time.

When she finished thinking through how she might reschedule her day, she turned back to the question of her son. She felt ashamed by the order and portioning of her worry.

"Is this why you've been so quiet this whole weekend?" Veronica asked when Diego finally got into the car.

"What?" Diego asked.

Diego knew the answer to both her question and his. On Saturday morning, he'd awoken to several different texts inquiring if he knew what had happened at the Cave House. Mateo, his closest friend among the Oaxacans, was the most succinct: "Shit went down with the white folks last night?" Diego didn't reply to the others and just sent a shrug emoji to Mateo. As the day had passed, he'd heard nothing official about it. He'd allowed himself to believe that after the melodrama of Stanley's return to the party he was somehow alright. But on Sunday morning, he'd gotten on a call with MJ and Vikram, who told him about the email their parents had just received. If Diego's mother had gotten the email, she had not mentioned it. Once again, MJ implored the other two to say nothing to anyone, to wait to hear how Stanley was going to describe the evening. "Let him show his cards first," MJ had said. Then they would respond accordingly. The rest of that day, as Diego waited for his mother to mention the email, he'd helped his uncle prepare and roll homemade pasta, using a technique Alex had learned in a Roman cooking class. The distraction had helped Diego keep himself silent.

Veronica held up her phone and he glanced at the email. He put his head down, his gut now suddenly ablaze.

"What happened?" she asked, assuming it had to be some kind of mistake, and if it wasn't, there had to be a simple explanation. Diego never got into trouble. She'd worked very hard to assure that he was tracked in the right kind of classes; she'd kept a close eye on his friends. She knew that the school was just waiting for boys like

Diego to mess up. So she simply hadn't let him. Diego had done his own part. Whether football worked out or not, his primary focus was getting into a good college. He'd heard his mother talk about how life-changing it had been for her and he wanted to feel the same way. He was curious; he wanted to know new things.

Diego opened the car door that he'd just closed.

"Where are you going?" she asked, perplexed at why Diego had not simply answered her question.

"Not school," he said with a hint of defiance. "At least not yet."

"Get back in here."

Diego got back in the car.

"What happened?"

Diego didn't say anything. Now the worry began to take shape in her lower back.

"You're going to need to tell me what happened before we go see the principal."

Diego continued to sit there silently.

"I have a flight that leaves at ten A.M. and now I need to be at your school. I'm going to trust that you'll remember what happened very shortly. I'm not playing around here. It sounds like someone is really hurt. Did you have anything to do with this?"

She looked at Diego, who seemed like he was trying very hard to stifle his tears. After he gathered himself, he continued to sit there silently. She tried a different tactic.

"If you don't play this Friday, there are no playoffs. And if there are no playoffs, there is no real football ahead. And I know that you want it to be ahead."

"I think you want it to be ahead more than me," Diego finally said, his voice barely audible.

"What did you say?" Veronica asked, having heard exactly what he'd said. "I wouldn't care if you quit right now."

"Really?" Diego asked, at last turning to face his mother. "OK."

He left the car and went back into the house to wait out the next hour. Veronica sat there, trying to parse what had just happened.

Exactly five minutes before, she had been looking up tea shops in the small town she was visiting. She liked buying expensive first-flush teas from faraway places. She wanted to like green tea, but she really didn't. She preferred the black.

The Diego who had just stepped out of the car seemed different from the Diego she'd cooked eggs for earlier that morning. His curtness worried her. The weekend that had just passed now worried her. Diego had loafed around the house, getting a drink from the kitchen, watching TV in the family room, texting on his phone. Diego had been no different than normal, though perhaps a little more quiet than usual. Something had happened on Friday night, and yet he seemed to be going about his business as if nothing had happened. She was convincing herself that his silence was less defiance and more fear.

However, it was his sudden turn away from football, even if said in the heat of their exchange, and the prospect of his missing out on playoff football, which he loved, that worried her. Something serious must have gone down.

She sat in her car, emailing her hosts about the slight change of plans. Hopefully, only the lunch would have to be canceled. She changed flights using an app on her phone, sensing that she might not make the flight at all.

———————————

An hour later and a mile away, Michael was sitting in his car, thinking that the statute of limitations had clearly expired on the phone tag he and his father's friend Tom Regan had been playing for nearly ten days. Tom had returned from vacation over the weekend and a phone conversation needed to happen today. To avoid his raw, frayed nerves about the call, Michael was thinking about what MJ could have possibly done. As if to make Shirley and MJ come to the car already, he had started the engine, and as he was mouthing the opening lines of what he wanted to say to Tom, the engine ran a full thirty

seconds before he realized that he was still in the garage. He immediately hit the controller that opened the garage, relieved that he'd
realized it before Shirley arrived, less because he was worried about
the fumes and more because Shirley would have entertained the
possibility that he was trying to kill himself, subconsciously or otherwise. If he had said he wasn't, she would have pulled out some basic
USC undergrad Freud about how he was in denial.

Shirley and MJ walked out the door that led to the garage. Shirley was dressed like she was meeting her friends for lunch—silk,
cashmere, pearls. Per usual, MJ was wearing shorts, a T-shirt, and no
shoes.

"Go put on a proper shirt and some pants and shoes," Michael
said, trying to contain his sudden rage that was focused on how both
his wife and son were dressed.

MJ continued walking past him and opened the back door to get
in. "Easy there."

"Go back into the fucking house and get properly dressed," Michael thundered. "I don't care if you don't respect us. But have some
respect for the principal who has called us in for whatever stupid
thing you've done."

MJ looked stricken, as if his father had just slapped him. Michael
seldom raised his voice. His own father had been a yeller and he had
vowed not to be. And he barely used the word *fuck*, which he found
to be inelegant. MJ went back into the house. Michael and Shirley
just sat there.

"Everything OK?" Shirley tiptoed.

"No," he said. "He doesn't understand the value of everything he
has. People who don't have shoes are actually the ones who are the
most desperate for them. He doesn't need to spend a year in Africa
to appreciate that."

Michael had opened the email soon after it arrived on Sunday
morning, in the breather he took between *The New York Times* and
The Wall Street Journal. He had shown it to Shirley before asking MJ

about it. They'd decided that Shirley would approach MJ first, given that he was more likely to talk to her. He'd said nothing to either of them. They'd reached a moment in their relationship when threatening to take something away—a toy, the phone, a driver's license—no longer worked as a bargaining technique. For years, they'd celebrated and marveled at how passionate and certain MJ was in his opinions and pursuits. Now they could both sense that his ideas were hardening into something unmalleable.

But the fact that MJ had gone in and returned with pants and shoes allowed Michael to think he might still be able to reach his son.

Chilesworth High School had first opened in the 1950s and the main three-story building, with its beautiful stone façade, had a certain Spanish hacienda grandness that announced that it took the business of education, and the necessary moments of teenage joy and school pride, seriously. There were two similar, smaller buildings on both sides of the main building and over the years, a growing set of prefab temporary classrooms had been added that were now essentially permanent. Gyms and fields and tennis courts were on the periphery of campus and all the various structures were connected by stone walkways, some of them now in serious disrepair.

Above the large doors that led into the main hallway was a Latin phrase etched in stone, which no one bothered to translate anymore. Filled with classrooms and the school administration offices and senior lockers, the main hallway was both the guts and the pumping heart of the school. Between classes it was loud and boisterous and exuberant and angry, clogged with students going in every direction. The walls were covered by framed 8x10 photos, one side with the Athletic Hall of Fame and the other with "Chilesworth Citizens"— graduates who had contributed to strengthening the social fabric of the city, state, or nation. The most famous athlete the school had produced was a running back for the Houston Oilers in the 1980s, and its most famous citizen was their current ten-term congressman.

Gita, Gautam, and Vikram were the first to arrive. Classes were in session, but despite that there were plenty of kids here and there in the main hallway, a few of whom approached Vikram and initiated friendly high fives, congratulating him on the game.

"Friends?" Gita asked.

"Never met them," Vikram said, shrugging but enjoying the attention.

The secretary in the principal's office—aging Charlotte, who'd held the job across thirty years, five different principals, and the same bouffant—directed them to an empty science classroom down the hallway, where the meeting would take place. If they weren't there under such duress, Gita might have luxuriated in a bit of nostalgia at the periodic table of elements hanging on the wall. She'd ruled class-rooms like this when she was a student: a 4.2 GPA; 1480 on the SAT on the first try; 5s on the four AP exams she took; varsity letters in swimming and track and field. She could outrun everybody. Now she did little running except her thrice-weekly 5K loop around town.

"Do you have a class in here?" Gautam asked.

The sound of his voice, far more upbeat than the moment de-manded, irritated Gita.

Gautam was preoccupied. All weekend long, he'd been checking his email to see if Rohan Doshi had made a decision and thus had not seriously engaged with the fact that Vikram had gone silent when Gita asked him what happened on Friday night. All the space in his mind had been occupied by how well he'd given his presenta-tion and what a huge sale might mean.

"I do," Vikram said. "Fourth period."

Once Vikram had shut down, Gita knew from her experience with their daughter not to push too hard. For much of the Sunday after they received the email, Gita had been in the kitchen, first cooking and then trying to manage an ant infestation. Every time she sealed up a source of their entry, another source seemed to open up. At some level, she appreciated the insistent, unending march of the ants. It would take more than an exterminator to fix this kitchen. They would need to tear the whole thing down to the studs. There was no other way.

With two silent, distracted men in the house, Gita had gone for a run. She'd finished her normal loop and then did it all over again. By the time she returned home, she had completed a very long conversation in her head with her son and was now agitated. In all his years of school, none of his teachers had said one negative thing about Vikram. He'd never gotten into major trouble.

"Look, I'm really trying to give you your space, but this email sounds very troubling," she'd said to him, standing in the kitchen, dripping in sweat from her run. "There's a boy in the hospital. You need to tell us what's going on. Now."

Vikram had not been the type to keep secrets from his parents. But between MJ's insistence that they not say anything and his worry about what had actually happened to Stanley, Vikram had remained silent, though it was getting harder and harder.

"There's some mix-up here. I really don't know what's going on."

"I don't think you're even convincing yourself with that," Gita said. "Are your new teammates involved in this? If they are, remember: You don't even know them. You don't need to cover for them. They're not your friends."

"Yes they are," Vikram said. Just because you don't really have any friends doesn't mean I don't, Vikram thought, but wisely didn't say.

Gautam had been looking down at his phone as he walked into the kitchen.

"Please say something to him," Gita said to her husband, her voice now slightly raised. "I need you to be engaged with this."

"Why are you yelling at Dad?"

"I'm not yelling at him. But neither of you understand how serious this is."

Gautam quickly placed the phone in his pocket, looking ashamed.

"I don't want to be embarrassed in this meeting," Gita continued.

"Is that your worry?" Vikram asked. "Your embarrassment?"

"No," Gita said. "You're my worry."

After that, Gita hadn't pushed him further, hoping that sooner rather than later he would tell her everything. That's what he'd always done when he got into minor trouble: silence followed by full confession. But sooner had turned into later, and they'd arrived at the high school without him having shared anything.

They were alone for five minutes, because they were a good five minutes early. Getting somewhere early was something Gita and Gautam still agreed on. Veronica and Diego came in next, right at 10 A.M. A minute later, Michael, Shirley, and MJ joined them. The parents briefly introduced themselves to one another before squeezing into the old one-piece chair-desks. They all sat in the front row, with an empty desk between each family.

"I don't remember these desks being so small," Michael said.

The others smiled stiffly but didn't respond.

At a bit past ten, Principal Helen Mitchell approached the classroom. A generation or two before, the men who'd occupied her office needed only a BA in English from a decent liberal arts college, a few years of inspired *To Kill a Mockingbird* teaching, and the ability to speak with certainty about things they didn't know before they were promoted to the top job. She'd gotten a PhD in education and had spent a decade in the classroom before she'd made her way up.

She stopped about a foot from the closed door, close enough so that she could peek through the small window and far enough away so that no one inside could see her looking in. She knew these boys. She was no longer teaching by the time they arrived, but she kept a particular eye on those getting ready to drop out and those on the verge of great things. Together, the three were a laminated poster for the public school way: academically strong, athletically nimble, racially diverse. She'd met Veronica once when she'd come to speak to one of the history classes about slavery. She'd never met the Berringers or the Shastris. But looking into the classroom now, seeing that none of them were speaking to one another, and recognizing the seriousness of the situation, she knew this wasn't going to be easy.

"Hello, hello," the principal said, stepping into the classroom. "My name is Helen Mitchell. The students affectionately call me 'Dr. Helen.' And less affectionately, 'Dr. Hell.' You're welcome to use either. I'm sorry I'm late. I was putting out a fire. Someone lit a brown paper bag full of excrement in the bathroom."

All three boys smiled but then seemed to remember why they were there.

"Hopefully it gave you a moment to get to know one another, unless you've met already."

Michael looked around the room and inched slightly closer to Shirley.

"Of course, I know Michael and Shirley through the years in football," Veronica said, nodding to the Berringers. She'd spent plenty of time with them at games and year-end banquets, but though they lived pretty close to one another, they'd never socialized outside of football. "But I hadn't met Vikram's parents. I was hoping that the first time we met would be under different circumstances so that I could congratulate them on Vikram's command performance last Friday."

Gita and Gautam nodded to the others around the room.

"Yes," Gita said. "That was a fun game. And I'm sorry too that we all have to meet like this for the first time."

"Can we know why exactly we're here?" Michael said, barely a second after Gita had finished talking. "Since we received your email, we have threatened our son, and if he wasn't bigger than me, I would have taken a belt out. But he refuses to say what happened." Michael paused to see how this was landing. "And for the record, I would never have actually taken my belt out."

There was nervous laughter around the room.

"My usually talkative son has been unusually quiet as well," Veronica said.

Gita looked at Veronica and then Michael, trying to assess them and what they'd just said. Why were they already throwing their sons under the bus? It had to be a strategy of some sort. Didn't they have the same bad feeling in their guts that she did, that whatever had happened could imperil the future of their sons? She didn't say anything to ally herself with them. She was thinking about how, after staying on course for so long, she'd been weak by letting Vikram play football. He'd had a nice small group of school friends—the golf guys—all competing to see which one could get early admission to Stanford. It was what bright young things did in California these days, knowing the admission would put them on the fast track to a destination where they would never have to apologize for knowing the answer to something before the questioner had finished half the question. She'd thought football would allow Vikram to inch slightly ahead of his studious golf friends.

Dr. Helen looked at the three boys, all of whom had their eyes facing their laps.

"Let me tell you what I know," she began.

At this, the three boys raised their heads and looked at one another. This was what they'd been waiting for. The first salvo.

"Please correct me if I get anything wrong. After the game on Friday, there was a party that all three of your sons attended. In an old, abandoned house up in the hills. This fact does not seem to be in dispute as far as I can tell. I've talked to students who said your sons were there. In fact, I've seen pictures of them up there."

Gita took a side glance at Vikram. On Saturday morning, she'd asked him how his night went and he'd said that they had gotten Indian food and walked around for a while, and then one of his friends had dropped him off at home.

"Yes, your children go to parties and don't tell you about it," Dr. Helen said, giving Gita a slight smile.

Gita suddenly felt vulnerable. She looked over at Gautam; the principal finally had his attention.

"There were nearly a hundred other students there," Dr. Helen continued. "The police have made clear to me that everyone was trespassing on private property. And to make things worse, many of them seemed to have gone into a set of caves above the house, which are all protected Native American heritage sites. On Saturday afternoon, I received a distressed phone call from the mother of a young man named Stanley Kincaid, who was also there. He had to be taken to the hospital on Friday night to remove spines of cactus from all over his body. I went to see him in the hospital yesterday afternoon. He was in terrible shape, fighting off an infection and, even with antibiotics, holding steady at a 103 temperature. Today he's going to have surgery on his right hand and arm because the wounds and deep cuts have to be surgically washed out and drained. But that's not even the worst of it. I've been teaching at public schools my whole career and I've seen my share of fights. I don't think I've ever seen a face as swollen as Stanley's. Black eyes, a fractured nose. Plus two cracked ribs."

The principal paused. "He said he was having a quiet moment in the caves, appreciating their natural beauty, when the three of you confronted him, beat him up, and left him in the cave. He said he couldn't understand why because you'd all had a nice dinner together earlier in the evening. And then, according to him, to make things worse, one of you came *back* to attack him again and because it was night and he was so disoriented in the darkness of the cave, he couldn't see who it was. After getting beaten up again, he pretended to pass out. When he was alone, he walked out of the cave and as he was running in fear, he fell off the trail into cactus and brush."

"Stanley is a liar," MJ said, his voice strong and confident. "For as long as I've known him, he lies and exaggerates. It's the only way he knows how to get attention."

Michael and Shirley turned to their suddenly talkative son.

"Then why don't you tell me *your* account of things," Dr. Helen said.

MJ retreated, as if he'd just remembered their pact to stay quiet. Vikram and Diego remained stone-faced.

Gita was listening carefully to what the principal had just described. She was no fool. She knew that kids got into trouble, did stupid things. But the description of events genuinely didn't com- pute in her mind. An image of ten-year-old Vikram playing soccer popped into her head. The game was in full force and Vikram had suddenly stopped running midfield and knelt on the ground. When the referee finally called a time-out, they'd discovered that Vikram was hovering over a small wounded bird. Gita knew it was naïve to base her sense of her son on this one act, but she would think back to this moment now and again when she felt like she was failing as a parent. She'd done this one thing right. He'd known when to stop and protect. "This is not something my son could have done," she said. She kept her eyes on the principal, and then added, with the slightest drop in her voice, "We're not that type of family."

Even Gita knew, as the words were coming out of her mouth, that she'd just removed the pin from a small grenade and carefully placed it on the dirty tile floor between them. A chemistry classroom was as good a place as any for an explosion. She sensed how all this was going to play out. She'd read the emails that the principal had been sending over the past year about equity and fairness in public schools and how certain groups had unfairly and disproportionately been affected by a traditional education system. The emails were thought- ful and thorough and eloquent. A few years back, she'd seen a story in the local paper about the principal's son, who'd been the first Af- rican American student in the history of the school to have achieved the Ivy holy trinity: admission into Harvard, Yale, *and* Princeton. On all counts, it was a remarkable achievement. And while Gita was keenly aware of the complicated racial histories that both the princi- pal and Veronica must have lived, she'd sensed a certain familiarity between them when the principal had walked in. The principal was going to protect Diego because brown boys like Vikram didn't get protected while brown boys like Diego did. And the Berringers, both dressed as if they were headed to a golf club for lunch after the con- clusion of the meeting, needed no protection. They had probably lawyered up already. Vikram was going to be left out in the cold and she wasn't going to allow that.

"What does that mean?" Veronica asked, turning to face Gita directly. "That the rest of us *are* that type of family? That we encourage our kids to jump other kids in caves?"

"I was questioning what this student is accusing our children of," Gita said. "That's it. And I'm only talking about Vikram here. I know my son. I know what he is and what he isn't capable of." She should have stopped. "But let's be honest. You encourage your son to play football, don't you? What difference is there between how he hits people on the field and how he may hit them off it? It's a thin line. And yes, we let our son play. It's the worst mistake I've made as a parent. I don't actually know your son. But I do know mine."

"First, spare us all the silliness about how violent sports make violent kids," Veronica said. "And second, don't take that tone with me."

"What tone is that?" Gita asked. "The only tone I hear is care and worry."

"You know exactly what tone."

"Let's not do this right now," Gita said. "In front of our boys."

Veronica gave Gita a hard stare. "But you're the one who started it."

"*I started it?* We're not on a playground." Gita looked at the soft space on her arm where a nurse usually looked for a vein to draw blood. "*Ouch,*" she said louder than she'd intended. A particularly aggressive ant was freely marching on her. She pushed it down with her thumb and then flicked it off. "Sorry. We have an ant problem at home."

"We know our child," Michael said, entering the slight opening created by the ant. "As well as you know yours."

Gita looked over at Michael and then Veronica, knowing that it was now two families against one. Fine, she thought. I'm up for this.

"I know all your children," Dr. Helen interjected. "They're smart, kind, driven boys with very bright futures ahead of them. That's not in doubt. But maybe the point here is that perhaps you don't know them as well as you think you do. I've spent my entire career with young people. And they're a complicated, wonderful bunch, who sometimes say too much and other times not nearly enough. This is what I do know. There's an injured young man saying your sons landed him in the hospital. That is a very serious charge. And at least one of your children is saying that he is lying."

"He is lying," both Diego and Vikram said in unison.

"So here's where we're at," the principal said.

"Why don't we bring this boy in," Veronica said. "Let's hear his side of the story."

"We did hear his side of the story. I just told you. The young man is traumatized. And rightfully so. I'm not bringing him in here. He's considering pressing criminal charges. I really don't want to bring the police into this. I want to keep it a school matter. But with every passing moment I'm starting to think that is unavoidable."

Vikram noticed MJ and Diego making eye contact. They must have talked alone at some point over the weekend. Given the connection they had on the field, they'd easily sacrifice him off it.

"Let me get this straight," Michael said. "Our sons are being accused of having done something based on what *one* kid says. And based on that alone, they've been suspended. What happened to innocent until proven guilty?"

"All they have to say is that they are innocent," the principal said. "That they had no altercation with the young man."

The attention in the room turned toward the boys. The boys looked at one another and then at the ground and then at one another again. The principal let a full twenty seconds pass.

"Were you there that night?" Dr. Helen asked Vikram, breaking the silence. "Can we at least establish that?"

"Yes," Vikram said.

"Why are you just asking him?" Gita asked.

"If you give me a second, Mrs. Shastri, I'll ask the others too." The principal turned to MJ and Diego and asked the same question.

"Yes," they both said.

"OK. We're getting somewhere." This time Dr. Helen turned her attention directly to the boys. "I know all three of you. And you all know me. I think I'm fair and balanced. You're good, smart kids. It breaks my heart whenever kids are in the middle of something, but I felt particularly sad when Stanley mentioned your names. Sad that he's hurt, and really sad that you three might be involved. But unless you start talking, this is going to end badly for all of you. You're not coming back to school until I know exactly what happened. And no school means no football. I know that you have a very important game this Friday. Our dear Coach Smith, who likes to say very little, had all sorts of words for me this morning. MJ, that nice commitment you have is not without strings. I know that they're very excited to have you, but they'll cut you off if the need arises. I know how these fancy universities operate. And Vikram and Diego, you know better than me that this year is the most important for college applications. You don't want to be absent for too long."

"Are you threatening my child?" Michael asked. "Just so I'm clear."

"Because it sure sounds that way," Veronica added.

Gita wanted to join in with the other parents against the principal, but since she'd already struck out on her own, she didn't know how to ease herself back in.

"No, I'm most certainly not. I'm just making clear to all three of them the stakes involved here. I think they don't quite understand the severity of the situation and until they do, their future is in jeopardy. I know that sounds a bit overdramatic. But trust me. All this is very dramatic. And I'm not just talking about college here. There's a very hurt young man in the hospital. If he gets any worse, things are going to get really complicated for us all. There's never a good time to bring up Richard Nixon, but there's a lesson to be learned from him. The cover-up is often worse than the crime. Just tell me what you know and we can figure out how to move on."

A flock of pigeons was cooing their deep-voiced song right outside the classroom window.

"So I ask again, what happened?"

"I know that house," Shirley said, breaking the silence. She had remained quiet for the whole conversation, observing everyone in the room. "I grew up going to parties up there. My parents were frequent guests. And I don't know what happened on Friday night, but honestly, it couldn't have been anything crazier than the things I saw when I was a kid. I know we're in mixed company here, but let's just say that there were mouths where they shouldn't have been."

She let out a slight snort.

"Mom," MJ said. "Stop."

Shirley waved her son off.

"Here's my point. Crazy things happen at parties. And crazy things have happened at this particular party over the years. Maybe these boys did what you're accusing them of or maybe they didn't. Who knows. If I had to guess, the truth is probably somewhere between what this Stanley is saying and what the boys are saying."

"That's the problem," the principal said. "Your boys aren't saying anything. If they do, then we'll have something to work from. Stanley is the only one talking."

"Is this the same Stanley that's been around the house now and again?" Shirley asked her son.

MJ nodded.

"Oh," Shirley said, as if she'd just found the missing piece of a puzzle. "That changes everything. That boy is a disaster. He's certainly not a reliable narrator in any of this."

Gita would be the first to admit that she'd underestimated Shirley, as if the pearls around her neck negated anything smart coming out of her mouth. This was an important detail to bring up. She'd heard the principal mention Stanley's name earlier but had not made the connection to the kid who'd been in her house. "I completely agree. He's been bothering Vikram since the very first day of high school. He's a menace."

"I know about some of the run-ins Stanley has had with other kids, but until I hear a different story, Stanley's is the only story I have," the principal said. "And it doesn't change the fact that he's the one in the hospital."

She gave the boys one more chance to say something. They didn't.

"This is not how I expected this meeting to go. But this is not the first time I've had mute boys sitting in front of me. I know your silence very well. I know that you can't wait to get out of here so that you can talk and figure out how to line up your stories. And I know lined-up stories when I hear them, just like your teachers know when you've 'borrowed' things from the internet for your essays." She paused and shifted her attention to the parents. "I'm certainly not going to tell you how to parent, but I'd keep these boys separated for now if I were you. And talk to your sons. Encourage them to be open and truthful. I'm going to figure out what happened in that cave. They can help me or hinder me. It'll be much better for your kids if they help. Let's plan on meeting back here, say, Thursday at the same time."

She needed time to talk to other students. "I have another appointment now and a couple of fully packed days of meetings in the district office. I do have an entire school to run. I'm hoping that by Thursday, you'll have changed your minds and gotten some clarity. But of course, if you remember what happened before then, please let me know and we can meet earlier. And if you want to talk to me individually, we can do that as well." Here she paused before continuing, "In fact, I'd like to talk to each of you boys on your own. I'll have my secretary be in touch to set up times. And I'll certainly be in touch if Stanley's condition worsens. Let's hope for all of us that that doesn't happen."

She intently looked at the boys and parents as she finished. It was clear to everyone in the room what she'd just done when she said that she would talk to each of the boys individually. How long could their silence last if there was the possibility of one of the others talking? Who would crack?

"I do not give you permission to speak to Diego alone," Veronica said. "It's either both of us or neither."

"Suit yourself. I was just trying to keep our lines of communication open." Dr. Helen turned to the other parents. "You feel the same way?"

"You talk to him, you talk to me," Michael said.

"We'd like to be there as well," Gita said.

"This really doesn't need to be adversarial. I know you want to protect your children, but they're also not children anymore. We can all do this like adults."

With that, she left the room. In any other circumstance, she would have said her goodbyes to the parents at the end of a meeting. But to convey her anger, she did not.

Gita waited to see if any of the other parents were going to say anything. For a fleeting moment, she considered apologizing for what she'd said earlier. When no one said anything, Gita tapped the knees of her men and the three of them walked out first, with Gita and Vikram ahead. Gautam followed a few feet behind.

ELEVEN

Gautam had stayed quiet for the entire meeting because it was his style. In and out of work meetings, he'd always been a better listener than talker. His reticence surprised people. He physically filled the corner of whatever room he was in, and yet remained enclosed, never insisting on seeping into other parts of the room. And so people tended to pay just a little more attention when he finally did speak. But this strategy had not always served him well during sales meetings, which depended on the salesman overtalking, overpromising, overovering.

"I'm not starting this car until you tell us what exactly happened," Gautam said softly and without force. "Did you hit this boy?"

Gautam was looking at Vikram in the rearview mirror. Even before he'd completed his ultimatum, he saw Vikram trying to fight back his tears, which he did by keeping his lips shut tight. Gita looked back at her son and tapped Gautam's knee, signaling him to drive away, lest any of Vikram's classmates see him.

Gautam started the car. "There's nothing you can't tell us," he said. "There's nothing for you to be afraid of."

They drove home in silence as Vikram figured out what to say.

"I'm sorry I didn't tell you that I went to that party," he said as they reached their driveway. "I should have. I know that placed you in an awkward position with the principal. And also, I ate chicken when we went out to dinner."

"It's OK, sweetheart," Gita said, appreciating the levity in a moment she knew was about to get heavy. "You can eat all the chicken you want. And we don't mind you going to parties. In fact, we've encouraged it. You just have to tell us. Stanley is that redheaded boy we saw after your first practice, right?"

"Yes."

Vikram then described driving to the party, emphasizing just how much of an irritant Stanley had been all night, needling all of them. "MJ and I had gone up to check out the caves. And Stanley was in one of them, acting all crazy. He'd had too much to drink and was arguing with Diego. We were just trying to defuse the situation. But then he lunged at us. All we did was calm him down. That's it. We left him in the cave. And the next thing we see, like an hour later maybe, is him running down with all these cactus needles in him."

"What do you mean 'calm him down'?" Gautam asked.

"I mean he was punching and kicking us and we were trying to deflect and may have thrown a few back just to mellow him out."

"Why didn't you say any of this to us earlier?" Gautam asked. "And to the principal just now? It all seems pretty straightforward self-defense."

"I don't know," Vikram said, scratching at his head. He looked like the child he'd been, confused about which toy he wanted at the store. "I don't know. I didn't want to be the snitch. And I don't want to get in trouble for something I didn't do. I don't know. MJ and Diego weren't saying anything. They said not to say anything. And now I'm afraid they're talking to each other without me. And blaming me for this whole thing. Especially now that they know that Stanley is really hurt. They've played together forever and barely know me."

"Is there anything else that you'd like to tell us?" Gita asked.

"No," Vikram said immediately. "I promise. I just want to get back to school like normal."

"Why don't you go on inside," Gita said.

"What are we going to do?" Vikram asked.

"Let your dad and me figure that out."

Vikram got out of the car and headed to the front door. Gautam watched him go.

Gautam loved his children purely and unconditionally, but there was a way in which he felt he couldn't really know them. He was born in a different country, in a different world. He knew enough about how the brain works to understand that things and ideas had been stuffed in the soft space of his mind during his first thirteen years spent in India. He would never be able to undo that. He couldn't understand how it was possible for his son to sit on this information for so long. All he needed to do was admit what he'd done and then they could move on. That's certainly what he would have done. But maybe this wasn't about those first thirteen years at all. Maybe they were just different. It wasn't just a one-way street. Once, a few years before, Gautam and Vikram had been driving around and Gautam was listening to some Hindi music—the soundtrack to the film *Veer-Zaara,* which had been all over the radio when he had visited India one summer. As he sang along, he'd noticed Vikram looking at him, befuddled, as if he couldn't understand the part of his father that felt the rhythm and the content of the music.

"I can see why he didn't say anything earlier," Gita said. "He's scared of messing up. We've made it hard for him to mess up."

Gautam knew how Gita would answer, and yet he still asked, "Is he telling us everything he knows? I just have a feeling that there's something more."

"Of course he is," she said immediately. She was trying not to be angry at her son for not telling her all this earlier. She believed he was telling them everything now, given her memory of the bird and given that she had birthed him. She believed because otherwise she didn't know either of her children. And if she didn't, where did that leave her? "Did you hear what the principal said at the end? That we'd meet on Thursday, but she would talk to any of the families individually. We need to get in there before anyone else does. She needs to hear Vikram's side of the story. *Now*. Before the others go in."

"Let's take a breather and see how this progresses."

"Taking a breather is your excuse to not make a decision. You always postpone the hard stuff. And stop looking at your phone! You checked it throughout the meeting. There's no miraculous sale coming. We need your head here."

Gautam kept his eyes off Gita lest he say something he'd regret later.

"I'm sorry." Gita sighed. "This whole thing is making me stressed. Vikram has worked way too hard and for way too long for it to disappear overnight. For something he didn't do."

"But he did do it," Gautam said. "At least part of it. And he didn't tell us about it."

Gita didn't respond. She knew she was protecting her son. But wasn't that, after all, her primary job?

"Let me go in and talk to him alone," Gautam said. "And then we can figure out what to do next."

Gautam opened his car door but sat there for a moment, taking a quick glance at his wife, who still had not unbuckled her seat belt. He had bitten his tongue with each thing Gita had just said. But the elbow about a sale not coming had been particularly sharp. He felt ashamed for how excited he'd been that maybe his work life was finally changing.

He had met Gita at a party on the Upper West Side, in the crowded, hot apartment of a mutual friend who was getting a PhD in something at Columbia. Gautam was going through a phase. Every Indian woman he met was his mother, a similarity he didn't like. Gita was more active in her distaste of Indian men, all of whom reminded her of her know-it-all uncles. Gautam was sitting on the balcony, smoking a cigarette, when she came out and asked for one.

They smoked through an entire pack of Camel Lights and talked and forgot about the party inside. The attraction they felt for each other through the smoke was clear. They made a very handsome couple. The night after they met, they went to dinner at peak-era Balthazar because Gita had heard of it and really wanted to go. They didn't have a reservation. The place was loud and packed and there were twenty-some people waiting outside. When they asked about a table, the hostess looked at them and she immediately said, "Welcome back," and took them to a corner table.

"Who do they think we are?" Gautam asked, trying to pretend this was normal.

"No clue. A Bollywood couple?"

Both of them liked the feeling that, together, they looked like a couple people wanted to know. And despite their reservations about being with another Indian, they collided in the safety and familiarity of each other.

They were married in the summer of 2000. It wasn't arranged, but once they knew they were serious about one another, further introductions were made and arrangements occurred. Her father warned her about marrying a Punjabi. It was originally his joke.

To them, it felt like a good omen to begin their lives together at the start of a century. And that first year had been pure. The passing years chipped away at that purity, but they were too busy with work and children to notice. Soon after their honeymoon, they made two major purchases: Gautam wanted a fancy washer and dryer and Gita wanted a BMW. He liked washing and carefully drying his shirts so that they wouldn't shrink. She kept the car impeccably clean, barely driving it to avoid putting too many miles on the odometer, just in case she wanted to trade it in.

And so it was a confused anger she felt when on the evening of September 11, 2001, she found a bumper sticker of the American flag affixed to the back of her car.

"Did you do that?" she'd asked, storming into the Marina apartment he'd moved into after they got married.

"What?" Gautam asked. He was in a nauseated daze from watching TV for most of the day.

"The sticker."

"Yes," Gautam said.

"Why?"

"Because it's about to get bad for us here."

He'd grown up in the rougher outskirts of Berkeley and understood how these things worked. Gita had gone from the west side of L.A. to Cornell to the East Village and now the fancy part of San Francisco.

"No they're not," Gita said. "And even if they do, having that stupid sticker is not going to help. Some asshole is not going to suddenly stop when he sees the sticker, and think, 'Oh, patriots. I'll leave them alone.'"

"Are you mad that I put the flag on or are you mad that I messed up the car?"

"You know how clean I like to keep it."

"That's the problem."

"That's the problem? That I'm taking care of something?"

This memory popped into Gautam's mind more frequently than he liked. Now, years later, he couldn't be sure if he'd affixed the sticker out of genuine fear or a desire to punish Gita just a bit for his secret worry that she'd settled for him after some other relationship had soured.

As Gautam was about to get out of the car, Gita put her hand on his arm.

"We need to figure out how we're going to move forward," Gita said. "Whatever happens, this MJ will be fine. He'll become one of the asshole sales guys you hate. And colleges are falling over themselves to get Diegos into their ranks. That principal is not going to help us. I could see her making eye contact with Veronica. They'll stick together. Vikram will be left out. He's our child and we have to protect him."

"I know," Gautam said. "But I think college is the least of our problems right now. The principal said twice that this boy is really hurt. We need to hope that he gets better very soon. And yes, we'll protect Vikram. But let's figure out the best way to do so. He at least has to be honest with us. Let me go check in on him."

He stepped out of the car but looked back in one more time. "Have we met this woman Veronica somewhere else? Diego's mother. Some school function or something? Did the kids go to the same elementary school?"

"I don't think so. I'd remember her."

"She just seems familiar."

Gautam walked into the house and found Vikram standing in the kitchen as if he'd forgotten why he was there.

"Come on in here," Gautam said, inviting his son in for a hug. "No need to leave room for Ganesh."

Vikram cracked a smile.

When Vikram was in junior high, Gautam, wanting to get involved in the lives of his children, had volunteered to chaperone a dance. His job was to make sure that there was enough space between the kids during the slow dances, and he had taken to walking around and saying, "Leave enough room in there for Ganesh." During the dance, it had embarrassed Vikram, but since, it had been a source of their shared humor.

Vikram leaned in and gave his father a long hug.

"You know I wouldn't just go around beating up a kid. I just wouldn't do that."

"I know," Gautam said. The image of Vikram knocking his opponent flat on the football field flashed through his mind. "I know. We'll figure this out."

When Gita walked into the house, Gautam was leaving for work. He wanted to blame her for deflating the excitement that had been building in him about the sale. But she was right. Maybe the sale was not coming after all. And even if it was, no single sale would fix the nagging feeling that he had simply not made enough sales in his life.

"Let's let him have the rest of the day," Gautam said. "I'll talk to him again tonight and we can see the principal tomorrow."

Gita wanted to go back to the school right then, but this was a fair compromise.

"Try to get home early." Gita paused and then carefully added, "I'm sure the paint guy will be in touch soon with good news."

Gautam walked out without responding.

—————»»»»»—————

During their whole drive home, it was Diego who kept asking his mother to say something, anything. And she didn't say a word until they got home: "I'm not talking until you start talking."

Diego was about to step out of the car, but he stopped and parsed what his mom had just said. "I've done everything you've asked of me. I've studied when you wanted, ran with the football when you wanted, made friends with the kids you thought I needed to make friends with. All of it without complaint. And I appreciate it all because I know you're just trying to keep me safe. But now, I need a moment to work through this on my own. And so please give me that moment."

"OK," Veronica said, taken aback by the clarity of his request. "OK. I'll give you your space. And there is plenty of it around this house, where you're going to stay until this is cleared up."

"That's not fair."

"You know what's not fair? A kid getting beaten to a pulp and landing in the hospital. That's not fair. And you staying quiet about it when you clearly know something about what went down. So yes, take all the moments you need, but in the four walls of this house." She took a breath. "Look, sweetheart, this is really serious. I'm here for you, but you have to come toward me. You have to trust me in this and not your friends."

Veronica had always struggled with how much to tell Diego about the reality of being brown in the predominantly white places they occupied. Tell him too much and she was over-shaping his sense of the world. Not tell him enough and he'd hit a brick wall that he didn't know was in front of him. "I'm just nervous that those boys will turn on you if things get really bad."

"Yes, Mom. Race. I know."

Veronica paused, noticing the time on the car clock. "OK," she said, and thought, OK. I'll give you some room to figure this out. "I need to get going."

"Of course you need to get going. To fly off somewhere important. To get that work done."

One's child had the unique ability to reduce a lifetime of intense work, anxiety, and determination to shards of glass, dressed up as easy, throwaway lines. Veronica took a deep breath to hold in the tears that seemed to have suddenly arrived.

"Careful. You have your quiet and safe walk home after school because I fly off somewhere important."

Diego went into the house and straight to the family room and his video games.

Veronica followed him in to get some water before heading out.

"What happened?" Alex asked.

"Why are you still here?" Veronica snapped. "You show up and you don't know how long you're staying. I'm trying to keep my family together."

"That's all I needed to hear," Alex said. "I'll pack up now."

Alex began moving toward the spare room that he'd used as a base of operations for the past couple of weeks. He'd not been there the whole time. He'd taken work trips to the Bay Area and to Los Angeles. And Veronica had really enjoyed his presence. It was the first time since Diego was born that she could be home and not be fully emotionally responsible for her son.

"I'm sorry." Veronica instantly retreated. "I'm really sorry." She glanced into the family room and saw that Diego had put on the large headset he used to play video games and tune out the world. She then briefly explained what had happened at the party on Friday night. "Will you talk to him? Get him to tell you his side of the story. Because I certainly can't, and he needs to start talking soon. I'm so nervous that one of these other two kids is going to place the blame on Diego because they can. And now I need to go and catch this stupid plane. I should have just canceled the trip this morning. It's a dumb, no-nothing invitation. Please tell me you're staying. I might even see if I can take a late flight home tonight."

"I'll be here." Alex paused. "On one condition. If you come see Mom with me."

"You're a terrorist."

"We'll make it a quick visit. I promise. A day trip. Now go. Do what you do well. We'll be here when you get back. And I'll have extracted some information from Diego."

Veronica wanted to go into her family room and give Diego a kiss goodbye. But she didn't, partly because he'd asked for space but mainly because she wanted to keep some power, which she feared she was quickly losing.

"I may have gone a little agro on him," Veronica said. "Why don't you play it soft?"

After Veronica left, and as Alex got some work done in his room, Diego stopped his game to get a drink and make sure his mom was gone and that the door to his uncle's room was closed. He then went back into the family room and texted MJ and Vikram to see if they wanted to play *Fortnite*. They'd played together a couple of times after Vikram joined the team as a way to break the ice. Now, once they were connected on the game and able to talk through the headphones, they began happily shooting and talking about game strategy so as to not show that all three of them were completely rattled by the events of the morning.

"That was nuts," Diego finally ventured after they'd been playing for five minutes. "Vikram, your mom and mine should go get drinks and hug it out."

Vikram laughed nervously. "Really not sure what was going on there."

"Please tell me you two have held strong and haven't talked to your parents about Friday night," MJ said, the impatience clear in his voice.

"I didn't," Vikram said immediately.

It was a lie he couldn't have told if they had been talking in person.

"Neither did I," Diego said.

"You think Stanley is really as hurt as Dr. Helen says he is?" Vikram asked.

"She has no reason to lie," Diego said. "But he also has reason to pretend to be more hurt than he is. What was all that bullshit about us having a nice dinner together? And that he was just relaxing in the cave? He has plenty of reasons not to be telling the whole story either. And that's why we have to get back in there. She needs to hear our side of the story."

For the following several minutes, all their concentration returned to the game. It was demanding their focus. And the longer they were submerged in the world, the longer they could avoid the difficult conversation they needed to have.

"I kinda agree with Diego," Vikram said. "I don't know what we gain now by staying quiet. MJ, you said that we should wait to hear what Stanley says. We heard it. The less we say now, the more guilty we look."

"You're probably right," MJ said. "But we have to go together. We don't have to talk to the principal when she calls us in. We don't have to go in alone."

"She's trying to break us up," Diego said.

"But we can't just say no if she calls us in," Vikram said. "That makes us look guilty. Like we're trying to line up our stories. I'd rather just talk to her and tell her that Stanley was going crazy and we calmed him down. All of us can say the same thing, one by one."

"Vikram, why do you keep talking about being guilty?" MJ asked.

"Because we are. And so is he. We need to explain that."

"I don't know, man," Diego said. "It kinda sounds like you want to go in there by yourself."

"I really don't," Vikram insisted. "And I won't."

"See," MJ said. "Dr. Helen's trick is working. We're not trusting each other. We just need to hold strong and go together. Let's figure out the right time. Are we good?"

"Yes," Vikram said immediately. "We're good."

"For sure," Diego added.

Just as they were getting back into the game, Vikram pulled them out.

"I'm really trying not to make this shit complicated, but if we go in together now, Dr. Helen will know we all talked and arranged it. It's what she told us not to do."

"That's why I'm saying that we need to be patient and not say anything yet," MJ said. It was a lesson he'd learned on the field. If he stayed patient in the pocket, the options of who he could throw to and what he could do would increase with every passing second. But at the same time, it also increased his chances of getting pummeled by a lineman.

Since telling his parents, Vikram felt that part of his guilty conscience had been cleansed. But certainly not all of it.

"You all heard Dr. Helen say that Stanley said one of us went back up?" Vikram asked through his microphone.

The ten seconds or so of silence that followed could have been because of a glitch in their headphones. But they all sensed a different kind of glitch. About half an hour, maybe more, had passed between the three of them coming down from the cave and Stanley coming down screaming, during which they'd not really crossed paths with one another. Had anyone gone back up? One of them? Two of them?

In fact, separately, each had gone back up on their own. But none of them were ready to admit this yet.

"Yeah, I don't know what the fuck he's talking about," Diego finally said.

"I don't either," MJ added.

"It's just him yapping," Vikram said.

"Let's give it the rest of the day and then we'll go see her," MJ said.

They continued shooting in the game.

"I gotta go," Vikram suddenly said. "My mom is coming."

"What do you think?" Diego asked after seeing that Vikram had logged off. "Is he going to go see Dr. Hell alone?"

"No," MJ said. "He's fine. Shit, he did the least damage up there. You and I went in on the fucker hard."

"Maybe that's why he'll go in. To save his ass and point the finger at us. He's gonna rat. I just know it."

TWELVE

When Veronica boarded her plane to Portland, a part of her wanted to be home, close to her son. The other part was happy for the temporary distance.

Her seat was right up front and she ordered a glass of wine as the other passengers walked past her. She sipped slowly and Googled "Gita Shastri." She found plenty of Gita Shastris—a lawyer in D.C., a pediatric heart surgeon in Houston, a banker in San Francisco. But none who seemed to be the one she'd just met. It was hard to trust someone who left such faint fingerprints online. Though she trusted the Berringers even less, she knew who they were. She could predict what they would think and what they would do and where they would be open and where they'd be closed. In the minutes before the principal had arrived, she had been glad the Shastris were there. At least they would be able to talk reasonably through the issues. But the second the principal had walked in, she'd noticed Gita's body tighten.

For a completely unnecessary comparison, Veronica Googled herself, which she did now and again. There were pages and pages of hits—videos of talks, reviews of books, links to her essays. Everything about her *work;* nothing about *her.* Over the years, she had been approached by alumni magazines for profiles, which she consistently refused because she believed that the only way to continue building the life she had created was to not look back, to not talk about the person she was before. The picture of her that kept coming up was from several years ago; she needed a new headshot. The only new thing she found was the very niche world on Instagram where readers posted her latest book as if it was the centerpiece of a still life. She wasn't sure if any of them had read the book, but it was slowly becoming a signal of one's deeper engagement with the world. *Want to have a deeper, doper trip to Brazil? I am so obsessed with Veronica Cruz.* If only this could lead to her being popular amongst *New Yorker* readers and finding a place on their coffee tables, alongside *Orientalism, The Tipping Point,* and *Beloved.*

Wine in the afternoon might have been a good idea for some—most of western Europe, say—but it was not a good idea for Veronica. She would be sleepy by the late afternoon, when she needed to be awake and sharp. But something about Diego's silence had unnerved her. Even when they disagreed about things, she never doubted her ability to reach him, to talk to him. Now it felt like they might be on the verge of something new, something where she'd done all the mothering she could do. He needed some fathering. She was thankful that Alex had arrived when he had.

She'd finished the wine by the time the plane headed to the runway.

"Portland is home?" the man sitting next to her asked.

She'd kept the pages of her talk on her lap, just in case a neighbor started chatting her up. She had given the talk several times already—excerpts from her new book, along with some further reflections and thoughts for future work. She didn't need to look it over, but she liked having it close as an escape route. For longer flights, she usually sat in business class, but this was short and so she sat in first. Invariably during flights, the men sitting next to her—and they always seemed to be men—would look her over to figure out what exactly she was doing in the nice seats. Gloria Estefan? Eva Longoria?

"No," Veronica said. "Quick work trip."

The man looked to be in his early forties. He was of a certain breed that she saw more and more of in the fancy seats. Lean, in shape, with facial hair somewhere between heavy stubble and an actual beard. This one in particular was dressed in post-Lululemon male weekend wear. Were those pants or sweats? She had noticed his ugly shoes when he first boarded. They were a type of square sneaker that signaled that he was a climber or long-distance runner or something that required deep lungs. Veronica, on the other hand, always dressed up to fly, with a cashmere shawl as a protective layer. He could have been a tech millionaire or a trust funder or the CEO of a company harvesting and selling boutique honey that the one-percenters in China had to have for their morning smoothies. If he said he ran the child labor division at Nike, Veronica wouldn't have been surprised. But she would have taken the opportunity to hit him up for some rare Jordans that Diego was coveting. Maybe that would get Diego to talk.

"What do you do for work?" the man asked.

Usually, they didn't ask about work, assuming that she probably didn't have a job.

"I'm an academic," Veronica replied.

Scholar was too heavy; *writer* wasn't quite right. *Academic* wasn't perfect, but it was effective with men. It usually shut them up.

"What kind?" The man's eyes lit up just a bit.

"I'm a historian. Of South America." And then she added, for a bit of fun, "Of the Atlantic slave trade."

"That's amazing," he said. "I'm assuming there are lots of your books at my local bookstore."

"A few."

"I was kind of on that same route once. I did a PhD in classics."

"From where?" She knew he wanted to be asked.

"Penn."

He had not said much, but he'd said so much. That he knew Greek and Latin and then probably a few other Romance languages because that's what those degrees required. You couldn't just read the stuff in translation. And that after that, he had moved on to something else. She hoped he was wise enough not to say: There weren't many jobs for guys like me.

"You're not doing that anymore?" Veronica asked.

"It wasn't right for me. I got antsy with the research. I didn't have the discipline to write books."

"What do you do now?"

"Private equity."

He said the two words as if he was showing her his perfectly calibrated penis: I dabbled in your world, but now I've moved on to the serious matter of money, which, when all is said and done, is the only thing that matters. Sure, it doesn't make me happy. But it makes my life way more comfortable. Isn't my penis perfect?

She'd met this guy too many times before. Now he was going to transition to Trump and the failures of democracy. Or perhaps how the Piedmont region is a highly underrated Italian wine destination. If somehow DACA came up, she was going to ask for a change of seats; she'd happily take a middle seat near the bathrooms. Her instinct was to borrow a plastic knife from the flight attendant and carve him up, but there was a part of her that wondered if his insecurity was as inflated as his bank account.

"And you do this private equity in Portland?"

"I did my New York stint. And I had enough. I wanted to come home."

"And do you enjoy doing this private equity?"

"It pays the bills. I take nice vacations."

"And how much longer will you do this private equity?"

"I feel like you're making fun of me. It seems that you should at least know my name before you do that."

"I'm not making fun of you. I have a brother who's done similar work. What's your name, private equity?"

"Peter."

"Hi, Peter. I'm Veronica."

"Can I buy you another glass of wine, Veronica?"

"Sure. That would be great." She paused and was about to call him by his new nickname one more time, but then decided not to.

Peter flagged down the flight attendant. "I'd like to buy a free glass of wine for the both of us."

Veronica appreciated a man who could take a poke to the ribs.

It was Peter who asked the questions. About each of her books. About teaching at a university. "Do you get nervous up there in front of students? I hear that they are very vocal now about their likes and dislikes." About the talk she was scheduled to give. Maybe it was the conversation, maybe it was the second glass of wine, but before she knew it, the plane began its descent into Portland. For the better part of the trip, she and Peter were involved in such an engaging conversation that she hadn't noticed any of the passengers around her. She suddenly felt self-conscious. Had they heard her talking? Did she sound pretentious? Flirty? As the plane inched closer to the gate, she took out her cell phone and turned it on so that she would have something to do with her hands. For a brief span, she'd forgotten about Diego's problems and she only remembered when there was no text from him. Usually, after they'd had some small disagreement, he would send an emoji or a meme to announce that things were good again.

"Can I borrow your phone?" Peter asked.

He was looking at his own phone.

"Sure."

He began maneuvering around it and several seconds later handed it back to her. "In case you get bored while you're here and need a decent meal. I know of an excellent South Indian place that makes the perfect dosa."

When she took the phone back, she fumbled it in her hand. She assumed he'd entered himself into her contacts; it seemed like an incredibly forward, intimate thing for him to do. Is this what they did now? She hadn't been on an actual date for some years. When the flight attendant opened the plane door, she thanked Peter for the conversation and the wine. She was the first one off the plane.

Because of the change in plans, she'd told her host that she'd take an Uber to the hotel, freshen up, and then head to the college. But when she walked to the airport exit, two young women were waiting for her. One looked slightly older than the other, but they both looked like children.

"Professor Cruz," the older one said, raising her hand.

Veronica appreciated meeting and teaching students; she loved that part of her job. But she sensed already what the younger one was going to say to her. How important Veronica's work had been to her. How much it had made her life, and the life of her family, feel it could be the subject of history. Veronica appreciated these moments. She really did. But right then, she just needed the quiet of a solo ride. She wanted to work through her conversation with Peter. Maybe send him a quick text. Was there a dosa emoji?

"It's so nice to meet you. My name is Maggie. I'm a graduate student and I teach classes at the college. And this is Natalia, one of our bright undergraduates. The college asked us to pick you up. Do you have any checked bags?"

Veronica shook her head. "Nice to meet you both."

If she had to guess, Maggie had probably graduated from Mount Holyoke or perhaps Swarthmore and had had a girlfriend for a while but was now with a sweet boy who was a labor organizer. She was getting a PhD that would not earn her the kind of job that her very encouraging undergraduate professors had intimated would be waiting for her after all the work was done. Hopefully, she had parents who saw her degree as one long study abroad and would help her with a soft landing. Natalia, on the other hand, was probably Native. Maybe not. Perhaps Veronica could get her opinions on how her son had trampled upon sacred land and was now being mum about it.

They headed out of the airport.

The young women hadn't spoken on the way to the car and now

Veronica wished that they would say something. Wasn't that part of their job, in addition to giving her a ride? And the ride? An old Civic that Maggie had clearly taken to the car wash before picking her up. The inside smelled like air freshener.

"We've been reading all your work in class in preparation for this visit," Natalia began from the back seat as soon as they got on the freeway. "It's really incredible. I appreciate it so much. As you probably know, our campus is about as white as it can be without being an all-white college. And so we appreciate you spending time with us."

Veronica turned her head and gave Natalia half a smile. This was coming from an undergraduate. She had a confidence that Veronica both appreciated and found insufferable. When Veronica was her age, she barely spoke, thinking it presumptuous. And yet she could not begrudge the fact that this young woman had found her voice so early. Natalia was so clear and direct.

"The college lured me," Natalia continued, "by telling me that there would be faculty who would teach classes on Natives in the Northwest. And there's not been much of that at all."

"Natalia has been leading a campus charge to diversify both the faculty and the curriculum," Maggie said. "She's quite the force on her own."

"I was choosing between coming here and Dartmouth," Natalia said. "I think I made a huge mistake."

"First of all, congratulations on getting into such great colleges. That's no easy task. Maybe when my son is ready to apply to schools, you can look over his essay for him. But in the meanwhile, I'm meeting with the president of the college this evening. I'll certainly reiterate some of these concerns you have. They're perfectly valid."

Suddenly, the five thousand dollars didn't seem like a high-enough payment. She didn't mind being the go-between, but it was exhausting. As they drove on, she looked through her contacts. Peter had added himself as "Private Equity." She couldn't contain her smile.

When they dropped Veronica off in front of her very nice hotel, she felt bad. The cost of one night's lodging was probably half the value of that car.

"I'll pick you up at four-thirty," Maggie said. "I'm sorry that doesn't leave you much time."

It was three already.

"No worries. I'll have a cup of coffee and be ready. It's a short walk, yes?"

"Very quick."

"Then I'll walk myself."

"You can walk onto campus and ask for Anderson Hall. It has the big theater space where you're going to speak."

Veronica checked in to the hotel, asked for a pot of coffee to be delivered to her room, and then lay on the incredibly soft duvet on the bed. She closed her eyes for just a minute. She might have slept through her talk if it weren't for the knock on the door: her coffee.

Berringer. It had a ring to it. Schwab. Goldman. Morgan. Stanley. The kind of name that could be trusted for a solid 7, 8 percent, with occasional forays into 10- and 12-ville when the market was humming. Michael had built his business around the solid middle. He would never let things dip down to a paltry 3 to 4 percent. Those were savings and loan figures.

Early on, Michael got clients because he had gone to Yale and because his father knew so many people in town. For a while, he'd done fine, less because of his acumen in understanding the market than because the market was on a massive upward turn and he was skilled at staying out of his own way. Eventually he began losing clients, not because he was losing money, but because he wasn't making the kind of money they wanted. They already had plenty of it; they just wanted more. There were now younger guys in town, math guys and physics PhDs and dudes on the spectrum who drove Ferraris because they knew how to get 15 percent in a really good year. Mad numbers.

Over the last few years, Michael had become the guy his clients gave a hundred, two hundred thousand to grow safely and steadily. But he was now down to five clients, an embarrassingly small number. The money he made off them was barely enough to pay the rent for the office he'd had for well over a decade. In the flush days, every desk in the office had been occupied by an employee, he had client lunches three out of five days, and he and Shirley threw an extravagant annual Christmas party where Michael opened both his wine cellar and his checkbook for generous year-end bonuses. In the week between Christmas and New Year, he'd close the office and the family would fly to Kauai. Michael and Shirley would sit on the beach, watching their growing children swim farther and farther out into the Pacific. Later, in bed, tasting the salt on Shirley's lean body, Michael would think that life was sweet.

Now he hadn't replaced his last junior analyst when he left for business school; he'd let his secretary go months ago, replaced by a woman in India who managed to be the secretary for ten different clients. She had an English lilt to her accent that his remaining clients loved.

Since arriving at the office after the meeting at the high school, he'd read the *Financial Times* and then had spent much of the day fiddling with an email to Tom Regan. He'd decided that email was better for what he wanted to explain. Just as he was finishing the email, Shirley called.

"Let's have them over."

"Who?"

"The other parents."

"Why would we do that?" Michael asked.

"Because it's important that we get to know them. This problem is not going away by itself. You can make some good drinks. I'll cook a nice meal. We need to decrease the temperature after that meeting at school. Especially if MJ continues being AWOL."

After the meeting, MJ had said he would walk home alone. He'd been in his room for a bit and then left the house.

"Fine," Michael said. "When?"

"Let's suggest tomorrow night. I can send a note out now."

"OK."

Michael went back to the email: "My advice is that you not get out of this market right now. I know it's a bit of a cliché, but we have to think about the long game. But I won't fight you if you decide to go another way. I can have the money transferred to your account by the end of the week."

Michael did not, in fact, have Tom Regan's money. He had used it to pay back another client who had wanted out. Now he had no money to pay anyone. He owed Tom roughly $125,000. In his mind, it was not that much cash. But he didn't have a liquid version of it. He didn't even have that amount in his personal savings.

Legally, Michael and Shirley's assets were all joint property. But in everyday life the accounts were separate. Even though they'd never sat down and explicitly talked about it, they had a basic financial agreement. Shirley had contributed the nice house without a mortgage and had her own accounts that she'd inherited directly from her parents. It was Michael's responsibility to take care of all other expenses—vacations, house upkeep, property taxes, college tuition when it was time. For years when the market was good and steady, he'd handled it all. But now he owed Tom money and he had no way to pay for tuition when MJ started college next fall. All along he'd just thought that he would make the right pick at the right time and he'd be flush again. He'd assumed that there was something good around the next corner, an assumption he'd made his whole life. But the right pick and the right corner seemed more and more elusive as the amount he owed grew.

Since MJ had chosen Yale, there was nothing Michael looked

forward to more than that moment the following fall when there
was a sharp chill in the air and he could sit in the Yale Bowl, watching his son warm up his arm. In warming it up, he would somehow
be warming up the arms of both Michael and his father. And yet
there was some small part of him, very small and very submerged,
that felt a sliver of relief when he had heard the principal describe
what the boys had done to Stanley. Could MJ's decisions relieve him
of a big check he could not, at the moment, write? Michael felt guilty
even letting the thought out into the light, lest it travel from the far
depth of his mind into the world and become a reality he had mani-
fested into existence.

He'd somehow figure out the tuition money, but he didn't know
where to get Tom's money on such short notice. And this was tightening his lower back as he sent the email.

The yes emails tended to arrive sooner than expected; the no's were
always later because no one wanted to write that email. In that inter-
stitial space between sooner and later, after Gautam had refreshed
his email roughly one hundred times through the course of the day,
the Indian CEO finally replied, cc'ing his chief operating officer.

Gautam read the email once and then twice, and with his heart
knocking against his chest, walked straight to the CEO Ryan's desk
and asked him to come with him to the enclosed conference room,
the only private space in the office. Gautam's immediate boss Bryan
had watched him walk over to Ryan and followed as well.

"Bryan, I'm glad you're here, too," Gautam began. "I had a meeting late last week with a guy named Rohan Doshi. Don't worry. I'd
not heard of him either. He owns a conglomerate of companies involved primarily in paints, headquartered in Gujarat, with offices in
Cape Town, Lagos, Cairo, Dubai, and London. He is looking to
open an American office. At our meeting, he explained to me how he
needed his employees to better communicate with one another

across some pretty serious linguistic and geographic divides. And I showed him how, with the added bonus that he'd no longer need to pay for his employees to fly across the world to miscommunicate with one another in person. I just got an email from him. He wants to do a trial, but a huge trial. They have twenty thousand global employees. And if our software fits their needs, he'd like to make the relationship more permanent." Gautam looked down at the email on his phone and read from it. "'I also know of a few other Indian companies that might be interested in this product.'" He looked up. "Rohan and his company are good enough on their own, but if his paint is the gateway to Reliance and the Ambanis or the Tatas, my god. There is a lot of money in the new India."

Gautam was trying to contain his smile, but Ryan couldn't contain his, especially because Ryan had been the one to push for Gautam's hiring. "Starting when?" Ryan asked.

"Yesterday," Gautam said. "Or as soon as possible."

Bryan had been on his phone the second Gautam had mentioned the CEO's name, balancing out listening and searching. When Gautam was done with his initial explanation, Bryan held up the phone, displaying a photograph. "This your guy? Hanging out with Pol Pot."

It was a photo of Rohan and Prime Minister Narendra Modi at a ribbon-cutting ceremony.

Bryan was Gautam's boss and he did vaguely bossy things to him. But this felt hostile.

"Ah," Gautam said, not biting back his comeback. "Someone has been reading *The Economist*."

Gautam's family had always been Gandhi and Nehru people, and his father in particular had been deeply troubled by the rise of Modi and his Hindu nationalism. Gautam didn't like it either and wanted to visit India less and less. But hearing the critique from Bryan, less political and more personal, made him almost want to defend Modi.

"We just need to be careful about who we're getting in bed with," Bryan continued.

"Two weeks ago, literally where we're standing now, you pressed me about not getting a big sale. And let's be clear, none of the other guys have gotten a huge one either. Now that I've gotten a massive one, with more in the pipeline, you've suddenly gone ethical on me. We've taken VC funding from banks wet from fossil fuels."

"Fossil fuels and fascists aren't the same thing," Bryan said.

"Rohan Doshi is not a fascist. He sells paint to the third world and he needs our help to keep his employees in close communication."

"I'm not saying we shouldn't do this," Bryan said. "We just need some due diligence before we get too excited. We have Muslim programmers here from Pakistan. How would they feel?"

Before Gautam could respond, Ryan did: "And we will do our due diligence. But more immediately, let's just take a moment to enjoy what this could mean for all of us. Amazing work, Gautam. Why don't you write him back and say we'll get the paperwork started on our end? That'll buy us some time. And then I think the three of us need to go get a celebratory drink. We all need this little victory."

"Yes," Bryan said, looking straight at Ryan. "Drinks would be great."

There was no way Bryan was going to miss out on drinks and be left out of the loop.

Adrenaline was now pumping through Gautam's body. "Bryan, I have to say that envy is not a good look on you."

"I'd be really careful about what you say from here on out," Bryan said, walking out of the conference room.

Veronica drank two cups of coffee, changed into a dark blue suit, and put on the gold hoop earrings she'd bought herself when she'd earned tenure. She checked her messages for the last time before putting her phone aside for the evening. Nothing from Diego. However, there was an email from Shirley Berringer. Dinner with that group sounded like an Agatha Christie murder mystery without any of the fun. But could she say no?

This town was built around the college. There was a square in the middle, surrounded by cafés, bars, a hardware store, the one very nice hotel for visiting dignitaries, a greasy spoon, and the requisite place where the chef probably liked spending the morning foraging for edible flowers. Surely this was where they would end up at the end of the evening.

The campus was even closer than she'd thought. She went through an ornate gate. The grass was impossibly green; the buildings looked like they had either been built in the nineteenth century or were constructed more recently to look like they had been. All the buildings were uniform—stone and eaves; Gothic liberal arts college chic—except the library, a work of trickle-down modernism comprised of glass, steel, and sharp corners. Veronica had seen this a lot: colleges spending millions on a new, modern library, thinking that they could lure more students in, when in reality, it remained largely empty. She loved these small college campuses and the towns built adjacent to them because they were charming and lovely and the last place she would ever end up. They were simply too small. The pleasure of her job was that she rarely bumped into any of her colleagues when she wasn't on campus.

She made her way to the main auditorium where she was going to give her talk. Most of the students walking around were white and looked healthy and happy and handsome, as if they spent a majority of their time on mountain bikes and in hot springs. The small handfuls of non-white students did a double take when they saw Veronica. They recognized her from the posters hung around campus advertising her visit.

"Veronica?"

There was a woman standing on the steps of the building.

"Susan," Veronica said, walking up to the woman, who was in her mid-fifties.

Susan Michaels, a historian of Latin America who worked primarily on Argentina, had invited Veronica. She'd written a terrific book on political violence but had published nothing else. Colleges like this expected a lot of face time with students.

"I'm so sorry about the delay today," Veronica said.

"No worries. Is everything OK with your son?"

"Same old teenage stuff."

Susan didn't reply. Either she didn't have kids or her version of "teenage stuff" was much different.

"Do you need anything?" Susan asked. "The auditorium is filling up. Everyone is really excited about your visit. I'm glad we'll get some quiet time at dinner."

"I've been looking forward to this. Why don't we go inside?"

It was still half an hour before the start of the talk and half the auditorium was already full. Susan took Veronica up to the front and introduced her to her colleagues, all of whom were exceedingly kind, treating her like she was some kind of visiting diplomat. As they were chatting near the stage, a man in a suit walked up to them and the mood among the faculty standing with her shifted. Everyone's spines straightened.

"Veronica, I want to introduce you to the president of the college. His generosity allowed us to invite you."

In another life, he would have been the CEO of a solid, midlevel food-and-beverage company. The only thing that signaled his scholarliness were his rimless glasses.

"Very nice to meet you," Veronica said. "Thank you for having me."

"I'm looking forward to our dinner together," he said. "But before that, I'm looking forward to your talk. I read that amazing write-up in *The New York Review of Books*."

"It was very kind," Veronica said.

The review probably had done more to legitimize Veronica in the mind of the president than her twenty-page CV.

Susan led Veronica to a seat in the front row.

"I'll give you a few minutes," Susan said.

Veronica looked over her notes, and every minute or so, looked back at the crowd. The auditorium was filling up quickly. A little before five o'clock, Susan went up to the podium and began the evening. She gave a very nice introduction to Veronica and her work and said that after the talk, there would be a Q&A and some brief closing remarks by the president.

Veronica had done this more times than she could remember. Still, as she was getting ready to stand up, she was overtaken by a passing anxiety. What if she forgot how to read? What if her mind short-circuited and she couldn't make out the words? She walked up to the podium and looked out at the audience. It seemed like all the students of color were here at the talk, making up roughly half the audience. It didn't say much about the recruiting efforts of the college.

"Thank you, Professor Michaels, for that warm introduction. You're all very lucky to have her here."

Veronica spoke for roughly forty minutes: on Latin American history, Slave Z.105, Brazil, and music, with quick asides on Melville and Shakira. She worked mostly from her notes, with the beginning and ending a little more off-the-cuff. She knew this material. Really well. There were stretches when she didn't need to read directly from the pages. Throughout the talk, she noticed the president taking diligent notes in his notebook. Maybe she had underestimated him.

The first couple of questions in the Q&A were easy ones about her writing process. Veronica was particularly skilled at taking softballs and making them into something more interesting and substantive. It made her sound smart and it made the questioner feel smart. There were a couple of questions from the faculty, which were less questions than demonstrations of their own work and showing that they had read Veronica's books.

After the talk and roughly fifteen minutes of questions, Veronica began to feel herself fading. The stress of the morning, the wine, and then the second glass and then the coffee were all mixing together. As if the moderator Susan sensed this, she announced that Veronica had time for one more question. Veronica's shoulders eased up. She was almost done. Now just a decadent meal and then she could rest and watch TV in her room. Maybe send Private Equity a quick text hello. He could send a driverless car for her.

The microphone was passed to the bright undergraduate Natalia. Veronica took a sip of water. She could almost taste the cool dry white that they would start with at dinner.

"Professor Cruz. Thank you for that wonderful, informative talk."

As she listened, Veronica noticed that Natalia had changed since seeing her last. She was now wearing a nice black dress. In fact, most of the students were dressed up. In the checklist they sent to incoming freshmen, did they ask the women to bring a nice dress and the men a sports coat, along with bedsheets and a mini fridge? The lecture hall looked like an intellectual cotillion.

"You tell this story of Afro-Latino history in this book," Natalia continued, "and I so very much appreciate it."

Even from the distance between them, Veronica could tell that she was nervous speaking in front of everyone. Just go ahead. It's going to be OK. "Thank you," Veronica said as if to encourage her.

"But from what I gather from your talk, there is a serious elision of the history of the *Native* populations of Brazil. It seems to me that they were silenced once in history and now you have silenced them again. Can you comment on your participation in this textual genocide?"

Serious elision. In scholarly talk, this was the equivalent of telling someone to fuck off. But *genocide*? That was next level.

Veronica looked at Natalia and Natalia looked right back at her without flinching. This nice young woman had chosen this moment to accuse her, in front of roughly 150 people, of leaving out important history. It was a serious accusation, one that had been leveled at Veronica in the early part of her career. Now when it happened, she usually pointed out that much of her second book had been devoted to the history of Native populations of Brazil as a way of providing a corrective for precisely the thing that this young woman was accusing Veronica of. She'd spent a better part of six years researching and writing that second book. She took a deep breath. This was not entirely Natalia's fault. She had taken classes at this college, which somebody paid seventy-five thousand dollars a year for her to attend, where she learned about the ways in which important histories had been elided from traditional narratives. The faculty sitting there in that front row had given her this precise language. And now she was rightfully using it.

Veronica looked at Natalia again and then glanced at the president, who she would be dining with shortly. Susan, the faculty member who had invited her, had said that the college was trying to manage its past sins of not thinking about diversity and the president had given a substantial sum of money to invite luminaries. She'd mentioned that he wanted to talk to Veronica over dinner about what the college could do to move forward, to best serve its changing student population. Maybe at some point he would hire her to help make the changes. The consulting fees would be handsome. Perhaps there was even a vice provost position in the offering.

She had signed a contract that didn't really exist. In exchange for the generous honorarium, she had to play nice, to make the students feel good. Her job was to challenge them but not so much so that they would feel uncomfortable.

Because Veronica didn't immediately respond, Natalia must have felt emboldened that her first statement had not been instantly shot down. She took one more step toward Veronica: "I think you need to understand how neoliberalism has not only destroyed Native life; it has destroyed the stories we can tell. And you and your work have internalized the neoliberal order."

"I appreciate your question," Veronica began, imploring herself to take three deep breaths. All she needed to do was thank Natalia for being so engaged and point her to her second book. After the talk, she would think of the perfect answer that would have pushed back at Natalia, but in a way that felt like she was holding her up at the same time. But that was later. "First of all, please stop Marxsplaining me with all this neoliberal talk." Until that very second, Veronica had never used that phrase. With it now out of her mouth, she couldn't contain the smile that was forming on her face. "Second, before accusing someone of elision, I would read the entirety of their work first. You and I chatted earlier. We had a really nice conversation and you said you've read my work. But clearly you haven't. There is no replacement for an actual engagement with the written word. Just because I didn't mention anything at this particular moment that you wanted to hear it doesn't mean I haven't thought of it." She looked out to the audience. She sensed the discomfort emanating from Natalia. That earlier confidence from the car was gone. "But what I really want to explore is the nature of your question: *Why is this missing?* Why is this the question that we always ask? Why are you more interested in what you think I have left out rather than what I have put in? Isn't that worth your time as well? I remember in graduate school a fellow student went on and on about how she hated Marx because he didn't take gender into account enough. True, he didn't. But he did take into account a lot of human history. I would have thought that was enough. But apparently, it's not. It's OK sometimes to omit. The whole is still good."

As these words came out of her mouth, she was blindsided by another threat of tears. She took a long sip of her water and didn't let herself go there. For a full ten seconds, she stood in a daze. But then she snapped back, trying to counter the emotion she could feel in her throat.

"So please, the next time you stand up and ask a question to someone older than you, who has been working on books as long as you have been alive, take a moment and a deep breath and ask them what they *have* done instead of what they *have not*. Be generous. Be respectful. There's a reason I am up here and you're down there."

By the time Veronica was finished, Natalia looked like she might faint. As the substance of her comments traveled across the auditorium, the room began to curdle. Groups of students started hissing and a few began walking out, followed by more.

Veronica immediately regretted what she'd said and what she'd done. For what she'd done all these years was to write and write and research and research and make as small of an actual footprint as possible. To make it just about the work and never herself. Now she had done exactly the opposite. She had made the moment about herself, even though she believed in the substance of what she had said. She felt lightheaded. She couldn't pinpoint what had pushed her over the edge this time. But she knew that since the conversation that morning with the principal, she'd been feeling irritable and combative.

Susan Michaels came onto the stage, and Veronica wisely stepped back.

"Let's thank Professor Cruz for a very engaging talk. And now the president would like to provide some closing remarks."

Veronica went and sat down in the front row. She took a deep breath. She felt disoriented. The president thanked her and then began talking broadly about creativity and the importance of critical inquiry during the college years, with bland references to Locke and Malcolm Gladwell and Albert Einstein. All that time he'd seemed to be taking notes during her talk, he had actually been preparing these remarks, which made no reference to anything Veronica had said.

The moment he finished, the remaining audience quickly left the auditorium, as if they were the last bit of water in a draining bathtub. Veronica just sat there, unsure of what was going to happen next.

Susan walked up to her. "Your work is really incredible. That talk was inspiring."

"Thank you, Susan. I'm sorry about scolding her like that. I really am. I'm not sure what got into me."

"Why don't we head out? We may all need a drink."

As they left the auditorium, Veronica noticed a young man sitting at a desk with a large stack of her latest book for sale. She was supposed to sign books, but there was not a single student in line. She smiled at the bookseller, slightly shrugged, and kept walking.

"I feel like I should be the one apologizing," Susan said when they were out of earshot of any students.

Veronica paused and looked very briefly at the other two faculty members that were with them, both young women. Both were probably still junior faculty. She remembered when she was in their shoes. She'd kept all her opinions to herself.

"It was my job to be the adult in the room," Veronica said. "But I couldn't understand what was happening. That young woman picked me up from the airport. She was exceedingly nice."

Veronica paused, thinking through what she wanted to say next. She had some sense of why Natalia had done what she'd done. She was earning her stripes in front of her fellow students, letting them know that she had the strength to go up against anyone, even someone like Veronica, who was in her camp. She'd done a bit of that herself in graduate school. But Veronica didn't want to share this with the other women, all of whom were white.

As Veronica had suspected, they ended up at the fancy restaurant several doors down from her hotel. They were seated at a table for five; the president's seat remained empty.

"He isn't coming, is he?" Veronica asked.

"I haven't heard either way," Susan said, and then lowered her voice. "But it will be better for all of us if he doesn't come. He's incredibly boring *and* patronizing. A terrible combination."

When the waiter came over, Susan asked the rest of the table if it was OK if she ordered the tasting menu for the whole group, with wine pairings. "The college is paying and I'm thirsty."

Veronica had no appetite, so it was ideal that each course was tiny and inconsequential. She had grown so tired of waiters reciting the exotic ingredients in each dish as if they were presenting the constituent elements of the smallpox vaccine. As the meal progressed, Veronica was thankful to her dinner companions for maintaining great cheer, gossiping lustily about their colleagues, and allowing Veronica to enter and exit the conversation as she wished.

But somewhere halfway through the meal, when they'd all had enough wine in them that whatever they said could later be blamed on the high quality of the grapes, Susan turned to Veronica: "Marxsplaining? That was hilarious."

"And so spot-on," the other women added in unison.

"Did you just come up with that?"

"For once in my life, yes. On the spot. It may be my greatest linguistic work ever. I've gotten used to it with my undergraduate and graduate student dudes, but she was really stepping on that neoliberal pedal. My guess is that she is a very, very bright young woman who may have just got caught up in the moment. I feel a little bad about it. In fact, a lot bad about it. She didn't deserve that. I'm going to send her a note apologizing."

The other women listened and nodded but didn't say anything. If Natalia was a student in their classes, they certainly weren't going to admit that now.

"Again," Veronica said as they stood outside the restaurant after dinner, "my apologies that I had to miss the lunch today. And sorry for being so quiet at dinner."

"It was a wonderful evening," Susan said. "Thank you so much for coming. I can have Maggie take you to the airport tomorrow, or if you would prefer, you can take a cab."

"I think a cab is best."

Back in the room, the first thing Veronica did was order room service. She had moved her food around on her plates all evening long and now she was finally hungry. She ate a hamburger, drank a beer, and watched *SportsCenter*. Then she picked up her phone and scrolled through the contacts. She stopped at Private Equity, thought about it, and then scrolled back to Diego's father and called.

"Everything OK? Diego OK?"

After all the fights over the years, including a recent one over alimony, Veronica and her ex-husband, Andre, had settled into utilitarian conversations. They were both tired of the bickering and disagreements.

"He's fine," Veronica said. She didn't want to get into it. Even from a distance, he would have ideas on how to handle it. "I need you to answer me something straight-up."

"OK."

"Have you been sending me letters?"

"Letters?"

"With my *name*?"

"No," he said immediately. "I'm a little annoyed that you'd ask. I've done my share of dumb things. But blackmail is beneath me."

Veronica laughed. For the thirty or so months they were in love, it was their banter she'd enjoyed the most.

"I'm sorry. I just needed to ask."

"Everything OK with you? You don't sound good."

Veronica paused, considering whether to say anything to him about Diego's time in the cave. Andre's late-night voice was still his late-night voice.

"Nothing I can't handle," she said. "Work is just a little complicated at the moment. And I think it's going to get a lot more complicated."

She was about to hang up, but she didn't.

"You know he needs you around a bit more."

She could hear Andre taking a deep breath. "You know you've usually discouraged that. I've been telling you that I've been doing much better."

They had married young, had Diego young, divorced young. And Andre had needed some time to get on track. Now he was. He worked in tech in Texas, which had become a thing, and he had a big, expansive family in San Antonio. Veronica knew that she should have encouraged Diego to see his dad more.

"Please don't put this on me."

"I'm not. It's on both of us."

"I agree. But this isn't an invitation for you to just show up. Just be in more regular touch with him. That's it."

"I am in regular touch," Andre said. "We talk every couple of weeks. He hasn't mentioned it?"

"I'm glad," she said, her eyes finally flooding with tears. "He needs you."

THIRTEEN

Vikram was sitting in his room with his door closed and his headphones on, trying to cancel out any outside noises, when he noticed a call from a number he didn't recognize. He let it ring once, twice, but then answered on the third ring.

"Hello?" he asked tentatively.

"Hey."

It was a female voice Vikram didn't recognize.

"I hope this is OK. Tyler gave me your number. It's Erin. Greene."

Vikram had stayed in bed for much of the day, getting up only to grab something to eat. His head felt foggy and his body was stiff from all the nonmovement. But now, as if the electricity had finally been turned on, his body suddenly crackled to life.

"Yeah, of course. I'm glad you called."

"How are you doing?"

"OK. I guess."

Vikram didn't know what Erin knew and so he wasn't sure what to say and what not to say. He was exhausted from the back-and-forth in his head. What to say to his parents? To Diego and MJ?

What to keep from the principal? There was something about her voice, melodic and soft, coming through the phone that made him want to tell her every detail of the evening, from start to finish.

"I wanted to talk to you about Friday," Erin said. "There are lots of stories swirling around school about what happened. There's a vague outline of you and Diego and MJ having a run-in with Stanley. And lots of pictures and videos when Stanley came down. All of this, but very little actual clarity."

Vikram wanted to ask about the pictures and videos but worried that he'd sound guilty and defensive if he did. On Saturday he'd seen pictures in various Instagram stories and on Snap, but nothing that was too incriminating. Since then, the feeds had moved on.

"You don't need to say anything to me if you don't want to," Erin continued.

This felt like an invitation, but he wasn't quite sure what he was being invited to.

"But you know that I work on the little paper we have at school."

Ah, Vikram thought, feeling stupid for what he'd been imagining about their future in the past minute. She just wanted information.

"But that's not why I called. I promise. If you want to tell me anything, fine. If not, that's fine as well. I just wanted to make sure you were OK."

Vikram wanted to trust her, and he wanted to keep talking to her. But had she made the same call to Diego? Having been in a few rumor mills himself, Vikram knew how stories traveled in high school. It was better for Erin to hear from him what Dr. Helen already knew. And he really wanted to keep talking to Erin.

"Yes, we had a little run-in with Stanley earlier in the evening. He was drunk and swinging his fists wildly. It was right after I saw you up at the caves. We calmed him down and left him to sober up. But I have no idea how he ended up in those bushes or so beat-up. It makes me sick thinking of him with all those cactus thorns poking out. We didn't do that to Stanley. We wouldn't."

"I believe you. I don't know you that well, but I kinda feel like you wouldn't be involved unless there was a right reason."

Vikram appreciated her faith and yet felt a little disappointed that she didn't think he would get into a brawl for the simple sake of getting into a brawl.

"But I also called for another reason. I'm sending you a photo right now. I took it and I haven't sent it to anyone else. And I don't intend to."

Vikram lowered his phone as a photo popped up. It was Stanley in the midst of his screaming. The photo was as clear as it was disturbing. Vikram enlarged portions of it to see Stanley's arms and legs covered in cactus spines and his face bloodied and beaten. He couldn't quite understand why Erin had sent it to him, but before he could ask, he noticed a figure in the background, standing behind and to Stanley's right side. He enlarged that portion and his whole face felt hot.

"Did you notice it?" Erin asked.

"Yeah."

"I know you were up at the caves earlier. That's not in question. But I guess why this worries me is that you're right behind Stanley, as if you're coming down the path just after he walked in, screaming. Like you had been up there with him."

"You get all that from this?" Vikram asked, feeling like he was going to be ill. He tried to remember the details of the evening as if he were watching a video on his phone. There were parts that were simply glitchy and unclear.

"I think you can get most anything from photos. And if I have this angle, I assume others have something similar. I know Dr. Helen has been talking to students. She's gonna get to me eventually. I just wanted you to know. I'm not gonna mention this picture."

"I was roaming around the party and just happened to be back there when he walked down," Vikram said. "That's it."

"That makes total sense. And I'm here anytime if you want to just chat."

"Why are you showing me this photo?" Vikram asked. He held two emotions simultaneously: a pleasant surprise that Erin had called and a pure panic that things were about to get real bad.

"I don't know. I just don't want you getting into trouble. That's it." Erin paused. "I should probably go."

"Can you do me a favor? Take good math notes for me. I'll be back soon."

"Sure," Erin said.

Just as he hung up the phone, he heard the front door open downstairs. He put his headphones back on. It was probably a good idea for him to go down and talk to his parents about this photo, but instead he just turned up the Nirvana he'd recently gotten into and tried to drown out everything else.

———— ⇒⇒⇒⇒⇒ ————

Gautam didn't get home from work until well after dinner. He hadn't called or texted to say he would be late. The longer she'd not heard from him, the more Gita assumed he'd gotten a no. When he walked into the kitchen, she could see he was not stable on his feet. There were plenty of things that annoyed her about him, but now she just felt pity.

"It's going through," Gautam said, tapping the counter. "And it's big. Bigger than anyone else has ever done. They have something like twenty thousand employees. RyanBryan and I went out for a few drinks."

The more drinks they'd had, the more they'd talked about what the sale would mean for the company and less about the due diligence they needed to complete. For whatever reason, by the time Bryan arrived at the bar, he'd backed off from his earlier critique.

"Oh." Gita felt sad that Gautam hadn't immediately called her when he heard the news. She tried swallowing it; at least he'd not called to punish her for her earlier lack of belief in the sale. "That's amazing news. Is there chatter?"

Chatter that an Indian American salesman had made a major sale to an Indian CEO.

"There'll be plenty from the sales guys when we announce it. But not yet. Bryan said some bullshit about the CEO being a Modi guy."

"Is he?"

"Honestly, I have no idea. If I don't get a proper promotion from this, I'm leaving. I should have Bryan's job. I understand sales *and* the technology."

Easy there, Gita thought. It was partly the alcohol talking and partly the fact that Gautam had never had the chance to be confident like this. But being happy for Gautam's work success was complicated. Gita was happy for their future bank account, and she knew how hard he'd worked. And yet this period of him switching from programming to sales had been difficult on their marriage. It had changed its internal mechanisms. Gautam had been angry a lot. And more alcohol forward.

"Can we get that kitchen now?" Gita asked, forcing a smile.

"Absolutely. Whatever you want."

"And can we talk about Vikram?"

"Yes. Is he still awake? Actually, I probably shouldn't talk to him now. I'm a little tipsy."

"Well, the quarterback's mother just invited us to dinner at their house tomorrow night. I'm sorry I didn't ask you, but I said yes. I thought it would be good for us all to gather."

"Let's do it," Gautam said. He paused and looked over at Gita. He moved a step toward her, noticing the lines to the side of her eyes that seemed to have appeared overnight. "I'm sorry. I'm really sorry about these past couple of years. It's been really hard on me. I'm hoping we can reset and start over."

He was speaking in generalities, but she knew the particularity he was talking about.

"Am I forgiven?" Gautam asked, tiptoeing closer to her.

Was he really bringing this up now?

Gautam had insisted that it had just been lunch. Two lunches.

Two work lunches at the last company he'd worked for. That's it. And Gita had, in the end, believed him. Believed him because he was not a liar. And believed him because she didn't think he would do something that might destroy his family for the sake of a young woman he'd met at work. Yet, in a weird way, she had also lost a little respect for him because he didn't have the courage to do something so stupid. It was such idiotic, insane logic, but it was her honest logic. There had been a part of her that wished something had happened, because that would have been better. Cornered, Gautam had blurted out: "She's Indian Indian. I feel more myself around her." Sex might have been easier to forgive. The honesty of the statement had been impossible for her to unhear.

Gita had only learned about the woman because she and Priya were out doing some shopping when Priya noticed her father and the woman sitting in a restaurant window. Even before she'd said, "Is that Dad?" Priya knew something was up. After that, she'd pulled away from her father and then her mother, who'd put all her sad energy into getting Priya into the right college.

"No," Gita said. "For that, you're not forgiven."

"I was just getting back at you. That's it."

"For what?" Gita asked. "There are other ways to get back at me. But there was nothing to get back at me *for*."

Between the drinks he'd had and the celebratory occasion for the drinks, Gautam felt dangerously free.

"You know as well as I do that there's a big part of you that wishes you'd ended up with some dude—Indian or not—who went to Stanford, did the consulting thing, and then headed off to business school at Wharton or Harvard." He paused. "It's why you're pushing Vikram so much. You want him to be that guy. If you couldn't marry him, at least you can raise him."

"You're drunk," Gita said, feeling like she'd just been slapped.

"I am. But that doesn't mean I don't see things clearly. Those lunches were nothing more than a chance to eat with someone whose eyes were not filled with disappointment."

"If you really think all this, Vikram beating up some kid is the least of our troubles."

The two were finally in agreement.

"Where are you going this late?" Alex asked.

It was nearly 10 P.M.

"For a quick run," Diego said, stretching out his legs near the front door. He'd spent an inordinate amount of time playing video games and was now in desperate need of fresh air. "No school and no practice is making me antsy."

"Please come back safely. Your mom will be pissed at me if you get kidnapped."

Diego smiled and stepped out into the cool night. At a solid clip, he jogged the mile through a few neighborhoods to MJ's house and stopped in front. "You up?" he texted. "I'm outside."

A minute later, MJ walked out of the door.

"I said no texting," MJ said.

"Half the party took photos Friday night. No one gives a shit about our texts. But sure, next time, I'll bring my messenger pigeon." Diego was tired of MJ's directives, on and off the field. "Why the fuck didn't you tell me those pills came from Stanley?"

"I didn't even know you really knew Stanley."

"Everyone knows Stanley," Diego said. "Now he has leverage over us."

"He doesn't have shit," MJ said. "We'll just deny it if he brings it up. No one is going to believe him."

Diego knew that Stanley was going to bring it up at some point because he didn't know how not to bring something up. Just the suggestion, even if people doubted Stanley, would make Diego look bad.

"Where did you think I got the weed we've smoked?" MJ asked. "Or when your rib hurt too much to play at the beginning of the season and you needed something for the pain? You can't get that shit from CVS."

"He's your dealer?"

"My dealer," MJ echoed mockingly. "We're not on *The Wire*. He just knows people. He steals some of it from his mom, who works at an old people's home. They have everything in there."

"So he *is* your dealer."

"And now yours."

"I've got to get back," Diego said. "I just wish you'd said where you had gotten them from."

"I wish you'd asked before you happily popped the pill."

"Fuck off."

With that, Diego ran back home. Since this whole thing had started, he'd been willing to let MJ take the lead. He didn't think that was a good idea anymore. Maybe Vikram was right; he needed to go see Dr. Helen himself.

"Do you actually like running?" Alex asked, when Diego came through the front door.

"No. But the better I get at it, the more I like it."

"You want one of these?" Alex asked. He was in the kitchen, making a PB&J. "When I lived in New York, I had an expense account, which meant I never paid for a meal. I ate a lot of very fancy, very expensive food. Sushi, steak, you name it. But I still think the humble peanut butter and jelly is the best, most perfect food."

"I can't say no now," Diego said. "Yes, I'd love one."

Alex made two sandwiches and they stood around the kitchen island eating them.

"I prefer the humble taco," Diego said. "But this is still pretty good."

For the whole day, Alex hadn't asked Diego anything. "You OK? You seem a little agitated."

"I am a lot agitated."

Diego finished half his sandwich and began by describing the first part of Friday evening when they all went out for dinner. He knew that Alex would tell his mom and he needed his family on his side. He certainly couldn't trust his friends. He explained how they went to the party and how he ended up in one of the caves, chatting with a girl that made him genuinely weak in the knees. Like he felt like he couldn't walk straight around her.

"Me and these football guys I was with wanted to leave the cave. We really did. But Stanley was drunk and talking crazy shit. We were trying to calm him down. That's it. I'll admit that I got some big hits in to make up for what an asshole he's been to me for years. I think even he knew that was coming. But what he looked like at the end of the night was not how we left him. We did not do that. I did not do that. I promise."

Diego looked at his uncle. He trusted him as much as he trusted his mother. He had more to say about the evening. "I need your help. I think I'm in huge trouble. Stanley thinks one of us came back after the first time and attacked him again. It got really weird when I was talking to Vikram and MJ about it earlier today. Like they knew something and weren't saying it."

"Did you go back up?" Alex asked.

Diego shook his head, thinking that if the shake was ambiguous, the actual answer could remain ambiguous.

"What does that mean?"

"Okay, I did. I was just so pissed at Stanley for messing things up with Erin. I just wanted to scream at him. But then I got there and saw him sitting on the ground, drunk and saying stupid shit. I left without saying or doing anything. Pissing himself was punishment enough. But if I admit to having gone back, the other two are just going to pin the shit on me and run."

"Let's talk to your mom about it when she's back," Alex said. "She'll know what to do."

"She tried to tell me this morning not to trust my friends and I was an asshole to her. Now I'm scared."

"You've got nothing to be scared about. Your mom and I will help you. As long as you explain everything you know, you'll be fine."

Diego heard his uncle say this, but he didn't really believe it. He wasn't ready to tell him about the pills. His mom was going to go ballistic on him when he told her.

Tuesday

FOURTEEN

By Tuesday morning, word of the events on Friday night had spread to the entire school. There wasn't a single student who hadn't heard some version of the story. The school newspaper, which had a deadline on Friday afternoon to put the monthly print issue to bed, had moved the existing main story below the fold and replaced it with a massive headline: WHAT HAPPENED IN THE CAVE? There was no accompanying article.

The majority opinion was spelled out on a banner that was already up in the main school hallway when students arrived. On most Fridays during the football season, there was an innocuous, encouraging banner in the same place—GO WILDCATS. Now there was this: STANLEY LIES. No one took responsibility, but one by one, students signed their names on the banner, doing it with a certain solemnity as if they were signatories to the UN's Universal Declaration of Human Rights.

About an hour later, another banner appeared at the opposite end of the same hallway: WE BELIEVE YOU, STANLEY. This one had fewer signatories, but with every passing moment during the seven minutes between first and second period, the numbers grew to a significant minority.

After the bell rang and the students settled into their classes, Erin Greene stepped into the empty hallway to use the restroom. Her class was close to the second banner and she stood in front of it, trying to decipher the various signatures. Some were messy scribbles, making it difficult to figure out the names. But most of the signatures were clear. One in particular was impossible to miss.

"Any idea who put these up?"

Dr. Helen had seen the banners and, wanting to take the pulse of school opinion, had instructed her staff to leave them up. She'd been in the hallway, clearing it of students, when she'd noticed Erin standing there.

"Hi," Erin said, suddenly feeling nervous. She shrugged her delicate shoulders and turned to the STANLEY LIES banner down the hall. "I think that one is the kind of performance art that Stephanie Cho would do. But I can't be sure."

"I understand you were at the party on Friday."

Dr. Helen had spent the better part of the previous day talking to students who'd been at the caves, trying to construct a timeline for Friday evening. Her secretary, Charlotte, despite her relatively advanced age, had become a bit of a wiz with social media, culling the various photos and videos that had been uploaded from the night. She'd found photos of each of the three boys in the frame with screaming Stanley. But that proved only that they were in proximity to Stanley, like so many other students.

"Yeah, I was there. It's not usually my thing. But I'd heard so much about the great Cave House and I wanted to check it out."

"And how was it?"

"The party?"

"The whole thing. The party, what happened after. Did you see anything unusual?"

"Not unless you think a bunch of high school kids hanging out in a broken-down old house is unusual." She paused, knowing that the principal was asking for something more, sensing that she was at one center of this story, even though she didn't want to be. "I was up in one of the caves with my friends. I know we weren't supposed to be there. I'm really sorry."

"Don't worry about that."

"I was chatting with Diego Cruz. He and I are in math together, which, if it counts for anything, he's freakishly good at. I was asking him about the game. Stanley Kincaid was there, too."

"What are your thoughts on Stanley?"

What intrigued Dr. Helen was that the first banner was not simply a statement of what Stanley had done—*lied*—but a statement on his being—*lies*.

"I don't really know him. I've never had a class with him. But he's always around. Seems harmless enough. He just doesn't know when not to talk. He interrupts people a lot. He kept interrupting Diego when we were trying to talk near the cave."

"Perhaps they were vying for your attention?"

"Perhaps," Erin said with a slight smile. A lot of boys tried to get her attention.

"Had he been drinking? Stanley."

Erin didn't say anything.

"Listen, no one is going to get in trouble for being there or drinking or any of it. I just need to figure out what happened between these boys in that cave."

"Yeah, he seemed a little drunk, kinda wobbly. Diego was drinking a beer too, but he was fine. He was just drunk with victory."

The principal smiled at Erin, thinking she was too smart for any of these boys.

"Did you see Vikram or MJ up there?"

"I saw both of them quickly as we were heading back down from the caves. They were going up. I didn't think much of it. And then later, I saw Vikram at the party and we chatted. He seemed fine. Excited about the game he'd just won. I made fun of him getting an A-minus in math."

"What about the other two? Did you see them at the party later?"

"It's a little fuzzy. But maybe I saw Diego? Like five minutes before I heard Stanley screaming. But I can't be sure. Stanley looked *bad*. How's he doing?"

"Not good." The principal paused. There were a couple of students hovering close to them, pretending they were in transit when really they wanted to hear a snippet of the conversation. Dr. Helen told them to get going to class and then turned back to Erin. "He's out of surgery, but I'm really worried about him. Is there anything else you can remember about that night? Anything."

Erin thought of Vikram's bleeding lip. She could feel the photo-filled phone in her pocket. She liked his sturdiness and the way in which he'd look at her and then quickly look away. She couldn't imagine him being involved in any of this.

"I'm sorry, but that's all I remember."

She kept quiet partly to protect Vikram but mainly because she wanted to piece together the story for the school paper. After a couple of years of writing articles about mold in the classrooms and features on retiring teachers, she knew she finally had a *story* in her hand.

"You should probably get back to class," the principal said.

Before Erin took a step away, she looked at the principal and then placed her finger on one signature on the WE BELIEVE YOU, STANLEY banner: Sara Humphries. MJ's girlfriend.

"Looks like Jay-Z and Beyoncé might be on the outs," Erin said with a slight smile.

With everything she needed to keep up with, Dr. Helen certainly could not keep up with the dating lives of her students. She didn't want to keep up with it.

"Maybe Sara put this one up," Erin said with a shrug. "And Stephanie the other one."

"Ah," Dr. Helen said, knowing the two people she needed to talk to next. "Now you're just stirring the pot. And before you go, have you signed?"

Erin knew that it was not a neutral question. "No. It's not a fair choice between the two." She took a step away but then stopped. "Or maybe I'll sign both. I know a lot of the kids are."

Erin went back to class without using the restroom.

———— ≫≫≫≫ ————

Vikram was sleeping in when his phone rang. The previous night, he'd fallen asleep late and hadn't been able to settle into deep sleep, his mind flooded with dreams and images he wouldn't remember later. He'd then woken up for an hour, scrolled on his phone, and fallen asleep again, only to be woken by a nightmare of himself in the cave, driving down on Stanley's face with his fists. Vikram could understand why he'd done it but that wouldn't rescue him from the guilt of having whaled on another person. He'd finally entered a deep sleep at 4 A.M.

"Hello?"

"Hey, Golden Boy."

He and his sister Priya went days and weeks without texting and then would have a span of days when they exchanged a terabyte of texts, discussing television, politics, memes, celebrities, the state of their parents' marriage. What they did not usually do was talk on the phone. It felt far too artificially intimate.

They'd FaceTimed occasionally since she left for college two months before but had not really spoken in any detail.

"How is it?" Vikram asked.

"Humboldt is a tad white. But I love my roommate, who is also a tad white. And I love how green everything is. We're planting winter veggies."

"You didn't have to do this. UCLA would have been much easier."

"And way too close to home."

"That's what the dorms are for."

"I didn't call to talk about me."

"Why are you calling? Did Dad tell you to call?"

"He just said you were in some kind of trouble," Priya said. "And he wanted me to check in on you. So I'm checking in. I also wanted to hear your voice. Have you gone through puberty since I left? Your voice sounds different."

"I don't need to be checked in on."

"So I'm not checking in on you."

"I don't think I want to go to med school anymore," Vikram said. "I think professional football is the route for me."

"Are you serious?"

"Not really. But kind of. The game is a blast. I was like the big star last Friday night. It was awesome."

"Vikram, what happened?"

He could hear the slight change in the register of her voice. A bit more serious. He missed Priya. She'd always protected him but knew to never stand too close. He hadn't had to study for his sophomore biology class because he'd used the impeccable notes that she'd taken; she'd known how to get him beer when he and his friends needed a six-pack. Her absence had left him a little rudderless.

"I broke through a bunch of tackles and scored two touchdowns."

Priya didn't respond.

"We got into a bit of a scuffle with a kid from school. And now he's making a big deal of it and all the parents are making a big deal of it. I just want to get back to class."

"Do you want to tell me what happened?"

Out of everyone in his life, Priya was the right person to talk to about his growing listlessness over the past year. He could tell her that while he had no interest in hanging from a walnut tree, he did understand his character's outward push to do all the right things—study hard, get into a good college—and his inward disgust with it all. That football, of all things, had jolted him out of these feelings, and that he desperately wanted to be back on the field. That the photo Erin had sent him didn't tell the whole story of Friday night and his involvement. He should have told her everything, at the very least, to get the words out, but he simply didn't have the strength or energy.

"I don't. But I'm sure Dad told you already."

"In fact, he didn't."

Vikram appreciated this about his father.

"I'll tell you at some other point. When are you coming home?"

"Christmas. I'm going to stay up here for Thanksgiving."

There was a pause.

"I think I gotta get going," Vikram said.

"Dude. You've been suspended. You have nowhere to go."

"True."

"There's a big world outside high school," Priya said. "You just need to keep your head down, finish up, and get out."

"Do I have to pay you for that advice?"

"No," Priya said. "I saw it on Instagram. I actually do have to go."

Vikram's phone was buzzing. Tyler was FaceTiming him on the other line. "I have to go, too."

They raced to see who could hang up first.

"This is why you didn't text me on Friday night? I thought you went to have chow mein with your parents and then home to sleep." Tyler was at school between classes and there were kids all around him. "You went to the Cave House without me? What the hell did you do?"

Tyler had been gone the whole weekend plus Monday on a golf trip to Bandon Dunes with his father. He'd heard some of the stories swirling around the school and his texts to Vikram had gone unanswered.

"Nothing."

Tyler held up his phone so that Vikram could see the first banner. "What is that?"

"It's in the main hallway. And now check this out."

The phone was shaky for several long seconds until Tyler reached the other end of the hall. He showed Vikram the other sign. And then he found a quiet corner to talk.

"Who put those up?" Vikram asked.

"I don't know. You gonna tell me what happened now?"

"We had a little run-in with Stanley on Friday night," Vikram said.

"It sounds like it was way more than that. The school is coalescing."

"Around what?"

"A bunch of kids think Stanley is lying, some others think he's not, and almost everybody agrees that you and Diego and MJ are douchebags."

"I'm not a douchebag," Vikram said.

"It's hard not to look like one in those jerseys. I know Stanley is annoying, but why'd you jump the kid? He's harmless."

"He's not harmless and we didn't jump him," Vikram said. "Is that what people think?"

"Most everybody."

Right then, still not fully awake, Vikram saw clearly that he wasn't going to wait until the principal called him in. He'd followed MJ's lead and waited for Stanley to explain the evening. And now, if Tyler was right, Stanley's explanation was the school's explanation. He needed to tell his side of the story. Quickly.

The bell for the next class rang.

"I gotta go."

"Will you be my ears?" Vikram asked.

"I'll try. But it's really noisy here."

———— ⟩⟩⟩⟩⟩ ————

Michael had arrived at his office that Tuesday morning to a response from Tom Regan, requesting that Michael transfer the money he'd invested to his bank account and send with it a full accounting of its ups and downs. "Can I buy you lunch this Friday at the Atherton for all the work you've done?"

Michael wrote back, saying he'd have one of his junior analysts put together the accounting and would have the money in his bank by the time they met for lunch. "Let's plan on noon," Michael wrote. "I'll make a reservation." Three days to come up with a solution for the $125,000 he didn't have. He was one decent trade from having fivefold that amount.

When, a little later, Michael received a second email from the principal informing the parents that Stanley's surgery had been successful but the infection that had started in his hand had now spread to the rest of his body, making for a very vulnerable situation, Michael was glad to be able to concentrate on another crisis. They'd given MJ enough rope and it was time to pull some of it back. MJ needed to talk.

Around 11 A.M., he heard the distinctive sound of his wife's old Jaguar—one part purring cat, two parts dying dog—as it pulled into a parking spot. It had been a few years since she'd come to his office. He looked out the window and saw both Shirley and MJ as they stepped out of the car. His first instinct was panic. Maybe he could run and meet them at the car, suggest they grab an early lunch of Cobb salad and have a serious conversation about Stanley's rising temperature. It was much easier to play a shell game when no one was keeping an eye on the shells. But somehow in that moment— and this genuinely surprised him—the panic was washed away by relief. Could he actually be honest with them? For nearly six months, he'd been coming into an empty office. Nothing made a day crawl more than pretending to work. Maybe Shirley could help him find a way forward. MJ seemed like he was in a phase where he thought of transparency as some kind of radical act.

Michael stepped out of his enclosed office and walked through the front room where his three junior analysts used to sit. The desks had all been cleaned out. In better days, Michael was both the principal and the chief investment officer and he would farm out analysis work to the analysts, who would sit at their desks for twelve hours a day, banging out reports. Just then, Shirley and MJ came through the front door. He watched Shirley as she glanced around the empty office, trying to piece things together. He couldn't think of a believable lie to explain.

"Where's Nancy?" Shirley asked, looking at the empty front desk. "Who answers your calls?"

Nancy had been the receptionist/secretary/pinch-hitting human resources chief. For several years, she picked out the birthday gifts that Michael had given Shirley, and those had been his most successful gift-giving years.

"I now have a secretary based in Mumbai, and it's so much cheaper," Michael said, knowing that his cheeriness was not going to fool anyone.

"That's all you want to know?" MJ asked his mother. "Who answers the calls?"

"No. I was asking about Nancy."

"I found her something more stable," Michael said. "I'm guessing from the look on both your faces that you have questions. And I have a few answers. But first, what brings you all down here? I can't remember the last time you came to visit."

"We did a little shopping for dinner tonight," Shirley said, trying to ignore what was clearly going on in the office. "Fish. Some greens. I thought I'd make a simple Niçoise."

"Fish?" MJ asked, incredulous. "Simple? Not just fish. Ahi that cost three hundred dollars. I suggested canned would be just as good."

Michael tried not to get bothered by the price, but it did bother him. It had always frustrated him that Shirley equated greater expense with quality. Was the bluefin, which he assumed she'd bought, that much better than the yellowfin?

"Trust me," Michael said to MJ. "The cost is well worth it."

"And it's in the car, so we can't really stay very long," Shirley said, taking a step back. "We just wanted to say a quick hello."

"It's a cool morning," Michael said. "It'll be fine for a few minutes. At that price, they should have sent you away with a proper cooler. Maybe even some caviar on the house."

"You were fine with it a minute ago," Shirley said, tightening her face to not show her annoyance. "And you've been fine when I usually buy it."

"Three hundred dollars for people we don't know?"

"Three hundred dollars to make nice with people so that we can put all this behind us. I don't know why you're making a big deal out of it. Your cellar has plenty of bottles well over that price."

"But I bought them cheap, knowing that they would appreciate."

"In that, at least, you're in the right business," Shirley said.

Michael couldn't figure out if she was being biting. She didn't need him to explain what was happening in the office for her to know what was happening in the office.

"Are we really arguing about tuna?" Shirley asked.

"We don't have to be. You could have just bought salmon fillets like everyone else."

"Salmon is an inelegant fish; the texture is all wrong."

The absurdity of the statement left Michael without a response. But it also gave him the push he needed. He knew that if he said nothing, Shirley would be willing to walk out of the office and return to her tuna and they could avoid the conversation altogether. If anything was going to change, he would have to be the one pushing.

"Well, as you can see, I've downsized a bit since you two were here last."

"It's nice," MJ said. "Lean. And here you were getting mad at me for my minimalism."

Michael smiled at MJ. It was the first moment of connection, bordering on intimacy, the two had shared in months. Michael had missed it. He had missed his son.

"Why don't we go into my office and sit down?"

They walked back. Michael took his customary seat behind his desk; the other two took the remaining chairs. There was still an opportunity to say just enough to satiate Shirley without having to tell her the whole story. She didn't need much to get on with her day.

"I'm not sure where to begin, so I'll just begin. MJ, it's no secret that I've tried reaching you these past couple of months. And I've mostly given up. I know you're a senior and you need your space. I get all that. Even though it doesn't seem like it now, I was there once. And your grandfather was not nearly as mellow about things as I've tried to be. He drove me hard."

"Is this the birds and bees talk we never had?" MJ asked.

"Different birds and different bees," Michael said.

Usually Michael would try to think through the consequences of what he was about to say. But he was tired of thinking ahead. It didn't seem to benefit him much.

"Whatever happened on Friday evening at that party is putting a wrench into some bigger, more complicated things. I can't make you talk. We tried. So I'll do the talking for now. Just give me a minute and listen. And then both of you can ask whatever questions you have, and I'll answer them as best I can."

Michael avoided looking at Shirley. He wasn't sure what he was going to say. But he was sure of the sudden burning feeling he now had in his gut. Wasn't this what she wanted from him? For him to be more honest with his feelings. To share more.

"The wonderful house we live in was paid for by your grandparents when they passed away. There's a part of me that's sad that I haven't been able to buy a house of my own. But I'm also no fool. We live in a lovely home. Trying to buy something equivalent now is nearly impossible unless you're the founder of a tech company or you're due a proper inheritance. This job I've had managing money has always been up and down. It's the way the business goes. And I have to admit that lately it has been mostly down. Really down. I can't blame the market for it. Despite my best efforts, I've not been very good at my job. I'm good at wine but not so much with stocks. It's not for a lack of trying. I can't see around a blind corner in the way that other, more successful managers can. And I don't have the stomach for crazy kinds of risk."

Now Michael wasn't looking at anyone. He felt like he was entering a bit of a haze. "What does this mean for you? Something and nothing. MJ, at this point it means that I don't really have enough money left to send you to college. But that could change. I always thought that when the time came, I would have finally been enough of a success to have proper money in the bank. As you've sensed, I've been pushing you in football lately and maybe, selfishly, I should have pushed you less. I guess if I was truly being selfish, I'd have pushed you to go to a place that paid for you to play. But now that you've chosen Yale, I don't have the funds for it. I barely have the funds to pay for this office and our family expenses. Maybe you can go to one of the other colleges that can pay your way through."

Finally Michael glanced up at Shirley, who looked like he'd just shared that he had a month to live. The last time he'd seen that look, she'd just learned that her father had had a heart attack. He couldn't believe he'd said all of that. He'd barely let himself think it.

"If this is meant to make me tell you what happened on Friday, it's kind of working," MJ said.

Michael laughed out loud.

"It's just meant to tell you what's up. I'm happy to give you the freedom that you want. But that freedom comes with its own price." He turned to Shirley. "I know I should have talked to you about this earlier. But I kept thinking I could fix it. And now I'm in a particularly bad jam that I need to deal with immediately."

"Just so that I'm clear," MJ said. "At this point, no matter what happens with Stanley, I'm on my own, in terms of paying for college. Even if this thing with Stanley hadn't happened, I'd be on my own."

"Yes. Unless something drastically changes this coming year. Or you pick someplace else to play that will give you a scholarship."

"This is amazing news," MJ said before his mom could respond.

There was a boyish glee in his voice that his parents hadn't heard for months.

"Which part?" Shirley asked.

"Now Dad can do what he wants to do," MJ said to his mother, but then turned to his father. "You don't want to manage rich people's money your whole life. You're free. Don't worry about me and college. I'll figure that out. And Kelly is both good at volleyball and loves it. She'll be fine too. Colleges are going to fall over themselves for a six-foot setter."

The train Michael was on was far too deep in its journey for him to suddenly get off now. There was no way of explaining this to MJ, who thought one could hop on and off trains at will.

"We need to get going," Shirley said, standing up. "The fish is in the car. It'll go bad."

"There's not much for me to explain about Friday night," MJ began. Shirley remained standing. "That kid Stanley was being crazy. The three of us tried to calm him down. I'm not going to pretend that we didn't rough him up. I went in on him hard. But when we left, he was basically fine. I've no idea how he got hurt like that. I think he was drunk, got really confused in those dark caves, and came running down the hill and fell. There was a rumor that there were mountain lions up there. Maybe he heard one of them, freaked out, and panicked. It's easier to blame someone than to say that you got disoriented and scared."

"Why didn't you say this yesterday?" Shirley asked. "It's pretty straightforward."

"I don't know," MJ said. He also didn't know why he didn't tell his parents he'd gone up a second time to check on Stanley.

If MJ had said this yesterday, maybe Michael wouldn't have had to have this talk with them. But now that he had, he felt relieved that it was finally out in the open.

"I don't know what to say to the two of you," Shirley said. "I've tried my hardest to create a nice home for us. Warm meals, cool rooms when we needed them, fires when it was cold out." She was on the verge of tears and before they fell, she walked out of the office. MJ remained seated.

"Go take care of your mom. And tell her I'll be home early to help with dinner."

MJ stood up and walked over to his father, who stood up as well. The two of them hugged.

"Please take a shower," Michael said, smiling. "Now go."

Michael sat in his office for a few minutes to give Shirley time to drive away. Maybe honesty was the key to fixing his problems. He may have lost Shirley temporarily, but he'd gotten MJ back. He felt incredibly exposed and vulnerable, and yet it was the exposure that also made him feel free.

Just as he was getting ready to close his office, Shirley walked back in by herself. Her gait had slowed, as if she were a cat. He knew this Shirley; it made him nervous.

"Hey," he said. He'd not planned to tell her about Tom Regan, but maybe he needed to.

"What are you doing?" she asked.

"I was going to go see my dad."

"No. I mean what are you doing, saying all this to our son? He doesn't need to hear any of it. He deserves to go to college where he was admitted. And it's been your one responsibility to make that happen. I wish you'd let me in on this a while ago. You make me out to be someone who only cares about ease and comfort. Sure, I like ease and comfort. But that's not all I like. We don't even talk about things. I deserved to have heard about our checkbook problems be-fore our son. That would have been the right thing to do." She paused and then added, "All that *talking*. I'm sorry. It was just too much. Please say less from now on."

"You do realize that all you've ever done is spend your parents' money," Michael responded, biting his bottom lip so that Shirley couldn't see it quiver.

"I think you have spent a lot of my parents' money, too," Shirley said coldly.

The two of them stood there, looking at each other in the empty office. This could get ugly really fast.

"In fact, I haven't spent much of it at all," Michael responded, ignoring the part of him that didn't want this to escalate. "You know why? Because I've no idea how much money we actually have."

Michael had his accounts, Shirley had hers. And for years, he didn't think much of this fact. Now, with his own accounts dwindling, he had begun to wonder about hers. They were, after all, married.

"I don't want your money," Michael continued. "I really don't. I just want to feel like our lives overlap. It just feels like you're always waving this threat in front of me. That you can walk at any moment."

"For the record, it would be you who would walk," Shirley said. "It is my house."

Michael looked at Shirley. "Isn't it a bit lonely? You and your money by yourself."

"In fact, it isn't. It's comforting. It's the only thing that's comforting. The only certainty. You know that and I know that. Why do you think people give you money to manage? To make it grow. To increase their certainty."

Michael waited for her to say something about his diminishing clients, but she didn't.

"It's unpleasant talking about this," she said. "Your responsibility is to take care of the kids' education. Please take care of it."

"We never actually agreed to that."

"Nor did we agree that you would never pay a dollar for a mortgage, but you seem fine with that unsaid agreement."

Shirley began walking out of the office. Seeing the sun streaming through the large windows, she remembered the first time she'd come here. It was the soft light she'd noticed. She had been the one to encourage Michael to rent the office, not only for the beauty of the space but also because it was the right time for Michael to hang out his own shingle. She'd believed he could take care of business.

And now that she knew he couldn't, she felt a pity for him that bordered on disgust.

Michael couldn't stop his legs from shaking.

"You saw that new email from the principal?" Shirley asked before she stepped out.

"I did."

"If something happens to that boy . . ." Shirley said, not finishing her thought.

"There's something about that night we still don't know," Michael said. "Something that just doesn't add up."

"I'm going to go," Shirley said. "All I need is for you to make some proper drinks tonight and be friendly and jovial. Is that going to work?"

Michael didn't respond. She left. He stayed in his office for a few more minutes before closing it up. In that moment, Michael wanted to leave Shirley. He could manage the physical distance they'd settled into, but he couldn't manage her humiliating him. But he had nowhere to go, no money to leave. And for that bit of humiliation, he couldn't really blame Shirley.

"If you're here to see me, you must need something."

Michael's father had never been a quiet man, but there was a way in which the occasion of his eighty-fifth birthday had removed the remaining filter between his mind and mouth. Michael knew this was happening, and he tried his best to not get his feelings hurt. But he had feelings and they tended to get hurt. His father was mostly unfiltered about the things he didn't like about Michael.

"Nice to see you too, Dad."

He went over and kissed his father on the cheek. Over the past few years, his father had developed a certain smell, which got stronger every time Michael visited.

"That thing with MJ resolved itself yet?"

"Who told you about that?"

"Shirley called to say hello."

"We're getting there," Michael said.

"Have him come over here. He'll talk to me."

"It's fine. He explained what happened."

Michael liked his father having a close relationship with his son. But this assumption he was making that he could parent him better? No.

"Maybe I'll get right to why I'm here," Michael said.

"Good."

They were sitting in his father's book-filled study. What was Michael going to do with all these books when his parents passed? There were no used bookstores anymore. Giving them to Goodwill seemed wrong.

"You may or may not have sensed that my work hasn't been going that well," Michael said. He'd just explained some version of this to his wife and son, which was embarrassing enough, but saying it now to his father felt awful. Or more accurately: shameful.

"That's what I hear."

"From whom?"

"Around town. This is a small place. With some small minds. People talk. Usually too much."

Maybe his father was on his side after all.

"Why didn't you tell me?"

"I assumed you heard the whispers, too. You have to keep your ears open."

"Dad, I think I'm in a bit of trouble. And coming to you like this is hard for me."

Michael noticed his father taking a deep breath.

"What kind of trouble?"

"I owe one of my clients some money, quite a bit of it, and I don't have it at the moment to give to him."

"Please don't say Tom."

Michael didn't respond.

"Why don't you have it?"

"I'm down to a handful of remaining clients. In order to keep them, I have to make them the kind of money they expect. And I'm simply not able to do that. I thought I could make everyone a good profit on one idea, but it didn't turn out that way." Michael paused. "I used Tom's investment to make the buy."

"You need to stop talking to me about this right now," Michael's father said. "The less I know the better it is for you legally. But I can't."

"Can't what?" Michael asked.

"I can't give you what you're asking for."

"You can't or you won't?"

"I should have cut off this kind of help years ago, and I was too afraid to do so. So I won't."

"I'm in trouble," Michael said.

"You're always in some kind of trouble. You've always been since you were a kid."

"That's not true."

"Admit that you did something wrong. Pay the penalty."

"The penalty may be jail. The penalty may be my inability to ever work in the business again. To make a living for my family."

"You really should have thought of that earlier."

"Why are you being so cruel to me right now? I don't understand."

Something about this question made Michael's father pause. He seemed to be parsing it in his mind.

"How old are you, Michael?"

Michael thought it was a rhetorical question, so he didn't answer.

"How old are you?"

His father didn't remember the age of his only son.

"Fifty-two."

"Do you know what I had done by fifty-two?"

"I do. Very well."

Michael did not want to hear this story again. The older his father got, the more he told it, always as if it was for the first time.

"I came from nothing, Michael. Nothing. I think you understand what that means, but I know you can't really feel it. I had ten lawyers working for me. And I didn't take a single one of them on as partners. I don't work well with others."

"I know," Michael mumbled.

"I know you don't want to hear this, but you've always been waiting for others to hand you things. And I've done that for years. I can't hand you things anymore."

"I'm not asking you to help me with an internship. I'm asking you to hand me my freedom. With the money you're going to give to me at some point anyway. Just give it to me now."

"I'm sorry. I can't believe I waited this long to say no."

As he had been driving to see his father, Michael had thought through how the conversation might go. In exchange for some genuflecting and genuine remorse, Michael would walk out with the money. He hadn't thought his father would actually say no. All this honesty and he still had no money?

"You're cruel. That's what you've always been. If I've been waiting for people to hand me things, you've been waiting for people to mess up so that you can step on them. I could go to jail and you're more worried about teaching me a lesson?"

FIFTEEN

Veronica reached home from Portland at noon. She heard shouting when she walked through the front door but knew in an instant it was of the joyous variety. She stood at the edge of the family room. Alex and Diego were still in their pajamas, playing video games. They suddenly stopped when they saw her. She wanted to laugh off the whole moment of them playing games in the middle of the day—of boys being boys—but she wasn't in the mood. The ease in the room disappeared. She went to the kitchen to make herself lunch.

A few minutes later, Alex walked into the kitchen.

"How was your trip?"

"Fine. I may have hit my limit with college visits." She paused. "I'm sorry again about what I said yesterday. It was shitty. I think the meeting with the principal was far more stressful than I realized."

"It was shitty."

"Would you like me to remind you of all the terrible things you've said? You were a cruel one in high school."

"I'm good." Alex leaned in and lowered his voice. "We finally talked last night. He'd been moody all day, then he went for a run to clear his head and then told me a bit of what happened on Friday. I think he was too nervous to tell you directly."

Veronica put down the knife she was using to cut tomatoes.

"Have you met this Stanley kid? Sounds like a bit of an ass. They all had dinner together and went to a party. At some point in the evening, he got a little crazy and Diego and his two friends tried to calm him down. He admits that they beat him up a bit, but only because he was drunk and swinging his arms and legs wildly. And the next thing they knew, nearly an hour later, he was screaming bloody murder."

"Why all the secrets, then? It's terrible that they got into a fight, but overall, that seems pretty tame."

"I think maybe he's not telling me everything."

Diego walked into the kitchen.

"You two do realize that I can hear everything, right? I'm sorry I didn't say anything earlier. I don't know why I didn't. I just needed a minute to sit on it."

Veronica looked at her son. He was sixteen years old. A man, really. A man able to knock other men who weighed 250 pounds on their backs. And yet, right then, he looked confused, ready to go silent again, or yell out, or speak from both sides of his mouth.

Diego looked back at his mother. He'd never really had any reason to keep anything from her. They were right that there were things he wasn't saying. He wanted to tell her about the pills from Stanley so that she'd feel like he was being open and honest with her. He was about to say something when the doorbell rang.

"You expecting anyone?" Veronica asked.

Diego shook his head.

Veronica went to the door and returned a minute later. "It's for you."

"Who is it?" Diego asked. "Should I be nervous?"

"I don't know. Should you be? It's the Oaxacans. They're welcome to come in."

Veronica had gotten to know the sweet, mammoth defensive linemen and their families through the years in football. They were good kids from families that struggled to pay the rent, to keep their other children out of trouble. She'd always felt a little guilty about the different paths ahead for Diego and the rest of them. Over the years, she'd given all of them rides at one point or another after practice and games, dropping them off at apartment complexes in various states of disrepair. They'd sat in the family room and played video games with Diego as she cooked them massive amounts of food that she was too happy to make. And she'd recently been playing the role of de facto college counselor to Mateo, Diego's closest friend in the group.

Four of the five had come. With their height and girth, they filled up the entire porch. Diego went to stand among them.

"What's good?" Diego asked.

"We gotta get back to school in a minute, but what's up with all this Stanley shit?" Mateo asked. He was the thick, strong defensive end, as voluble on the field as he was off it.

"What do you mean?"

"We don't care what happened or what you did or didn't do. White boy gets hurt and suddenly the whole school goes crazy. We just need to make sure you're back on the field this Friday. Coach said yesterday that you and MJ and Bin Laden are out. Just say what you need to say to get back on the field. We really need you."

It wasn't a threat and Mateo's tone wasn't menacing. It was just simple, direct language. Winning this game and getting into the playoffs were important to these guys. Not because they were being recruited for college or wanted to be recruited. Simply, they liked the game; they'd worked hard at their craft through the heat of the summer and the shortened days of fall, year after year; they were all graduating and moving on to lives that weren't yet clear to them; they wanted to win in order to connect the dots between working hard and winning. And they couldn't do it alone. They'd take care of the defense. They needed MJ and Diego, and now Vikram, to take care of the offense.

"It's not my decision," Diego said.

"Nah, man. Of course it is. You did it and so you can undo it. Just say sorry. That you won't do it again. *They* love apologies."

"I'll do what I can," Diego said.

"Do it quickly," Mateo said.

And with that, three of the guys returned to their cars. They were his teammates and he'd been through three years of exhausting off-seasons and intense seasons alongside them. He knew he had to get back on to the field. He owed them that.

Mateo remained on the porch with Diego.

"You know how this is going to go, right?" Mateo asked. "Don't let this house and this nice neighborhood fool you. They need to find some-one to blame. MJ's gonna float along like he always does. And when it really matters, Bin Laden is basically white and so he'll float up at some point, too. He's 7-Eleven brown, not 9/11 brown. That leaves you."

Diego didn't want to believe this, but he knew Mateo was right.

"I'm not as dumb about all this shit as you think I am."

"I know you're not. You gotta just be smart about it now." Mateo stepped off the porch and gestured toward the car. "They're not say-ing anything, but winning these games is really important to them."

Diego went back into the house and told his mother how he'd gone back up to the caves a second time to check on Stanley, taken a look to make sure he was OK, and then had come down a minute later without even talking to him.

"That makes all of this a little more complicated," Veronica said.

When Gautam had arrived at the office that morning, neither Ryan nor Bryan was there.

Gautam had proceeded with his day, communicating with Rohan's right-hand man about the details of their operation and their general needs. He'd not said anything about the sale to his coworkers, but everyone who had been in the office had seen Gautam, Ryan, and Bryan talking in the conference room and then later heading out together. They knew something was up. Eye contact from younger employees, who'd seen Gautam simply as someone *older*, lasted for just a second longer; there might have been a smile or two more. He had no experience being the center of attention in a workplace. The last time he'd had anything remotely close was his freshman year in college when he'd joined the intramural Ultimate team. In the final seconds of a game, with the score tied, he'd gone deep and noticed the Frisbee floating above his head, racing right past him. As it continued to spin and hover, he ran faster and faster until he finally just leapt, grabbing the disk, falling to the ground, and scoring. His teammates had gone wild. No one was going wild in the office, but perhaps they might at some point soon.

At a bit past two, when it was clear Ryan and Bryan weren't coming in, he left the office. Usually he was the first one there and the last one to leave, a Protestant or Gandhian work ethic that had not always benefited him. He wanted to do a little shopping; he'd always been very prudent in his purchases. Maybe check out an Apple Watch, or, if he was feeling particularly frisky, a simple Rolex. No checks had been cashed yet, but he was certain that it was certain.

En route to a watch shop, he was distracted by the cars. His Camry was getting old. What was it with Americans and their cars? He turned the question over and under as he made his way from one dealership to the next, each with their shiny, eyes-wide-open wares on display.

A BMW, even though it came with some awfully sweet, soft cow leather, was a little too Bavarian for his taste. And also, of course, a sore spot with Gita. Range Rover? He was no fool. Audi? He wasn't white. A Subaru? He hated the outdoors. For years, he'd told himself that when he could afford it, he'd get himself a seventies-era Mercedes sedan—preferably in silver or forest green—that he used to see driven by gangsters when he visited Bombay as a child. Maybe he needed to look at the Teslas. Most Indians he knew in the Bay Area had already bought one or two to mark their success.

As he stepped onto the Cadillac lot, which happened to be next to the Volvos he'd just eliminated, he had no intention of staying for more than a minute. But then a red sedan caught his eye. It looked clumsily futuristic, as if the designers were hoping for a product placement in a *Blade Runner* prequel. Something in him knew he was in trouble. The car felt like attainable luxury, which sounded like a commercial they'd already made with men like him in mind. Cadillacs, or any traditional American cars for that matter, weren't on his list.

He had been on the lot for exactly thirty seconds, gently tapping his fingers on the cars as if he were checking thread count, when a salesman started making his way toward him. When he saw Gautam see him, he swallowed a step. What system did salespeople have in place when a new customer arrived? A simple queue? Or did they, in mere seconds, negotiate among one another as they assessed the willingness of a customer to buy, based on, say, gender, in relation to pauses in front of particular cars and concerned glances at the sticker price? Had Gautam been haggled over? Had the salesman lost?

When Gautam took the car out on the freeway for a test drive, he quickly climbed to eighty miles per hour without realizing it.

"I love this car," Gautam said to the salesman as they drove back into the lot. "But the problem is that it doesn't match up with any part of who I am. I feel like I'm trying to be someone I'm not."

"I can understand that. But do you like the way it feels? Do you like the way it handles? Sometimes that's a better measure of figuring out who you are."

"You want to be my therapist as well?" Gautam asked.

"If the commitment feels too much at this point, you can always lease," the salesman said. "Barely anyone buys cars these days."

The mention of a lease broke the spell Gautam had been under during the test drive. He'd grown up with the clear lesson that buying things on credit was for other people. If you wanted something, you either had all the money for it or you didn't. Because this was a rule his father had lived by, his father had purchased a series of Honda Accords over the years: practical, affordable, long-lasting. Gautam really wanted the Cadillac, but he didn't have the stomach to pay full price for it. And even entertaining the idea of leasing felt illicit.

"I'm going to take a bit of a walk and think things over," Gautam said as he stepped out of the car.

"I'll be here for the rest of the day," the salesman said.

He made his way over to the Honda dealership, which he'd purposefully avoided because he knew driving away with a new car from there was going to be practical, guilt-free, and utterly boring. He scanned the lot and made his way to the Accords.

"You look like someone who knows his way around Hondas," the new salesman said as he walked up to Gautam.

This was entirely the wrong thing to say to Gautam, precisely because it was completely right.

"My family bought our first one in the eighties. I think I'd best keep the trend going."

After finishing all the paperwork, Gautam got home just a little before six, when they were due at the Berringers'. He rushed into the house, freshened up, and didn't say anything about the car. When he and Gita walked out together, she looked at the Cadillac, confused.

"What is this?" Gita asked.

"I've always wanted one," Gautam said. "Wait until you ride in it. It's incredible."

Gita screamed at him internally at the absurdity of it: Gautam's suddenly arrived midlife crisis, dressed up as a strut, when they were actually in the middle of a real crisis. In the midst of this, he went car shopping? The bright sheen of the red car looked beautiful in the evening light.

"We can afford this now?" Gita asked, trying to make it sound like a question about accounting.

"We'll be able to shortly."

"So the deal is done?"

"It's not, but it will be."

"You know best. But you also know that a deal isn't really done until the money appears in your bank account."

"Is that what this is about? Money?"

"Everything is about money. But this isn't. This is about you taking the little headspace you have away from work and using it to decide what kind of car to buy. During this of all weeks? I'm here for your midlife crisis. Mine is coming right around the corner once Vikram graduates from high school. I get it. I'm either going back to work or becoming some kind of online guru for sad white ladies. But right now, today, I needed you to be home and present, talking us through this. I can't figure it all out on my own, Gautam. I can feel Vikram disintegrating, sitting up on his bed."

"Gita, you don't work. This is your job. You keep insisting that being a mother is a job. And now I agree with you. So do it."

Gautam had opened the driver's-side door and was standing behind it, as if to protect himself from the sharp retort that was about to come his way.

Gita took a deep inhale, trying to calm herself. She had a sudden desire to kick the side of the car, hoping it would make a dent.

"Vikram is not my job. He's both our jobs. And it shouldn't feel like a job."

"Well, it sure feels like I leave my regular job and then come home to a whole new job in the evening. I'm hitting my limit. I just made a big deal, this should feel like a good shift, shouldn't it?"

The two of them stood there. Gita glanced at her watch.

"Red?" Gita asked. Their fight the previous night was the start of their cleaving, and this major purchase, when they'd always talked through big buys together, felt like a further splitting apart. But she also knew that if she didn't bring down the temperature of the conversation, they would arrive at this party separate when they needed to be together. "I hope it drives fast, because we're now late."

"You couldn't help yourself, could you?" Gautam asked. "Maybe let me have the pleasure of enjoying the car for one evening before laying into me about it. Just one evening."

———»»»»———

A student in the hallway had overheard Dr. Helen say that Stanley was "not good," and over the course of the day, these two simple words had been added to and expanded on so that a rumor spread that Stanley's temperature had been steadily rising. That information had been layered with a new detail that his heart had not been able to keep up with the sudden height increase he'd had in the past year, and that this medical condition, coupled with his body's stress of going through surgery, had led to his heart simply giving up. A question rather than a declarative statement had made its way from one phone to another of a majority of students: Is Stanley Kincaid dead?

SIXTEEN

Shirley was in her garden, carefully cutting pink roses and lavender, and, to lighten the mood a bit, adding a few olive branches. During the morning of errands, flowers were the one thing she had not bought. She took great pride in growing them herself. Dinner tables, she insisted, had to have a proper bouquet of freshly cut flowers to get the feng shui right.

"I think you're mixing metaphors," Michael offered.

They'd not spoken since she left his office earlier that day.

"I may be. But I still set a nice table. Make sure the bar is well stocked."

She wasn't sure what made her angrier at that moment: that Michael couldn't take care of his responsibilities or that he'd shared his inability with their son. The only things providing her solace were the complex layers in the roses she grew.

It was a warm night and Shirley had set the dinner table in the backyard. Three hundred dollars' worth of fish was one thing. Inviting near strangers into their dining room felt a little too intimate.

On a side table, Michael had laid out beer in a bucket of ice. From his cellar, he'd brought up several bottles of light reds and whites he liked, but nothing that was too extravagant. Just as he finished setting up the drinks, he heard someone come into the backyard. He'd left the front door open, with a note for the guests to find their way back.

Veronica was the first to arrive. Michael was on friendly terms with her, or as friendly as one gets when children are on a sports team together. They'd never met socially. He'd always wondered why an attractive woman like her had remained single all this time. And so it was a pleasant surprise when she arrived with a man.

"Nice to see you, Veronica," Michael said.

"Hi, Michael," Veronica said. "Thanks for the invitation. This is my brother, Alex."

It was precisely the quizzical look on Michael's face that had made Veronica think twice about bringing Alex with her.

There had been plenty of good since Veronica split with her husband, but the bad was that, as the years passed, she no longer got invited to dinner parties. People didn't know how to read her new status, and, because she traveled so much, she found herself declining the solo invitations early on. Soon enough, the invitations stopped coming altogether. But the invitation from the Berringers was less to a dinner party and more to a conversation over food. Veronica didn't want to go and she definitely didn't want to go alone.

"Nice to meet you, Alex. What are the two of you drinking?"

"What are you pouring?" Alex asked.

Alex was good at this kind of thing: taking a question, asking a question.

"Beer, wine, cocktails. Whatever you like."

Veronica knew the Berringers were well-off, but as she had walked through the house to the backyard, she'd pieced together that theirs was an old-school kind of well-off. She had to pay for every last thing that was in her house, and she sensed that there were inheritances all around this one, from the paintings on the walls to the books on the shelves. All this time, she'd assumed that Michael did particularly well at whatever his job was. Perhaps he did. But there were multiple sources of income here.

Just then, Shirley came out of the house, holding a jar of roses and wearing expensive white jeans and a cashmere sweater. She was the type of woman Veronica instantly disliked for the jobs she'd never worked. But it was hard to deny the subtlety of her taste: the placement of olive trees in the yard, an English garden that was both immaculate and unruly at the same time, a dining table with hearty earthenware. And now these damn beautiful flowers that she placed at the center of the table.

"I'm so happy you're here," Shirley said to Veronica.

It was a curious thing to say, given the circumstances. Veronica introduced Alex.

"Very nice to meet you, handsome Alex," Shirley said, holding out her hand so that he could shake it.

"Thanks for having us over," Alex said.

"Did Michael get you a drink?" Shirley asked, turning to her husband. "I've asked him for once to be useful."

"We were just about to get one."

Veronica suddenly felt the need for a strong drink.

"What did you decide?" Michael asked.

"What do you like to drink?" Veronica asked. "Something special you like to mix?"

"I make a terrific gimlet," Michael said.

"Works for me," Veronica said.

"Make it two," Alex added.

"Gin or vodka?"

"Gin," Veronica said. "It's a truth serum. We could all use some of that."

Michael made a show of walking over to a lime tree and picking out three choice limes. Veronica glanced at Alex. Yes, yes, we know you grew the fucking limes yourself.

While they were deciding on their drinks, Gautam and Gita arrived. Veronica looked at them and made eye contact with Gita, inviting them over. While she felt bad that they'd gotten off on the wrong foot during their first conversation, she didn't think she was in the wrong in pushing back at Gita. Veronica smiled; Gita tentatively smiled back. They walked over. Noticing the cold air between them, she guessed that Gita and Gautam might have had a fight on the way over. Sure, she didn't get invited to dinner parties, but she didn't have to deal with mid-marital fights either.

"Sorry we're late," Gita said. "We had some car issues."

"We just got here, too," Veronica said.

She introduced Alex.

"Michael is getting us a drink," Alex said. "Can I pour you two some wine? Or ask him to make you a drink as well?"

"Wine is great," Gita said.

Alex poured two glasses and then the four of them stood there awkwardly. There was a sharp noise and they all turned to it. Michael was vigorously shaking a cocktail shaker the size of a small missile.

"He's really going at that thing," Gautam said. "Seems well-acquainted with it."

Veronica smiled.

"You work for VirtualUN?" Alex asked Gautam.

Gautam was wearing a Patagonia vest with a logo that Veronica didn't recognize.

"I do," Gautam said.

"How is it going? I know you guys got quite a bit of funding early on."

"Too much, if you ask me," Gautam said, bolstered by the confidence he'd gained in the past week. "Made us a bit soft."

The two men started in on tech talk, which sounded not so different from sports talk.

Gita led Veronica a bit away. "You think maybe you and I can start over?" Gita asked. "My tone was a little off yesterday. This whole thing is making me into a ball of stress."

"We're all under that same stress," Veronica said, appreciating Gita's willingness to take a friendly step toward her. "We're good."

Veronica was good with conversation. Not always with starting one, but she knew how to keep things moving.

"Do you work in tech as well, like your husband?" Veronica asked. "And I'm not asking because you're Indian."

Gita flashed a smile.

"You're not that far off. I was a management consultant until my older child was born. I haven't worked since. I burned myself out and didn't go back. But I really hate the phrase 'stay-at-home mom.'"

Gita not working didn't annoy Veronica nearly as much as Shirley not working.

"You?"

"I write books that most people skim."

"Romance novels?"

"You skim romance novels?"

"For the juicy bits."

Maybe she and Gita had a future after all. Veronica had not made many friends in town. Was it possible, after this, that they could be founding members of a book group? A knitting circle?

"I write about slavery and Brazil. And so maybe the exact opposite of romance novels."

"That sounds genuinely interesting," Gita said. "I'm afraid I didn't know there were slaves in Brazil. I can find you on Amazon?"

"In the Amazon and on Amazon." Veronica paused and smiled. "Sorry."

"Wow, a real-life author."

"In the flesh," Veronica said, knowing how absurd it was.

On one hand, Gita was being friendly, making up for the distinct unfriendliness of their first meeting. But Veronica also sensed that she had a book brewing somewhere inside her. The ones who did always marveled at Veronica's writing a bit more than others.

Michael came over with three perfect-looking martini glasses on a tray; the liquid had a tint of green. He held the tray in front of Veronica, who took one. She couldn't quite put her finger on it, but

Michael had a certain arrhythmia about him. She'd not spent enough time around Gautam to know his rhythms, but he seemed to be humming along. Alex, of course, had made his cash already and so his crisis would be of a different nature.

"I think you might want one, too," Michael said, looking at Gita. "You won't be disappointed."

"I just got this wine," Gita said.

"That can be your second course," Michael said.

Gita placed her wineglass on the tray and took the gimlet. Michael handed the third one to Alex. Veronica took a careful sip and could instantly feel the heat of the alcohol, followed by the tiniest shards of ice.

"That's delicious," Veronica said.

"It's all in the shake," Michael said, moving his hand up and down.

Michael returned to the kitchen. Gita took a sip of the drink.

"It tastes like fire with a hint of lime," Gita said. "I think I feel it already."

A few minutes later, Shirley came out with a glass of wine, followed by Michael, who had made himself his own gimlet. He placed the large cocktail shaker on the dinner table.

Shirley led the group to a set of six chairs around a lit firepit. They all sat down.

"We wanted to bring us all together so that we could get to know one another," Michael began. "If our sons won't do any talking, the least we can do is talk together and figure out a way forward."

Just as he finished, Veronica heard a creaking sound and looked up. MJ was standing on the balcony overlooking the garden below, gazing down at the party. He didn't say a word. He made eye contact with Veronica and then his parents and then walked back inside.

"I pushed Diego," Veronica began, not knowing how guarded she needed to be. The drink was making her less so by the sip. "He still didn't say anything to me. But he did tell Alex that they were trying to calm this kid Stanley down. I've met him. Stanley. He used to come around the house. Eddie Haskell crossed with a psychopath in the making. He ate a lot and never really wanted to leave. Diego said he has no idea how Stanley ended up so bloodied and battered at the end of the night."

"I'm happy to hear that," Gita said. "Well, not *happy* to hear it. But that's about the story we've gotten from Vikram."

"That's what MJ finally eked out as well," Shirley added.

"I'm not sure what else there's to do at this point," Gita said. "We can go back to the principal with this and hopefully we can be done. The boys were defending themselves."

"I think there's more to the story than what we've heard," Veronica said. She took a careful sip of her drink. She looked across at Michael, who was already done with his. Either he was now drunk or he was such an alcoholic that he didn't feel a thing. "Something isn't adding up. I thought the threat of being held out of the game was going to be enough for them to tell us everything immediately. I know how important these games are to Diego. Or at least I thought I did. But the fact that he didn't say anything at first makes me think something more is up." She was going to protect her son, but she wanted to get a sense of what the other parents were thinking.

"I could not care less about the football game," Gita said, the gin making her tongue looser than it might have been with only the wine.

For a minute, it had felt like Gita and Veronica were on the same side.

"Admittedly," Gita continued, "I thought being on the football team would increase his chances of getting into a good college. But this is actually going to ruin them. I wish we'd never agreed to let him play."

Why did this woman think this was still about their kids getting into college? Had she not read the second email from the principal about Stanley's fever?

"It's going to ruin all our sons' chances," Veronica said. "If this continues down the path it's going, we'll be lucky if their college plans taking a hit is the worst thing to come."

Veronica noticed Gautam placing his hand on his wife's hand. She couldn't tell if it was a sign of support or he was imploring her to stop talking.

"But go ahead, Gita," Veronica said. "Honestly. Say what you wish to say. Get it out. That's why we're all here, isn't it? To clear the air. The clearer it is, the better for all of us. All this silence is really getting to me."

"I'm going to need a second drink for this," Michael said, getting up. "Can you give me one minute?"

Without waiting for an answer, he walked over to the dining table and quickly returned with another full gimlet. In the few minutes he was gone, the remaining group talked awkwardly about the charcuterie board Shirley had prepared.

"I don't want to mess it up," Alex said.

"You couldn't mess anything up," Shirley said.

Veronica glanced at her brother. This woman was not being shy in her flirtation, even with her husband so close by.

Shirley provided a brief guided tour of the wooden block where she'd arranged the coppa and the jamón, the hard and soft cheeses, with figs and pecans, crackers, and fresh rosemary in the interstices. "I want all this gone before we have dinner."

The group tried the various cheeses and cured meats.

"You were saying," Veronica said, turning to Gita when Michael returned to his seat.

Veronica took yet another tiny sip of her drink, enough to numb her just a little for what was to come, but not so much that she wouldn't know how to respond.

"Well, this is America, after all," Gita began. "Despite the sport they're playing, I understand from Vikram that both Diego and MJ are very good students. I think we can agree that all three boys are very smart, and maybe that's one of the reasons this is so worrisome to us. They all have bright futures ahead of them. But what I've been trying to figure out is how much of a head start each of them will get as they move toward college. You've asked me to be honest and so I'm being honest." She took another sip, as if to give her the courage to continue. "MJ gets to go to Yale and Diego will, I would think for very real and legitimate reasons, get other help when his time is ready. What does Vikram get? I think I know the answer and that makes me nervous."

Everyone kept their eyes on the gas-powered flame in front of them.

"Well," Veronica said, with a slight smile, "I appreciate the clarity of your opinion."

Veronica made a very good living by making carefully constructed arguments. In everyday life, she was not a fan of arguments and confrontation. But there was no way of just letting Gita say what she thought without challenging it. And yet she just wanted to have her drink and try out the aged manchego.

"MJ doesn't *get* to go to Yale," Michael said. "Just to be clear. He earned his way in. And yes, before you ask, I went there and so did my father. And I know all that is unfair. And yet MJ has nearly perfect SATs, a perfect GPA, and a pretty strong throwing arm. He would have gotten in even if I hadn't gone there. All the other universities that have shown an interest in him based on his grades and football prove that."

"MJ has worked as hard as anyone else," Shirley added. "Things may look easy, but they're not."

"There are hundreds of kids with perfect grades and scores," Gita said. "It's the sport that got him in."

"That I can't help," Michael said. "He's playing within a system. I didn't make it. He didn't make it."

"Will you do me a favor, Gita?" Veronica said. "Can you clearly say what you're trying to say about Diego? Just so that we are on the same page."

"You and Diego are Latino, correct?"

Veronica nodded. *"Correct."*

"And I say this knowing full well the terrible history of this country. But bright Latino boys like Diego have every college door open to them. My son, on the other hand, gets neither the Yale pat on the back nor the helping hand. I'm afraid he just gets slapped around. In some cases, literally." Gita paused. Her eyes had suddenly gotten moist. "He has to work hard and still may end up with nothing. And that's why I think that while we're all in this together, the crisis is not the same for all of us."

"It's not my job to educate you on why I think you're wrong," Veronica said. She could sense that there was some detail about Vikram that Gita wasn't sharing. But at the moment, her only concern was Diego. "Let me ask you a question. Where did you go to college?"

"Cornell."

"Your father? Grandfather."

Gita paused, realizing what Veronica was up to.

"Carnegie Mellon. MIT. I know what you're doing."

"What am I doing?" Veronica asked.

"Simply put, Vikram will not get the same benefits as MJ when they enter the same room, no matter the similarity of where their parents went to college. And Vikram is much darker than Diego and yet doesn't have the benefits of a last name that triggers some algorithm."

Veronica could feel her temperature rising. But she knew that if she let go, only her son would be hurt. They all needed to work together to resolve what was in front of them.

"Their skin color might be different, but an application with 'Cruz' versus 'Shastri' will be treated very differently," Veronica said. "You seem like a very bright woman, Gita. Whatever their skin color, you know as well as I do that an Indian kid and a Latino kid are not going to be treated the same. Never. Most of Diego's teachers look at his name and assume it's a mistake he's in an honors class. I bet you don't have that problem with Vikram."

"But I have plenty of other problems."

Gita and Veronica were looking at each other across the fire as they talked. The rest of the group continued to keep their eyes on the flame.

"We're now beginning to sound like a shitty Fox News segment on affirmative action," Veronica said. "Can we just agree that our boys will have different advantages and disadvantages? Then maybe we can sort all this out so that we can get to minimizing the disadvantages and leaning into the advantages."

"Am I the Ann Coulter in this scenario?" Gita asked.

There was a sudden increase in tension around the firepit.

"Because I'd really prefer to be Sean Hannity," Gita continued, now with a smile. "I think he gets better ratings." She raised her glass. "Here's to our insane boys never getting into college. And to Stanley getting better soon."

"I'll drink to that," Michael said.

"And please eat to that," Shirley added, pushing the cheese.

"Before we move off the serious topics," Michael said, "I have just one other question. What do we think about the principal?"

By itself, it was an innocuous question. But then he followed up.

"Can we trust her?"

Veronica looked around. It had gotten darker and now the fire from the pit was a primary source of light.

"What do you mean?" Veronica asked, knowing exactly what he meant.

"I mean, is she going to be fair and balanced?"

"I've interacted with her on a couple of occasions. And she has been nothing but up-front and gracious. I think we'll be fine."

"I do get a no-nonsense vibe from her," Gita added.

Gita and Veronica made the slightest eye contact.

Shirley, noticing them doing so, stood up. "Now that the hard stuff is out of the way, I'm going to get dinner ready for us," she said.

"Can I help?" Veronica asked. "Gita, you want to come with? So we can really make the gender differences clear."

The men laughed, but none of them bothered to stand up and volunteer their help.

Veronica had expected Shirley's kitchen to be large and airy and immaculate, and it was exactly that. Lots of marble and a cooking range fit for a nice restaurant. On the counter there were six plates prepared already with fresh greens, a perfectly sliced egg, and green beans. Shirley walked over to the refrigerator and removed a platter of raw fish with a purple-pink hue. Even from a slight distance away, Veronica knew that the fish was fresh and expensive. It was one of her indulgences. She wanted to be invited to speak in Japan so that she and Diego could eat their way through the country.

Shirley turned on the stove and grabbed a cast-iron pan hanging above her. As the oil heated up, Veronica could feel her chest tighten. The heat was going to destroy the fish.

"How can we help?" Veronica asked.

"By drinking my husband's expensive wine," Shirley said. "Just relax and enjoy. I wanted to give us a break from the men."

There was a bottle on the counter and Shirley expertly uncorked it and poured three liberal glasses.

"I hope you don't mind the simplicity of this meal, but since this was all last-minute, I just put some things together."

"It looks amazing," Gita said.

"If I'm honest," Shirley said as she placed the first piece of fish in the pan, "MJ has been drifting from us, little by little, for years. I know that he'll be leaving for college next year, but it feels like he's left already. We're here and he's there, and I don't think we're crossing paths anymore. I think the hardest thing about parenting is watching your kids live and make decisions, decisions you might not make, and then loving them in the face of it all. There's no other relationship like it, is there? To see the differences, to engage with them. Sure, you can bail or be unavailable or punishing in your judgment. But if you have any desire to look back and say to yourself, 'I tried to be a good parent,' you have to be able to withstand the different choices they're making."

She let the tuna heat for roughly thirty seconds and then quickly turned it over for thirty more seconds. She then placed the seared flesh onto one plate. She began repeating the same move for each piece of fish.

"I don't understand boys," Veronica said. "I thought I did. At first, I was glad to have a boy because I was afraid that I was going to clash with a girl. And for many years, it was great. Diego and I have always been close. I've prided myself on the fact that I always keep lines of communication open between us. He can tell me anything. And I mean *anything*. But it feels like that's changing. Like it changed over the weekend."

Shirley was done with two plates. Gita reached for them.

"Can we wait a minute?" Shirley asked, placing her hand on Gita's. "We're not going to get anywhere if we let those guys out there manage this situation. The three of us need to figure it out."

"Yes," Gita agreed. "The less we involve them, the better."

"Look," Shirley said. "I think I know my son. Better than I think I know myself. But I also can't possibly know all of him. He may have done what this boy is accusing him of. I mean, this whole thing, according to the principal, is about one of them going back up to the cave after the three of them had tried subduing him. I genuinely don't think MJ did, but I can't completely rule it out, and I don't think you two can for your sons either. And I know I don't know your sons. So I'm not accusing anyone of anything."

"I'm aware enough as a parent to know that I can't be aware enough to know everything that's going on with these kids," Veronica said. "Sometimes it's hard to know the difference between what we want them to be and who they end up being. And so, yes, of course, I think Diego could have done it. But I too would like to hope that he didn't."

There was a pause and both turned to Gita, who took another sip of her wine.

"I agree," Gita said. "I really don't know what these boys are capable of."

Since these conversations had started, Gita seemed to keep certain things close to her chest while being open and frank about others. When it came to Vikram being responsible for anything, she always seemed to get quiet.

"But we do have some clarity about the evening," Veronica said. "We can go into this meeting with the principal and present that to her. The boys were up in the caves and they got into it with Stanley, tried to calm him down, and then went back to the party."

"And we can tell our own stories about our interactions with Stanley, who's not the best person to trust in all this," Gita added.

Shirley continued searing as the two others sipped their wine, seated on the stools at the far end of the island.

In the large, airy space that encompassed the kitchen and the family room, there was one wall filled with framed photographs. Veronica noticed it and Shirley noticed her noticing it.

"May I?" Veronica asked. She didn't know Shirley, and it felt like she was assuming an intimacy they didn't have if she just went and looked at their family photos.

"Of course."

Veronica walked over with her wine. On the wall were roughly thirty framed photographs of different sizes: a pictorial representation of lives well lived. Farthest to the left were black-and-white photos of young couples she assumed to be Shirley's and Michael's parents. The more she moved to the right, the more color appeared: a young MJ posing in a Little League uniform; a few photographs of a girl playing volleyball; the whole family at the Grand Canyon; Shirley and the volleyball player in front of the Eiffel Tower; Michael and several friends all in cycling gear with their bikes, an imposing mountain range in the background.

It made her sad to think about what a similar wall might look like in her house.

One photo somewhere in the middle of the chronology caught Veronica's eye. She leaned forward to get a closer look. She looked over and saw that Shirley was still working on the fish and chatting with Gita. Veronica tried removing the framed photograph; it came off the wall easily. She walked back to the kitchen island and placed it on the island. Shirley glanced at it and continued her work.

"Everyone seems to notice that one," Shirley said. "I may need to retire it soon, or at least transfer it to somewhere more hidden in the house."

Veronica had noticed it, and presumably others before her had noticed it, because it didn't fit with the life implied by the rest of those photographs. It certainly didn't fit with this kitchen and this house. Veronica appreciated that Shirley had not said what was certainly sitting right on the tip of her tongue: Not what you expected?

It was a color photograph of a young Shirley and two skinny, handsome young white men, one of whom was Michael. Standing between them were two young African children who looked like the malnourished kids that were often paraded around on TV during the Live Aid era.

"Our *Heart of Darkness* year," Shirley said, carefully placing a seared tuna on the final plate. She looked at Veronica and Gita to see if the joke had landed. "Meaning, of course, that Michael and I were the dumb colonists."

"Where is this?" Veronica asked.

"Uganda," Shirley said, glancing quickly over at Gita. "Peace Corps."

Veronica didn't know the history that well, but Shirley seemed to know it. There had been Indians who had migrated to Uganda in the nineteenth and twentieth centuries and made their lives there for generations, but after Uganda gained independence from the British, the ruler Idi Amin kicked all the Indians out.

"'Africa is for Africans, black Africans,'" Gita said in some kind of accent meant to emulate an African accent. "*Mississippi Masala.* Did you two see it? It made quite the impression on young me. Correction: Denzel Washington made quite the impression on young me. It's set partly in Uganda, right?"

"I can't believe I missed it," Shirley said. "I'll find it." She turned to the photo. "This is where I met Michael. I'd gone after I graduated from college. I was all sorts of ambitious then. I taught English in a small rural village. The other guy here is my college boyfriend, Willy. I should have known from the name it was never going to work out. But then I thought it was some sign that both of us had gotten into the Peace Corps and both of us had been assigned to Uganda. It seemed like fate. The best thing about him was that he made me never believe in fate again. This was the first day Michael and I met. He and Willy had become friends. Michael worked in a little town nearby, helping set up a small credit union. I remember how funny he was back then."

"He still seems funny now," Gita said.

"I guess he was a different funny. Young, careless funny. I went with Willy and I came back with Michael. I knew I was going to be with him when we both got malaria within weeks of each other. So maybe I did still believe in fate a little."

Veronica didn't have *Shirley in Africa* on her bingo card and Shirley, of course, knew that. "I'm not entirely sure how one goes from the Shirley in the photo to the Shirley being super-careful about not messing up the tuna. But here I am."

Veronica had been asking herself this very same question. She went and hung the photo back on the wall. Just after she did, she looked out the window and saw the three men drinking and talking and then Alex stepping away to take a phone call.

Since they'd first sat down, Gautam had been looking at Michael's wristwatch. For nearly a decade, Gautam had proudly worn his Casio G-Shock with a bit of pride. It worked well, and it kept working. But he'd wondered if he'd been so devoted to it because he was actually coveting something more expensive.

For the twentieth anniversary of the family restaurant, Gautam and his mother had gotten his father a special gift. They'd never been a gift-giving family, but even his mother thought the moment required marking in some special way. Gautam's father had a thing for punctuality. He opened the restaurant on time and he closed it on time. He felt insulted when someone arrived late to a meeting. Being early was excusable, but being late was not. And so Gautam had decided to get his father a watch, a nice one he could still wear but would replace the Timex he'd purchased from Kmart soon after they had first arrived in America. The Tissot that Gautam bought wasn't that expensive in the universe of expensive things—four hundred dollars. But he knew that anything more expensive would have upset his father. The watch had a simple, classic look, with a bit of weight that replaced the slightly tinnier face of the Timex. His father had been very gracious when accepting the gift, but Gautam never saw him wear it. When his old Timex finally conked out, his father had bought another Timex. The nicer watch had remained in his drawer.

"What is that beautiful thing?" Gautam asked, sensing that Michael was now drunk enough in case Gautam was breaking some rule of WASP engagement in asking about the watch. Michael either wouldn't mind or wouldn't remember it in the morning.

"My thirtieth birthday gift from my father. I think I have worn it literally every day since. I'm nervous about what would happen if I didn't wear it."

"What would happen?"

"I don't know. California might fall into the ocean. Maybe it would rain frogs."

Michael removed it from his wrist and laid it on the table in front of Gautam, who took a closer look. It was as simple as it could get, but it was the simplicity that made it so alluring. Patek Philippe. He knew they were expensive, but he didn't know just how expensive. Ten thousand dollars? He'd never pay that much for a watch.

"It's beautiful," Gautam said.

"Try it on," Michael offered.

Gautam's first thought was about germs. You've just been sweating in that thing. But his next instinct was a little more amorphous. It was as if Michael was offering to let Gautam try on his favorite boxers or his wedding ring—things that were his and his alone.

But not wanting to be ungracious in his home, Gautam tried on the watch. None of his own watches had ever fit quite like this one. It had the perfect weight: enough to be serious, not so much to weigh him down. He needed something like this to go with his Cadillac.

"It looks good on you," Michael said. He drank the last of his second gimlet. "Why don't you keep it?"

"Ha." Gautam began removing the watch instantly. "It's made for your wrist."

"I'm serious, Gautam. My father has a thing for watches. Growing up, every time he won a big case—and he won a lot of big cases—he went out and bought himself a fancy new watch. Rolex, Omega, Cartier, you name it. At some point, I'm going to inherit a baker's dozen of them."

Gautam suddenly felt uncomfortable. Michael didn't seem to be joking. He'd just said that he'd worn the watch nonstop for twenty years. Gautam wanted nothing to do with the weird karma that had greased the fancy gears in the Patek.

"Please keep it," Michael said. "I'm asking."

"There is no way. I can't."

"You can't? Or you won't?"

"I can't and I won't. I have my own watch, Michael."

"That thing?" Michael said, looking at Gautam's wrist. "You can get that out of a vending machine."

There was a slight menace in his voice.

"I'm good," Gautam said, trying to laugh it all off.

Michael took his watch back and quickly put it on. "I'm just kidding," he said. "This watch might be worth fifty K at this point. A collector's item."

It now looked very heavy on Michael's wrist.

"Who's ready to eat?" Shirley asked, stepping into the backyard.

The three women came out of the house, each carrying two plates of food. As they put them on the table, Michael went and opened two more bottles of wine for the table and poured glasses for all six of them. Shirley gracefully showed the guests where to sit, the couples and siblings next to each other.

They'd all barely settled into their seats when Veronica took a knife and sliced into her fish. The inside was uncooked and pink and perfect. She took a bite.

"Where did you get this?" Veronica asked, surprised at just how well Shirley had cooked the fish. "I've never tasted anything so delicious."

Shirley glanced at Michael and then told Veronica the name of the market. "For some reason, Tuesday mornings are when the fish is the freshest. Right off the boat."

For the next several minutes, everyone busied themselves eating and taking sips of the wine. Everyone except the Shastris, who were eating the greens, but only taking small, careful bites of the fish.

"Oh my god," Shirley said. "I didn't even think about it. Are you two vegetarians? How am I so horrible that I didn't ask?"

"No, not at all," Gita said. "The food is really lovely."

"Is it too raw? I can place it back on the stove for a little longer."

"It's perfect," Gautam said. "I see why the Japanese eat the stuff up. And why they're so damn healthy and handsome."

As the dinner progressed, Michael made sure that no wineglass stayed empty for long. The guests shifted around so that the women spoke to one another at one end of the table and the men gathered at the other.

As the meal ended, Michael finished his glass of wine, reached into his pocket, came out with a quarter, and tapped it against his wineglass to get everyone's attention.

"Absolutely not, Michael," Shirley said. She looked horrified. "We've made some strides tonight. This will seriously set us all back. It's a bad idea."

Michael had had plenty to drink. They all had.

"What's a bad idea?" Alex asked, looking at Shirley. "I love bad ideas."

"It's never a bad idea," Michael said, turning to the rest of the group. "I'd like us to play a game before dessert. We've already broken the ice, but this will really break things wide open. We will all be best friends after this."

"There's no dessert if we play," Shirley said, without a hint of playfulness in her voice.

"Hey," Michael said. "No threats here. We gathered to get to know one another. I can't think of a better way."

Veronica couldn't figure out what exactly was happening between the couple. Was this friendly banter? Were they angry at each other? Did this have anything to do with Willy?

Michael stood up and placed his empty wineglass on the ground in the open space between the dinner table and the firepit. The rest of the group watched as Michael took the quarter and affixed it, on the outside of his khakis, into the space between his hefty butt cheeks. It took him a couple of tries to get it right.

Veronica glanced at her brother, who had the most incredulous look on his face: Yes, this is going to be a spectacular car crash. He took a big sip of his wine, as if it were popcorn and a terrible movie was about to start.

"Luckily, we're all wearing pants, but this is going to be hard if they're tight," Michael said, standing there looking as uncomfortable as a person might be if they were not accustomed to a quarter being stuck in their ass. Michael glanced around. "The idea is to walk a few feet toward the glass without letting the quarter fall out, and then, when you get right above it, aim and relax so that the quarter falls into the glass. One point for making it in. The first team to three wins. *Butt Darts*. A brilliant game. Up there with chess in terms of the strategy and guile necessary to win."

"Where does one learn a game like this?" Alex asked. "Yale?"

Michael just smiled and began waddling toward his wineglass. When he reached it, he stood above the glass, slightly squatted, and then relaxed his bottom. The coin dropped, and a split second later, fell into the glass, making a loud ringing sound. "One-nothing-nothing."

He leaned down and retrieved his quarter. He looked very self-satisfied and quite drunk.

"I'm not doing this," Veronica said immediately.

"Veronica, you cannot live in fear," Michael said. "You're welcome to wave the white flag. There's no shame in it. But I want you to embrace this moment."

Despite herself, despite his frat-boy antics, Veronica liked Michael at this moment. She wished she had brought Private Equity with her instead of her brother.

Veronica fished out a quarter from her purse.

"My suggestion is that you don't share quarters, but since your partner will be your spouse or sibling, it's up to you."

Veronica went next. The quarter fell out even before she'd taken her first step.

"You get a mulligan," Michael said. "Try again. You have to strike a fine balance between being at attention and at ease. It's a metaphor for life, really."

Veronica tried again. This time, she reached the glass, but the quarter hit the ground. Despite the absurdity of the game, she now wanted to win. To hell with decorum.

"What the hell are they doing?" Stephanie Cho asked. She was watching the proceedings from MJ's bedroom window.

MJ had invited her over and she'd just arrived. He knew his parents and these parties. There was plenty to drink and so they wouldn't really notice who was in the house and who wasn't. Even when they weren't drinking and there was no one over, they really didn't notice who was where.

Over the past few weeks, there had been a slow-burning, distinctly lo-fi energy between MJ and Stephanie. They liked sketching in notebooks; they liked reading aloud together. A little portraiture here, a little Ta-Nehisi Coates on reparations there. They were learning things together, but really, MJ was still a boy in a man's body and Stephanie was emotionally and intellectually well into her college years.

"It's my dad's favorite game," MJ said. "He only pulls it out on rare occasions. Either he is feeling really comfortable or he's feeling super-awkward."

The two of them watched the game for a minute; MJ recorded it on his phone and sent the video to Diego and Vikram.

"Have you heard?" Stephanie asked.

"What?"

Stephanie handed him her phone. She had several different messages from her friends asking the same question: "Is Stanley Kincaid dead?"

"What is this?" MJ asked. In his head, he knew it couldn't be true. But it wasn't his head that worried him. His chest and stomach felt ablaze.

"People seem to think that he had a heart attack in the hospital today and died," Stephanie said. "Some kid's dad works at the hospital."

"That's the stupidest thing I've heard," MJ said. "There's no way that happened."

"How do you know?"

Over the weekend, MJ had told her what he'd eventually told his parents. But there was something he'd not revealed to either of them. "You really can't tell anyone this, but I went back up to the cave after you and I talked on Friday night. To check in on him. He was fine. Still drunk. There's no way he went from that to dead. No possible way."

"You really can't know that for certain. Things happen."

"Yes, I can." MJ then added, trying to convince himself, "I promise you, he's fine."

He had invited Stephanie over to see her but also to ask a favor of her, which he now turned to in order to stop talking about the prospect of a dead Stanley. "I wonder if you can do something for me."

"Now?" Stephanie asked, giving MJ a coy smile, wanting to break the tension that had been rising in the room.

MJ turned his eyes from her in shyness. "For the past couple of years, Stanley has been getting me stuff. Edibles at first and, lately, pills mostly."

"Oh, c'mon," Stephanie said, feeling the tension return. "Are you serious?"

"I've stopped. I've detoxed from it all. Mostly. I went back to the cave to make sure he was going to shut up about it. As long as he stayed quiet, I'd stay quiet. But here's the thing." MJ paused, nervously picking at his fingernails. "I have a little leftover stuff sitting in my locker at school. I certainly can't get it, and I'm wondering if you can get it for me tomorrow."

"Are you kidding?" Stephanie asked. "Why would you do something so stupid? And none of that is going to matter if he's dead."

"It is going to matter. He's fine. Can you just please do me this one favor?"

As Stephanie sat on MJ's bed, trying to work through his request, MJ sent another text to Vikram and Diego, ignoring his own directive about texts. "We need to meet tmr. Coffee place near theater. @9. Fuck. Fuck."

There was a knock on the bedroom door.

"Come in," MJ said, knowing it was his sister, Kelly. She had very strict ideas about privacy, so she never entered his room unless he was clear in the invitation. Over the past year or so, the siblings had simply stopped interacting very much, despite the fact that they shared a wall and went to the same school. He didn't want her to come in. She was squarely and unambiguously on Team Sara and she was not going to like that Stephanie was here.

Kelly opened the door and stepped in.

"Hi," Kelly said, the displeasure clear on her face when she saw Stephanie there.

"You know Stephanie?" MJ asked. "I don't know if you've met at school."

"We have met," Kelly said, remembering how often her mother instructed her not to be rude to guests, no matter what she felt about them. "Sorry to barge in. My iPad is glitching. Can I use yours?"

MJ glanced at his desk. Kelly walked over and picked it up. "Really nice seeing you," she said as she was about to leave. "By the way, I saw the banners in the hall today." She looked first at Stephanie and then at MJ. "I signed the one for Stanley."

"Are you serious?" MJ asked.

"I am."

"Then you can't use the iPad," MJ said.

"Are *you* serious?"

"Very."

Kelly gave MJ a dirty look and placed the tablet on a table and walked out.

"That was awkward," Stephanie said.

"She's awkward. She's just getting back at me because I won't drive her to school."

"I think I'm going to go," Stephanie said. "Putting up the banner was one thing. But this is getting a little out of control."

"Please," MJ said. "It's just in the back of the locker, under my books in a plastic bag."

As Stephanie left, MJ looked out the window as the competition in the yard below increased.

Both members of each team got a try, and for the first several rounds, Michael's initial score was the only point on the board. The less they all scored, the more Michael refilled their wineglasses, and the more difficult it became for the quarter to find its target. Despite her protestations, even Shirley got into the game, and she was actually quite good at it. Perhaps the lack of body fat in certain areas was the key to success. She scored their second point.

Finally, Gautam scored. "Ah," he said. "I now understand how this works. It's simple physics."

"How is it simple physics?" Alex asked. He and Veronica had not scored yet.

"I'll tell you after we win."

Gita scored their second point. When Gautam dropped in the final quarter to reach three points, with Michael and Shirley stuck on two, and Alex and Veronica at zero, he circled the glass like a rooster.

Michael went around and hugged each of the competitors. "We've battled against each other and now we're stronger for it. I really love you all and all our beautiful boys. We'll get through this together."

Shirley looked really embarrassed for her husband. And herself.

In the complex ecosystem that is the dinner party with near strangers, things had been winding down when Michael brought out his quarter. Now, post-quarters, there was a newfound energy among the guests. New conversations started as Shirley went back into the house to get the dessert. Michael followed her in and went straight to his cellar before she had a chance to criticize him about the game.

Standing in front of roughly four hundred bottles, Michael was feeling a few things strongly: drunk; disappointed that he'd not won a game he'd introduced, a game he had the most practice with; annoyed that Gautam had been so expressive in victory. He wanted to finish the night with a big bottle. He doubted any of his guests would know the bigness of the bottle. But he'd know, and at that moment, it was more important to him than anything else. He pulled down a 2016 Heitz Cellar. If Shirley could spend three hundred dollars on fish, he could do the same on proper grapes. Michael didn't have the budget to be a French wine snob, but he was very particular about California.

He was walking through the kitchen with it when Shirley saw him.

"You don't need to open one more. Everyone's had enough."

"There's never enough," Michael said, grabbing three new glasses. He paused and for a moment seemed to be completely sober. "I know you're embarrassed by me. But it's no more embarrassing than your flirting with Veronica's kid brother."

"I'm just being a good host," Shirley said.

Michael stepped out into the night. He didn't offer the wine to the women. He uncorked the bottle carefully. He didn't bother with letting it breathe. "The really good stuff."

Both Gautam and Alex signaled to him to not pour too much.

"You'll want more," Michael said, making two conservative pours and a liberal one for himself.

"I don't know what it is," Gautam said, taking a sip, "but it is nectar."

Michael and Alex had had roughly equal amounts to drink and were now roughly equally drunk. But in matters of drunkenness, Alex took his cue from the Stoics and Michael from Nero.

"What do you do again, Alex? You're a lawyer? I hope you're not a lawyer. I really hate lawyers."

"I work for—"

Three random names of three random men who together ran one of the better-known venture capital firms in Silicon Valley. Names that meant something to Alex, Michael, and Gautam. Men like them were all about the Valley, even when they weren't involved in it. It was where all the heat resided.

"That's amazing," Michael said. "I hear it's quite the shop."

"It's a nice place," Alex said. "A lot of very smart people who're able to see around very tight corners."

Gautam had leaned away from them and was talking to Veronica.

Michael leaned in toward Alex and lowered his voice. "You have to know something good. Something crazy."

"I know that this wine is very, very good."

"C'mon."

"Gautam's company is certainly a sure bet, especially now."

"I'll keep an eye out for them. But they're not even public yet."

"I've got nothing."

"That's so not true. But I can understand why you can't say anything."

A few seconds after it came out of his mouth, Alex wasn't sure whether he had said it or not. A company he knew that was about to get bought by another bigger company. And he wasn't sure if Michael had heard it. They were both in a bit of a wine haze.

Michael reached over to pour more wine for Alex and Gautam. Both instinctively placed their hands over their glasses.

"What? This isn't good enough for you?" Michael asked, the question aimed more at Gautam than Alex.

"I've just had more than my share," Gautam said.

"Me too," Alex added, to give Gautam cover.

"Well," Michael said. "Me three, then."

He took the bottle of wine that was in his hand and, out of a combination of drunkenness, an attempt to be lively, and an embrace of the shame and anger that had been building in him steadily since his talks with Shirley and his father earlier that day, he flung it up in the air. The men watched it fly upward, suspend for an instant, and then start to drop and somehow land in the center of the carefully placed stones of the firepit. The glass shattered and the small fire suddenly grew tall and wide.

The women were sitting a little bit away and quickly turned to the loud noise and the intense flash of light and heat.

"Michael," Shirley yelled into the night air.

He calmly stood up and walked over to the firepit and turned a lever, shutting off the gas. The fire lowered.

"I guess the party is over," Michael said, turning to the group.

SEVENTEEN

Neither of the Shastris was in any shape to drive.

"It's not that far," Gautam insisted, getting into the car.

Gita was about to protest, but she was in no mood to stand in the Berringers' driveway waiting for an Uber.

"What the hell was that?" Gita asked.

"What I'd do to know what Shirley is saying to him right now."

They drove away from the house.

"God, I hate her," Gita said.

"Shirley?"

"Shirley is harmless. The other one. Why do these professors think they understand everything better than the rest of us? She works at a university. Why is that any better than where the rest of us work?"

"You said to her that her son would get into college easily because of his last name."

"Did I say something wrong?"

"You said that his name is all he needs."

"I made it clear that he's a bright kid. What's wrong with saying that both MJ and Diego will get a helping hand that Vikram won't? In fact, most of these colleges claim they already have too many Indians. They don't seem to worry when there are too many white kids."

"I'm just saying that you'll want to be a little more careful on Thursday."

"We'll see. By the way, that fish was disgusting. I know it's supposed to be sophisticated to like raw fish. But I don't. I never have. I watched her barely cook it. I thought I was going to be sick. I should have said something."

"What did you do with yours?" Gautam asked.

"I hid most of it under the greens. She'll see it when she clears the plate. I don't really care."

Gautam had intended to take some side streets, but he forgot the second he started driving. As he drove, he saw a McDonald's. He looked over at Gita.

Neither of them ate burgers. But once, long ago, when they were just getting to know each other, they had connected over the one thing their parents allowed them to order at McDonald's when they were young: the Filet-O-Fish. As if it was much safer, compared to the distinctly unvegetarian Big Mac.

They ordered at the drive-through and then sat in the parking lot, eating the fish, sharing a large fries, and sucking on thick chocolate milkshakes.

"All she needed to do was cook the damn thing," Gita said. "That's it."

"We're fucking Brahmins," Gautam said, perhaps a little tipsier than he'd thought. "We oppress everyone below us and we don't eat raw fish. How hard is that to remember?" Gautam was eating several french fries at a time. "You know these things taste so good because they're still fried in beef fat?"

"They don't do that anymore. It's vegetable oil now. It was such a controversy in our household when we found out about the lard. My dad was angrier than I'd ever seen him. He has not had a McDonald's french fry since."

"I think it was a controversy in every Indian family in the mid-eighties," Gautam said. "You can imagine how my parents reacted. It convinced them that the American Dream was in fact fried in bad oil."

"That is very clever, my friend," Gita said, slapping the dashboard. "Very clever."

"Easy," Gautam said. "That's brand-new. But thank you. See. I make a big sale, I become clever."

For the moment, they allowed themselves to not think about the things they had said to each other over the past day. The two finished their meals and headed home.

"I know I know her," Gautam said as they drove into the garage. "Your new best friend, Veronica. I asked her at one point during dinner where she went to college, and she was super cagey about it. She was all about asking you where you went to college. Finally she admitted that she went to Berkeley, too. We must have had a class together, though she had some useless major that I hadn't even heard of. What the hell is Rhetoric? An entire major about public speaking?"

When Gita and Gautam entered the house, it was quiet. Gita had vacillated between being angry at Vikram and feeling a deep, visceral love for him. Now, with that gimlet and wine in her and her belly full, she felt the deep love. She went up to his room to find him. His light was on, but he was fast asleep. He still slept in the twin bed they'd bought him years ago, and now his feet and arms hung off the sides.

"Vikram?" she whispered.

In the silence, she heard a slight bit of snoring. She walked over to the bed and kissed him on his forehead, which she now only did at these quiet moments when he was asleep. He didn't stir. As she was about to turn off his light, she noticed his cell phone. She looked at it for several seconds, turned off the light, and then walked out of the room with it.

She knew Gautam would come at her with some high moralism

about invading their son's privacy. She went into their bedroom and punched in three different attempts at the code. None of them worked. She walked back into the hall and was about to return the phone but instead she went downstairs.

"Is he asleep?"

"Fast."

She handed the phone to Gautam. "What's this?" he asked.

"Can you put your face up to it?" Gita asked. "The facial recognition might work with you."

"Absolutely not. Are you crazy?"

"We've given him plenty of time and opportunity. Now we need to do something. You're the one who said that there is more than what he's telling us. And I don't trust those moms. They're going to show up to this meeting on Thursday armed and ready. They're jackals in cashmere."

"What do you think you're going to find in there? A confession tucked into Notes?"

"Please see if you can open it."

"Let me be clear. If he finds out, we're going to be worse off than we already are. The only thing we have is the trust between us. Once that's broken, there's no going back."

Gita was unable to contain her laughter. "Please, no lectures about *trust*. Just see if you can open it."

Gautam placed his face in front of the phone, and dutifully the phone unlocked. He handed it back to her. "Fucking Apple racists."

Gita held the phone in her hand and quickly began looking through it, afraid that it would close again if she waited too long. Like her, Vikram was orderly and neat about everything. His room was immaculate; his backpack was perfectly clean, even though he had had it for five years. He made his shoes last longer than they should have. But the phone was a mess, the digital equivalent of a dirty old wallet with receipts from a decade before. She opened Notes and found nothing there. She opened the emails and found only a bunch from school. She already followed him on all his social media accounts, so there was nothing new there. The only real hidden things were his text messages. Carefully and hopefully she opened them. There were messages between her and him. And there were messages between him and his sister. For a second, she considered not looking at them, but then she did. The early ones were mostly messages from Priya complaining about Gita. She already knew these complaints. She had tried to deal with the hurt of how much her daughter disliked her. She didn't need to read more about it. When she saw a response from Vikram agreeing that he too found Gita annoying lately, she quickly turned to another set of messages. She was still a little drunk and that slightly dulled her sadness. She went to the thread she was looking for, between Vikram, MJ, and Diego.

> . . .
>
> MJ: You two want to roll?
> Diego: Smaller the better.
> Vikram: Is this meant for me too?
> MJ: I wrote you, didn't I? ☺
>
> . . .
>
> MJ: Your parents are having dinner with mine. WTF? D,
> your dad is blond?
> Diego: Uncle
> Vikram: What are they saying?
> MJ: Bullsht. Blah, blah, blah. My mom is such a bitch.
> Vikram: Mine too.
>
> . . .

A few hours later, MJ had sent a video. Gita turned it on. It was of them playing Butt Darts.

> Diego: What the actual fuk?
> MJ: Our parents are putting quarters up their asses and
> dropping them in a wineglass.

. . .

   MJ: We need to meet tmr. Coffee place near theater. @9.
   Fuck. Fuck.
   Vikram: See you there.
   Diego: Yep

   . . .

Gita went back to the messages between her kids.
   Vikram: Can you come before Xmas? Need backup.
   Mom on rampage.
   Priya: Ima try.

   . . .

There was nothing in the text string about how Vikram and Priya found Gautam annoying. Without any warning, her eyes suddenly flooded with tears.

Right before she went upstairs to return the phone, she looked at it once again. She opened his photos and found too many that were out of focus. She scrolled through them and found the ones from the previous Friday. There were plenty from the football game, before and then after. And then there was one other thing. A video. She hit the play button. At first, it was hard to figure out what was going on. The video was jittery. She heard voices. There was darkness and light. Then suddenly, the video came into focus, and Gita could make out three figures. Stanley was on the ground and MJ and Diego were leaning down, throwing punches.

She watched the video and then watched a second time. It made her entire diaphragm burn. Vikram wasn't in it but had stood there, filming it all. For a moment, she thought of sending the video to her phone so that she would have it as well. But then Vikram would know. So what? At least she would have it. She went back and forth in her fuzzy head before finally deciding not to send it to herself, wanting to maintain Vikram's trust and hoping he had enough self-preservation to not erase it.

She went upstairs to return the phone. Vikram seemed to be still asleep. She placed the phone down, and just as she walked away, she heard Vikram stir.

"Did you find anything interesting?" he asked.

Gita felt hot all over. "Let's talk about it in the morning."

"You shouldn't have done that. It's my phone."

Gita went downstairs and into the kitchen. Gautam was no longer there. She went to the cupboards and began emptying them, one by one. First she tried to maintain some order, stacking the plates carefully, making sure all the glasses were together. But then she just started stacking everything on the dining room table. The pots and pans now seemed old and dingy to her. Some were dusty from underuse; others browned from overuse. She decided that she was going to throw them all out. The better thing might have been to drop them off at the Goodwill, but she would never buy secondhand plates, and so she didn't think it was right giving them away so that someone else could.

When the cupboards were completely empty, she went into the garage and rummaged through the tools. She found a hammer and a crowbar. She could guess some origin story for the hammer, but how did the crowbar get there? She brought both into the kitchen and began dismantling the cupboards, one by one. As sturdy as they looked, they came off the walls surprisingly easily. At first she tried to be quiet, but as she got into it, as she enjoyed the process of destruction, she paid less attention to the noise she was making and more to ripping every cabinet fully out of the wall.

Vikram either didn't hear it or chose to ignore it. But Gautam did and came down.

"What are you doing?" he asked, looking at the mess in the kitchen.

"Remodeling," Gita said. "These cupboards are disgusting. I can't look at them anymore. And I can't deal with the ants. I spend so much time in here and it's filthy."

"But it could be months before we have cabinets again."

Gita shrugged and continued her work. "You get a Cadillac. I get the cabinets and counter I want." Her eyes filled with tears again. "When do I get to be sick of everyone like everyone seems to be sick of me?"

Wednesday

EIGHTEEN

By Wednesday morning, this is what Dr. Helen knew.

She couldn't confirm what had happened in the cave, but there were enough students who could at least place all three boys and Stanley up there. Until the three started talking or Stanley gained some clarity, she couldn't know exactly what had happened. She had some sense that roughly thirty minutes to an hour had passed between the three boys returning to the party and Stanley coming down from the cave badly beaten, with hundreds of small cactus spines sticking out of his body. She had seen too many pictures and videos of Stanley screaming in pain, and Charlotte had located all three boys in them. That this was all she had at this point was making her nervous.

With a timeline in mind, she'd talked to a lot of students, and it was no surprise that there were plenty of conflicting theories about what had happened in the cave. The students were most opinionated about two people in particular: MJ and Stanley. The have and the have-not. The chosen and the forgotten. In the first school where she'd taught, there had been gangs, and the teachers could always sense when things were not quite right, when the main hall was about to become a narrow space of chaos. She didn't quite have the same feeling now, but she could clearly see a cleaving, a fault line running the length of the main hallway, starting at one sign and ending at the other. She just couldn't make sense of who was on which side and why.

Dr. Helen had talked to various teachers but hadn't learned anything new. Yes, the three football players were all very bright; Stanley had decent grades his freshman year, but since then they'd all dipped into the low C and D range.

"You have anything for me?" Dr. Helen had asked Mr. Walters, the English teacher who'd taught all three football players.

"Vikram is a really bright kid," he said, sliding his short story toward her. "Even with the story, he's not the one who worries me. If I had to guess who's at the center of this, it's MJ. He brings people into his orbit and sucks them toward him."

"He's worried me the most as well," Dr. Helen said, "because I understand him the least."

———

Gautam went into Vikram's room before he left for work. When he walked in, Vikram was turning from his side onto his back. The room had the lived-in look and smell of summer, when he stayed in it for too many hours of the day.

"Hey, Dad," Vikram said, peering through his barely open eyes.

"Did you sleep OK?"

"Yeah."

Gautam waited for several seconds to make sure that Vikram was not slipping back into sleep. Vikram used his elbows to push himself up and leaned his head and neck against the wall.

"Listen. I know she's going to be too nervous to say anything directly to you, but I think your mom is very sorry about what she did last night. She shouldn't have done that."

"What did she think she'd find?"

"I don't know," Gautam said. "But she did say she found a video. I didn't look at it. I don't want to look at it. I just want to hear whatever you might have to say about it."

"I've already told you what happened. The video doesn't change that. It just confirms it. But it does make things look bad."

"I think your mom's stress level, *our* stress level, is high at the moment." He thought about the dismantled kitchen, but he didn't quite know how to explain it. "You can understand that. It's good we're meeting with the principal again tomorrow. Hopefully we can put all this behind us, and you can get back to school and regular life on Friday."

Vikram didn't respond.

"Do you think the other two boys took their own videos?" Gautam asked.

"I don't know. Probably."

"Maybe you ought to see your principal today. Tell her what you told us."

"I can't do that," Vikram said.

"Why not?"

The question hung in the air between them, unanswered.

Gautam looked around the room. The framed photograph that usually hung in the corner of the living room was now on Vikram's desk.

The photo had been on the front page of most Indian newspapers in March 1930. Gautam's teenage grandfather had seen Gandhi come through his village on his Salt March and had walked the length of the village alongside him. A photographer had captured the image and sold it to newspaper after newspaper across India and eventually across various parts of the world. In many ways, the moment had been the genesis of the twentieth-century Shastris. Gautam's grandfather had become a devout Gandhian—taking part in rallies, spinning his own cotton, becoming a kind of everyday ascetic for the cause of national freedom. Gautam's parents had traveled to America with the original photo—torn from age and humidity—in their carry-on. When they opened their restaurant in Berkeley, they'd named it after the patron saint of the family and hung the framed photo behind the counter. And now Gautam had a digitized version of it in his house, complete with the tear. He'd hung it up without thinking much about it. Looking at it now, he wondered if the long shadow cast by Gandhi and the Gandhian life—of simplicity and austerity and nonviolence—had been too much pressure for them, too much for anyone. All these years, had feeling guilty about wanting to make proper money prevented him from really succeeding? He certainly didn't feel the guilt now. Buying the red Cadillac was the most post-Gandhian thing he'd ever done.

And yet a little bit of Gandhi was like a little bit of Catholic guilt. Useful at times.

"I forget how amazing this photo is," Gautam said. "I'm the first to admit that I get a bit exhausted by all the Gandhian pieties, but the message really never gets old, does it?"

"I guess not. I'm using it for an AP English assignment. Might as well work on it. I have the time."

Because he thought that he'd never quite been settled in his work life, Gautam had never been patient enough to be fully present with his kids. Gita was correct in saying that he had always been there for the macro moments, but he'd left the more difficult, everyday micro moments of parenting to her. Feeling like he'd turned a massive work corner for once, he settled into the chair next to Vikram's bed. Perhaps if he'd been more engaged in his son's life, he wouldn't be stumbling around now for information from Vikram.

"What's the assignment?"

"It's kinda stupid. Don't get me wrong. I really like the teacher. But he wants us to do archival work to show us how archives are everywhere."

"This sounds nothing like my English class. We had to memorize poems."

"Do you remember them?"

Gautam shook his head.

"'An Archive of the Self.' That's the assignment. To find some object that we can use to write about ourselves. The whole thing is really corny. But the cornier I am, the better grade I'll get. I'm using the photo."

"Can I read it after you're done?"

"No, you cannot," Vikram said, smiling.

Gautam looked at Vikram and tried to figure out what was going on in that head of his. He tried to remember what it was like when he was his age. He didn't much like thinking about that time.

Srikanth Murthy had arrived at Gautam's high school in Berkeley when Gautam was a junior and Srikanth a senior. Gautam had gone by *Tam*, because it was high school and it was the very early nineties and he'd been referred to as *Go-Tam* one too many times, partly out of confusion, mostly out of mockery. The first thing he noticed about Srikanth was how he introduced himself. One word; barely a breath between syllables; no *Sri* silliness. The second thing was the distinct English accent that made him sound posh among the Californians, as if he'd been knighted already. And third, he'd shown up that first day of school wearing a yellow Campagnolo bicycling cap, a fashion choice that made much better sense after they watched *Breaking Away* together. He had the right-sized head for it.

Srikanth's arrival made Gautam realize something about rules and regulations. He had been working his way up the high school hierarchy slowly but surely. Freshman year was terrible. Sophomore year was a bit better. He was excited about what new joys being a junior would bring. The new students who came in as upperclassmen did not simply jump in with the rest of their class. At least for a while, they had to do their time in the sticks. But it was different for Srikanth. He went right in with the other seniors. One of the older school counselors who paid special attention to the kids who wanted to go to fancy colleges saw the same future that Srikanth saw for himself. The really attractive girls, who were just slightly different from the popular ones, found him intriguing, exotic. And it was Gautam he chose to show him around the school.

"Are we the only two Indians here?" he'd asked, introducing himself.

"Yep," Gautam said. "But plenty of cowboys."

"Let's get to it then, partner."

"Get to what?" Gautam had asked, not knowing how to keep up the banter.

"Everything."

Until then, Gautam had had friends here and there but no one who was loyal to him. Within days of his arrival, Srikanth didn't do anything unless he asked Gautam first. At the end of the first week, Gautam spent the night at Srikanth's palatial house in the Berkeley Hills. His parents seemed far more urbane than Gautam's. His father had been transferred for work, and his mother was busy setting up their house, which was easily twice the size of Gautam's family's home. The mini fridge in the downstairs TV room was filled with very cold Cokes and Michelobs.

"Go ahead," Srikanth said.

"They don't mind?"

"They know I'm going to drink, so why sneak around?"

That night, Gautam learned about The Who, had his first beer, and watched *The Evil Dead*.

That fall, Srikanth applied to colleges and went on bike rides in the hills that stretched behind the East Bay. When he wasn't working at his parents' restaurant, Gautam spent most of his time at Srikanth's house. They could go the full two days of a weekend without running into Srikanth's parents. One day when Gautam was over there was a brand-new racing bike in the garage. A perfect red Specialized.

"My dad bought it for himself. But why don't you use it for now? He's too busy with work."

It wasn't until years later that Gautam realized that Srikanth had bought the bike himself, using his parents' money, knowing that Gautam wouldn't be able to afford it. No matter how many dosas his parents sold to Berkeley undergraduates, it would never be enough for this bike.

And so they rode.

For the most part, Srikanth was skinny and seemed unathletic. But on the bicycle, he looked like his legs were attached to the pedals. Gautam, on the other hand, did not have the body for long-distance biking. He had very strong legs but already, while still in high school, he had begun to look like a former wrestler. He had too much bulk to sustain the long distances. He always started strong and then ended with a whimper.

Over the course of the school year, the two were always together. The next summer, before Srikanth needed to make his way east to Princeton (he had chosen it over Amherst, a school Gautam had never heard of), they packed up a car and headed out for a road trip.

On the first night, as they were checking in to a campground somewhere south of Eureka, the man in the office asked them if they were related to the Ayatollah.

"Only by marriage," Srikanth replied.

It took him a second to realize that the man wasn't joking.

"Absolutely not," Srikanth added. "I'm as Californian as a hippie."

This didn't seem to help matters much.

"You don't sound Californian."

Over the next ten days, they camped and hiked and heated soup from cans. They played Frisbee on the white sands of the Oregon coast, the stars that night shining extra brightly because of the shrooms they'd had with their dinner. As they were driving home, filthy from barely taking showers, they both knew they were coming to the end of something good. Srikanth would spend the next week packing his things before heading to New Jersey. Gautam had long assumed he would end up going to Berkeley or maybe UCLA. But now that he'd spent the year with Srikanth and seen the number of schools he'd gotten into, when it came time for Gautam to apply to colleges, he wanted to aim higher than state schools, even though he knew that he didn't really have the grades or the money to do so.

When Srikanth turned the corner to get to Gautam's house, he kept his eyes on the road. "I just wanted to say that this past year has been better than anything I expected. I thought my life was over when we left London. And I know how sick you must be of hearing about my life there. It'll be fun for me to show you around the city at some point." The car was getting closer to Gautam's driveway. "I just wanted to let you know that I love you, man."

For a second, the words didn't compute. They were words Gautam had heard on television. His parents, of course, never uttered them. He wasn't sure exactly what they meant coming from Srikanth. Repeating them back to him felt cheap. Not repeating them wasn't an option.

"I love you, too," Gautam said, looking straight ahead, seeing that his parents were in the front yard, working in the garden. He got out of the car as soon as Srikanth stopped.

This moment in the car turned out to be their goodbye. Srikanth's life got hectic over the next week. The plan was that he'd be back for Thanksgiving. But he didn't come back for Thanksgiving. Gautam waited for a message or a phone call. The Friday afterward, he went to Srikanth's house. It was empty. His parents had moved out.

He never heard from him again. Nothing. Absolute silence. It was, in some ways, an abandoning that had shaped Gautam's inability to make friends as he got older. After Google became a thing, Gautam had found Srikanth practicing medicine in Atlanta. Urology.

"Dad," Vikram said. "Everything OK?"

"Yes, yes," Gautam said. His eyes had glazed over a bit. "Sorry. These boys, Diego and MJ. Are you friends with them?"

"I know them. I've been in classes with them. But I don't really think of them as friends."

"Unless you know them well, I wouldn't trust them," Gautam

said. "Think about going to see the principal today. I wouldn't be surprised if they've seen her already. You going in by yourself will be more effective than all three of us going together."

Gautam stepped out of the room. As Srikanth had come into his mind and then out, as he tended to do now and again, someone else from that period suddenly came into focus. He had let Srikanth take the lead in everything. What they did, what they watched, what they listened to, what they drank: all a sort of brown boy sentimental education. The only thing that Gautam had done on his own was be a part of the debate team. He thought back then that he might go to law school, vaguely following in Gandhi's footsteps. There were competitions on the weekends that included debate and other forms of public speaking. For a couple of years, Gautam had done Expository, where he competed with other students over who could explain a topic with the most clarity. His talk was on the stock market his freshman year and on terrorism his sophomore year. By the time he was a junior, he needed a change and convinced Srikanth to try debate with him. They could do either team debate or Lincoln-Douglas, in which they'd argue opposite sides of a topic. Srikanth had suggested the team version, but Gautam had insisted on going solo. He didn't want to be deadweight to anyone.

The economic, social, and cultural good brought by British colonialism outweighs the bad. How could he ever forget the topic they debated for the fall season? Gautam and Srikanth had high-fived when they heard the topic announced. In preparation for a major fall tournament, they researched and worked together, sharing material and ideas. Gautam seldom had an advantage in anything. He certainly wasn't naturally bright like Srikanth. But in this case, he had an ace in the pocket: his family's Gandhian past.

The tournament was held at a local high school on a chilly November morning. Gautam had borrowed the one suit his father owned. The wool was itchy. If they made their way through the preliminary rounds, they would have to speak in both agreement and disagreement with the topic.

In the first round, Gautam had to disagree, and he went in feeling confident. When he arrived in the room where he was supposed to debate, his opponent was already there, an unremarkable-looking young woman from his rival high school, wearing a plaid skirt. When the debate started, she took a knife out of her bag and proceeded to carve Gautam into neat, tiny pieces. By the time it was his turn for a closing argument, he had nothing left to say. For her closing argument, she'd put her notes aside and looked Gautam right in the eye, hammering down on the argument that British colonialism had been particularly beneficial in India, which was on the cusp of going the way of Africa before the British arrived. He didn't need to hear from the judge to know he'd lost.

She went up against another teammate of his in the next round and this time she had to disagree. As forcefully as she'd argued for India's savagery, she then provided an eloquent account of what she called the "Native knowledge" that had been lost in the colonial period. Listening to her, Gautam couldn't decipher what she actually believed.

Later that weekend, the same young woman made it to the finals, going up against Srikanth, who had made his way through several rounds without much trouble. Even in this one thing that was supposed to be Gautam's strength, Srikanth had inched well ahead.

Everyone at the tournament came to watch. For the final, she debated for the affirmative. While Srikanth put up a decent fight, she was always in control. Srikanth used Gandhi to talk about the immorality of colonial rule. She countered with an argument that Gandhi's ideas were taken from the American Transcendentalists and European liberal philosophers, and so he couldn't have made his arguments without the gifts brought by colonialism. Even Gandhi's rightful protest, she said in her closing argument, was made possible by the fact of colonialism.

In those days, the debate competitors were mostly white with the smallest scattering of Black and Asian kids. The high school where the competition was held and that the young woman attended was predominantly Black. Most of the bright white kids there joined the debate team and stuck together weekend after weekend.

After the debate was complete, the young woman shook Srikanth's hand and then walked over to her friends, all of whom were white. At the awards ceremony later that afternoon, when her victory was announced, she accepted the trophy as if she knew it was meant for her all along.

As Gautam made his way downstairs from Vikram's room, he couldn't be entirely certain because his memory was hazy. But he was pretty sure that the young woman who had crushed both him and Srikanth was Diego's mother, Veronica. But she'd had a different name on the nametag she wore all weekend. And Veronica Cruz was not the name the judge announced at the ceremony. It had been something else. But Gautam couldn't remember what.

"We went to opposing high schools," Gautam said excitedly, stepping into the destroyed kitchen where Gita was making tea. "I knew I knew Veronica."

Michael was a lucky drinker, able to sweat out all the alcohol as he slept. But this time, he'd simply had too much, including finishing the dregs of various wine bottles after everyone had left. He woke up to his head feeling heavy. After all these years of drinking and socializing, Michael was clear about one thing: He was an introvert with ambitions of being an extrovert. At parties, he drank to keep the fun buzz going. He spoke with guests, and, as he was speaking with them, felt confident and smart and charming. Occasionally he placed quarters in his butt, but that he kept in his back pocket for special gatherings. Because Shirley tended to be quiet, he felt the need to make up for her. But this also meant that the next morning he regretted everything he'd said.

"How are you feeling?" Shirley asked, walking into the room. She wasn't truly interested in how he was feeling; she only wanted to know if he felt bad. She wanted him to feel bad for making the evening have such an embarrassing turn. The game was one thing. The wine bottle was something else entirely.

"You know. Not my best. But I think we should be proud of what we accomplished last night."

"What was that? Showing that we're the kind of family that sticks objects up where they shouldn't be and tosses wine bottles into the fire? That we are a stone's throw from chaos?"

"The game was a hit. I promise. Our goal was to get to know one another a bit better. And we did that."

He didn't want to talk about the wine and the shards of glass he would need to fish out of the firepit later.

"At least I know next time not to serve fish to this group," Shirley said. "The fish on two of the plates was nearly untouched. The Shastris, I assume. I feel bad that I didn't think to ask them about dietary restrictions."

"I bet they'd have eaten salmon."

Shirley refused to crack the tiniest of smiles. Michael let out a slight groan.

The doorbell rang. It was a sound that Shirley knew well growing up, but no one rang the doorbell anymore because people no longer just showed up.

Shirley went down and returned a minute later.

"It's for you."

Michael suddenly felt nervous. Had Tom Regan come to personally collect? All the drinks the previous night had helped push away the simple fact that he didn't have the cash. Now sober, what was he going to do? He could sell his watch and get some of the money. What else in the house could he pawn without Shirley noticing? He could go back and take another watch from his father, who would certainly not notice anything missing at this point. As long as he got the cash to Tom, he could buy the time to put together the financial paperwork for him. "Who is it?"

"Veronica's brother, Alex. Why is he here?"

"Maybe he's here for you," Michael said. "I bet he wants some of our leftover fish."

Shirley gave him a look of irritation. She was tired of his little jokes and asides. Michael made his way downstairs. Alex was sitting at the kitchen table, looking clean and refreshed, as if he'd already run a 10K in the hills and needed only hot water and lemon to fuel it. Michael was in his bathrobe.

"I thought you might want a cup of coffee," Alex said. He had two to-go cups.

Michael smiled. "I appreciate it."

"I'm sorry for just showing up like this. I realized that I don't have your number or your email. And a conversation in person is better."

"Should I be worried?" Michael asked.

Alex could have Shirley as long as Michael got to keep the house.

"No," Alex said, not sounding very self-assured. "First of all, thank you for last night. Everything was great. The wine, the food. When the evening started, I didn't think we were going to play games or that Gautam was going to be the one to come out on top. But he won fair and square. I won't judge a book by its cover anymore."

"Being just slightly uptight is the key to the game," Michael said.

"Well, I think the Gautams are going to rule our world soon enough," Alex said, as if he were talking about the inevitability of climate change. "I've worked with a lot of them."

"I wish he were just a little more graceful in victory."

They sipped their coffees.

"You've probably guessed why I'm here."

"In fact, I haven't."

"You and I had a conversation toward the end of the night that I would not normally have if two gimlets and a very heavy Napa Cab weren't coursing through my veins."

"What conversation?"

Alex cocked his head slightly.

There were stretches of the previous evening that Michael didn't clearly remember. But he definitely remembered the name of the company Alex had mentioned.

"The company I may or not have mentioned is privileged information I should not have. And therefore, it is information you shouldn't have. I certainly can't act on the information and no one I know can act on it either. Martha Stewart learned that lesson the hard way."

"So this is information you shouldn't have told me?" Michael asked.

"I didn't tell you anything. If asked, I'll say that. But acting on that information would also not be a good idea. It may raise red flags and it would certainly be illegal."

"Is it illegal if you don't get caught? Hypothetically speaking."

"Yes. Nonhypothetically speaking. My strong recommendation is that you forget all about it."

Alex and Michael sat across from each other at the kitchen table, with the morning sun streaming in.

"This is very good coffee," Michael said.

"For a while, I was all-in on the cappuccinos. But now, in the mornings, I just want a simple cup of coffee. A splash of cream. One sugar."

"Make coffee great again."

Alex gave a tight smile.

"You joining us for this lovefest with the principal tomorrow?"

"I'm not sure," Alex said. "Maybe. It's up to Veronica. Thanks again for last night."

After Alex left, Michael sat at the table, tapping on his watch. No one was going to really notice a fifty-thousand-dollar stock buy.

—➤➤➤——

Before he went to meet MJ and Diego, Vikram stopped by the school, unsure what he'd do upon arrival. He'd been thinking about what his dad had said. He really didn't know MJ and Diego at all, and yet he'd been making decisions based on what they wanted to do.

He arrived at the school when he knew classes were already in session. Only when he was skulking through the hall did he realize that he was probably not allowed to be there. He made it to the principal's office without seeing anyone he knew.

"Is she here?" he asked Charlotte in a near whisper.

He'd never been in the office before, but the secretary seemed to know exactly who he was.

"She is. But she's with someone. She'll be right out."

Charlotte pointed to an empty chair near the principal's closed door. Vikram sat down. He sat there playing on his phone, and as his ears became more accustomed to the sounds around him, he could make out two muffled voices behind the door. He assumed one was Dr. Helen's; he didn't know the other. But the other voice kept getting louder.

"I really don't want to. But what choice do I have now but to bring the police in?"

Just then, the door opened slightly, but no one came out. Vikram and the secretary made eye contact.

"Please just give me another day," Dr. Helen responded. "I'm close to figuring it out."

The door opened fully and a woman in nurse's scrubs walked out. Dr. Helen followed her. Both of them noticed Vikram. Vikram had never met the woman, but he knew she was Stanley's mother.

"You're that boy? Stanley's friend Vikram?"

Is that what he'd told his mother? That they were friends?

Her tone wasn't accusatory. It just seemed dipped in sadness.

"Why would you do this? You're friends. I know Stanley can be a little intense, but he didn't deserve this."

She was now standing over Vikram, and he suddenly felt scared, even though all he needed to do was stand up and he would be taller than her by nearly a foot.

Dr. Helen saw the look on Vikram's face.

"Mrs. Kincaid. Please let me manage this."

Stanley's mother took a step away.

"Why would you do this?" she asked again, as she was leaving the office. "He likes you so much. He says you're one of his closest friends."

"Why don't you go on in?" Dr. Helen said to Vikram. "I'll be right there."

Vikram walked into the office, his knees suddenly feeling weak. The office was a bright, airy room with high ceilings. Vikram looked around and walked toward a wall that had two large bookshelves filled with books. He glanced at the various titles. He could make out what the different books were about, urban education and sociology, but there was not a single one familiar to him. Among them, on a shelf, was an 8x10 diploma leaning against some of the books. Vikram took a closer look, as if it were a piece of diamond: Helen Mitchell. Doctorate of Education. Harvard University.

"What was it like?" Vikram asked when the principal returned, trying to pretend that Mrs. Kincaid hadn't rattled him.

Dr. Helen noticed him hovering around the diploma.

"First of all, I'm sorry about that. She's understandably upset, but she shouldn't have talked to you like that. And second, it was intimidating at first. But then I got used to it. I wanted to hate all the pomp and circumstance, but then it seeps into you and suddenly you're buying your whole family cheesy school sweatshirts for Christmas. You think you might apply?"

"I'm not getting in," Vikram said matter-of-factly. "And besides, I want to stay in California. Cold weather scares me."

"You should apply," Dr. Helen said. "You're very strong in science and math, and as I understand it, you're also quite the writer. That will come in handy when writing the essay."

The principal held Vikram's gaze.

"Mr. Walters showed you?"

"I've been chatting with all your teachers, trying to figure out what's up and what's down. He didn't mention it at first. But he had to pass it along."

"It's just a story," Vikram said. "I promise."

"Oh, I know. And you're a good storyteller."

"There's no connection between what that character is going through and me. Please don't use it to explain what happened on Friday night. I'm not depressed. In fact, just the opposite. I've never felt as great as I did after that game. Besides, we don't even have a strong-enough tree in our yard."

"Don't worry. I'm just treating it like a story. But I'm also hoping you're here to tell me what happened Friday night. That's the real story I need to hear."

Vikram stood there. He could still walk out without saying any-thing.

"Have Diego and MJ come in?" Vikram asked.

The principal kept her face completely still, with a slight, calm smile.

Knowing that he now needed to make his own decision, Vikram told her what he'd told his parents but added details that Dr. Helen, knowing who Stanley was, would understand. "Him saying that we had a nice dinner together is a full lie. We had a minute of friendli-ness before he began badgering us. That's what he does. Later, at the party when MJ and I were up exploring the caves, we saw that he was badgering Diego."

"Over Erin Greene?"

"Yep. At that point, he was totally drunk. He started swinging at us wildly and we just tried calming him down, but things got a little intense. We finally mellowed him out and then afterward made our way down."

The principal had talked to a lot of students in the last few days and had seen too many videos of Stanley screaming in agony. But now she'd gotten some clarity on what may have happened inside the cave from someone besides Stanley. She knew enough about

Stanley to not believe everything he'd told her. If she was lucky, she could gather all the different accounts of the evening and piece together some semblance of the truth. With that, she could apportion blame and responsibility.

"You couldn't say any of this on Monday?"

At this point in her career, Dr. Helen did not make too many assumptions about the silence of teenage boys.

"I should have. Stanley is pretending that he's innocent in all this. He's innocent in nothing."

"I know that. Is there anything else you want to tell me?"

For the entire morning, Vikram had been debating whether to erase the video on his phone. He had already broken whatever pact existed between him, MJ, and Diego by speaking to the principal. If he really wanted to separate himself, all he had to do was show her the clip.

"That's it," Vikram said.

"There is one last thing I want to ask you," Dr. Helen said.

She opened her laptop, searched around, and then turned the screen so that Vikram could see. It was a photo very similar to the one Erin had sent him. He couldn't be sure whether it was the same one.

"Who sent this to you?" Vikram asked.

"I can't say."

"Now you're the one not talking?" Vikram said, trying to mask with humor the panic he felt.

"Did you go up to the cave a second time? I really need for you to be truthful."

Vikram's ears began to ring. After days of going back and forth in his head about what to say and what not to, he was simply tired.

"I did," Vikram said. He looked at the photo. "I know it looks like I'm coming down behind him, but I just happened to be in that part of the house at that point. That's it. I'd gone up for like a minute, twenty minutes before this photo was taken. I've never gotten into any kind of fight before. I couldn't think straight, but I'm not a psycho. I had to go check on him. He seemed fine. So I made my way down."

Dr. Helen looked at him.

"Do you believe me?"

"At this point I don't know what to believe."

Vikram had admitted to going a second time, thinking it would demonstrate to Dr. Helen that he was being truthful. He wasn't sure how the information was landing. "Do you know what I hear from some of the guys on the team and then a lot from Stanley?"

Dr. Helen sensed what he was going to say but stayed quiet so that he could say it.

"A lot of 7-Eleven and terrorist jokes. Constantly."

Vikram felt embarrassed having to admit this.

"I'm very sorry to hear that," Dr. Helen said. "I really am. And we'll deal with it seriously when we are done with this other thing. Is there anything else you want to tell me?"

Vikram shook his head.

She stood up from behind her desk. "I'll see you here tomorrow, then. I really appreciate you coming in like this, without being forced to do so."

Vikram began to leave, but then stopped and turned around. "Would you ever write me a letter?"

The principal looked confused.

"Of recommendation. If I applied to Harvard."

Vikram glanced at the diploma.

"Let's see how this turns out," she said, and then added, "I would really like to."

Dr. Helen stepped out of her office a minute later. Vikram was gone.

"Did you put him in that chair on purpose?" Dr. Helen asked Charlotte.

She just shrugged. "I didn't think it would hurt for him to hear snippets of your conversation."

"If MJ or Diego comes in, you put them in that same seat, even if I'm not talking to anyone."

She had been waiting to see which of the boys would come in on their own.

Vikram made his way to a side entrance, hoping no one would see him. But in the empty hallway, with the students all in class, he noticed Stephanie Cho standing at an open locker, talking to Sara Humphries. In the quiet of the hall, Vikram's footsteps echoed and the two looked up from their conversation toward him. He considered stopping, turning around, and finding another way out of school. But it was too late now. In any other circumstance, he would have been happy to chat with these two.

"Hey," he said gingerly as he walked up to them.

He glanced into the locker, which had several varsity letters attached to the back with duct tape. He figured it was MJ's locker.

"Maybe I'm not going to ask what's going on here?"

"Maybe you shouldn't," Sara said. "Or maybe you should. Stephanie here is retrieving something for your friend MJ, and I think it's something that doesn't belong to her."

Stephanie had opened the locker but had not found the sandwich bag MJ had assured her would be at the back, below the copy of *Of Mice and Men* that he'd not returned since freshman year. Sara had walked out of a nearby classroom and seen Stephanie.

"I'm just picking up some books for him," Stephanie said. "So he can keep up with schoolwork."

"The locker is school property," Sara said. "And you know as well as I do that he isn't keeping up with schoolwork."

"Are you suddenly working for the school?"

"Are you suddenly working for MJ?"

Vikram could feel the tension rising between them.

Stephanie closed the locker. "I need to get back to class," she said.

Sara shook her head. "This whole thing is so stupid. I'm not getting into trouble over MJ. He's simply not worth it. Neither should you."

Stephanie began feeling the panic MJ would feel when she told him that the pills weren't in the locker.

"Are you even supposed to be on school grounds?" Stephanie asked Vikram. Before he could answer, she asked him a more important question. "You hear anything about Stanley having a heart attack? That he might be dead?"

Vikram didn't know how to compute the questions. "No. There is no way that's true. It can't be. I just saw his mom." He looked at the time on his phone. "I gotta go," he said. He quickly walked away and headed to the café to meet MJ and Diego. With each step, his panic kept rising. By the time he got there, he had trouble breathing.

"It's not true," MJ said when he saw the look on Vikram's face. "They're just bullshit rumors."

"How do you know?" Vikram asked.

"There's just no way." MJ paused. "What were you doing at school? Stephanie just texted me and said she saw you there."

"I was just picking up some books from my locker," Vikram said.

"Just books?" MJ asked without blinking.

"Yeah, my mom is on my ass about not falling behind because of this. Bro, who are all these people?"

There were a few customers talking to one another, but mostly the café was filled with solos on their laptops wearing incredibly large, expensive headphones.

"Screenwriters," Diego said. "Programmers? Trust-funders. I don't know."

All three went to the counter and ordered mochas with whipped cream.

"How's it going out there?" MJ asked when the other two were back at the table.

Diego and Vikram looked at each other.

"Shitty," Vikram said. "My parents are having a complete meltdown. Actually my mom is having the meltdown. My dad is just at work for longer and longer. She thinks I won't get into college. And my dad went out and bought himself a new car. Considering that he never spends money, I bet he doesn't think I'm going to college either and is spending the money he's saved up."

"If Stanley files a police report, you'll still get into college, but you'll have a police record," MJ offered. "College is going to be fine."

"You don't have to worry about that," Diego said with a bit of accusation in his voice.

"About what?"

"Going to college."

"That's the thing," MJ said. "I might not be going. This whole moment has given me the clarity I needed."

"I'm sorry, but that's about the stupidest thing I've ever heard," Vikram said. "Yale *wants* you. The two of us will be begging colleges to take us."

"There's the problem," MJ said. "They don't really want me. They want my arm. And they kinda want my name so they can ask my parents and grandparents for money later."

"You need to stop spending so much of your time with Stephanie Cho," Vikram said. "Is she a Leninist now? She's got all kinds of ideas and I'm sure she also has all kinds of trust funds."

"She's not wrong," MJ said. "I have ill-gotten gains."

"I say this with love and respect," Diego said, "but shut the fuck up. What're you going to do? Hang out at home while she gets into whatever place she's going to get into?"

"We can talk about my future later," MJ said. "Right now we need to figure out what we're going to say tomorrow."

"Before we do that," Vikram said, "can you explain that video of our parents?"

"There's no explanation," MJ said. "You just had to be there. They were putting quarters up their asses and walking around with them. And they were all pretty juiced."

MJ brought out his phone and played the video again.

"I hope they threw those quarters away," Diego said.

They all laughed.

Though none of the three said it, they all felt it: There'd be a limit to how much their parents could insist that they do the right thing with Stanley. Making false equivalences was the specialty of sixteen-year-olds.

"We need to take charge of the meeting tomorrow," Diego said when MJ put away his phone. "We say what I told my mom already. By the way, I told her. I wasn't going to be able to keep her off my back if I didn't give her something."

"Me too," Vikram said.

"I knew you two would be weak." MJ paused for effect. "I told my parents, too."

The three of them smiled.

"We explain how each of us knows Stanley," Diego continued. "We tell her about dinner, his drinking, heading up the hill, and what happened when you two showed up in the cave. That he'd stumbled and we tried to stabilize him, but he began kicking and punching. We tried to chill him out and may have thrown a few punches, but nothing to cause what he looked like. That maybe he fell going down. The three of us could tell that story over and over again, and it would be the same thing because it's the truth. I'm assuming this is the story you've told your parents, too."

"That's what I told my parents," Vikram said. "But you know that's not going to be enough. My mom may want to believe what she wants to believe, but Dr. Helen has X-ray vision for bullshit. She scares me."

For a few long seconds, all three kept their eyes down on their drinks.

Vikram leaned in and lowered his voice. "Like maybe an hour passed between when we first came down and when screaming Stanley arrived. We need to talk about that. Did either of you go back up there?"

They looked at one another. Each had been annoyed by something the others had done, and yet there was still some trust between them, an optimism about their goodness.

"I did," MJ said with a solemnity in his voice. "We all came back down and I saw Sara and we had a stupid fight. Then I found Stephanie. I didn't tell her about what had happened. But when I didn't see Stanley come down, I got a little worried about the fucker and went to check on him. He was still there, and he started screaming at me. I didn't say anything and just left him there to sober up. I made my way down again, and twenty minutes later, he came down screaming murder. I've no idea what happened."

Diego and Vikram looked at one another.

"You going to tell Dr. Helen about this?" Vikram asked.

"Going up a second time solo is much worse than the one time with all of us," MJ said. "So I'm not sure."

"I went up there, too," Vikram said, feeling relieved as he said it. "Just to check on him."

"I went up there to hurt him some more," Diego said. "But I didn't have the heart."

Diego took a look around the café and then turned back to his friends. "So here we are."

The three had barely touched their drinks.

"We should have gotten boba," Vikram said, pushing the drink away from him. "This shit sucks."

It brought back some levity between them.

"Let's go in and explain why we did it," MJ said. "Explain who Stanley is. The fact that we went back after—that should be off the table. It will only muddy the waters. Personally, I think he just woke up, got freaked out, and slipped and fell in the bushes on his way down. He doesn't want to admit that's what happened and so is blaming one of us. It's way more dramatic. The principal has to believe us. She'll believe us. Stanley was drunk. He's not going to be able to say anything for certain. He probably pissed himself and wants an excuse for it."

They all agreed to this path forward and to seal the agreement, they decided to get some boba.

"I actually have to get going," MJ said.

"Getting your Asian tapioca somewhere else?" Diego asked, unable to contain his grin.

"That's some racist shit," MJ said.

"Are you serious?" Diego asked.

"I am and it is," MJ said. "I need to run a quick errand, but wanna maybe meet at the hospital in a bit? We probably won't get in, but let's see if can get a little peek in on Stanley."

They agreed to meet in front of the hospital in an hour. MJ walked away.

"You still have time for boba?" Vikram asked.

"Time is all I have."

"One thing I wanted to tell you," Vikram said. "Erin and I were just talking about math at the party. That's it."

"We're good," Diego said. "I don't think she's interested in any of us."

"I'll admit, though," Vikram said, thinking that Diego was not completely right about that, "she's very library hot."

The two began meandering down the street, looking at their phones and talking as if everything in their lives was fine.

NINETEEN

When Vikram was growing up, *friends* was a weird category in the Shastri household. The four of them were always a unit, taking frequent trips to visit Gautam's parents in the East Bay and Gita's parents on the west side of L.A. The family was the inner circle and no one else could enter. But whenever Vikram had been to his friends' houses, his presence there was never in conflict with their family. He could eat at their dinner tables, hang around their living rooms. He had made plenty of friends through the years, but there was no one he had gotten really close with, no one who came and spent time at his house. It was one of the reasons, it seemed to him, that his mother was always asking about other Indian kids. Maybe, according to her logic, an Indian kid could be both a friend and family-adjacent.

"What's up with MJ?" Vikram asked. "I mean really up with him. He and Sara looked like they should be on a TV show. It just feels like something weird is going on with him right now. He's had this whole disheveled look going, but today he actually *seemed* disheveled.

Like he couldn't take the boba joke? He doesn't get to be offended by that."

"No he does not," Diego said.

They walked along.

"Your parents going crazy over this, too?" Vikram asked.

"My mom is pissed. My dad lives in Texas and I don't see him much. I just want to get back to school. I miss the everyday stuff of classes. I didn't think I would. And the practices. I go right from football to basketball season. I'm better at football, but I actually like basketball more. I don't want any of this to mess with my playing time."

"Whatever happens, we gotta get ourselves out of this," Vikram said. "I need to get my ass into college and out of the house. Speaking of which, you been working on that stupid archive assignment?"

"I've been wanting to, but I can't think of anything to use. What are you using?"

"This photo of my great-grandfather and Gandhi. You gotta have something similar in your family. Who's the Mexican Gandhi?"

"I'm not Mexican," Diego said, sounding a bit offended. "My mom is Brazilian and my dad is from Texas. His parents are Mexican, but still."

"Che? Was he Brazilian? I've seen you in one of those T-shirts."

Diego laughed. "You're an idiot. But I need something fast here. When is it due?"

"Next Monday."

They got their bobas and sat on the curb outside. Vikram looked over at Diego. He'd seen him around school for a couple of years, even had a class or two with him. But he'd only really known him these past few weeks. Not enough time to really know him. Or fully trust him.

"You went back up, right?" Vikram asked. "You weren't just saying that because MJ said it?"

"Oh yeah, I went up there. And I'm so glad he was that drunk. If he hadn't been, I would have done something really stupid."

"Same," Vikram said immediately. "Same."

Diego took a sip of his drink. "I'm not gonna lie. It's weird when the little balls go through the straw and pop in your mouth."

Vikram laughed and took a big sip.

"Hello, gentlemen."

Diego and Vikram looked up and saw their coach standing in front of them. He was holding the finger of a young girl, barely five, though neither Diego or Vikram could read the age of a kid that young. Nor could they tell how old the coach was. Thirty? Fifty?

"Hey, Coach," both boys said, standing up at attention.

"Take it easy. We're not at practice."

"Is this your daughter?" Diego asked.

"Yes. Say hello to Jasmine. Jasmine, say hello to Diego and Vik-ram. They run very fast."

"Hello, Diego and Vikram," Jasmine said. "Do you two play with my dad?"

"Yes, sweetheart," the coach said. "We all play together. If I give you this bill, can you go in and order what you normally do?"

"Can I get the big one?"

"No," the coach said, but nodding yes.

"Thanks, Dad," Jasmine said.

With that, she was gone.

"I spend half my salary here," the coach said, keeping one eye on his daughter through the glass door. "She loves this place."

Vikram was afraid that he'd gotten rid of his daughter so that he could yell at him and Diego with some freedom and vigor.

"From what I hear," the coach continued, in a soft, even-keeled voice, "you two and MJ have had quite the week."

"Are you mad at us?" Diego asked.

"For being sixteen-year-olds? Of course I am. But I don't blame you. I think I did some pretty dumb things at sixteen, too. But it's funny I bumped into you two today. I don't think this meeting is just random. I know you'll turn to each other when I'm gone and say that

I'm a little kooky, but I'm a big believer in fate. I had decided that I was not going to say this if I didn't see you in person this week. I didn't want to force the issue over the phone. And here you are."

Both the boys were confused by what the coach was saying.

"Diego, remember that friend of mine I told you about, the running backs coach at Cal?"

"Of course."

"They're playing UCLA this weekend, and he's making a little pit stop here. He was originally coming just to check out Diego, but I sent him a short video of Indian Marshawn Lynch here. So he's going to hit two birds with one stop."

Diego and Vikram looked at each other.

"So you find yourself in a bit of a moral quandary here, don't you?" the coach continued. "I understand that the principal is not letting you play until you explain what happened last Friday night. I'm not even sure she'll let you play after you do explain it. She's been keeping me updated. But now, suddenly, you find yourselves wanting to get this thing over with as quickly as possible. Am I right?"

Both boys nodded.

"I bet the two of you have your sights set on Stanford, but Berkeley is really the way to go. You don't want to miss this chance at getting properly looked at. You have to figure out what's more important: whatever reason you're not talking about last Friday or your desire to play this Friday. I'll leave it up to you. It's a tough one."

Jasmine walked out with her boba.

"Hope to see you gentlemen on Friday," the coach said. "But I genuinely respect whatever decision you make."

With that, the coach and his daughter and her giant plastic cup of boba walked down the street.

"Why was he talking so weird?" Vikram asked. "Like some kind of guru."

"Why was he only talking to you?"

"What are you talking about?"

"He didn't say I was the Latino Marshawn Lynch."

"First of all, he was talking to both of us. And second, he only said that because it sounds so fucking absurd."

"Whatever, man," Diego said.

Vikram allowed himself for a second to imagine the ludicrous fantasy of getting recruited to play Division I football, all because he could run a forty in 4.5 seconds and had the build of the Punjabi he was not. He had never thought to want this, and now that it was remotely possible, he wanted it badly.

"You wanna head over to meet MJ?" Vikram asked.

"Sure."

They walked the mile or so to the hospital without saying much.

The hospital was not guarded like a prison, but it wasn't open for anyone to just go in and out. Both the emergency room and the ICU were off-limits, but the floors above, with rooms for patients, were not that airtight.

"Do you know where he is?" Vikram asked MJ when they met out front.

"No idea," MJ said.

"We can't just go from floor to floor until we find him," Vikram said.

"That's exactly what we can do," MJ said. "We just walk like we're headed somewhere. People only question you when you stop. If you keep walking, they think you have purpose."

Diego and Vikram looked at each other.

"What?"

"I think that's *your* experience of being where you shouldn't be," Diego said.

"Or being where you should be," Vikram added.

"Fair," MJ said. "I guess at the moment, I'm our primary hope of getting in there and being left alone."

"Why don't we just see if they have visiting hours?" Vikram asked.

"We'd have to sign our names," MJ said. "I don't think we want them to know we were here."

With the plan to go from floor to floor in mind, they walked through the main entrance and took the elevator up. They made their way through the entire second floor without being stopped or finding Stanley. Each of the rooms had a small window next to the door. Some blinds were drawn, while others were partly open. The names of current patients were written by the door, but the print was too small for the boys to read as they moved quickly from room to room.

"We're not going to find him," Diego said as they climbed the stairs from the second to the third floor. "We'll have better luck asking about visiting hours."

They were halfway through the third floor when they passed an open window.

"That's him," Diego whispered as they walked past.

They stopped at the end of the hall, away from the nurses' station.

"Are you sure?" MJ asked.

"No."

MJ walked back down the hall, slowed down, and then lingered by Stanley's door for a moment. Then he made his way back quickly. There was something genuine and distressed on MJ's face as he made his way back toward them. As if now, finally, it had dawned on him that they were in real trouble. Stanley was not on a ventilator but he was attached to an IV and a heart monitor. He looked listless in bed. MJ knew in his gut that the rumors weren't true, but the reality that Stanley was seriously hurt was hitting him hard.

"It's him," MJ said. "Fuck, fuck."

Vikram went to take a look. He didn't pretend to linger or stop to check something. He just stood in front of the window and peered inside, then quickly turned around, almost running down the hall.

The door to the room suddenly opened.

"Hey," Stanley's mother said firmly. "What are you doing?"

Vikram was far enough away so that she could neither catch up with him nor absolutely identify him. When she looked down at the other end of the hall, MJ and Diego had already disappeared through the doors that led to the stairs. They did not stop until they were out of the hospital. They looked around, but Vikram was nowhere to be seen.

"Where did he go?" Diego asked.

"Wherever he went, I'm beginning to think we can't really trust him at that meeting tomorrow. Something is off with him. He looks scared."

"I think we're all fucking scared."

When MJ got home, his mother was in the kitchen.

"You hungry?" Shirley asked. There was a time when she'd grown sick of preparing meal after meal for her children. Now she missed it.

"I am."

"There's some leftover fish from last night. I can grill it."

"Can you just make me a peanut butter and jelly sandwich?"

"I'd love to."

Shirley brought out the ingredients. MJ sat on a stool at the island and watched as she expertly spread the peanut butter on both pieces of bread. Maybe this was the key to why her sandwiches always tasted so good.

"Don't worry about money for college," she said, putting the plate in front of him. She got him a glass of milk. "I'll figure all that out. You just do what you want to do."

He ate the sandwich as if he'd not eaten in days. Shirley made him another without asking.

"I don't know what I want to do," MJ finally said. "I think that's the problem."

"Would you like some advice? Or maybe just a thought?"

"Sure."

"I wouldn't normally say this to you. But you've always been well beyond your age in understanding, so I think I can say it. I've been through what you're going through. Maybe not the bare feet part. But some version of it. My rebellion was a little later when I went off to a Ugandan village to teach English. You're wanting to figure out who you are. Your job is to do that, and our job as your parents is to provide you some guardrails. No matter how sick you are of this house and all we have, you won't always be. I think you'll want to come back to some version of this. That's just how it works. So for now, go ahead and be honest with yourself about what you want and don't want. But also recognize that you'll want to give yourself some options if and when you change your mind."

MJ finished his second sandwich and nodded.

"Right before the game, I took a pill to perk me up and help me focus," MJ said. "Since you're being honest with me, I want to be honest with you. I got it from Stanley, who I think stole it from his brother."

"What exactly did you take?" Shirley asked, her voice suddenly rising with concern. She'd read countless stories about the pill-popping revolution among teenagers and how a benign-looking multivitamin could be the fentanyl or ketamine that would kill you. This worried her more than any of the dangers lurking around her children.

"It was just Adderall." MJ shrugged. "In case it comes up, I wanted you to know. Stanley's been getting me stuff now and again for the past year. So that I can experiment."

"Like what?"

"Nothing that serious. A little Ecstasy. Some other random stuff. But I'm done with it. I had some in my locker at school. I asked a friend of mine to get it for me and it's not there anymore. I think the principal went through our lockers, which I think the school has the right to do. It's going to come up tomorrow at the meeting."

Throughout the week, Shirley had been worried. But she'd countered it the way she'd always countered worry: They could throw money at it. This last piece of news made her think that money wasn't going to help. She was thinking that she was now very angry at the two men in her house, who had all the opportunities they needed and were figuring out ways to squander them. "I'm here for you," she began, trying and already failing to remain even-keeled. "But you've been making some stupid decisions. It's not that hard if you simply think one or two steps in front of you. That's all you need to do. Think about consequences. It's really that straightforward."

"I know," MJ said. "I know." He stood up and placed the plate in the dishwasher. "Thanks for the sandwiches. I'm sorry I've messed everything up. We went to see Stanley today. In the hospital. He looks really bad, Mom. I really don't understand what happened. I don't know how he ended up like that. It wasn't us."

"Did you talk to him?"

"We were going to. But his mom was there and she looked mad. Like she had no interest in talking to any of us. We were just there to see how he was doing."

Perhaps she needed to see the principal herself.

Veronica was picking out the best plums at the farmer's market when she heard a vaguely familiar voice.

"Veronica?"

Often she bumped into moms from school so that's what she assumed when she turned to the sound of the voice.

It was not one of the moms. It was Jane Marcus—a junior faculty member in her department who'd been hired a few years before. After they'd hired her, she had reached out to Veronica several times, wanting her to be her mentor. Veronica had no patience to mentor a grown adult.

"What are you doing here?" Jane asked.

"I live here," Veronica said. "Do you?"

"We're up here with some friends for a rock-climbing trip. There are amazing boulders in the area."

There were many things about young people that Veronica did not understand. But she didn't think she'd taken a single day off for the ten years after starting her first academic job. There were books to write, hustles to be hustled. Rock-climbing? On a Wednesday afternoon? She'd worked very hard to earn this weekly ritual, happily overspending for truly flavorful fruits and vegetables.

"Have you always lived up here?" Jane asked.

"Yeah," Veronica said. "It's nice to have some distance from the campus."

Veronica suddenly felt nervous, as if Jane had walked in on her doing something she shouldn't have. Shopping for fruit suddenly felt illicit.

As they were talking, a man was hovering around Jane. She motioned him to come closer.

"Have you met my partner, Aaron?"

Aaron was Korean American and had high, sharp cheekbones. Veronica had to look away for a second. Aaron was alarmingly handsome, and he and Jane—her prep-school pedigree turned radical historian—made a striking couple.

"Hi, Aaron," Veronica said. "I hear that there are rocks to be climbed today."

"Yes," Aaron said. "We're picking up some provisions for our night in the backcountry."

Now Veronica really couldn't understand these people.

"It's really nice meeting you," Veronica said, beginning to step away, trying to cut the conversation short.

But before she could escape, Alex appeared at her elbow.

"I found incredible mushrooms," he said. "I spent fifty dollars on them, but still."

Veronica stood between Jane and her very blond and very green-eyed brother. Jane looked at Veronica this time as if she had caught her in an affair, or perhaps worse, overspending on chanterelles.

"This is my brother, Alex," Veronica said, reading Jane's mind. "Alex, this is Jane and Aaron. Jane is the French historian in our department. She studies the Revolution."

"Oh," Jane said, not trying very hard to hide her confusion. "I didn't know you had a brother."

Veronica didn't respond. Things suddenly got awkward at the five-second mark after no one had said anything.

"What are you going to do with those mushrooms?" Aaron asked.

"Butter. That's all they need. And this." In his other hand, Alex had a loaf of sourdough. "And goat cheese. Why don't the two of you come for lunch? I'm cooking."

Jane stood there, not knowing what to say.

"You're welcome to," Veronica said. "But they're headed into the backcountry."

"A rain check, then," Alex said.

As Veronica began inching away, Jane turned to Veronica. "Can I chat with you for a second?"

The two of them moved toward a stand selling fresh, bright yellow lemons.

"So nice seeing you, Veronica. I haven't seen you around the department."

"It's a nonteaching quarter for me."

"It's so great I bumped into you like this. I wanted to ask you a quick question. Did you give a talk in Portland earlier this week?"

Veronica nodded. "I did. Why?"

"I have a friend from graduate school who is junior faculty at the college."

"Were they in the audience?"

"Yes. She was excited to hear you speak."

If Veronica could have remembered the names of the two young female faculty members who'd joined her for dinner, she would have asked if it was one of them.

"And what did she say?"

"That you were dazzling. She went on and on about it. That you brought up *Moby-Dick* in the context of the slave trade, which made her want to read the novel. She also said that you had a run-in with a student."

"Is that what she really said?"

"Not exactly."

"What *exactly* did she say?"

"That you verbally attacked a student. A Native American student."

There was something in Jane's tone. Some change, as if she relished this moment. Veronica had a powerful presence in the department. A presence that she took advantage of. Now, suddenly, she had a vulnerability, and Jane was the one taking advantage.

"She said you called the student something. Some phrase. You didn't curse at her, did you? Not that I'd blame you. Students can be exhausting."

"I wanted to," Veronica said. "But of course I didn't. I gave her a compliment. I called her a 'Marxsplainer.' She was giving me a lecture on archival elision and neoliberalism. The term fit."

Jane thought about it for a few seconds. "That is genuinely funny. If it's OK with you, may I use it when the moment arises?"

"I have released it into the public domain. Do with it what you may."

Maybe if the two of them had started on this foot when they first met, things could have been different. Even so, there was something about Jane that Veronica simply hadn't liked and didn't like. And it wasn't just the Spence-Columbia-Yale dripping off her.

"Do you have another question for me, Jane?" Veronica asked. "Or do you just want a sense of my lecture schedule?"

"It was nice seeing you, Veronica. I hope to see you soon."

Jane and Aaron moved on to get the rest of their provisions, and Alex went off to get more things. Veronica just stood there in the middle of the farmer's market on a sunny day, angry at herself for responding in the way she had to Natalia, the bright young student in Oregon. Considering how quickly word had traveled down the West Coast, she feared she'd cracked open a door she'd kept shut for a long time and had now invited people to come in and dig around. In the larger scheme of things, Veronica was not very consequential, but in the small world she occupied, she had, through the years, asked enough hard questions from others in her field and taken enough jobs that others had wanted to make enemies. If they heard that Veronica had humiliated a young Native American student, they would start asking questions. About what Veronica had done. About Veronica.

How was she going to tell this story, her story, which somebody somewhere was now going to want to be told? She sensed that there were lots of questions coming.

Veronica had graduated from Berkeley with a double major in History and Rhetoric. While she'd not left a huge footprint in either department, she'd been admitted to several graduate programs and had arrived at Brown to study nineteenth-century American women's history. She'd applied as Veronica Matthews and had lasted in the program exactly one year. She couldn't figure out what the problem was. It was as if, for that whole year, she was wearing a sweater that never fit properly. It was too tight or too itchy or the wrong color. Was it Providence? The East Coast? Maybe her cohort, all of whom she hated. The only saving grace that year was that she met, fell in love with, and married Andre Cruz, whom she had connected with in the first wave of online dating. They'd honeymooned in Brazil, and shortly before, had discovered that on her father's side, her great-grandfather had migrated to the U.S. from Brazil via Hawaii. She'd made a trip to the village where he'd come from and, while she'd found no clues about his life, she had returned with a project about the slave trade in Brazil.

Andre was from San Antonio and wanted to return to Texas. Veronica didn't feel ready to give up on the scholarly life. She was good at languages. She'd studied Spanish through high school and some in college; she took an intensive Portuguese class after they returned from Brazil. And she applied to other graduate programs, this time in Latin American history, using her married name: Veronica Cruz. Once she got into the University of Texas, she didn't bother to think about other schools.

At the department orientation at the start of the year, Veronica just felt different. Where she'd been at the margins in Providence, she was in the deep center in Austin. In the first seminar she took, the class presentations each week by the students switched between English and Spanish. For her presentation, she spoke entirely in Spanish. At the holiday dinner held at the chair's house at the end of that first semester, she brought Andre along. This seemed to seal the deal. Between her name and the olive hue of her skin, her working knowledge of both Spanish and Portuguese, and now her husband, her fellow graduate students and the mostly white faculty made assumptions about how recently her family had immigrated from Brazil.

When the time came, she asked one of her female white professors to be the chair of her committee. She agreed immediately, as did the three other historians Veronica approached. They all seemed to have a deep investment in her success. By the time she finished her dissertation, she had a young child and was divorced from Andre. She went off to her first job in Boston. When her first book came out, she was already being recruited by other universities. Over the next decade, there wasn't a year when she was not going on campus visits or negotiating with a dean. With each passing year, she got further away from whoever Veronica Matthews had been. She'd already had a limited relationship with her parents growing up, so her estrangement from them did not feel like such a big loss.

But then those two letters had arrived in the mail, weeks apart, addressed to VERONICA MATTHEWS in large letters. Andre knew about her name change; Alex knew about it. But her suspicions had landed on one of her colleagues. They were all master archivists. It was not a hard thing to uncover.

What could Jane possibly do now? Tell her colleagues that Veronica had a blond brother? That she'd had a run-in with a student? Would they make Veronica take a DNA test? What would that prove? If she had to take one, they should all have to take one.

She went back for more plums, deciding that she was going to bake a big, beautiful tart. Maybe she could bring it to the meeting with the principal.

When Veronica and Alex reached home, Diego was sitting on the steps of the porch, thinking about how much both MJ and Vikram were getting under his skin. After all this time playing together, Diego had grown tired of the way MJ always needed to be in control, even as he insisted that he had no interest in control. With Vikram, Diego was beginning to admit something to himself that he didn't want to admit: Perhaps Vikram was a better player. That admission made him hungrier to be back on the field.

"You going somewhere?" Veronica asked.

"I was going to go see the principal."

This is exactly what Veronica had wanted him to do, but she'd not said it to him because that was a sure way for him to not do it.

"Do you want me to come with you?"

"I do, but I think I better do this alone."

"Have Vikram and MJ talked to her already?"

"I don't know. But we saw him today."

"Who?"

"Stanley."

"Where?"

"At the hospital. We went to visit him. Just to make sure he was OK. He was in bed, sleeping. Mom, I didn't do that to him. Something happened, but that wasn't me."

Diego sounded scared.

"It's OK. Talk to her. Tell her everything. C'mon. I'm going to drive you."

Alex had already gone inside the house.

"I'll walk home," Diego said, getting out of the car at school.

Diego arrived at school after classes were done for the day. He stopped first at the football field and, from a distance, watched as his team practiced. He missed being out there with his teammates. Perhaps he was imagining it, but they looked bad and out of sync and unhappy. He could hear the head coach's voice from a distance. He was never this loud.

"Can I ask why you're here?" Dr. Helen asked after he was seated in front of her desk.

"Because you asked us to come in," Diego said.

"Of course. But besides that. Why are *you* here?"

Diego paused to consider the question. "I want to tell you my side of the story."

He told her his side of the story. As she listened, she noted how much it sounded like the story Vikram had told her. That could have been because the two of them were there together and now remembered the same details or because they had agreed that this was the story they'd tell.

Diego shuffled in his seat and then leaned forward. "I've told you already how much Stanley used to mess with me. Constantly. Up there in the cave, he did some of that again when I was trying to talk to Erin. Making fun of me for being short when I first started high school, as if that was going to help his chances with Erin. Of course, I didn't do anything when Erin was there, but after she and her friends left, I tried to keep my cool. Even before Vikram and MJ showed up, he'd tried to throw a punch at me. When I asked him what he was doing, he said he was just messing around. He tried laughing it off. After MJ and Vikram arrived and things got a little crazy, I snapped a bit. I was just getting back at him. That's it. But we didn't land him in the hospital. He'd taken a hit or two, sure, but he looked fine enough when we left him in the cave. He even had a smirk on his face."

Diego looked up and paused.

"And now that I have told you, I want to ask you to consider letting us play Friday night. I honestly don't care if we win or lose. But I have played with some of these guys for years. We have had some terrible seasons together and one really good one last year. This year has been tough. I just want to be out there with them. I've told you everything I know about the evening. I promise."

When she'd spoken to them, both Vikram and Diego had sounded pretty honest, and while both their lockers were criminally dirty, she'd found nothing incriminating in them. MJ, on the other hand, had not come to see her and she'd found enough in his locker to get him into genuine trouble. She knew so much more than she had on Monday, yet she felt like she was being played by these boys. And she did not appreciate being played.

"Let's see what happens at our meeting tomorrow," Dr. Helen said.

Thursday

TWENTY

At a little past 8 A.M. on Thursday morning, MJ entered Coach Smith's physics classroom. For the past couple of years, it had served as an early-morning haven when he'd needed it. The coach usually had a pot of coffee on and music coming from the speakers on his computer, occasionally reggae or sitar, but mostly jazz and classical. The coach prepared for classes and games during that quiet hour and anyone was welcome.

"Hey," Coach Smith said when MJ walked in. He was sitting at his desk. He placed his pen down and noticed MJ's feet. "Shoes. It must be serious."

"Big meeting," MJ said, walking over to the coffee and pouring himself a cup. "What are we listening to?"

"A French composer. He wrote this piece when he was in a German prison camp during World War Two."

MJ listened to it for several long seconds. "Clarinet?"

"Indeed. I used to play it in junior high. I was solidly mediocre."

"It's hard for me to imagine you in junior high," MJ said.

"I looked about the same as now. More hair, maybe. I thought I might have a real future in the jazzy clarinet."

The coach waited a minute for a movement to end.

"It's called 'Quartet for the End of Time,'" the coach deadpanned. "That's our mood?"

"Not really. It's all about the clarinet."

"How's the team?" MJ asked.

The football practices during the week had been a combination of high-pitched excitement and short-circuiting nerves. The game on Friday had stakes: win or the season ends.

"We simply don't have the firepower without the three of you. So I'm concentrating on defense. Andrews has been taking your snaps in practice. But he's been so nervous that ten-yard passes hit the ground soon after they leave his hands. The physics are nearly impossible, and yet he manages it."

"I'm sorry. I know this was really bad timing on our part."

"I have some sense of what happened. And honestly, I don't want to know more. But can I give you one piece of advice?" He didn't wait for MJ to answer before proceeding. "We may well lose tomorrow night. I'd like to win, but I'm not going to be heartbroken with a loss. I like winning, but I don't *need* it. I know you're meeting with the principal this morning. Maybe she'll let you play, maybe she won't. But I think you don't want to miss out on your last high school game. I know it may not seem like much of a thing right now. But in a couple of years, maybe more, you'll want to have really taken this game in. You've worked very hard these past four years. Win or lose, you deserve to be there."

MJ listened to what the coach had said. "I really don't think any of it is in my control anymore. I wish it was."

"I think you have far more control than you realize."

The smart kids liked to say that the coach was often very *poetic* in the classroom. MJ had always assumed that they meant he knew how to turn a phrase at the right moment. But his poetry was more than that. He chose his words and lines to mean more than one thing at a time. With the idea of control buzzing around in his head, MJ remained in the classroom for ten more minutes, listening to the music as the coach got ready for his first class.

"I'll see you soon," MJ said as he stepped out.

"I hope so."

On his way in, he'd seen the two banners in the hall but didn't have a chance to examine them. He first went and stood in front of STANLEY LIES. Every last bit of white space had been filled with signatures. When there was no room left, students had signed on top of others, as if they didn't want to be left behind. He turned around and made his way to the other banner. He had been standing there for about a minute when he felt a strong presence behind him. First period would start soon, and he didn't want to be there when the hall was full.

"Clearly there are more on the other one, but I'm surprised that there are as many on this as there are."

MJ noticed Sara's arrival. They'd not spoken or texted since Friday night.

"There should be more," she continued, motioning to the left side of the banner. "But it's hard to go up against majority opinion."

MJ examined the banner like it was a pointillist painting that required a closer look to appreciate the brilliance of detail and technique. He noticed Sara's signature. He looked back at her and she just held his gaze.

"Really?" MJ asked. "I know we've had our issues. But this hurts."

"I can believe you and him at the same time, can't I?"

"You signed the other one, too?"

Sara shook her head.

"Why would you believe him?"

"Because I don't know what you did in that cave. But I know that he's hurt. I saw him."

"He was being an asshole. We were defending ourselves. That's it."

"When you and I argued at the party, you had just come down from the caves, right?"

MJ thought through the timeline. He nodded.

"You were all weird and out of breath. I thought it was from something else. You didn't say anything to me. But I knew something was up."

"What did you want me to say? 'Yo, we just knocked around Stanley and he's lying up there drunk and done.'"

"Yes. Something serious could have happened."

"Well, something serious did happen. But we didn't do that to him. We saw Stanley in the hospital yesterday."

"You visited him?"

"Not really. He didn't look good, Sara." However much he had drifted from her in the past few months, the two had also spent a lot of time together. She knew him well; he felt comfortable with her.

"I'm scared for him. And I'm scared for us. This thing has gotten completely out of hand. I don't know how to fix it."

MJ took one step toward Sara, as if he was asking for warmth. She took a step back.

"It's not your job to fix it," Sara said. "Just tell the principal everything you know. That's all you can do."

The five-minute bell rang, signaling the approach of first period. The hallway was filling up with students.

"I wish you'd just told me all this," Sara continued. "I wish you'd told me about Stephanie."

"There's nothing to tell about her," MJ said weakly, tired of pretending.

"Did she tell you that she and I had a little chat?"

"She did."

"I really don't understand what's happened to you," Sara said.

"I don't either," MJ replied.

That morning his parents had suggested that they go to the meeting with the principal together, but he'd said he wanted to go in

earlier on his own. Now, as the hallway filled with students, he felt
alone.

Vikram had been a little wobbly as he made his way downstairs. He
had been wobbly since he left the hospital the previous day and
walked all the way home without stopping.

His parents were waiting for him in the car.

"So I was thinking," Gita said as they began driving, "that we
should have a clear game plan about what's going to happen at this
meeting. We can't just wing it."

"*Game plan?*" Gautam asked. "This isn't a game."

"Oh yes it is," Gita said. "One which we need to win. Losing isn't
an option."

"Will you two just stop," Vikram said from the back seat, his voice
louder than he intended. He liked it better when they argued in silence. "I cannot listen to the two of you fighting over everything
anymore. I'll say whatever you think I should say, but can we just
have some peace on the way there?"

Gita and Gautam looked at each other.

"You just explain the first part of the evening and that's it," Gita said.
"And honestly describe your experiences with Stanley." There was that
video on his phone that they'd not talked about. Gita assumed Vikram
knew that she'd watched it. It was an ace if and when she needed it.

"Fine," Vikram said softly from the back seat.

It did sound fine to him, but he wasn't entirely sure what he was
going to say or leave out. He'd slept badly the night before, thinking
about Stanley in that hospital bed.

When they arrived at school, the Shastris and Veronica, Alex, and
Diego happened to park their cars close to one another. As they
walked toward the building, they kept their distance. But once in the
main hallway, Gautam called out softly, "Veronica."

Veronica and her family turned around in the empty hallway. They all stood there.

"I'll see you in the classroom," Vikram said, noticing the STANLEY LIES banner.

"Me too," Diego said.

The two walked toward the banner.

"What the fuck is this?" Diego asked.

Vikram looked at it closely.

"Our safety net, I think," Vikram said. "The principal has to believe us. Most of the school does."

"Why did you take off yesterday?" Diego asked, lowering his voice. "We couldn't find you afterward."

"Did you see him lying there?" Vikram asked. "He looked terrible."

"He was fine," Diego said. "It's not like he needed help breathing. They were probably just giving him liquids. You know Stanley. He's probably been telling the doctors he's more hurt than he is to get their attention."

Vikram turned to face Diego. "He looked bad. You're not actually this cold-blooded, are you?"

"Of course not. But remember who we're dealing with." Diego paused and looked around. "Man, I need this whole thing to be over. I want to be back at school and I really want to play tomorrow. We just tell the principal the story openly and truthfully. That's it. I bet we'll be done with the meeting in like ten minutes."

Down the hall, Gita and Gautam and Alex and Veronica stood together.

"Veronica, I may be totally off here, but do I remember correctly that you were once a great debater at Roosevelt High?" Gautam asked.

The slightest twitch on Veronica's face told Gautam that he had, indeed, remembered correctly.

"Did we go to high school together?" Veronica asked.

Gautam had not been sure what he was going to say if she was the person he remembered. But he found it annoying and a little hurtful that she didn't remember him—that she had no recognition at all. She didn't even pretend. Was he so forgettable?

"No," Gautam said. "I went to El Monte."

"Ah. Our friendly rivals."

Veronica took a step as if to continue down the hall.

"I think you beat me pretty badly one time at a debate," Gautam continued. "If I remember correctly, you were a huge fan of British colonialism."

Veronica gave half a smile, as if she was now vaguely recalling this.

"I think I was just a good debater, able to argue passionately from either side."

"Yes. I suppose that's true. I just couldn't see both sides equally on that one. Because, you know . . ." Gautam shrugged.

"I can understand that."

"You seemed different then," Gautam said.

"We were all different then," she said.

Gita gave Gautam a puzzled look. He pointed down the hall. He had shared his suspicions with Gita the previous morning when she was making her tea.

"We'll see you in the classroom in a minute," Gita said.

"Do you need me to stay?" Alex asked his sister.

"I'm fine."

Gita and Alex began walking down the hall.

"You beat my friend Srikanth in the debate finals," Gautam said.

"English-accent guy?"

Gautam nodded. Of course she remembered him.

Being in the main hallway reminded him of how lonely his own high school experience had been. Recalling these feelings, sensing them in his chest, he turned to Veronica.

"I may not have the right language for this, and forgive me since I'm a humble computer programmer, but I don't remember all this passionate Latino stuff when we were in high school. I remember quite clearly that you and all your debate friends took pride, and perhaps some understandable solace, in being the small group of white kids in a predominantly Black high school. What was Roosevelt? Ninety-four, ninety-five percent Black? In that way, I suppose, you and I weren't that different. I was one of two Indian kids at El Monte."

"Is that what you remember?" Veronica asked.

"That's what I remember."

"Well, let me assure you that it's far more complicated than that."

"Which part?"

"All of it. You went to El Monte. You know clearly what it was like. The white kids hung out with the white kids, the Black kids with the Black kids. I guess you hung out with the other Indian kid?"

Gautam smiled.

"At Roosevelt, you had to take care going back and forth to school. You did what you had to. Stuck with who you had to not get jumped."

"I can understand that," Gautam said. "As I said, I don't understand a lot of this stuff. American race talk has always confused me. But you pretending to be something and someone you're not—your whole thing being a lie—is not going to be the stick you use to beat down my son."

"First of all, there is no lie. And second, no one is beating down your son, Gautam. Certainly not me."

"Really? Because that's what it sounded like on Monday and then again at dinner at the Berringers'. Whatever it is, however this goes down from here on out, I'll be protecting my child."

"And I'll be doing the same," Veronica said. "But forgive me for thinking that this is some kind of threat. How does this play out in your head? That you keep whatever secret you think I have if Diego takes the responsibility for everything?"

"Oh no," Gautam said. "Nothing like that. I'm just sharing information."

"Thank you for sharing that information. You're welcome to share whatever information you think you have. But there's nothing there."

The two of them stood across from each other for a few seconds. Veronica needed to work through this, but she was not going to work through it with Gautam.

Gautam said, smiling, "I'll give it to you, though. You wiped me in that debate. Left behind a pile of ashes."

"I should have probably gone to law school," Veronica said before heading down the hall. "It would have solved a lot of problems."

When Gautam and Veronica entered the classroom, everyone else was already there, including the Berringers who had arrived separately from their son. Gautam gave Gita a slight smile as he sat down next to her, as if he had finally found that one piece of the puzzle that had been eluding them.

The classroom was dappled in the morning light, the sun coming through the trees outside the windows. On Monday, the principal had mostly stood for their meeting. Now she was seated behind the teacher's desk up front. She'd had one of her secretaries arrange it so that there were three clusters of chairs pulled out from the rest, one for each family.

Sitting there, the principal looked like the judge in a small, jury-less bench trial.

"Come on in," Dr. Helen said, waiting for Gautam and Veronica to settle into their seats. "I'll mark you both down for being tardy." She said it as a joke, but her facial expression made it clear that she was all done with jokes. "Veronica, I just met your brother. Welcome to him and thank you all for being here again. Boys, I've taken a few days to speak with a lot of your classmates who were at this party. I want to make clear that I'm tired of this situation we have here. I've just spoken with Stanley and his mother again. They're waiting to hear from the three of you before they decide how they want to move forward and whether the police have to get involved. I have a feeling that your contrition in this matter will go a long way toward helping put all this behind us. So tell me, how are we moving forward?"

Dr. Helen looked at the three families seated in front of her. On Monday, they'd all looked confused and uncertain, slouched back in their chairs. Now the adults were sitting up, their backs straight, ready perhaps to pounce. The boys were still slouching.

As if they had prepared and were now giving a group presentation on "major themes in *The Catcher in the Rye*," each of the boys, with the right amount of humility and regret, explained the first part of the evening, the part they had already told their parents, the part they'd agreed to tell. Their intention was to take turns, but once one started, the others joined in. "We were all going crazy over the win," MJ began. "And then we decided to grab dinner at this Indian place," Diego continued. "And while we were sitting there," Vikram said, "Stanley showed up. We really didn't want him to join, but he did. I have a bad history with him picking on me and I think these two do as well. But not so bad that we'd try to hurt him that much." MJ leaned into the group. "Up at the cave, we tried subduing him. We really did. He was drunk and crazy." And then Diego took the story home: "We made our way back down and like half an hour later, Stanley came down, screaming murder."

The boys had remained seated as they shared all this.

"Why didn't you tell me this on Monday?" the principal finally said, looking impatient. "It could have saved us so much time. While I appreciate hearing it now, as I did when a couple of you came to talk to me, it also doesn't explain how Stanley ended up in the bushes, nearly impaled by cactus, so many that his right hand is now full of tubes to make sure it drains properly."

The three boys looked at one another. Diego and Vikram were the first to look away from MJ.

"You talked to her?" MJ asked the other two under his breath.

Diego and Vikram kept their heads down.

"I agree that the boys needed to have told you this earlier," Gita said. After losing it on the kitchen cabinets, she was now back to beastly management consultant mode. Vacated of feeling about who would be fired, her only job was to protect her client, who in this case was her son. "And I suspect there are all sorts of complicated, unformed-frontal-lobe reasons they didn't. But they're coming clean now. That's important, I think. I can hear the contrition in their voices. And while none of us would ever blame the victim, in this case Stanley is not an innocent bystander. I've had him at our house. I think all the parents have. Something is not right with that boy."

While the parents had certainly not made Gita their spokeswoman, they would have conveyed a similar sentiment if given the chance. They all nodded as Gita spoke. "The boys did something bad, but not that bad, and they've paid the price, and now they should be able to move on."

"I don't know what it is, but I have this feeling that there's still more to this story," the principal said, looking at each of the boys individually. "There is, isn't there? Something more happened that evening. I don't know why I know. But I do. From what I've seen in the signatures on those banners outside, the school knows something more happened. I've done this job long enough to recognize the difference between an empty silence and a pregnant one. These have definitely been very pregnant. This is your last opportunity to say anything you want to say. When I walk out this door, I'm not walking back in. This is your last chance to tell your story in full."

The pigeons outside the window were there again, even louder this time.

"Stanley is highly skilled at getting under people's skin in one way or another," Diego began, his voice low and steady. Since his conversation with Mateo about the nuances of American race relations, he'd been thinking hard about how he wanted all this to play out. He'd decided he was just going to tell Dr. Helen the truth. "In my case, he got more than under my skin. I hinted at this when I came to see you yesterday, but for most of my freshman year, he liked beating on me before the start of class. And not just a slap here and there. Knuckles and full strength. Beat-downs."

"Did you ever tell anyone?" the principal asked.

"Snitch?"

"Report."

Diego shook his head. "Things don't work that way. Kids beat up

on other kids all the time. And mostly, we take care of it among ourselves. On our own. I don't think any of you really know how much
that happens." Diego paused as if he wanted the adults in the room,
particularly the mothers, to reflect on the point he'd just made.
"We're living in a jungle out here, folks, while keeping up with math
and chemistry. And I don't mean *jungle* in a racist way."

The principal gave Diego a slight smile. "You're good. Go on."

No one else in the room could hear it, but Veronica knew that
despite how calm Diego sounded, he was on the verge of tears. She
desperately wanted to reach out and hold him but knew that doing
so would only bring the tears on.

"There are so many things I've learned in all my various classes,"
Vikram said when Diego didn't continue. "How to solve for *x*, how
to write a solid thesis statement, how to take multiple-choice exams.
But I wish I'd been taught some other things early on. Like a periodic table of who to make eye contact with in school and who not to.
Or how to train your body to not need to use the bathroom during
school hours. Or maybe an entire class on active and passive listening. How to not listen to most things people say to you. That would
be a great class to take."

Vikram's leg was shaking as he spoke. Gita noticed this, and because she was his mother, she placed her hand on his thigh, hoping
her touch would bring him some calm.

"Stop!" Vikram said, turning on his mother. He realized that he'd
just snapped at her in front of all these people. "All of you stop. I'm
sick of these meetings. I'm sick of this week. I need all this to stop."

Gita was horrified that Vikram had snapped at her. Gautam
looked at his son and couldn't fight the feeling that this was happening because he'd been a terrible father.

There was a marked silence in the room as each of the adults engaged with what Diego had said and what Vikram was now saying.
Michael and Shirley glanced at each other. After all his silence this
week, they were glad that now MJ just sat there without saying anything. Let the other two talk and trip over themselves. Shirley looked

at Alex and was embarrassed at the way she'd flirted with him at the party. He was, however, quite handsome.

Alex could sense his sister's tension, but in this room, it would have been too weird to place his hand on top of hers. Veronica just sat there, thinking through how Gautam could possibly use her past against her. She was realizing she might have to tell Diego.

"I appreciate what each of you are saying here," the principal said. "I really do. I know how tough these years are, and I recognize the grace with which all three of you have walked through them. The more I've thought about it, the more I realize that this situation is much bigger than who did what." She paused. "And yet we still have an issue in front of us that we need to manage. I'm going to return to Stanley and his mother and explain your version of what happened that evening. It's then up to Stanley how he wants to proceed. If he wants to press assault charges, I won't stand in his way. You'll serve out your suspensions for the rest of the week and then you can come back to school on Monday."

Each of the parents clearly understood what they'd feared all week. In one way or another, small or large, this moment was going to change the lives of the children that they'd worked so hard to protect. And that made all of them very nervous.

"This is ridiculous," Michael said. "The boys have been punished enough, don't you think? A week for a scuffle?"

"No, no, no," Veronica added. She'd remained quiet since her conversation with Gautam. "At the least, let them play in the game tomorrow."

"Are you really asking me this? None of these boys will step on the field for the rest of the season."

"You don't have the power to do that," Michael said.

The principal just looked at Michael.

"Listen, I don't have much power, but I do have this power. In fact, I have the power to do more. I'm showing restraint here." She turned to MJ and held his gaze. He was the only one of the boys who'd not spoken up, and she was beginning to think there was a reason for that. "If you want to challenge me, feel free. Now, I have other things to take care of."

"Please," Vikram said.

"What's that, Vikram?" the principal asked.

"Please, Dr. Helen. We'd like to play tomorrow night. I know it's a lot to ask. I'm not even sure my parents will let me. We messed up. We admitted it. We now just want to play."

"We owe it to our teammates," Diego said.

"If I had some greater clarity about what happened that evening, I would consider it. But things still feel murky."

Gita kept her eyes glued to the blank space in front of her. "I know we keep going back and forth about what these boys could and could not have done. And I hate to do this. I really do. But I spoke with Shirley and Veronica earlier this week in some detail. They both said that their sons were capable of really hurting Stanley. I agreed so that they wouldn't feel strange about admitting it. But in my case I don't believe it. I keep trying to tell you that my son could not have done this."

"Mom," Vikram said, turning again to his mother. "Stop it."

"You're a terrible woman," Veronica said, looking straight at her and then Gautam. "I keep wanting to think otherwise. But all you've cared about since this thing started is saving your son. You don't care about who else gets hurt."

"Please don't talk to my mother that way," Vikram barked.

"I speak respectfully to your mom," Diego said. "So you do the same with mine."

Veronica was about to say something to Vikram.

"Don't say a word to our son," Gautam interjected and then looked to the rest of the room. "This is white-on-white crime. Plain and simple. Whatever else happened up there, our son wasn't involved."

Everyone in the room except Veronica was confused about what Gautam had just blurted.

"Listen, Gautam, you say whatever you want about me here," Veronica said. "I really don't care anymore. I'm an open book. I was just going to apologize to Vikram for raising my voice. I shouldn't have done that. Gita has the right to her opinions, no matter how much I think they are categorically wrong and stupid."

"Gita," the principal interjected before things got too out of hand, "I appreciate this input from you. But interestingly, it isn't that different from the input Veronica gave me on the phone yesterday." The principal looked over at Veronica. "I will not share the details of our conversation because it was private. Or the thoughts I received from Shirley over email. All of you think your boys can do no wrong."

After the farmer's market, and before returning home, Veronica had given the principal a call. Shirley had emailed right after she and MJ had talked about the pills. Both had talked about what good students and citizens their sons had always been.

Diego looked at his mother. "What did you say to her?"

"Nothing very interesting," Veronica said. "If it had been something interesting, we wouldn't be here right now."

The principal looked at her watch, as if to signal that they were running out of time to save their children.

"Before you go, there is one last thing," Gautam said. "I promise. Vikram, can you hand me your phone?"

"Don't do this, Dad," Vikram said.

"Just trust me. Hand me the phone." Gautam paused. "And unlock it."

"Please, no. I'm asking."

Gautam just held his hand out. Vikram was about to hand him the phone but instead tossed it toward him. The phone flew in the air and just as Gautam was about to catch it, it bounced off his hand and landed screen-first on the tiled floor. He leaned down and saw that one large crack had appeared on the screen. Gautam held his face to the screen and the phone unlocked.

"I'm not sure what you're going to show me," the principal said. "But honestly, I've already seen too many videos in my time here, especially too many videos of Stanley screaming in agony at the party. As many students who came to help him, there were even more who instinctively turned on their cameras. I'll look at whatever you want me to see if you think it's vital. But I really need you to take a moment to think about showing it to me. I can't unwatch it, and I wish I could unwatch most of the videos I have seen through the years."

Gautam's only concern at that moment was saving Vikram. He barely heard the substance of what the principal had said.

Gita had told him about the video, and until this moment, he didn't know what to do about its existence. He hadn't actually seen it because he thought he was respecting Vikram by not looking at it. But they'd entered desperate territory, knowing that if they walked out now, all three boys would be held equally responsible for the events. Maybe the video wasn't even there anymore. But he found it, hit play, and held up the phone so that everyone could see.

At first there was just darkness. Then a light came on and one could begin to make out contours of what was happening. Stanley was on the ground, yelling something indecipherable.

"Stay down, bro," Diego could be heard pleading. He was standing near Stanley, who then grabbed hold of his right ankle. Reacting, Diego pulled his leg free and pushed Stanley away with his right foot. "Stop."

Then, as if to to put an end to the back-and-forth, MJ leaned down and landed a swift punch to Stanley's mouth. Diego then stepped in and kicked him in the ribs.

"Fuck," Vikram could be heard saying clearly on the video, as if he was speaking for everyone in that chemistry classroom.

Just like that, the video ended. Ten seconds.

Gautam looked at his son, who seemed like he was going to be ill. He was about to say something, but Gautam just shook his head.

"This doesn't prove anything," Michael said. "Or rather, it proves that Vikram filmed himself some insurance at the right time. And that he's willing to sell out his friends. He's already admitted to participating."

"I'm not the one who showed it to you," Vikram said. "If you want to blame anyone, blame my parents." He then turned to MJ and Diego. "I didn't film it for insurance. I swear. I was holding up the light and I just somehow started filming."

"Somehow?" Diego asked under his breath. "Fuck off. You should have told us you had it."

"I'm sorry," Vikram said.

"You have nothing to apologize for," Gita said. "You did the right thing."

Gautam handed the phone to the principal so that she could see it more clearly. She watched the video again and looked up. "Do you two have videos you want to show me as well?" she asked MJ and Diego.

They both shook their heads.

"Please email that video to me," the principal said to Gautam, handing the phone back to Vikram. "For now, my earlier decision still stands. I don't like what I see, but it doesn't substantively change anything."

"Dr. Helen already knows about this photo and so the rest of you might as well see it," Vikram said, his voice shaky. He pulled up the photo Erin had sent to him and showed it to the group. "If the video makes it look like I had nothing to do with it, this photo makes me look like I'm the one who went up that second time. None of these photos or videos prove anything."

Gita looked at her son in disbelief, partly because she'd not seen the photo when she went through his phone. Vikram looked at MJ and Diego. Yes, they weren't his friends. But he also didn't want to lose them or throw them under the bus.

Dr. Helen stood up from the desk. She was angry at herself for not having figured all this out. Who went up to the cave once? Who went twice? There was just too much confusion.

"Just one more minute of your time," MJ said, finally speaking.

"No more," Dr. Helen said.

"One more. I promise to make it worth your while."

"What do you have to say?"

MJ looked at his mother and then his father. Not to get their permission to speak but to appreciate them for all that they had done for him. They'd been nothing but giving and present—though perhaps a little too giving and present. He felt like he was now done with them.

"It's not a mystery why the three of us really dislike Stanley," MJ began. "We were up there trying to defend ourselves and things got out of hand. We can all agree on that. But as you can see in the video, I'm the only one really hitting him. Diego got in his lick, but he didn't do much more. The three of us went down to the party after. And then like twenty minutes later, I made my way back up there. I felt bad that we had left him alone, and I knew that he had been drinking. I didn't want him passing out and choking on his vomit or something. But when I reentered the cave, the place stank. Like he'd peed on himself or something." MJ paused, as if to gather himself for the rest of the story. "Before I knew what was going on, he lunged at me. But this time, I moved out of the way and something in me just snapped. Like I went into survival mode. I started punching him, harder than I realized. Again and again. By the time I stopped, he was bleeding out of his mouth. I left him there. And then he must have stumbled down the hill and fell in the bushes."

Stanley had first given the principal this exact account of the evening, which the three boys had vehemently denied.

"Vikram and Diego should not get dragged into this," MJ continued. "It's not fair to them. I'm the one who told Vikram that he should come to the party. He wanted to just go home. And Diego? If he doesn't make it in football, he's going to be some kind of math genius. Let them both be. I went back up. By myself."

Gita placed her hand on Vikram's hand and squeezed it, as if to say that he was to remain absolutely silent. Vikram flexed his fingers and Gita's hand fell right off.

"One last thing and then I'm done talking," MJ said. "Stanley offered me some pills last week to increase my focus. And I took one for the game. I shouldn't have, but I did. I just wanted to put that out there as well, in case he brings it up. Dr. Helen, I think you have the rest of my pills from my locker. I don't have any to show."

He didn't look at Diego as he said this.

The principal sat behind the desk and tapped her fingers on the wood.

"You did all that?" the principal asked.

"I did. I'm just sorry it took me this long to admit it. I needed to get some things straight in my head."

MJ looked over at his parents. Shirley's eyes were filled with tears. "I'm really sorry, Mom."

The principal looked right at MJ.

"What are you doing?"

"I'm telling you the truth," MJ said.

The principal didn't say anything. Instead, she let the room marinate in the silence. She looked over at Diego and Vikram, both of whom seemed confused.

"I'm giving up what I have—and what I have is crazy and unearned and unfair—for the sake of others who don't have it." MJ took a few more seconds to line up his words. "I'm making reparations."

Veronica let out the tiniest laugh.

"What did you say?" the principal asked.

"You know, when individuals and society atone . . ."

"I know what *reparations* are," Dr. Helen said, her tone both stern and annoyed.

"I'm taking responsibility for this. End of story. I am begging you not to involve Diego or Vikram anymore. Let them play tomorrow. You can keep me out of school for as long as you wish. You can expel me if you like. You do whatever you need to do to make this right. That video is all the evidence you need. Vikram's dad is right. It's white-on-white crime."

"Sweetheart," Shirley said, "will you please, for the love of god, shut up. I'm not sure what you're doing, but it's not helping anyone."

"Please," Alex said. He knew he had no place to talk at all. But he saw a clear lane for his nephew, and he was intrigued by what MJ was saying. "Let him finish. I want to hear everything he has to say."

Michael turned to Alex. "You keep your mouth shut. I think both of us know that you're a bit too loose-lipped for your own good."

The principal sat there, looking at each of the three families. She sensed that things were headed further south. She checked her watch, stood up, and as she stepped out of the classroom, she said, "I'll be right back." She walked several doors down to her office and brought Stanley and his mother back with her.

Stanley walked into the classroom with his mother alongside him, her hand at his back to keep him stable. His right hand was in a cast; he had bandages on different parts of his arms and legs; he had a black eye that was now a light shade of purple. Every other time the boys had seen him, Stanley had always been up to something. Scheming, talking, mocking. This time, he was quiet and subdued, as if he was still high on painkillers. His mother was dressed simply, in jeans and a cotton cardigan.

There was a uniform look on the faces of the other parents in the room: one that showed they had been blindsided by this little stunt, that the principal should have told them she was going to bring in Stanley and his mother. But mostly, it was the look of deep, unmitigated shame: Their children, the children that they had birthed and raised and played with and loved unconditionally had done this to Stanley. They could go back and forth about who was to blame for what, who went up once to the caves, who went up twice, who had a head start and who didn't, but they would always be left with the fact that their children had given this boy a solid beating.

The principal pulled out chairs for Stanley and his mother. As he began lowering himself onto the chair, he winced in pain. The room was absolutely silent, as if the parents understood that after all the talking, their primary job now was to keep their mouths shut.

"Principal Mitchell invited us to come to this meeting," Stanley's mother began, her eyes not making contact with anyone in the room.

"But I wasn't entirely sure we were going to make it. We've had a couple of scary days in the hospital, but things are getting better. All the cactus needles are finally out of Stanley's body." She paused and now carefully looked at each parent and each boy in turn, to have a clear visual of the people who had caused her son so much pain. "I didn't want to come, but Stanley really did. He said he wanted to talk this out with you. He thinks talking can fix it." She paused, this time looking only at the parents. "I don't. There is no way to fix the pain we've felt."

"What up, all-stars?" Stanley said to the boys, as if to lighten the heavy mood his mother had created.

"Hey, man," MJ said. "That hurt?"

"It all hurts. Cactus is evil. But this is the worst." Stanley held up his cast. "There's tubes and shit in here right now." He looked over at the principal. "Sorry. Tubes and stuff."

The principal gave him a smile.

Vikram glanced over at his parents, confused by all that had occurred that morning. Gautam nodded to him in the way he might have in grade school when Vikram was feeling nervous about the first day: Go on in, sweetheart. I'll be here.

"We've had some things between us, but last Friday got out of hand," Vikram said, his eyes darting from the floor to the ceiling to the trees outside. He wasn't sure if he was going to break down in tears or simply break down, so he wanted to get his words out.

"They really did," Stanley replied. "Honestly, I want to put this all behind me and have a chill last couple of years in high school. I actually blame the night on the Indian food. It must have been juiced up somehow. Because that would explain it, right? Explain how savage you all were with me up there."

The boys looked nervous.

"The okra seeds are lethal," Stanley continued, in control of the mood in the room and yet unsure of how angry he wanted to remain or what he wanted to do with this newfound power over them. "That's why I avoid the stuff."

"I'm really sorry," Vikram said, forcing himself to say the words and look Stanley right in the eye.

"The eggplant did it for me," Diego said. "I've sworn it off." Diego paused and looked straight at Stanley. "Honestly. It won't happen again."

"You shouldn't have ordered the chicken tikka masala," MJ said. "It would have been a very different night if you'd gone with the vindaloo, or, of course, the butter like the rest of us. But whatever chicken you ordered, you didn't deserve all that. Maybe a small bit. But not all of it. And not like that."

"I knew it," Stanley said. "I knew you were all looking at me funny when I ordered that. Like I was some idiot. In the hospital, I've had some time to think, some time to research. Do you know the name Ali Ahmed Aslam? I bet you don't. He was born in Lahore, Pakistan, and moved to Glasgow in the sixties and opened an Indian restaurant. Or should I say Pakistani restaurant? He invented the chicken tikka masala for the poor Scots who thought pepper was too spicy. I know you guys think it's lame. But I have some belly issues. The tomato sauce helps mellow the spice. It's delicious. And for the fucking record, if it wasn't three against one, I could have had a fighting chance."

The principal stood there, neither frowning nor smiling.

"So what now?" Stanley asked, turning to Dr. Helen.

"Well, MJ here says that he's the one that came up by himself the second time and that you lunged at him and he lunged right back."

"That sounds about right," Stanley said. "I can't really remember much from the night. But I think that covers it. You've seen how far QB One here can throw the ball. He's got a really strong arm." Stanley paused.

"This whole thing is a sham," Michael said to the principal. "And you know it."

Stanley turned his eyes down to his feet, addressing no one in particular. "Do any of you know what it's like to be ignored, year after year? I've just wanted a friend. That's it. Someone to hang with."

For all the sarcasm and light derision in everything the boys said day in and day out, Stanley had spoken simply and with heart. Before any of the other boys felt compelled to respond, Stanley turned to the principal and said, "I think we're good."

"I'm going to need a little time to think this through," Dr. Helen said, getting up from her chair. In the intensity of the conversations they'd been having, she didn't hear the sound of the bell that marked the end of second period. "You'll all be hearing from me shortly. In the meantime, Stanley, can you and your mother walk over to my office with me? I'd like to chat with you about a few more things."

"Before we go," Stanley's mother said. She kept her eyes down like her son had a minute before, feeling ashamed. "As you can imagine, this whole period has been difficult for us. For me and my boys. I work hard. And I don't have much left over at the end of the month. My insurance covers some of Stanley's hospital costs, but not all of it. We are really not sure what we are going to do."

"You don't have to worry about that," MJ interjected. "My parents will take care of it. They have plenty of money."

At this point, Michael and Shirley looked nonplussed.

"I think the three sets of parents here will help cover those costs," Shirley said quickly.

"I'll let you all manage that," Dr. Helen said.

The families walked out of the classroom, one by one.

––––––––➤➤➤➤➤––––––––

Four cars left the school parking lot around the same time.

In the old Saab, MJ was unsure of where he was headed. What if he just went south and stopped after reaching Mexico? He could survive on warm tortillas and cold beer.

In the Jaguar, after a week of MJ's silence, Shirley and Michael were now silent until they reached their driveway.

"I wish I could slap all that reparations talk out of his mouth," Michael said. "I've been wanting to get a handle on him sooner, but you insisted that he'd return to some normalcy on his own. You've been way too soft on him and his antics."

"You'll not place this on me," Shirley said. "I need a break. From our son. From you. From everything."

"What does that mean?" Michael asked.

"I'm not entirely sure," Shirley said. "But you'll know. In the meanwhile, I need you to get yourself in order. Pay your debts."

Michael got out of the car and headed into the house. Shirley remained in the car.

In the Tesla, the car was silent, but the passengers weren't. They weren't jubilant, and yet for the first time in a week, Veronica, Diego, and Alex drove with some ease. They stopped for an early sushi lunch and talked about the Raiders and Niners and the upcoming basketball season, and Veronica kept thinking about what Gautam had said to her.

In the Cadillac, Vikram was the first to talk. "Can we never talk about what happened in there again? I just want to have things go back to normal now."

"They will be," Gita said. "I promise."

"If the principal lets us, I'd really like to play in the game tomorrow," Vikram said.

Gita and Gautam looked at each other. "I think you're old enough to make that decision on your own," Gautam said.

Vikram was the first to get out when they reached home. His parents sat in the car for a minute.

"I'm glad this is over," Gita said.

"*This?*" Gautam asked. "Us?"

Gita smiled wearily. The two of them had said some hard things to each other, but she was deeply thankful for the way Gautam had protected their son.

Friday

TWENTY-ONE

On Friday morning, Veronica came out of her bedroom to make coffee and found Diego sitting in the living room, reading.

"You're up early," she said as she went past him into the kitchen.

"I have an English thing due on Monday and I haven't started yet. Any word?"

"Nothing."

The principal had ended the meeting the day before by saying that she would be in touch shortly about her decision on how to proceed. Neither Stanley nor his mother had said anything about pressing criminal charges. She did want the hospital bills paid and maybe something for pain and suffering as well. The parents planned to figure out how to split the bills. And so whatever the principal decided was going to be the end of it.

Veronica made her coffee, then removed eggs from the fridge and cracked several of them in a bowl.

"Who's sending mail to Veronica Matthews?" Diego asked from the other room. He knew it was his mother's birth name and had seen the name *Alex Matthews* written out plenty of times in the letters and postcards his uncle had sent from across the world. But he'd only known his mother as Veronica Cruz and seeing this other name on a mailed letter felt odd and out of place.

The question had a banal tone. Can I get some toilet paper? When will dinner be ready?

Veronica heard the question and took a deep breath. She finished making her coffee, added cream and an extra bit of sugar, and went into the living room. When she'd walked by the first time, she had not noticed that Diego was reading her first book. He was sitting on the comfortable leather couch, looking relaxed and at ease, with the book open in front of him.

"What's the assignment?" Veronica asked, her heart now starting to beat heavily.

"We have to write about some sort of archive about ourselves," Diego said. "The teacher likes clever. So I picked your book to write about. You're a pretty good writer. Who knew?" He pulled out an envelope and held it up. "I found this in here. It has our address."

Perhaps at some level, between her conscious life and her unconscious muck, she'd placed the envelope in that book because Diego was more likely to open it up than any other book on that shelf. He knew how important it was to his mother. If she'd never wanted him to find the letter, or for that matter for anyone to ever find it, she would have placed it in her unmarked copy of *Of Grammatology*.

After Portland and the vague threats from her colleague Jane, she'd heard nothing further. Maybe she was in the clear. Maybe she wasn't. But Diego was owed the story before anyone else heard it. And she owed it to him that he didn't hear it from anyone else. But if she'd feared that she was losing him earlier that week when he'd gone mute, she would certainly lose him now. There had been a certain strange innocence in them sitting on the couch on Sunday afternoons and watching grown, enormous men pounding each other on TV.

"It's me, before I married your dad."

"I know that. But have you changed it back?"

He was asking a simple question about this random envelope with a recent stamp.

"No, I haven't. So, *Matthews* is a Portuguese name, I think. *Mateus* in Portuguese before it was Anglicized. When the Portuguese colonized Brazil, the name traveled. And it eventually traveled to America."

"I'm already getting a history lesson here," Diego said, holding up the book, smiling at his mother. Through the years, he'd gotten plenty of history lessons, over ice cream, on the way to school, driving to away games.

Veronica continued, now taking a seat across from Diego. "When I was your age, I didn't know any of this or think much of my name. In high school, I was a debate nerd and had, like, two close friends and we were obsessed with The Cure."

"So you were basically emo?"

"Something like that," Veronica said. She had another sip of her coffee, placed the mug on the coffee table between them, and took a deep breath, as if she was about to dive underwater. "I only learned of this history—and our family history—much later, when I was in graduate school. My great-grandfather went from Portugal to Brazil and then eventually ended up in California. Knowing that kind of opened the world to me. By that time, I'd met your dad and we went to live together in Texas, where he had this big Mexican family. I felt at home for the first time. I took his name and it all just fit. I felt like I belonged to something for the first time in my life. It was like I'd finally found my right skin, uncovering a heritage that felt most true."

There. She'd said it for the first time aloud. Veronica didn't fully spell everything out. She didn't think she needed to. But she could see Diego doing the calculus in his head.

"Graduate school? But we took those trips together in the summers," Diego said. "You showed me the village and made it seem like you grew up in Rio, like we were born with this strong Brazilian heritage. Not three or four generations removed."

Technically I never actually said that, Veronica wanted to say.

"So we are not Brazilian, we're Portuguese, and barely even that?"

"This doesn't change who you are," Veronica said, even though she could see from his face that it was already changing who he was.

"Of course it does," Diego said. "The Oaxacans like joking that I'm bougie. What's going to happen when they hear that my mother is white? That's what you're telling me, right?"

Maybe she could take another job and they could just start over.

"So you've been lying my whole life?" Diego continued.

"It's complicated." It was complicated because growing up and ambition and race were all complicated. But she knew that these were public and private history lessons that Diego was in no mood to hear. "I didn't lie. But I didn't tell the truth either. I made decisions long ago, never thinking that the ripples would extend this far into our future. I'm really sorry I didn't tell you earlier."

"No, it's not that complicated. You either lie or tell the truth. You've been on me this entire week, making me feel like shit for not telling the truth."

Alex had been standing at the edge of the room. Diego noticed him.

"You've known this?" Diego asked Alex.

He nodded.

"What's the matter with you two?"

Diego returned the book to the bookshelf and went into his room. Veronica and Alex heard the door slam.

"He's going to need some time with this one," Alex said.

Veronica was trying to think of something to say. But she had nothing. She went and sat down on the couch and let herself fully sink in. As quickly as Diego had slammed his door, she heard it open. Diego walked back into the living room and went to the bookshelf without saying anything or looking at anyone. He removed Veronica's book and then said to the room, "This is, in fact, perfect for this assignment." And with that, he returned to his room, this time closing the door carefully.

———≫≫≫———

"I've been getting complaints about the music in here," Dr. Helen said, walking into Coach Smith's classroom before his first class started. "That it's too depressing."

Kind of Blue was coming out of his computer speakers.

"Jazz is not depressing," Coach Smith said. "It's a mood."

"A depressing mood."

"I hear you've had quite the week. You have good news for me?"

"I have good and bad news. You get your running backs back."

"That's very good. But I also need my quarterback. Desperately."

"I've lost quite a bit of sleep this week. On one hand, I don't want any of them to play. And on the other, I need us and the school to move on. I think Diego and Vikram will. Even Stanley will once he heals up. But I'm mostly worried about MJ. He's going off some deep end, but I don't know what end it is. He doesn't want to come back—to school, to the field. Even if he did, he in particular, can't play. I'm sorry. I've talked to a lot of kids about what happened. That cave sucks everything in, and then spits out random pieces of information. I still don't feel like I have a real handle on what happened up there. It's just too dark in those caves to see. But MJ is taking responsibility for it all."

"MJ was in here yesterday. He's just not the kid I've coached these past four years. But still. He's a good kid. They're all good kids. I know Vikram the least, but I almost trust him the most. He has a good head on his shoulders. Just like Diego."

"Hopefully, the kids are going to be fine. It's the parents I can't deal with. I wish they'd just stop clutching their pearls about the lives of these boys. At first, I was wary of the moms. But then the dads got into it at the meeting. Another five minutes and I think I would have been trying to pull them apart." Dr. Helen paused. "I really tried to listen to what all three boys had to say to me. It wasn't just that I couldn't tell truth from lies. Their heads are filled with so many echoes of what their parents think they should be doing, what they think they should be saying, what they hear from their friends, what they see on their phones. So they don't even know what they're really saying or even thinking."

"And I thought my job was hard," the coach said. "Speaking of which, you coming to the game tonight?"

"Are you kidding? I hate football. It's grotesque what you all do out there. But I'm glad you got your runners back. Good luck." Dr. Helen began walking out of the room. "Maybe I'll come out if you make the playoffs."

"We'll make the playoffs if you give us MJ back."

"It's out of my control now," she said with a shrug.

———————

The Atherton was one of the nicest hotels in town and inside was a fancy restaurant, Atherton Eats, which had gained a bit of a reputation as the power lunch spot in town. Gautam was meeting Ryan for a celebratory lunch. Since that initial squawking about Rohan Doshi's politics, Gautam had heard nothing.

Gautam arrived first, driving right up to the front and handing the keys to his now beloved Cadillac to the valet. Just as he got out of his car, Ryan rode up on his very nice mountain bike that he used to go from meeting to meeting around town.

"I'm not usually a drink-at-lunch person," Ryan said when they sat down. "But I think maybe we can make an exception today."

When the waiter brought two glasses of champagne, the two toasted awkwardly.

"Congratulations, Gautam," Ryan said. "I mean really. You may have opened the floodgates. I'm not quite sure how I can thank you."

"Well," Gautam said, smiling, "I can think of some ways."

"Yes, of course. This is a celebratory lunch. But also a bit of a negotiation session. Why don't we order and then we can get down to business?"

Just as they were about to order, Gautam noticed Michael Berringer walking into the restaurant with an older man he assumed was his father. The two of them were walking toward Gautam and Ryan's table to get to their own.

"What are we celebrating?" Michael asked cheerily when he stopped at the table, as if the events of the previous day were already forgotten.

"It's a Friday," Gautam said, remaining vague.

Gautam introduced Ryan.

"Ah," Michael said. "The VirtualUN brain trust. This is Tom Regan, an old friend of my father's and a trusted client of mine. We'll leave you to your lunch, but if I may, the crab cakes here are exceptional." He paused and looked over at Gautam. "They cook them through beautifully."

Gautam smiled. Tom and Michael continued to their seats.

"That dude is a little stiff," Ryan said after they'd passed.

"Our boys have been up to no good together this week," Gautam said. "We've been dealing with the fallout. He's fun when he drinks, though. I think he's a little pissed that I beat him at a party game we played."

"What game?"

"Next time we're really drinking together, I'll show you."

Gautam ordered the crab cakes. Ryan got a Cobb.

"So, let's get to it," Ryan said. "What do you envision for yourself moving forward? Rohan Doshi is going to be a cornerstone for us. The next round of funders will come to us, instead of us having to go to them. I am now, of course, embarrassed that we said that sales may not be your strong suit."

Any complaints Ryan or Bryan had about Modi's politics had suddenly stopped the moment they saw the kind of numbers the Doshi sale would bring in.

"I appreciate you saying that. I've had a few moments myself when I've thought the same. Clearly, there's a director of sales already. I really like Bryan and so this is not meant as a hostile takeover. But I think I should be in that job. Traditionally, the salesmen and programmers have never gotten along. The sales guys think the programmers are nerds, and the programmers think the sales guys shovel bullshit. I think there is truth on both sides. And since I can do both, speak the language of both, I can bring the two parts of this company together."

"I think you're describing my job," Ryan said.

Before, Gautam might have shirked from this moment. This time, he remained in it. He smiled and shrugged. "When we go public and you want to go find yourself by hiking the Himalayas for a year, I could hold down the fort. You can be the visionary, sending us voice memos from Everest base camp."

"It feels like you've thought this out."

"Some of us just take time to find our niche. Maybe I've finally found mine. Here, or, I suppose, somewhere else. I'd rather it be here."

Gautam could barely recognize the person saying all this. But for once in his work life, he had a sliver of power and he wasn't going to part with it easily.

They talked salary figures and the organizational chart for the next ten minutes. Then Gautam got up to use the restroom.

As he passed the table where Michael was seated, he could sense the tension in the conversation. On the way back, he kept his ears open and slightly slowed his walk. He heard the older man say, "You know I'm going to have to take you to court on this."

It sounded like Michael was having a very bad week.

"Do you ski?" Ryan asked when Gautam sat back down.

The food had arrived while he was gone.

"Not if I can help it. It's just too cold."

"Well, my wife and I have a cabin in the mountains. It sleeps six comfortably. You're welcome to use it anytime."

"Can we go up and not ski?"

"I go up and don't ski all the time. And the fact is, I don't go up nearly enough. I always feel guilty that it's sitting there empty. Please use it."

After lunch, Ryan rode back to work and Gautam handed his ticket to the valet.

As he waited for his car, he noticed Michael exiting the hotel as well. The two men nodded at each other. They stood there, about fifteen yards apart, waiting for their cars.

"The crab cakes were delicious," Gautam said.

"See," Michael said, coming closer. "I should have gotten them."

"I'm not quite sure how to describe that meeting yesterday," Gautam said.

"Pure disaster for me. If there's one thing I've learned about my son, I can't make him change his mind once it's made up. Maybe the one thing we learned is that we should have gotten the four boys together in the first place and let them hash this out like they did. Vikram playing tonight?"

"I prefer him not to," Gautam said, "but I think he is. MJ?"

Michael just shook his head, now looking agitated. He resented the fact that his son was taking the fall for Vikram and Diego, even if he'd volunteered. He deserved to be out there. He was the heartbeat of that team. "This whole thing is a mess."

As they were standing there, a very nice Audi sedan eased into the front of the hotel. Gautam had checked out one of these in his car shopping. Its price hovered around ninety thousand.

A teenager in the back seat got out first. He was wearing a T-shirt and shorts that both read Harvard-Westlake. His mother got out of the passenger seat. Attractive, but perhaps more so because of her wealth. Jeans, stylish cowboy boots. It was a Friday afternoon. A man got out of the driver's seat and waited for a valet, all of whom were either brown or Black. He had pulled a hundred out of his wallet and was playing with it, stretching it out, as if it was a trick he had learned in an eighties movie about rich people. Two valets approached. One broke the hundred for him. He handed a twenty to the other, who was about to park his car.

"Keep the change."

The father and son were skinny, tall, with terrible haircuts on the wrong part. The family of three strolled into the hotel.

Gautam looked over at Michael and Michael looked back at him. It was Michael who first shook his head.

"I wish MJ were playing tonight," Gautam said. "The team needs him."

"So do I."

The two of them stood there awkwardly for another minute.

The valet drove up with Gautam's car. He began moving toward it when he noticed that the family that had just gone in was now exiting the main door. The valet who had parked their Audi had just returned. The father noticed him and walked over. "The restaurant is closing. Can we get our car?" He paused and then added, "And can I get that twenty back?"

Gautam heard and saw this and couldn't believe it. The valet had completed his job. He'd parked the car and now he would retrieve it. It wasn't his fault that only two minutes had passed between those two acts. The middle time was not his responsibility. Michael had also heard the exchange.

The man held out his hand. The valet reached into his pocket and handed him the twenty-dollar bill.

Gautam's car was ready and his instinct was to get in and drive away. But he paused. He wanted to hand the valet a twenty himself in front of the man, and his vaguely pretty wife, and the son who was picking up all the signals on how to live in the world from this father. He reached into his wallet and got out two twenties. One for his valet and one for the other.

Just as Gautam took a step forward, Michael did as well.

"What are you doing?"

For a second, Gautam thought Michael was talking to him. But Michael's eyes were on the tall man, who looked over at Michael.

"Yes, I'm talking to you," Michael continued.

Now the whole family, and the two valets, turned toward Michael.

"Why are you asking for your money back? You rolled in here with your nice car. They parked the car for you and now they're bringing it back. You pay for the services they have provided."

"Mind your own business."

"It's my business when someone acts like an asshole."

Now the son looked worried.

"Don't call my dad an asshole."

"I didn't call him an asshole. I said he was acting like one."

"Don't talk to my son," the wife said.

Gautam just stood there, watching all this go down. The valets stood there as well, unsure of what to do with this cockfight.

"Can you get my car, please?" the man said to the valet. "We need to go."

"As long as you give him back the twenty," Michael said. "Then you can go."

"You're going to make me?" the man asked.

"I'm not. Not here in front of your wife and son. We'll look like fools. But what I am going to do is give this man the money he deserves."

Michael reached into his pocket.

"No," the man said. He shoved the twenty he had taken back in front of the valet. "Take it." The valet took it.

Michael and the tall man were now directly facing each other. The thing was done. The money had been returned to the rightful owner. Everyone needed to back away. But starting something was easy enough. Ending it was far more difficult.

It was hard to tell who leaned in first, who didn't back away, but suddenly there, in front of the hotel, as people waited for their cars,

Michael and the tall man were tangled up together, each throwing punches that never landed anywhere they could actually hurt. One landed on a shoulder, another barely grazed a cheek, both fighters sounding like they were in the eighth round of a ten-round fight. Two men in their fifties, flailing their arms and legs, panting and out of breath.

"Sir." One of the valets jumped in and pulled the Audi man back.

"Let me go," he yelled and went back at Michael.

As he was moving forward, Michael swung his right hand and just before he made contact with the man's jaw, his fist came undone and he half-slapped, half-punched the man, who, on contact, snapped his head back. This seemed to put an end to it.

His lip had started bleeding. "Everyone saw that," he said.

"You started it, I just finished it," Michael said, repeating a version of a phrase he had last used in the seventh grade.

And just when it seemed like it was over, the two of them started pulling and pushing at each other again. In the first round, the two men had remained mostly defensive, as if they were doing this on purpose to get a sense of the tendencies of their opponent, but this time they swung wildly. It was as if both had been waiting their whole lives for this moment. To swing away. And they did. This time, the punches landed. Hard. Over and over. It looked like a video game—*Punch-Out* with one skinny man and another one with a slight belly. Back and forth.

The two had crossed into an invisible bubble that could only be broken when they were done, when they had spent themselves. With every punch that landed, the sound of the thud made Gautam and the man's wife and son and the other guests and the valets feel ill, as if they might throw up.

Finally, with both men exhausted, the other guy grabbed hold of Michael's shirt and started pulling at it, as if to keep himself upright.

"Let go," Michael said.

"You let go first."

The two men finally separated and as Michael staggered back, his opponent ripped his shirt before letting go.

Gautam had been standing there and quickly moved forward, helping to steady Michael.

"Are you OK?" Gautam asked.

The two men looked at each other, knowing that the week that had passed was now not the only thing they shared. Gautam respected Michael for having done the right thing.

"I'm fine," Michael said, standing there with his shirt torn open. He didn't try to cover himself up. He didn't look embarrassed. Gautam noticed a tattoo on Michael's upper right arm that he would have never guessed was there. He quickly read the lines, vaguely recognizing them, and then mouthed the first line to himself.

Gautam glanced at the tall man and then saw that his wife had a look on her face that he couldn't quite decipher. The son was standing several feet away from his father.

"What can I do?" Gautam asked Michael. "Call the police? Drive you home?"

"Nothing," Michael said matter-of-factly, as if he did this kind of thing often. "I'm good. You go. I'll figure this out."

"You're not good," the other man said to Michael. "You're going to jail for this."

"Shut up," Michael said dismissively. "We both started this."

Gautam got into his car and drove away, finding himself both disturbed by the moment and amused by the sight of two finely dressed middle-aged men clawing at each other. And as he drove, he understood the look on the wife's face: *sharam;* shame.

When he arrived back at his office, he sat in the car and Googled the words he had said to himself. He found the whole line, reading it once and then twice and thrice.

The world is what it is;
men who are nothing,

who allow themselves
to become nothing,
have no place in it.

For the first time in his adult life, Gautam felt like he was something.

※※※※

During a difficult week filled with dwindling options, Coach Smith
had devised a basic game plan. The JV quarterback could manage to
hand off the football but nothing more. The problem was that his
two main running backs were not going to be on the field. Since the
quarterback had no one to hand the ball off to, the coach had no real
offensive game plan. He had then turned his attention to his defense
so that, at the very least, they wouldn't be humiliated on their home
field. Once he learned that he would be getting two of his missing
three players back, he devised a whole new plan.

Through their scouting, the opposing team would be expecting
MJ at quarterback and Diego carrying the ball. Vikram had not
played enough for word to have spread about his skill set. Knowing
that their opponents had an equally beastly defense and an anemic
offense, the coach's new plan leaned on the surprise and confusion of
a wildcat offense. Diego would play quarterback and spend most of
his time running with the ball, handing it off to Vikram, or throwing
very short passes; they would do this for the better part of three and
a half quarters, exhausting their opponents with short, quick runs,
and when their opponents were gassed, they'd keep attacking; the
defense would need to keep the score close.

It was a game plan that Diego would have been thrilled with
most of the time, except for this evening, when the promised running backs coach did indeed show up, standing on the sideline in a
Cal hat that looked roughly twenty years old.

"Don't worry," the coach assured Diego as he ran him through the changes in the pregame meeting. "He'll see you doing plenty of running. He's not here to see you play a position. He's here to see you on the field. He wants to see how you move and watch you make decisions. That's all you need to concentrate on: the decisions."

The home side of the stadium was fully packed, with excited students and adults squeezed in tightly. The visitor section was sparsely occupied.

When the game started, the air had a late November chill. Vikram and Diego stood on the sideline as they neared kickoff, blowing warm air into their cupped hands.

"We good?" Vikram asked through his helmet. "I promise I wasn't filming to get anyone in trouble."

"We're good," Diego said immediately. "It's all past."

None of it was past: the fact that Vikram had filmed them; the realization that the Cal coach was going to see Vikram get touch after touch; the revised history his mother had presented to him that morning.

"You and me are going to smash through these fat dudes," Vikram said, knowing it was silly bravado and knowing that silly bravado was the only thing that was going to help them withstand roughly a thousand pounds of a defensive line.

"Run and block," Diego said. "Run and block. That's all we do. I'm not even going to throw this shit. You run, I run, we win."

They stood there as a little guy on the opposing team caught the football and weaved and bounced and jumped and ran himself through the secondary and scored immediately. Fifteen seconds into the game and they were down 7–0. The stadium was silent.

Vikram and Diego looked at each other without saying anything, the bravado leaking out of them.

In the bleachers, Veronica asked, "Do you see him?"

"It's the dude in the Cal hat," Alex said.

"You'd think he'd be a little less conspicuous."

"I bet he enjoys the power he has over all these boys."

With the week they'd had, Veronica was in no mood to be at the game. But there she was, hoping somehow that Diego's return to the field meant a partial return to what they'd been. He'd not said a word to her since their conversation that morning.

For their first offensive play, the coach drew up options. Diego could go down the field with a pass. If no one was clearly open, he could run with it. And if there were no holes for him, he could dump it off to Vikram. Three workable options. Diego just needed to decide which was best. Because he wanted to show his coach that him passing the ball was a terrible game plan, he stood in the pocket after the snap, half-closed his eyes, and threw the ball down the field, high up into the sky. When he opened his eyes, he saw the ball sailing through the lights, and as it came down, the wide receiver caught it in full stride and was immediately pushed out of bounds. A forty-yard gain. The part of the stadium that had gone mute after the kick-off return was now full of stomping feet on the bleachers. Holy fuck, Diego thought. This is why being quarterback was such a sweet deal. You don't get hit and you get all the love.

For the very next play, this time feeling more confident and wanting more love, Diego set up to throw again, but just as he readied himself, a large man hit him square in the chest. As promised and feared, the defensive line.

After that first major gain, they had trouble getting a first down on that possession and the next three.

"You have no opinions about this position change?" Alex asked.

"I have too many opinions, especially on this night. But I'm trying to be Zen. And you asking me about it is messing with my Zen."

Alex smiled. "I'm liking this new Veronica."

"I'm not."

In an early huddle, Diego made it clear to the rest of the team, without actually saying it, that if they were to have any chance of winning, they'd all need to help Vikram and Diego advance the ball. In other words, Diego and Vikram would talk and the rest of them would listen and block. With each successive huddle, the two talked, as if they were trying to solve a particularly complicated math problem, attempting to figure out the defensive system and find holes and determine the weakest defensive links. Early on, they had been getting three or four yards per carry if they were lucky, and they were now slowly climbing to five and ten yards, with Vikram finally breaking out for fifteen on one, setting them up for a field goal as the first half came to an end. 7–3.

As he ran back into the locker room, Diego tried not to pay too much attention to the fact that the coach was calling play after play for Vikram to run with the ball.

Gita and Gautam were sitting in the stands. "This is getting a little boring," she said, only half joking. They were ignoring all that had been brewing between them. Gautam was certainly rooting for his son and the team to win, but he was going to be just as satisfied if they lost and brought this little football experiment to a quick close. Since lunch, he'd not been able to get the incident with Michael out of his mind.

"I know what you're thinking," Coach Smith said to Diego in the locker room at the half. "But for now, can you please continue to throw short passes or hand off to Vikram? You need to be patient. We need to be patient. And you have to trust me on this."

MJ arrived at the game just as the team ran back onto the field for the second half. He found the seat farthest away from the field, in the opposing team's section. He didn't want to play in the last game but he didn't want to miss it. Most of all, he wanted some peace and quiet to enjoy what was probably the last time he'd be in this stadium as a student.

He had played JV his freshman year and got the starting job for varsity halfway through his sophomore season. He had spent more actual hours in the stadium—playing, practicing, running—than he had in any one classroom at the school. The stadium itself was unremarkable. But it was a simplicity that he had come to love. And one that he would miss.

He was happy to see the score so close. He knew Diego could do this. When the second half opened with a pair of completions from

Diego, MJ had to wonder whether the wide receivers had suddenly gained sticky hands now that Diego was throwing. Maybe they didn't like MJ after all. If that was the case, he was fine with it. But when Diego threw two more times, his easily catchable balls were dropped and the team returned to a running game.

It took Coach Smith three full quarters to feel confident and assured that the game plan he'd mapped out was the right one. The opponents were indeed remarkable defenders, but they did not have a very strong offense. Despite scoring that early touchdown, their offense had gone completely inert. If Diego and Vikram could get the ball into the end zone just once, it might be enough to win the game. Coach Smith had been calling offensive plays that allowed the opposing coach to figure out something himself: Vikram, this new weapon of theirs, was the Wildcats' only real option on offense, and if they shut him down, they could shut the whole team down.

When the fourth quarter hit the halfway point, the home team had possession and was hovering around their opponents' thirty-yard line, the closest they'd gotten to the opposing end zone all game. Sensing that this was the moment to strike, Coach Smith drew up a play during a time-out and quickly explained it to Diego, who took it gleefully into the huddle.

"It's the okey-doke, motherfuckers," Diego began, and quickly reminded his teammates of the play they'd often practiced.

Vikram would stand to Diego's right, and when the ball was snapped, Vikram would run about ten yards forward and then make a hard cut to the left and into the middle. The defense would be expecting the throw to go to him and in that moment, they would all move his way. Over the course of the game, Vikram had rightfully earned their attention and respect. Diego would pretend to throw to him and, in the same motion, move to his right, run down the right side of the field, and, if he was speedy enough, rush into the end zone.

They'd never used the play in a game because MJ was simply not fast enough to outrun the defense once they realized that they'd been duped. But Diego loved this play for himself. After taking so many hits through the game on runs that went nowhere, he'd finally be able to show off how well he could run with the football when it really mattered.

"Don't wait too long to make the hard cut," Diego said to Vikram as he readied to break the huddle. "I need these dumbasses to run to you. Make it all look real."

"This is all you," Vikram said with encouragement. "Just run like you're trying to make it over that border."

Diego smiled through his helmet. "Solid work, Apu. Now make the fucking cut."

From his seat high in the stands, MJ sensed this play was coming from the way everyone had lined up. It was perfect. There was poetry in the fact that Diego would score the winning touchdown for them, this time from a completely different position. He wanted this for Diego, but he suddenly wanted it for himself, too. What was he doing up there, on the wrong side of the stadium?

The center snapped the ball to Diego, and MJ watched as Vikram ran straight ahead and then made a beautiful, graceful cut to the middle. His strides were long and majestic. The two safeties thought that the ball was going to Vikram and began moving toward him. With Vikram demanding all their defensive attention, MJ could see the slipstream Diego had into the end zone.

Diego pulled his arm back, but as it sprang forward, the ball came out of his hand, a perfect, screaming spiral heading straight to the numbers on Vikram's jersey. Gita and Gautam were watching; Veronica and Alex were watching; the entire stadium was watching.

Vikram caught the ball and before he could take a step or protect himself, the first safety hit him. It looked like Vikram had withstood the hit. But then a second, more vicious blow arrived. Vikram's head snapped forward and then back. When he hit the ground, his head bounced up and down on the artificial grass, once and then again.

From his vantage point, Diego saw the moment play out and immediately, as if he had been the one who got hit, his head began to pound. He ran toward Vikram as the referees' whistles screamed into the night air.

During the entire time it took for Gautam and Gita to leap out of their seats, rush down the bleacher stairs, and make it onto the field, Vikram did not move. He just lay there, watching the bright stars beyond the stadium lights.

Part III

FAMILY TIME

TWENTY-TWO

Veronica was on the dry 405, stuck in a hellhole of a traffic jam. She was out of range for the public radio station she'd been listening to and, as she tried to find a different one, Joni Mitchell slinked out of her nice speakers. She'd had phases when she'd listened to *Blue* again and again. But at some point Mitchell's voice began to get on her nerves, and she couldn't understand how she had allowed Mitchell to give voice to her own longing. *Court and Spark* had done nothing for her, and yet, that morning, when the first chords of "Free Man in Paris" started, she let it play. It was a cheese puff of a song, really. But with traffic stopped and Veronica not having to maneuver through cars on an L.A. freeway, she listened to the song. Carefully. By the end she was, despite herself, sobbing—for the way, in a matter of one month since the three boys had entered that cave, her life had changed so that the certainty and predictability she had worked so hard to create as her cornerstones were quickly crumbling; for the way Diego had now actually gone silent on her and that he felt that she'd lied to him all these years; for the sliver of unfettered freedom she felt. The tears lasted well past the end of the song, until she passed the cause of the backup—two ambulances, firetrucks, police cars, and at the center of them all, a small Honda Civic that looked like it had been split exactly in half. The scene jolted her away from her Joni Mitchell–induced self-pity.

A young, intrepid journalist from *The Chronicle of Higher Education* had been tipped off about Veronica's talk at the college outside of Portland, and as she dug into it, she'd found the much bigger, much more interesting story of the two Veronicas. She'd tracked down a couple of people who'd been graduate students with Veronica Cruz at UT. But she'd found it difficult to find anyone who remembered Veronica Matthews at Brown, even though there were student records of her. She spoke with Veronica's colleagues throughout her field. The historian who'd written the rave in *The New York Review of Books* said, in essence, that she could only comment on the work, and the work in her estimation was undiminished. The prominent, damning pull quote had come from Veronica's junior colleague Jane Marcus—she of the rock-climbing skills and the absurdly handsome boyfriend: "I feel, *we* feel, betrayed by Professor Cruz. People will certainly talk about the greatness of the books she has written. But what do we do if the very heart, the very moral authority of these books about slaves and their descendants is based on a lie?"

Veronica was now pretty sure that Jane was the one who'd uncovered her secret some time ago and that she'd been sitting on it, waiting to use it. The letters in the mail were just for the sheer sport. After hearing of Veronica's run-in with the student in Portland and then meeting her at the farmer's market with Alex, Jane had seen her opening and tipped off the reporter. And for what? Because Veronica hadn't given her the time and attention she felt she deserved?

When the story had finally come out, with the headline "Award-Winning 'Latina' Historian Tests Limits of Racial Performance," the breadth of the research the journalist had done was impressive. Veronica had gone back and forth in her mind, but in the end, had decided not to sit down for an interview. Maybe she would write about this herself at some point.

The piece had, of course, caused quite a bit of chatter among her colleagues and in the discipline at large, on and off history forums. Veronica's local paper had done a short follow-up article. The reporter had spoken with people around town about her, asking whether they knew that she was living a "double life." The most prominent quote in the piece was from a vendor Veronica liked to frequent at the farmer's market. "I don't know about all this, but I will say she has impeccable taste in vegetables. She loves the leeks." Veronica had been nervous that the *Chronicle* story would go viral, but days had passed and nothing had happened. She was relieved, but then also strangely a bit disappointed that she wasn't worthy of a bigger controversy.

After she passed the accident, the road to campus was smooth. For years, she'd been figuring out ways to stay away for longer and longer periods so that she could write her books. The more she'd stayed away, the more she'd been promoted. But now that her place on campus was perhaps in question, everything and everyone looked beautiful and sun-kissed as she walked from her car to a café near the engineering school. She was meeting Mary Stone, her department chair, and here they wouldn't see anyone they knew and could talk, they hoped, without being interrupted.

"Nice to see you," Mary said when Veronica arrived. Per her namesake, her face didn't betray whatever she now felt about Veronica. But she stood up and gave Veronica a hearty hug. "How are you?"

Mary was a historian of Han China and a generation older than Veronica. Over the years, they had not been on the friendliest of terms. But they had always respected each other. Mary was part of the first generation of women who had entered the academy in relatively large numbers. Veronica had followed in the generation after. In the time since Veronica's news had broken, it was the younger wing of the department that had been most vocal in voicing their displeasure and disappointment with Veronica. No voice was louder than Jane's.

"Considering that most of our younger colleagues think I'm a fraud, I'm doing pretty well," Veronica said. "How are you?"

"I'm almost done with being the chair. And for the past couple of months, I've been quietly congratulating myself on getting through nearly five years without any major controversy. This is now, of course, my fault. I introduced that idea to the universe."

"I'm sorry to make your life difficult." Veronica paused. "That didn't come out the way I wanted it to. Genuinely, I'm sorry. And I know that I haven't always been the easiest person to deal with over those five years."

"You've been great," Mary said. "You were simply asking for the things you richly deserved."

Mary had found a seat at one of the outside tables. She already had her coffee.

"Why don't you grab yourself something and then we can talk?" Mary said.

"Can I get you anything else?"

"I'm fine."

Veronica returned several minutes later with a cappuccino.

"When is our dear colleague arriving?"

Mary looked at her watch. "We have plenty of time to talk properly. Thank you for agreeing to meet with her. You certainly didn't have to."

"Oh, no. I'd really like to chat with Jane. It will be good for all of us. I've been having a lot of clear-the-air conversations lately. They are strangely cathartic—and have the potential for positive chaos."

She'd put the change from her coffee in the tip jar but had kept a quarter, which she placed on the table. Having a quarter handy had become a strange kind of security blanket for her, reminding her that in its entirety, the world was absurd.

"I know it's a long way for a cup of coffee, but I really wanted to hear your side of the story," Mary said. "In real time."

"Where do you want me to start?"

"Wherever you like. But before you do, can I ask a question?"

As a historian, Mary's fame rested on a certain avant-garde approach to archives. Yet there was something old-school about her unwillingness to keep up with changing trends in how academics spoke. Old-school and kind of charming. Veronica braced herself for the question that was coming.

"Of course. Whatever you like."

"So you're . . ." she began, but then stumbled over her words. "Never mind. Can you start where you want to start?"

"From the beginning?" Veronica asked.

She felt an affection for Mary in that moment; she herself was entering a phase when the everyday meaning of things was becoming more and more confusing.

"That would be helpful."

"My great-grandfather was Portuguese, a laborer who worked the sugar cane fields in Hawaii, where he had come via Brazil. He eventually married a white American woman and they moved to California, where they had kids and settled down. My father was their oldest grandchild. My mother's side of the family is from the Central Valley. Farmers from Hanford. My mother is blond and blue-eyed and pretty clearly what you would call white American. I got my father's olive genes and my brother inherited my mother's blond ones. As you know, I was an undergraduate at Berkeley. I did a double degree in History and Rhetoric but took plenty of classes elsewhere. I was very impressionable and a lot of impressions were made. I just knew that I wanted to be a historian, even though it was not the kind of thing my family did. Because I was so good in high school debate, my parents hoped I would become a lawyer and help support them. Neither of them went to college. When I first arrived at Brown, I had a terrible time. It was partly to do with me, partly to do with the school. At that point, I didn't know anything about my father's family history. He'd never talked about it."

Veronica took a breath and a sip of her cappuccino. "To answer your initial question, I arrived as your basic, well-read young white female graduate student, wanting to study the early suffragettes.

After a year, I left the program. I'd met my ex-husband and we got married. It was only when I told my father that we were going to Rio for our honeymoon that he told me the story of his grandfather. Before we went to Brazil, I did a little research and found the place where he may have lived. And suddenly a book idea was born, about voluntary and involuntary migrations to Brazil. When I reapplied to graduate school, this time with my married name—Veronica Cruz— and with this new project, things were suddenly much better for me. I didn't lie about my name on the applications. It was my new legal name. My transcripts, my letters of rec, all had my old name. I wasn't pretending to be someone I wasn't. But when I arrived, my cohort assumed I was Latina. The faculty I took classes with all seemed ex- cited to work with me. It was a brand-new feeling and I really liked it. And so it just stuck. It wasn't that I was introducing myself in a particular way. It was just that people made their assumptions, and I didn't correct them. I became Brazilian, Chicana, Latina, whatever they thought I was. And then, eventually, my books started coming out. My Portuguese is impeccable, as is my Spanish. That can take you a long way. But let me be clear: I did all that work myself. I was the one who spent the time in the archives. I was the one who wrote each of these books. And I know that I haven't been the friendliest presence in the department, but I have only asked for the things I deserved. You, of all people, know what I mean."

Mary just nodded. Veronica continued.

"I didn't set out to lie"—she placed air quotes around the word *lie*–"but I knew that, even back then, there was no way I was going to be able to really do the work and the research I wanted to do if people knew that I was white and grew up in the Bay Area. It was weird. I changed my name and people just treated me differently. I was the same person who worked very, very hard. Things just felt dif- ferent. Nobody ever asked me anything about it. You don't do a DNA test when you get a job. You know the rest. My books, as I said, are good. But I know no one is going to read them again. Trust me, I understand the moment we're in, and I understand why people might be angry. But something isn't right. I think I worked harder on those books precisely with this possibility in the back of my mind. I knew at some point things would probably come to light."

"They're good. Slave Z is as memorable a character as I have read in a novel."

"I worked hard on Z," Veronica said, sounding wistful.

"I know you did. We certainly can't take that away from you."

"What *can* you take away from me?"

"That's where things get a little more complicated. The soon-to-be retirees in the department are thrilled to finally get back at you. The young folks feel betrayed by you. Ultimately, it's the young ones I'm worried about. There are a lot more of them. As far as I can tell, your job is technically safe. For now. I don't think there is any legal standing for the university to mess with you, but I really don't know the law. I'll be honest. I'm not sure what your way forward here is going to look like. Are any of your colleagues here and across the field interested in talking to you? I doubt it. And I'm not sure what classes will be like. I'm glad you're not teaching this term. You can hope all this will blow over soon enough and the students will have moved on to some other controversy. But every time you question a student on academic integrity, all they have to do is Google you."

On the drive to campus, Veronica had assumed that after a big mea culpa, they could all move forward. Obviously it wasn't going to be that easy. Could she negotiate some kind of early retirement?

"I won't mind if the students do get upset," Veronica said, feeling defiant. "We could talk about it. What's worse than their indifference? But please make it clear to my colleagues that I'm not going anywhere. I'm taking a little break from campus, but I'll be back next fall, ready to go."

"Is it fair to say that you misrepresented yourself all these years?"

Veronica took a breath. There was a technical way of answering this question.

"Maybe I did. But a slight misrepresentation is not a crime. And I never actually lied. At the same time, however, I have the family history that I have. I didn't make that up. My great-grandfather did come from Brazil. But, sure, I let assumptions be made. I'm taking responsibility. But others have responsibility to take as well. My dissertation committee at Texas? Fawning all over me because they thought I was this Latina woman made good." Veronica paused and took a long sip of her coffee, trying to locate herself all those years ago. "I was young and ambitious and sensing that the marriage I'd rushed into was coming to a quick close. Being Veronica Cruz meant success. It meant I could properly support myself and this young child I had. Being Veronica Matthews meant being ignored. I made the logical choice. The only choice."

Mary continued to listen, taking it all in.

"Should I think about getting a lawyer?"

"That's up to you. But if you want one, I have a name for you."

Mary went into her purse and came out with a pen. She took one of the clean napkins on the table and wrote a name on it and pushed the napkin over to Veronica. She was about to ask Mary to email it to her, but she appreciated the quaintness of the name on a napkin.

"You know I've suspected something for a while," Mary said. "For a few years, in fact. I'm a pretty good archivist."

Had she sent the letters?

"Really? How did you find out?"

"An old friend of mine started graduate school at Brown around the same time as you, back when you went by your birth name. She left the academy years ago. She was at my house and noticed your book and we got to talking. She told me she knew a Veronica in graduate school but then lost touch with her. I started digging around after that."

Veronica wanted to ask the woman's name, but there were other pressing issues.

"I have questions," Veronica said.

"I'm sure you do."

"How long have you had suspicions?"

"Since your second book came out."

"Why didn't you say anything?"

"It wasn't my place. I'm not going to get in the way of the work you've been doing. I think what you did was wrong. Your committee and their desire to make good on their gooey, liberal ideas were in the wrong, too. But you ultimately made the decision not to clarify things. With that said, I still think your work deserves all the praise it's gotten."

Veronica's mouth was suddenly dry. There had been some part of her that thought Mary was going to support her unconditionally.

Just then, Jane showed up.

"I hope I'm not early," she said.

When she'd seen her at the farmer's market, Jane had looked very sporty in her Patagonia. But Veronica didn't know what she was like on campus. There was a chill in the air, and Jane was wearing a wool blazer, a crisp white shirt, and very expensive-looking sunglasses. Lady Di out for a Sunday ride if she'd gotten a PhD in French history. She sat down and took off her glasses. There was a light in her eyes.

"How was your climb?" Veronica asked.

At this, Jane seemed to get flustered. Veronica, right out of the gate, was laying bare exactly what was going on between them.

"You know, the rock-climbing."

"Ah, spectacular," Jane said, regaining her confidence. "How were the mushrooms?"

"I could take them or leave them. Not a big fan."

"Do you want to grab something?" Mary asked Jane, sensing the window of small talk quickly closing.

Jane tapped at a recyclable cup she held in her hand and took a seat. "I'm good."

"Then maybe we can get started," Mary said. "It seems that at my age, I've become a bit of the Nancy Pelosi of the history department, getting legislation through, whipping up votes. I'm trying to stay neutral, but I certainly have a vote and lots of thoughts. Let me give you a sense of where we're at and the impasse we've reached. I just had a very productive conversation with Veronica, where she explained her history to me. And I think it would benefit us all if she were to perhaps write down what she said to me in a letter to the department. I really hate to use this phrase, but it's a bit of a teaching moment for us. There is one faction of the department that I suspect would be happy to read this letter, think about it, and return to the business of teaching and writing. I fall into this category. Whatever punishment we wish to levy against Veronica is nothing compared to the punishment she's going to receive from historians in the field. But there is another contingent that feels that ideally Veronica should resign from her post and if not, face some serious questions from the department."

"Let me stop you there," Jane said. "Our concerns are a bit more nuanced."

"I think I know your concerns," Veronica said. "I read about them in the *Chronicle*."

"I don't think you do," Jane said, now using a tone that she used for her male undergraduate students who thought they could take a shot at her during lecture. "By pretending to be someone you're not, you have used your privileges unjustly. You've used them to harm communities that cannot speak for themselves. You took on their voice when you had no right. And you've used them for monetary gain, which, considering that our salaries are public information, I know has been quite substantial. This requires a real reckoning. Not just a letter to the department."

"Just so that we are clear here, Jane. In terms of this conversation around privileges: I helped hire you. I read your file in detail. I remember you saying during the interview that you were very excited, after having been in private institutions for your entire life, to finally give back at a public institution. So let's get that straight. As my son might say, you're one privileged white girl."

"And it turns out," Jane said without skipping a beat, "so are you."

Mary looked between the two women.

"You don't actually know anything about me at all," Veronica said. "About where I've been and what I've done to get here. I hardly think your experience at Spence or Choate or wherever you went is anything like my public high school. I thought I wanted to have this conversation to clear the air, but it turns out the air is just rancid. I appreciate all the moral outrage. But that's not what this is about. It's about you wanting to climb your way up. I get it. Mary did it; I did it. But we did it by writing important books. We didn't do it this way. We didn't do it by sending creepy letters in the mail."

"What creepy letters?" Jane asked, looking confused.

"The innocent bit is boring. You know exactly what I mean."

"I do not."

"You pointed the *Chronicle* reporter toward me, and you sent letters with my birth name on them to my home address."

"I have no problem admitting that I pointed the reporter toward you. It was because of your run-in with the student in Portland. I thought that moment deserved some proper attention. You attacked a kid. But then the reporter did her own work and found all this other stuff. But do not accuse me of something I didn't do with these letters. I've no idea what you're talking about."

After feeling wavering confidence in her conversation with Mary, Veronica again found the ground beneath her soften so that she had no proper footing. She could engage in these conversations and get into arguments as long as she knew she could get back in her car and return to her house and cook a meal for her son. But Diego had been spending less and less time at home.

"Mary, I'm leaving. You all decide what you want to do. But I'm not going anywhere when it comes to my job. I have tenure. And I'm not going up in front of this tribunal Jane wants. Fuck that."

"You don't get to just walk away from this," Jane said.

Veronica really didn't condone violence of any sort, but in that moment, she felt just a slight desire to slap Jane and felt a little closer to what might have been going on in Diego's head in that cave with Stanley.

"I'm not walking away. I'm leaving before I say or do something stupid."

"I think you better sit," Jane said. "Your job is more precarious than you think it is. There are provisions in the bylaws that allow the university to fire you for not being forthcoming about important details. They can fire you for saying you have a degree when you don't. At the very least, I have the support of most of the department to censure you. And that's just the start."

"Am I getting fired?" Veronica asked Mary.

"There's a distinct movement for it."

Veronica took another sip of her coffee and toyed with the quarter in her hand. Mary had left this information out of their earlier conversation.

"What do you want, Jane?"

"We want you to apologize to the department and to the university. And we want you to apologize to the community of historians for writing books based on a lie. The books should be pulped."

She could manage the apologies to the department and the university. But the books? They were hers, and saying that they were based on a lie was saying that she was based on a lie. That she was a lie.

"Who's this *we*? I think it's what *you* want. And I can't figure out why."

"Because I can," Jane said.

Veronica appreciated the clarity of the response. It was a knife fight and her knife, at the moment, was dull.

"You do whatever you want."

Veronica stood up and walked away. She felt exhausted. She had been in a cycle for as long as she could remember. She did not want to be discovered, and because she did not want to think about being discovered, she had worked harder and harder. She never took time off. With every book she finished, she felt panic that she wasn't far enough along on the next. The sense of calm she hoped to find with each big publication never seemed to arrive. She had believed that if she worked hard and produced good, important work, that if the truth came out, they would forgive her. They would say, Fine. Your work stands. And her work had stood. It had stood its ground and then some. It was one of the reasons that she didn't really have any friends among her colleagues. Her books won awards. Big ones. Again and again. And that meant she got job offers. And that meant her salary kept rising. Some of her colleagues assumed that it was her last name that had won her the prizes; others assumed that she won the prizes despite it.

Somehow there was barely any Friday afternoon traffic as she made her way home. She actually wouldn't have minded it; a little more time in the world before she returned to an empty house. But when she returned home, Diego was there.

"Something up at school?" Veronica asked.

"We had early dismissal."

A couple of weeks earlier, soon after Diego and Veronica had had their big conversation, Diego had gotten in touch with his father, wondering if he could visit him in Texas. With the football season over, he had more time. He'd left on a Friday morning and returned that Sunday. Veronica was ready with her reasoning on why it was a bad idea for him to move to Texas at this point, assuming he was going to bring it up. But he hadn't. Rather, he was in good spirits, and the trip, more than anything else, had created an opening to a new normalcy between them. She was insistent in her belief that she'd not kept father and son apart all this time, even though she knew she had.

After staying for weeks, Alex had finally packed up and returned to the Bay Area.

"How was work?" Diego asked.

For these past weeks, Diego hadn't been hostile to his mother, but they'd not had any kind of talk either. He'd been busy reestablishing himself in his classes. Not everyone at school had read the *Chronicle* article or the follow-up article in the local paper. But enough people had. Diego found himself spending even more time than he had with the Oaxacans, who did not say a single negative thing about the woman they'd affectionately called Mrs. Cruz for years.

Great, Veronica was about to say. It had been her tendency through the years to shield her son from the ups and downs of her work life. But instead she said, "It was fine. Not the best."

"Can they fire you?"

"They can't. At least, I don't think so. But they can make my life miserable, and I'm not sure I want to let them do that to me." She'd been thinking through her options on her drive home and she already knew that she would likely quit before they could fire her. She still didn't want to quit. She would be leaving a lifetime of security— and tidy monthly checks—on the table.

"Fuck them," Diego said.

It had been her job to protect him, to put her arms around him and shield him against anything and everything. Right then, it felt like he was doing the same for her.

"Yes," Veronica responded. "Fuck them."

Diego smiled.

"I want to tell you something," Diego said.

Finally, Veronica thought. She'd given her son all the time and space he needed to think through what she'd told him. She'd thought that maybe they could see a therapist together. Veronica readied herself for whatever was coming. She felt nervous. She could see that Diego was also nervous.

"I need you to know that I didn't throw that ball to Vikram on purpose, knowing he was going to get hit. I can tell everyone thinks it. Vikram thinks it. And I know you think it. I saw it in your eyes that night."

"No one thinks that," Veronica said immediately. "I certainly don't think it. He was open and you threw to him. It's that simple."

"Don't do that."

"What?"

"Trying to make everything OK. Vikram hasn't said a word to me since."

"He's still getting over his concussion. His head isn't straight."

"I had a clear path to the end zone. A run I'd been desperately looking for all game. But somehow, that ball just came out of my hand. I don't know why. I'm the one that knocked him out."

"You didn't knock Vikram out. He knocked himself out by stepping onto that field and the other players did by tackling him." Veronica paused, wondering if it was the right time to ask this next question. "Is this why you've been so quiet lately? You've been working through the game in your head?"

Diego looked at his mother and cocked his head to the right. "Are you kidding?"

"Maybe just hoping," Veronica said with a slight smile. "I'm really sorry."

Diego nodded. "I know."

In the stands, Veronica had watched the play unfold and watched as Diego was the first to rush to Vikram's side. The first thing out of her mouth had been: "Why did he throw it?" She'd spent the better part of these past weeks turning that question in her mind, as if she was loosening a screw. Was he sabotaging himself or Vikram? Or maybe the ball had just slipped out. Or maybe he was somehow getting back at her.

She stepped toward him, unsure if he would let her hug him. The moment he was in her arms, his strong body went loose and limp. He kissed the top of her head and then rested his head on top of hers.

"You did the right thing in throwing to the open man," Veronica said. "Vikram just got unlucky. That's it. End of story."

Diego went to the fridge to get himself something to drink.

"I'm doing a quick day trip tomorrow to see your grandparents," Veronica said. "I've kind of assumed that you didn't want to come with me. But I can easily get you a ticket."

"I really want to see them," Diego said. "But I have plans tomorrow. I can easily cancel them, though."

"There will be plenty of chances to see them," Veronica said. "We'll go up again soon."

The next morning, as Veronica was walking to her flight gate, she saw Gita Shastri walking toward her. They made eye contact. If they turned away now, they could never turn back. The last time they'd seen each other was at the football game. Veronica waited to see if Gita would slow her stride. She did.

"Hi, Gita."

"How are you, Veronica?"

They stood tentatively together as other travelers streamed past them.

"Vikram feeling better?"

The team had lost the game, ending their season. Vikram had suffered a grade three concussion. The X-rays had shown nothing more concerning and in the four weeks that had passed since the game, he had gotten much better.

"He was very bad right in the beginning but now he seems mostly fine. The symptoms seem to have all gone away, except he's just withdrawn. They don't mention that as a symptom."

"I'm sorry you and Gautam had to go through that. It was terrifying to see him get hit and then lying on the field. Diego had a concussion last year. Not nearly as bad. It just takes a little time to get back to normal."

Veronica had called Gita the day after Vikram's injury and left a message. Gita had called back and they'd had a brief, stilted conversation. Perhaps because the Shastris didn't know the ins and outs of the game, they didn't seem to think Diego had anything to do with their son's injury.

"The upside is that it knocked some sense into him. I think football might be over, though I really can't be sure."

Veronica hadn't even considered the possibility that Diego would
not play the following year.

"You headed somewhere?" she asked.

"No. I'm picking up my daughter for winter break. Who I haven't
seen for several months or really talked to in more than a year. I'm a
little nervous, to be honest."

For all the holding close to the chest before, Veronica appreciated
Gita's frankness now.

"I think it's a trend," Veronica said. "Children not talking to their
parents."

"Everything OK with Diego?"

"As OK as it can be for now. He's still a little mad at me. But it's
getting better."

"For that thing?" Gita asked.

"For that thing."

"The story in the *Voice* made it sound like you were a spy."

"It was hilarious."

Veronica noticed Gita glance at her watch.

"Do you need to go?"

"I do," Gita replied.

"I need to catch my flight as well," Veronica said. "Nice seeing
you."

The two women stood there for another few seconds, made eye
contact, and then headed in different directions.

When Veronica arrived at the Oakland airport, Alex was waiting
in his car at the curb. She had been back to Oakland and Berkeley
many times, watching them become cities they certainly weren't
when she was growing up. She had not, however, ventured north of
Berkeley in years. It was a line she didn't cross. Once they did cross
it, the freeway and the area surrounding it looked more and more
shabby, with garbage strewn on the sides of the road.

"The straight route or the scenic one?" Alex asked.

"Scenic."

Alex got off the freeway in Berkeley and began making his way down the decidedly unglamorous San Pablo Avenue. They passed the bowling alley where Veronica had smoked her first bowl. There was now a shopping area filled with every imaginable big-box store. The Nation's Giant Hamburgers was still somehow there. The places with the greatest staying power were the dive bars, which had miraculously remained divey for decades.

They drove past an Indian restaurant that had been there as long as Veronica could remember, which had a long line of customers out front.

"What's up with The Gandhi?" she asked.

"All the hipsters love it now," Alex said.

"Too bad."

After crossing into Richmond, Alex turned left off San Pablo onto Barrett Avenue. Perhaps the reason Veronica had been so insistent about having a nice house in a well-manicured neighborhood with an easy walk between it and Diego's schools was to make up for all she hadn't had.

"There was a part of me that assumed that you'd bought them a new place."

"Don't think I didn't try," Alex said. "Over and over again. There's a beautiful condo in Emeryville sitting empty, ready when they are."

"They'll never be ready," Veronica said.

"You don't know that," Alex said, sounding annoyed.

"You're right."

She didn't actually know who they were anymore.

Alex parked his car in front of the house. It looked even smaller than she remembered it. A combination living room and dining room, a kitchen, and two bedrooms. A house of this size could bring a family close together or push them far apart. But it had always been a warm house when Alex and Veronica were growing up.

"I really don't want to do this," Veronica said, feeling nervous.

It hadn't been that long since she'd been there. Maybe three years. But this arrival felt distinctly different. Before, the house was always a brief stop en route to some remarkable place she'd been going, but she now felt like she had returned to where she'd started with no clear sense of where she was going next.

Alex placed his hand on hers.

"It's just a meal. They can't wait to see you."

Inside the house, her father was on his recliner and her mother was just finishing preparing lunch. Veronica hugged them both. Of course they'd aged in the time since she saw them last. Her mother looked far more tired than she remembered. She regretted her absence in this particular passage of time.

"How are you feeling, Mom?"

"Your brother spent all this extra money to have a fancy doctor say exactly what my doctor already said to me: I'm fine."

Veronica couldn't remember the last time all four of them were together in this house.

"How's the book writing?" her father asked. "Got a Pulitzer yet?"

"Not yet, Dad," Veronica said. "But I may take a slight break. I'm thinking of trying something besides writing and teaching. I've done that too long."

Veronica and Alex looked at each other.

"My firm has a solid internship program," Alex said, and then suddenly looked worried. "Too soon?"

"No," Veronica said. "I'm going to wash my hands so we can eat whatever smells so good."

On the way to the bathroom, Veronica stepped into her old bedroom. In high school, she and Alex had shared the room, and after she'd left for college, Alex had taken it over. Her diploma, some varsity letters, and class pictures were pinned on a corkboard—mementos of who she'd been. Alongside them were Alex's diplomas from high school and USC and a piece of paper with Alex's full name in his steady, confident hand. When he was in high school, Alex had been quite the graphic designer, writing letters in black ink that looked as if they had been professionally printed. He'd thought he would do that for a living until he discovered that he liked math and risk and money. She was looking at his name—ALEXANDER MATTHEWS—when some mechanism in her head turned just a few degrees, as it might in a fancy watch. Over the years, the shape of Alex's writing had become so familiar to her that she didn't even associate it with him anymore. It was more of a font—The Alex—rather than Alex's actual handwriting.

She turned around to go find him, but he'd just entered the room. "Ready for lunch?" he asked.

"Not quite," she said, staring at the lettering again to make sure.

Veronica didn't know whether to be angry. And she didn't know how, after all these years, she had forgotten about Alex and his blocked, steady handwriting. She should have seen it the instant she looked at those envelopes.

"You sent them?"

Alex paused for a second before he responded.

"Yeah," he said, as if he was affirming that the Earth was round. "I just can't understand why it took you this long to figure it out."

"Why?"

Alex had been preparing an answer.

"At first, I sent it as a bit of a joke. To needle you. I was coming to visit and I didn't want to show up unannounced. I was sure you'd know it was me. But then I showed up and you were clearly un-nerved by it and I got too nervous to say anything. I remember your temper from when we shared this room. Now I'm not entirely sure that was the only reason." Here, Alex paused. "Maybe it was to get you back. Back to us. To remind you of who you were. Not in a shitty Klan way, but in a way to say that we've missed you. Mom and Dad have missed you. We don't understand why you've disavowed us."

"Are you fucking kidding, Alex?" Veronica asked, her voice soft only because she didn't want her parents to hear. "You stood in my living room when I told you about the envelopes and you didn't say anything? And don't give me this shit about my temper. You needed to tell me. It's been driving me insane. I've made a fool of myself accusing all these different people of sending them."

"I'm sorry I did that," Alex said. "I really am. But it still doesn't change the fact that you've not been here."

"I'm a grown woman, Alex. I can choose not to be here. That's *my* choice to make. Not yours. And sure, I can blame it on my work and how continuing to do well there meant not visiting here as often as I should have. But ultimately, I made the choice. And it's not like you've moved home. You've been gone, too."

"Yes, it is your choice. And we can be sad that you've made it."

Since Gautam had reminded her, Veronica had been thinking a lot about that seventeen-year-old she'd been. That person had been anxious and ready to leave this room and to leave this house to find herself, to specify who she was in the way a zoologist might specify a certain species. Now, having returned all these years later, arguing with her kid brother in the room they used to share, Veronica was right back to not knowing quite who she was. This, more than the letters Alex had sent, was the source of her anger and confusion. She felt stripped clean in a way that scared her.

"Yes, you can be sad about it," Veronica said. "But I can safely say that your sadness comes nowhere close to the sadness I'm managing now." She could feel the tears coming and she didn't want them because she didn't want her parents seeing her like that. "And about the only thing that can help that is Mom's cooking. Can we do that?"

TWENTY-THREE

Over the weekend after that last game, in the musty garden shed at the far corner of his backyard, MJ had set up his new living space. From the local Goodwill, he'd bought a Vietnam War–era army cot, and he used a battery-operated lantern for light. He came into the main house to use the bathroom and to shower on Wednesday and Sunday evenings. His diet now consisted mainly of peanut butter and honey sandwiches, so he had no need to use the family kitchen or eat with his parents. He let his phone run out of juice and didn't bother plugging it in again. When he returned to school on that Monday, one full week after he was first suspended, he seemed like a different person: a cross between a homeless teen and a burgeoning ascetic.

Most of his classmates assumed that he had had some kind of mental breakdown.

"Schizophrenia sometimes shows up in the teen years," Shirley had said to Michael.

"I don't think that's it."

They had not said anything when he began spending the nights out in the shed. But finally, after a few days, they paid him a visit. He was reading *On the Road* from the light provided by the lantern. On the makeshift night table, there was a paper copy of a thick Saab owner's manual.

"You going somewhere?" Michael asked.

"Not yet. But sometime, I suppose."

"Honey," Shirley said. "What's going on with you? What is all this?"

Shirley had asked the question expecting silence.

"Reparations," MJ said.

"Enough with that," Michael said.

"There can never be enough. For this house, my college admission, our lives. I don't want any of it. It's bought with blood money."

Both Michael and Shirley had walked back into the house knowing that some core mechanism in their son had shifted. The question was how long this particular phase was going to last and whether they needed to get their son professional help.

"Can you imagine me saying that to my dad when I left for the Peace Corps?" Michael asked Shirley. "On some vague level, I may have felt it."

"I kinda wish he was leaving for the Peace Corps," Shirley said. "At least that would make some sense. I think you and I had some serious feelings, but I don't think either of us felt that."

———— ≫≫≫≫ ————

On Saturday afternoons, Michael liked to cook. The kitchen window looked out into the backyard. As he cut onions and minced garlic, he heard the side gate open. A young woman walked through their yard toward the back of the property.

"Is Yoko back?" Shirley asked.

"You're going to say that by mistake in front of him, and that will really be the end of us," Michael said. "But yes, she's back."

Stephanie walked toward the garden shed with a thermos and a book. As she passed their kitchen, Shirley opened the window.

"Hi, Mrs. Berringer. I brought MJ some lunch." Stephanie held up the plaid thermos, which looked like it was from the fifties. "Tomato soup."

"Did you grow the tomatoes? He said something about only wanting to eat things he's grown."

In an empty cupboard in the kitchen, Shirley was now leaving an envelope with twenty-dollar bills along with the freshly ground peanut butter and Ojai honey MJ liked from the local natural foods store, as well as bread that she had baked herself. He picked up the provisions whenever he was in the house.

"Someone grew them," Stephanie said with a smile.

"Well, let him know that there is plenty of lunch for both of you in here if you want to join us. And a cake for after. Which I baked myself."

"That's very kind."

"Is that poetry?" Shirley asked, looking at the book in Stephanie's other hand. "Emily Dickinson, I hope. I loved her in college."

"Yes, poetry," Stephanie responded. "But Marianne Moore. If you excuse my terrible language, Emily Dickinson is, you know, a bit of a basic bitch. Ms. Moore, on the other hand, is another level entirely."

Shirley wasn't exactly sure how to respond to that. Was she, by implication, a basic bitch?

"We'll be here if you need anything."

Stephanie continued to the shed as Shirley closed the window.

"Whatever spell our son is under, that young woman is awfully good at casting it," Shirley said. "She's a stunner."

"You know who her father is, right?"

Shirley shook her head.

"He's a biotech guy. He patented some kind of arthritis drug. In their garden shed, they might as well mint money. In ours, we've got Ted Kaczynski."

"Use more flour on the dough," Shirley said. "It'll stick less."

Michael was experimenting with making his own sourdough.

The first thing Stephanie noticed when she stepped into the shed was the smell.

"Why's your mother being so nice to me? She invited us in. Maybe we should go in for dessert."

"You're welcome to," MJ said. "She's a master of the oven. But I'm fine here."

Stephanie poured some soup into the cup that came with the thermos. They took turns sipping from it and reading poems aloud to each other.

"What does that mean?" MJ asked at one point.

"Which part?"

He took the book from Stephanie and read aloud. "'The deepest feeling always shows itself in silence; / not in silence, but restraint.' I get the silence/restraint distinction. But why say that silence is the deepest feeling and then change your mind a line later?"

"It's the father in the poem speaking."

"I know that."

"I don't think he's changing his mind," Stephanie said. "He's adding a new layer of thought. And Moore is showing us his thinking process in real time."

"I think he's changing his mind," MJ said. "Maybe that's what Moore is trying to show. The change."

Stephanie couldn't understand why he didn't understand what the poem was doing.

"Can't it be both at the same time?"

MJ shook his head, took a sip of the soup, and said quietly, "You have to pick."

Stephanie turned to another poem but then closed the book.

"You going back Monday morning?" Stephanie asked.

A couple of days after MJ had returned to school, he had stopped going altogether.

"Why? I get AP Lit right here. And much better food than the cafeteria."

"You should probably get back to it. You can't just sit in here all day. Well, you could. But you'll get tired of it."

MJ hadn't heard from Yale. Presumably nothing about what had happened had reached that far east. In his mind, he was thinking that he was not going to go, or at the very least, put off his decision as long as he could. He and Stephanie had been discussing packing up his Saab and driving east. She had gotten into Williams early decision. He'd drop her off in Williamstown and maybe hang around for a little while before heading up to Nova Scotia.

They finished the soup.

"I hate to be so blunt," Stephanie said, "but I don't think there's going to be any fucking with you smelling so bad."

"I get it," MJ said. "I wouldn't want to fuck me either."

A few minutes later, with those last words buzzing in her head, Stephanie walked out of the shed, leaving the thermos behind but taking the book with her. Through the large windows in the back of the house, she could see Michael and Shirley in the kitchen. She knocked on the sliding door that was wide open.

"Can I join you for a second?"

"Of course," Shirley said. "We're just about to have a little sweet. Can I cut you a piece?"

"Yes, please," Stephanie said, stepping into the house. "My sweet tooth is a problem."

Shirley had baked a poppy seed cake, which was dense and low on the sugar.

They took their dessert into the living room.

"What was there?" Stephanie asked, looking above the fireplace where there was a paint discoloration the size of a large frame.

"A painting that I've looked at since I was born," Shirley said, melancholy suddenly creeping up on her. "An old Dutch master."

"You own one of those? Now I really want to see it. Is it here somewhere?"

Michael and Shirley glanced at each other. It wasn't exactly guilt that Michael felt. It was shame.

"It's not," Shirley said.

"What happened to it? Please tell me MJ didn't throw paint on it to protest climate change."

Shirley couldn't help but crack a smile. "We sold it."

"You *sold* a Dutch master? I hope you're flying the family to the Maldives first class. And you got me a ticket."

"It wasn't quite a Dutch master," Shirley added. "Maybe more a Dutch minor. And sometimes it's best to let go of things."

"Buddhist detachment," Michael added, both for Shirley's sake and Stephanie's.

Thinking that he'd never get caught, Michael had seriously considered making a big buy in the company Alex had mentioned. The merger would have happened soon after and he would have made out like the bandit he could have been. No one would have known. But ultimately, he hadn't. He hadn't because he didn't have the cash. Shirley had hatched a plan of her own soon after he told her about his run-in with the Audi driver and his family at Atherton Eats. He wasn't sure what Shirley's reaction would be when he returned home with his shirt torn, but she'd asked him for a detailed play-by-play. She didn't like her son getting into fights, but she found she did like the idea of her husband in one, doing the right thing.

Shirley had a friend in town who was an art broker, bringing together sellers and buyers. This friend had found a buyer, a couple who'd done a full genealogical check and found that the artist Erich van Royen was a distant relative. And because the husband had just cashed out of his company, they had silly money to spend, and because of the relationship, they wanted the painting. And so after commission and taxes, the Berringers had ended up with just south of two million dollars for the painting that had hung above the fireplace for two generations. A painting whose worth was mainly based on its age and its vague proximity to greatness.

Michael had used some of the money to pay off all his clients and had given Tom Regan a bit extra so that he'd wouldn't squawk about paperwork. They'd placed aside a large sum for college. Enough for both MJ and his sister.

As always, Shirley had assured the family their comfort. They wouldn't ever have to think about getting the salmon instead of the ahi. Michael was left with the lingering sadness of never having made a career and life of his own, a sadness that he could push down easily enough but could never quite extinguish. Shirley wouldn't let it be extinguished.

"We hear you got into Williams early decision," Shirley said.

"I did. The only place I planned to apply. Glad I got in."

"That was risky," Michael said.

"*Risky* is kind. My parents used the word *stupid*."

Stephanie took a bite of the cake and then a couple more.

"That was delicious," she said, placing the empty plate on the center table. "I should get going, but before I do, I just wanted to mention that I'm not entirely sure what's going on with your son. I'm a bit worried about him not wanting to go to school."

"He'll be fine," Shirley said immediately, the defensiveness clear in her voice.

"Yeah," Stephanie said, hearing it and retreating. "Maybe school is just too boring for him. I'm sure once he gets to New Haven, he'll thrive." Stephanie stood up. "Thanks for the delicious cake. Do you mind if I give this to you?"

It was the book of Moore poems.

"Sure," Shirley said. "Will this make me less basic?" she asked, and winked at Stephanie.

Shirley waited until Stephanie walked out the front door before turning to Michael. "She feeds all this craziness into his head, and now is worried about him?"

Michael's attention had returned to the wall where the painting had been. For so long, the Dutchman's sad eyes had watched over the room, and their absence now was more than just the empty space on the wall. It was as if a silent member of the family had left.

"What about that oaky and hilly watercolor that's in the hallway?" Michael asked. "It'll fit perfectly."

Michael and Shirley weren't art collectors, but there was plenty of very nice art spread throughout the house, purchased or inherited by Shirley's parents. Michael and Shirley had purchased several pieces of their own through the years. They'd displayed some of the smaller ones, but the bigger showpieces that they'd bought when they were in Uganda and during later travel in Asia had remained unhung and stored in a cool place in the garage.

"No," Shirley said, shaking her head. "That's not quite right. It's the kind of piece you walk by. We need something that will draw people in."

"What about the abstract in the family room?" Michael asked. "We can easily find something else to fill that space."

"That might work," Shirley said, knowing it wasn't going to.

They were having a conversation about interior design and art, but they both knew they were having a conversation about something else. Michael wanted to fill the space as quickly as possible in order to forget his own humiliation. Shirley wanted to keep it empty a little longer so that he wouldn't forget quite yet. Michael knew Shirley was doing this and there was nothing he could do.

"I was thinking maybe the landscape I bought in Kampala," Shirley said. She'd been missing that version of herself as she simultaneously worried about this new version of her son.

On their last weekend in Uganda, Shirley had gone into an art gallery near their hotel and purchased the painting. The combination of colors and the scale of the sky with the horizon had done what Shirley wanted art to do—it made her heart beat, it reminded her of the year she'd just spent, it helped her look back and forward at the same time. Michael had seen it and he didn't really get it or like it, nor did he understand how she'd spent so much money on it. For a while, she'd hung it in her nice walk-in closet because she wanted her own private relationship to it. But then, several years ago, she'd moved it down to the garage.

"Sure," Michael said. "I love that piece."

TWENTY-FOUR

Priya pretended to be a hurricane, but she was really a necessary summer rain, arriving suddenly, moving through quickly, leaving behind a layer of cool. She was wearing some old jeans, a nice long sweater, and an assortment of bangles on her wrists.

"You OK?" she asked her mother after they hugged.

"Of course," Gita said. "Why wouldn't I be? You're home."

"Because you usually give me the once-over on what I'm wearing, while pretending that you're not giving me the once-over. You didn't this time."

"I'm sorry if I've done that," Gita said, subdued. "I think my mom used to do it to me and I didn't realize I was doing it to you." Then Gita gave her daughter the once-over. "You look nice."

"Thank you," Priya said, holding up her wrists. "I'm going through my bangles phase."

"I've got plenty more if you want them."

They made their way to the car.

The air between them was much calmer than either had expected.

Maybe Priya had needed to finally leave the house to feel more comfortable when returning to it; maybe Gita needed to see the possibility of things really falling apart with her family for her to ease her foot from the pedal.

"How's he doing?" Priya asked.

"The doctor says he's fine. His neurological functions seem fine. He's just withdrawn and distant, which I think might be a lingering side effect. He says he gets headaches."

"Was it scary? Him on the field?"

"Terrifying. Remember when he split his forehead open in the sixth grade? That was nothing. Even from a distance, I could see his head bouncing on the ground. I'm stupid for letting him play. And to your dad's credit, he's not said 'I told you so' once."

"How's Pops?"

"Currently, on top of the world. Or on top of the VirtualUN world. Please don't make fun of his new car. He absolutely loves that thing."

"Vikram sent me a pic. Honestly, I have no comment. I mean I do. But."

"And he bought himself a fancy watch. He's a whole new thing."

As they were nearing the house, Gita glanced at Priya.

"I want to tell you something. I'm hoping you won't say anything to Vikram about it quite yet. But he'll know it soon enough. I think he already senses it. Your dad and I are going to experiment with taking some time by ourselves. To figure things out. I don't know exactly what that's going to look like. We need to figure out what we're going to do after Vikram leaves in a couple of years. I need to figure out what I want to do. More immediately, I'm thinking of doing a yoga retreat in Kerala in the new year."

Gita was now looking straight ahead and her eyes had suddenly filled with tears. Priya had never seen her mother cry. It wasn't what she did.

"We've had a rough go this past month and probably for longer than that. Your dad and I. I don't think he likes me much." I don't think any of you like me much, she wanted to add, but didn't because it would force Priya to disagree.

"He was an asshole for having lunch with that girl. All this isn't your fault."

"Don't call him an asshole."

"Butthead, then. You're not the only one responsible. He just disappears. Into his work. From us. From everything."

No matter how much Gita knew this to be true, she also knew it would break Gautam's heart that his daughter thought so.

"Is it over? I don't want it to be, but you should do whatever you need to do. Vikram and I will be fine."

Gita had not considered this question head-on, even though it was the only question she needed to answer. "I really don't know. I don't want it to be over. And I don't think your dad does either. But he and I have settled into these patterns of always walking and talking in opposite directions. For now, I really want to make our trip work. Can you get Vikram excited for it? He said he's coming, but I want him to be really in. It'll be good for us to be away and together. He just goes to school and then comes home. He's not really seeing friends. Nobody is coming over. Did he tell you about that weird visit he had?"

"No," Priya said.

At the end of the weekend after the last game, there had been a knock on the door.

"Hi, Mrs. Shastri. Is Vikram here?"

Gita stood at her front door, not entirely sure how to manage the visitor. There was certainly a part of her that wanted to shut the door on Stanley, or to tell him that she was glad he was feeling better, but that as much as her son had apologized to him, he also owed an apology to her son.

"He's upstairs in his room. The first door to the right."

Stanley stepped into the house and began removing his shoes.

"No, no," Gita insisted. "It's OK." She appreciated his gesture, but she also didn't want the removing of the shoes to translate in his mind as an opportunity to spend a couple of hours here. She wanted him in and out.

"They're already off," Stanley said, laboring to remove his high-top Converse.

Vikram had somewhere between a moderate and severe concussion. He'd not lost consciousness, and even though the X-rays had revealed nothing troubling, he'd had terrible headaches through the weekend. Though he was ready to get back to school, he wasn't in any shape to do so.

Stanley knocked on the door. Vikram assumed it was his mother, who never used to knock but had been since she'd looked through his phone.

"Hey," Stanley said, standing just outside the room. "Do you mind if I come in?"

Stanley was the last person Vikram thought would visit him. MJ had been by and Tyler had spent a chunk of Saturday afternoon in his room, playing video games as Vikram came in and out of sleep.

"Come in."

Vikram was sitting up in bed, looking at his phone. Stanley walked in and brought over the desk chair.

"How you feeling?" Vikram asked.

"Better every day," Stanley said. "You?"

"I felt like absolute shit right after and yesterday," Vikram said. "But now it's getting a little better. I should be back to school tomorrow. I can't miss any more school."

The two of them sat there, both aware of how strangely similar their realties had been recently.

"I came to see if you were OK," Stanley said. "But I also came to see if we can put all this behind us. I really don't want to think about any of it anymore. I shouldn't have been such a dick for so long and you guys shouldn't have been such dicks in the cave. Now that my memory of the night is a little clearer, I remember it was MJ who came back that second time and went in on me. He was the one who hit me the hardest the first time."

Vikram felt a sharp pain in his head. "You were really ripped that night. Whatever was in that flask was making you a little crazy."

"Please don't mention the flask. I don't think I'll ever touch tequila again."

"But I do think you're right about MJ," Vikram said.

Vikram didn't mention that he and Diego had also gone up a second time.

"Can we just be done with it?"

"Yes," Vikram said. "We're done." Vikram rubbed his temples. "You can stay for as long as you want, but I need to take a nap."

Stanley stood up to go. "Hopefully I'll see you tomorrow at school."

Gita had been standing outside the door and quickly walked away. She didn't tell Priya that part.

When they got home from the airport, Priya first hugged her father, who was packing the car.

"Sweet ride," Priya said.

"I appreciate you saying that," Gautam said. "I promise we'll buy electric when it's time to replace Mom's car."

"Maybe by then we'll all just be walking everywhere, living in villages."

She went upstairs to knock on Vikram's door, walking in without waiting for an answer. Vikram was just lying on his bed.

"Do you realize the kind of flight risk Mom must think you are if she called me in? I was thinking about just staying at school for the break. But she insisted I come home. She's not about to lose both of us. What's going on, buddy?"

Vikram sat up in bed, happy to see his sister. "You growing weed up there?"

"I don't need to grow it. I always thought I'd arrive at college and could be a dealer in my dorm room. A perfect side hustle. But it's legal now."

"There's other stuff you could sell."

"Yeah," she said. "But then I could get caught. Ladies jail is not my thing."

"You and Mom are talking now?"

"Only about you. Why aren't you two talking? Did you get an A-minus on something?"

Vikram shrugged.

"Please. Enough with the mute shit."

"She broke into my phone and read my messages."

"Dick pics?"

"That would have been fine. She broke my trust."

"She looked at your phone. That's nothing. She used to follow me around when I went out with my friends. Spy shit. I had to leave a party and tell her to go home. Once she starts doing that to you, you can complain."

Vikram had missed Priya. They protected each other from the things that their parents didn't understand, which in their eyes was pretty much everything. Priya had not been gone for that long, but he'd felt her absence.

"Seriously, are you OK? She says you've been moody and distant."

"I'm totally fine," Vikram said. "I told them that I have lingering effects from the concussion so they'll leave me alone. Headaches are useful when you want peace and quiet."

"That's fucking genius. You can say whatever you want and blame it on the head bump. Can you say some stuff for me?" Priya made eye contact with her brother. "But really. What's up?"

"I don't know," Vikram said. "I'm just kinda tired of it all. High school. Classes. Figuring out how to get into college."

Priya smiled. She knew this feeling well.

"I was totally into football, but then I got my head bashed in. And now all I think about is being back on that field and playing."

"But this isn't you. You don't like just lying around in bed, doing nothing. You actually love high school, and you want to go to college."

Vikram lay back in bed. Priya poked his side with her finger.

"'What is it you plan to do with your one wild and precious life?'"

"Is that Oprah?"

"Get your stuff together. Gita says you don't want to go to this weekend house. Have you seen the pictures? The place is ridiculous. They're packing the car now."

"I don't want to be with them all weekend long."

"I don't either. But if we're together, we can take edibles in the game room and play *Call of Duty* all weekend."

Vikram slowly got out of bed and started packing. Priya went downstairs to report to her mother.

"What exactly is happening in here?" Priya asked, looking around the mess of a kitchen.

"We're getting a new kitchen," Gautam said, winking. "From all the money we saved on your tuition."

Gita allowed herself to smile.

"He's game," Priya said to her mother. "I'm the Vikram whisperer."

Half an hour later, they piled into the new Cadillac for the three-hour drive.

"Just like old times," Gautam said, desperately wanting it to be like old times.

"The best way to make it like old times is to stop at Murphy's," Priya said as he drove out of their neighborhood.

The kids had always loved going to Murphy's because they were so generous with their scoops of ice cream. And Gita loved it for their pistachio. Though Gautam loved their mango, he'd never liked going there because the few parking spots out front were always taken.

"And don't worry," Priya said, "I think there'll be a perfect spot for you out front. You've karmically earned it."

And somehow there was. Gautam made eye contact with Priya in the rearview mirror.

"I'd go buy a lottery ticket if I were you," she said.

Gautam parked and they all went in and got their generous scoops. Vikram seemed to be perking up, either from the sugar or Priya's arrival.

"We can eat in the car," Gautam offered when he saw that the few seats in the parlor were occupied.

"You never let us eat in the car," Vikram said.

"See. Things are changing. Dad is loosening up."

They all sat in the car and ate their ice cream. Gautam wasn't ready to give up the parking spot yet, so after he finished his scoop, he checked his email one last time and then put an out-of-office message on. Ryan had offered the use of the cabin for a week, but their plan was to stay three nights. Gautam had been really looking forward to the long weekend. He'd bought himself a brown-checkered Pendleton shirt and a copy of *Lonesome Dove*. He wanted to read and play rummy with the kids and learn how to make a roaring fire. There wasn't any real snow yet, so maybe they'd take some hikes.

"Everyone ready? Anyone need to go to the bathroom?"

No one responded.

When he started the car, he took a quick peek in his rearview mirror. There was another car blocking his way. He turned off the engine and stepped out, thankful that he'd not just absentmindedly backed out. A shorter man in his early fifties had gotten out of his car as well. He was wearing Ray-Bans and a frayed tank top with the American flag on it. Gautam registered him but didn't really piece him together in that first moment. If he knew what the word meant, he might have thought of him as a dirtbag.

"Hey, I think you're blocking me," Gautam said in the casual tone he'd just used to ask for a taster of the salted caramel before ordering his usual mango.

"I know," the man said with a smile. "I noticed you sitting in your car for quite a while, hesitating about leaving the spot, and I wanted to give you a little nudge to get going. To let you know that there are others waiting. And that in America, we have rules."

Gautam looked at the man and his old Honda CR-V and now knew what the man was doing. Fuck you, you short fuck. Get out of my way, he wanted to say. But he sensed how this was going to proceed if he did say anything like that. The man was picking a fight, a fight that would only benefit him. There was no telling what he had hidden in the back of his car. A gun? A bat?

"If you move, I can let you have the spot," Gautam said, trying to remain calm. He just wanted to get going on their trip. He wished they'd not stopped for ice cream.

"You're not *letting* me have the spot. You're not *letting* me do anything."

Gautam could feel his body getting hot. Sure, he'd won already, with his lovely family and his nice car. And because of this, the man wanted the little victory that came from knowing that Gautam wasn't going to do anything to jeopardize that. As he stood there, Gautam could feel himself shrinking. He looked at the man and then looked at his family in the car. Vikram had turned around and was watching the exchange through the rear windshield. Gautam and Vikram made eye contact. He was certain that while Vikram had not heard the conversation, he knew exactly what was happening.

Gautam got back in his car.

"What's up?" Gita asked. "Everything OK?"

"Yeah," Gautam said, his voice now fallen, his heart beating wildly. "It's fine. This guy is being difficult."

Gautam waited as the CR-V moved out of the way. As Gautam backed up, there was a retaining wall close by, so he had to maneuver to get his car out. He noticed that the man in the CR-V was trying to show him with his hands how much room he had to back up. But Gautam didn't want his help, mainly because he wasn't sure if he was actually just mocking him. Gautam kept an eye on him in his periphery, while the man sat in his seat laughing, as if to underscore how idiotic Gautam looked driving his car forward and backward in two-inch increments.

Finally, Gautam had enough room to maneuver his car and straighten it out. He did so and, without making eye contact with the man in the CR-V, drove away. As he did, a sadness began to wash over him. He looked in the rearview mirror and saw Vikram looking at him. Why didn't you do anything? He quickly turned his eyes to the road. Gita placed her hand on his. He was about to pull his hand away, not because of the fights they'd had, but because her care for him in that moment made his humiliation worse. But he let her comfort him, and they began their drive.

They were on the freeway for the next two hours. The longer they drove and the farther they got into the mountain air, the more Gautam's earlier cheeriness returned. He insisted they stop at McDonald's for french fries. For the last hour, they were on a winding, wooded road. Finally they turned off toward the house.

Gita had never seen *Deliverance* but knew the vague outline, and so when Gautam had first suggested this trip, she had used it as evidence that a family, particularly one that looked like theirs, was not safe so far from the city. Gautam had countered that there was a grocery store that sold fancy cheeses a mile away from the house.

Gautam was the first to notice the deer that appeared cautiously out of a thicket of pine trees about twenty yards to their side. What is it about a deer that makes most everyone stop and gaze at it in wonder? As if it, more than any other animal, has the power to deliver them to a better, kinder place. Gautam slowed down, hoping that the deer would be a reset for them, a kind of portal.

"Look," he said, in that voice he used when the children were young and could be mesmerized by a caterpillar.

The deer bent down to forage in the dry, crackling ground. Gautam stopped the car. Gita reached her hand back and tapped the kids on their knees.

"So beautiful," she said in a whisper, rolling down her window.

Priya set her phone aside; Vikram removed his headphones. Right then it was so quiet and then so loud—birds in various registers they could hear but not see, a slight breeze rustling through the trees.

"This is nice," Gautam said. This is all that he'd wanted out of the weekend—the four of them gazing at an animal, with birds chirping in the background.

Nice was barely out of his mouth when something heavy and nimble dropped out of the tree above the deer and landed right on its neck. Before Gautam registered what exactly was happening, he felt the sheer delight of discovery. To *see* the mountain lion felt a little mythic. But the myth was quickly replaced by the reality of a ferocious animal attacking a sweet one. He thought the lion would be bigger, but it was big enough to rip the deer clean in half.

After landing on the deer's neck, it had submerged its jaws deep into the flesh. The deer made a desperate, whimpering sound as its whole body convulsed. Both animals thrashed around.

"Dad, do something," Priya screamed from the back seat.

"Drive the car toward them," Gita said.

Despite how little he knew about these things, he knew a dying animal when he saw one. Yet he pulled to the side of the road and tried to inch closer to the lion and the deer. The lion didn't bother to notice the car. It continued to dig deeper and deeper into the deer. Priya unbuckled her seat belt, reached over the front seat, and leaned on the horn. Finally, the lion looked up at them lustily, with the deer's throat still in its mouth. For the next several seconds, they all just looked at the lion, the sounds of the birds now replaced by all their hearts beating wild with irregularity.

When Priya pressed on the horn one more time, really leaning into it, the lion finally dropped the deer on the ground, and, as quickly as it had appeared, it vanished into the trees. They could hear the deer crying, the sound getting fainter with every passing second.

"We should call someone," Priya said, her voice breathless, looking down at her phone. "The ranger should still be able to save it."

"I'm sure they can," Gautam said, knowing that there was no saving that animal. "Did you find a number?"

"The reception is bad," Priya said.

"Let's drive up to the house. We can call from there."

"I really don't want it to be alone," Priya said.

Gita reached her hand back and Priya held it for several long seconds. And then Vikram, who'd not said a word throughout, let out the sharpest of cries from some deep fold inside him. The sound was just different. Gita and Gautam turned back to him; Priya looked to her side. Vikram was sitting there, the tears streaming down his face. And then, with the loving eyes of his family on him and finally unable to hold in what he'd been since that night in the cave, Vikram let himself go. His large, strong face collapsed. He started crying in heaves and spurts until it got so bad that he was struggling to breathe.

"I didn't mean to hurt him like that," Vikram said, for the sake of his parents. But he also knew, and wouldn't say, that he'd meant every punch and kick.

Gita felt like she was going to be ill. Somewhere in her, she had already known what Vikram was now admitting—not the details but the vague outline—because she was his mother and she knew these things. And yet, because she was his mother, she'd wanted to believe that he'd never do such a thing. She'd wanted to believe that he could not and would not have ever thrown the vicious punches that MJ and Diego had.

Gautam looked at Vikram, feeling a discomforting pride for his son and a deep shame for himself that he'd never been able to do what Vikram had done. That in the face of jeering, Vikram had refused to take it.

Priya offered her brother her hand, which he took.

"Can we head up to the house now?" Vikram asked. "I need to pee."

TWENTY-FIVE

Seated several feet apart, Vikram and Diego were lounging on the bleachers, their long, strong bodies covering three rows up and down. Well over a month had passed since the end of the season. The two had played video games together a few times and seen each other a lot in class, but they'd not spent any time alone. Now, without the distraction of MJ, football, or Stanley, the two were shy around each other, in a way boys could be when they were inching toward friendship. Vikram had been the one to reach out to see if Diego wanted to meet him at the field. He didn't mention that he'd not been back since his head had bounced on the turf.

"Good break?" Diego asked.

"Same old. Chilled at home. Now my dad is busy with work. My mom is on a yoga retreat in India, doing her eating and praying. And my sister is back at school. You?"

"Christmas with my dad and his family. Hung out after with my mom. She doesn't really teach anymore. She's working on a new book, banging away on that laptop. And I'm ready for school to start on Monday."

Vikram tried to think of something to say about Diego's mom but couldn't come up with anything.

"You hear anything from MJ?" Vikram asked.

He'd been back to school, arriving just as classes started and leaving right when they ended.

"We haven't talked, but I bet he's headed to Yale after all," Diego said.

"Of course he's going," Vikram said. "With shoes. Nice ones, too." He paused. "I hope he's doing OK."

The two of them sat there, looking down at the field. Diego's eyes fell onto the thirty-yard line, the place he'd been standing when he'd thrown that terrible pass.

"I've been meaning to tell you this for a while," Diego said. He had no intention to do so when he'd agreed to meet Vikram. But now it seemed wrong to not say anything. "You know, when you got hit on the head."

"I don't remember that at all," Vikram said, smiling.

"Well, I'd rather not remember it either. I think I was mad that you were getting all this attention. Mad that the Cal coach was there and you were getting so many touches. I didn't throw the ball at you thinking you were going to get hit, or get hit as hard as you did. And for sure I didn't think you were going to get a concussion. But somehow, the ball just came out of my hand. I don't think I did it on purpose, but maybe I did. And it was so stupid. I had a clear path into the end zone. You've no idea how shitty I felt after. How I've felt since. But maybe not as shitty as you when your head was on fire. I should have come to see you. I'm sorry I didn't."

Diego turned to look at Vikram to get a sense of how he was receiving this information.

"I was just faster than you," Vikram said. "I can understand why that may have been frustrating."

Diego smiled. "Fuck off."

Vikram was not accustomed to being the object of envy, and he liked the feeling.

"You gonna keep playing?" Vikram asked.

Optional spring workouts were not that far off.

"I don't know," Diego said. He'd been thinking a lot about how much his interest to be on the field had been tied to his mother's interest. He didn't know how he felt about it himself. "You?"

"I can't wait. No pressure, but you could just switch over to throwing the ball. We would cook." Vikram looked back to the field. "Hey, one other quick thing. Since we're sharing."

"If it's about Erin Greene, please don't tell me. I don't want to hear it. It'll make me too jealous."

"She's not interested in either of us. Certainly not me. It's something else."

Erin had written a story in the paper about the events in the cave. While reporting that MJ Berringer had taken responsibility, she had expressed her concern that the full truth of the evening had not been revealed.

Vikram had invited Diego to meet to tell him this because he simply needed to tell him. "That night, I made my way through the party and back up the pathway leading to the caves. Just like you and MJ. I told myself I was just going to check on Stanley. And that's really what I wanted to do. On my way up, I'd stopped and shined the light from my phone on one particularly magnificent, enormous agave. The one I think nearly impaled Stanley. I touched the silver-green tip of one of the large leaves, as big and sharp as a sword, with my finger, and if I'd pressed down any harder, I would have easily punctured my skin, drawing blood. I walked to the final cave and shined the light in and saw Stanley there. He put his hand in front of his eyes to avoid the light. I had no real intention of doing anything. But then Stanley called me something and I just lost it. I don't even remember what he said. *Fag, pussy, Bin Laden.* Whatever.

"I turned off my light and without saying a word, I took a step into the cave toward Stanley and wildly swung my fist, and despite the dark and the difficulty of telling up from down, I connected with his jaw. I could feel it rattle. I followed up with several more swift, hard punches to Stanley's chest and arms. And then again back to his face. I went in on the fucker. He could barely defend himself at that point. Then I walked out and back down. And like ten minutes later, he came down screaming. I assumed that Stanley would eventually point the finger at me, but I think he truly didn't remember. He was too drunk."

Vikram stopped and looked over at Diego.

There. He had said it all aloud. He could feel his eyes moisten. He looked back to the field.

They sat in silence for what felt like a long time while Diego tried to get his head around what Vikram had just told him.

"Holy shit," Diego finally said. "I really thought he just fell and hurt himself. I knew MJ hadn't done it because of all that reparations bullshit. And I knew I hadn't. And there was no way it was you."

"Why not?"

"C'mon, man," Diego said. "Indians don't do that kind of shit."

Vikram smiled.

"You lied the whole time?"

"No," Vikram said. "That's the thing. I couldn't think straight for a while. My head was like a hive of bees. But yes. I also lied."

They were not equal, the two stories they'd just told each other. And yet, for that one moment, the two of them felt just a bit lighter. They both felt the relief of confession.

"I haven't told anybody," Vikram said. "And I'm not planning to. You think you can keep it to yourself?"

"Of course. You gonna keep my story to yourself?"

"For sure."

They bumped fists, as if to retreat from the intimacy they'd just shared. And just as they did, they held the contact of their skin and bone for a second or two longer than usual. They liked the warmth.

———⟫⟫⟫⟫———

That night, Vikram sat at his desk and read over the "Archive of the Self" essay that he'd turned in for his English class. He'd written about the Gandhi photograph and Mr. Walters had given him an A-minus, along with a one-sentence note: "But where are *you*?" Mr. Walters allowed the students to revise their assignments until the end of the term and had given Vikram extra time because of his concussion. He hadn't known how to revise it. But the conversation with Diego had opened something inside him, perhaps locating the *you* Mr. Walters had been seeking. He wrote a whole new essay.

This is what he included:

He titled it "How I Went from the Gandhian Nonviolence of My Great-Grandfather to the Violence of the Gridiron," and wrote about the long shadow a Gandhian ethos of nonviolence, purity, sacrifice, and self-denial of pleasure had cast over the generations of men in his family. He wrote about being born in America, of playing American sports, of going to American schools. He wrote about the fear of one's weaknesses being exposed on the field of play, of the many school years saturated with violence—watching a fight in junior high when hair was pulled from a scalp; of bloodied and broken noses. He wrote about joining the football team, and, despite all his Gandhian baggage, strangely enjoying the purity of laying out an opponent. He wrote about going to a big party after an important victory and seeing a schoolmate there who'd bullied him for years. He wrote about how he and two of his teammates had ended up in a cave where the bully was drunk and belligerent and how, as they were trying to calm him down, the three of them had beaten him up out of self-defense. He wrote that the moment had changed his life and the lives of his two friends. It had caused a deep crisis in his family, but one they emerged from stronger and better. He wrote that at the end of it, despite the bully's longstanding provocations, he'd learned that violence could never be the answer. "In all this, after all these years, I have returned to my nonviolent Gandhian roots."

This is what he did not include:

That as he'd made his way down from the caves a second time, he couldn't understand his rage. It was partly to get back at Stanley, but they'd already done that earlier. Vikram had returned to the party and not ten minutes later, Stanley had appeared screaming into the night. Standing there, Vikram could almost feel the pain Stanley must have felt in having those sharp points of the cactus piercing his body.

He had not written about the guilt he'd felt for letting MJ take the blame for the whole thing. He'd let MJ take the blame because it allowed him to return to school, allowed him to get back on track, allowed him to play. Because it let him be OK with his parents, who could begin to understand the first moment in the cave but certainly not the second one.

He had not written about how ill he felt every time he thought about how much he'd liked punching Stanley. He didn't write about how his return to the cave would always stay with him. It was his. It was him. And as he grew older, the wound would remain, without the benefit of a scar. He was the one who had done it and tried to justify it. He hated Stanley for doing this to him. What would he tell his children about that night? He'd spend a better part of his life wondering why he'd done it and trying to make sure it never happened again. He'd not written about his sweet, sometimes meek father, who he didn't want to become, nor his mother, who was maybe just trying to move the men in her life along. And he'd not written about the feeling of power and fear and exhilaration now coursing through him.

He had not included any of this because he couldn't.

But this is what he did include at the end.

Vikram closed his essay with a copy of the photograph of his great-grandfather that had first appeared in *The Times of India* and had hung for years behind the register at his grandparents' restaurant and in his family's living room. He wrote about his deep affection for the photo and about how, after seeing it day after day, year after year, he felt like he was the one walking on that village road, smelling the dust in the air, feeling the heat on his skin, sensing that together they were all marching toward a brighter future. He saw himself in his great-grandfather's side glance at the mysterious, beatific presence next to him. And in looking back, Vikram knew that he'd been made by all the people that had come before him. He wondered what it would take for him to someday be his own people. And thought that maybe that someday had already arrived.

ACKNOWLEDGMENTS

Thank you to my friend and agent, Seth Fishman, who is always smart and clear in his counsel. And to Jack Gernert, who gave me great edits at the right time.

A heartfelt thank-you to Chelcee Johns, my wonderful editor, who shared my vision for this book and guided me in all of the right places with her keen eye. And to Sydney Collins and Anusha Khan for all their help. To Kathleen Fridella for the excellent copyediting. To the great design team. And to everyone else at Ballantine Books.

Fellow writers and friends were equal parts encouraging and incisive in their read of early drafts: Ryan Black, Leland Cheuk, Lacy Crawford, Keith Scribner, and John Weir.

Thank you to Peter Seaman for the gift of a great party game that makes an important appearance here.

I never met my maternal grandfather, Harilal Dave, who was a photographer and ran the Dave Brothers Studio in the Colaba neighborhood of Mumbai. The archive he left behind—from family portraits to documentary photos of the Indian independence movement—has been a continued source of inspiration. The photograph that appears at the end of this novel is one of my very favorite of his photos.

To my mother, Ragini, and my sisters, Uttara and Meeta, deep gratitude always. And to my in-laws, Andy and Yvonne, for all of your support.

My wife, Emilie, has read and reread everything I have written and published. She is my closest reader and my best friend.

And finally, to my beautiful boys, Ravi and Ishan. This book is for the two of you.

ABOUT THE AUTHOR

Sameer Pandya is the author of the novel *Members Only,* a finalist for the California Book Award and an NPR "Books We Love" of 2020, and the story collection *The Blind Writer,* longlisted for the PEN/ Open Book Award. His cultural criticism has appeared in a range of publications, including the *LA Review of Books, The Atlantic, Salon,* and *Sports Illustrated.* A recipient of the PEN/Civitella Fellowship, he is currently an associate professor of Asian American Studies at the University of California, Santa Barbara.

sameerpandya.net
X: @sameerpandya
Instagram: @sameerpandya524

ABOUT THE TYPE

This book was set in Caslon, a typeface first designed in 1722 by William Caslon (1692–1766). Its widespread use by most English printers in the early eighteenth century soon supplanted the Dutch typefaces that had formerly prevailed. The roman is considered a "workhorse" typeface due to its pleasant, open appearance, while the italic is exceedingly decorative.